Pure Bliss

Other Books by Lexi Blake

ROMANTIC SUSPENSE

Masters and Mercenaries
The Dom Who Loved Me
The Men With The Golden Cuffs
A Dom is Forever
On Her Master's Secret Service
Sanctum: A Masters and Mercenaries Novella
Love and Let Die
Unconditional: A Masters and Mercenaries Novella
Dungeon Royale
Dungeon Games: A Masters and Mercenaries Novella
A View to a Thrill
Cherished: A Masters and Mercenaries Novella
You Only Love Twice
Luscious: Masters and Mercenaries~Topped
Adored: A Masters and Mercenaries Novella
Master No
Just One Taste: Masters and Mercenaries~Topped 2
From Sanctum with Love
Devoted: A Masters and Mercenaries Novella
Dominance Never Dies
Submission is Not Enough
Master Bits and Mercenary Bites~The Secret Recipes of Topped
Perfectly Paired: Masters and Mercenaries~Topped 3
For His Eyes Only
Arranged: A Masters and Mercenaries Novella
Love Another Day
At Your Service: Masters and Mercenaries~Topped 4
Master Bits and Mercenary Bites~Girls Night
Nobody Does It Better
Close Cover
Protected: A Masters and Mercenaries Novella
Enchanted: A Masters and Mercenaries Novella
Charmed: A Masters and Mercenaries Novella
Treasured: A Masters and Mercenaries Novella, Coming June 29, 2021

Smoke and Sin
At the Pleasure of the President

URBAN FANTASY

Thieves
Steal the Light
Steal the Day
Steal the Moon
Steal the Sun
Steal the Night
Ripper
Addict
Sleeper
Outcast
Stealing Summer

LEXI BLAKE WRITING AS SOPHIE OAK

Texas Sirens
Small Town Siren
Siren in the City
Siren Enslaved
Siren Beloved
Siren in Waiting
Siren in Bloom
Siren Unleashed
Siren Reborn

Nights in Bliss, Colorado
Three to Ride
Two to Love
One to Keep
Lost in Bliss
Found in Bliss
Pure Bliss
Chasing Bliss
Once Upon a Time in Bliss
Back in Bliss
Sirens in Bliss

Happily Ever After in Bliss
Far From Bliss, Coming 2021

A Faery Story
Bound
Beast
Beauty

Standalone
Away From Me
Snowed In

Pure Bliss

Nights in Bliss, Colorado Book 6

Lexi Blake
writing as
Sophie Oak

Pure Bliss
Nights in Bliss, Colorado Book 6

Published by DLZ Entertainment LLC

Copyright 2018 DLZ Entertainment LLC
Edited by Chloe Vale
ISBN: 978-1942297-09-3

Sign up for Lexi Blake's newsletter
and be entered to win a $25 gift certificate
to the bookseller of your choice.

Join us for news, fun, and exclusive content
including free short stories.

There's a new contest every month!

Go to www.LexiBlake.net to subscribe.

Dedication

To my husband, for taking this amazing journey with me. Special thanks to Chloe Vale, Shayla Black, and Kris Cook for listening to me talk endlessly about this book.

As a note to readers unfamiliar with the Texas Sirens series, Trev McNamara's story is told in full in a book titled *Siren in Waiting*.

2019 Dedication

Dear Reader,

I'm about halfway through putting these books out again and I'm reflecting on the people who've come on this long journey with me. So much of Bliss is taken from my husband's memories of his childhood growing up in rural Colorado and the band of mountain men (they were boys) he called friends. I want to thank my husband for being okay with me fictionalizing those stories. I hope I stayed true to this special part of his life. To my children for supporting me. To my friends who are always there for me. To the fans who started out with me and these characters all those years ago.

When Pure Bliss first came out Noah Bennett was something of a controversial character, but I loved the idea of a second chance romance—between brothers. These books are about love in all its forms. Between lovers and friends. Between family members, both blood and found. Between friends. And sometimes it's about finding a way to love ourselves. This is one of those stories.

You are enough.

Have fun in Bliss!

Love,

Lexi

Prologue

Five years before

James looked at his brother, his heart in his throat. They didn't share a drop of blood, but they'd shared every damn thing else since the day Noah's father and James's father had decided to marry the same woman. For almost seventeen years, it had been him and Noah and the odd family their parents had created.

How could Noah walk away when James needed him most? How could he not understand how much trouble they were all going to be in soon?

"You promised to come back here and start a practice." James had said the words about three hundred times since his brother announced he was leaving Bliss at his father's funeral the day before. James was down a dad. How the hell was he supposed to get through this? Brian Bennett's grave was in the small private cemetery on Glen land. Their mom died the year before, and he didn't give his own biological father more than a year or so. Fred Glen already looked lost without the two people he'd spent his life with. He wouldn't eat. He barely slept. His dad was going to fade away.

And then he would be utterly alone with a huge herd. He was going to have to keep the ranch going all on his own. So many people depending on him. So much history riding on his dumbass shoulders. He wasn't ready for it. He needed his brother.

Noah frowned, but he didn't stop shoving clothes into his suitcase. "I can't, Jamie. You know how bad I feel about this. I can't let Ally go all the way to New York without me. You know I'll do anything else I can to help out."

Ally. Ally was the reason his whole world was falling apart. And he had no one to blame but himself. He'd been the one to bring Ally into their lives. She was a gorgeous raven-haired beauty with a banging bod and an open mind. He'd thought she was the perfect woman to share with Noah. Seemingly fun loving, and with a healthy enough sex drive to keep up with two men, Ally was a good-time girl.

Except she'd decided to play some nasty games with them. And Noah had bought it hook, line, and sinker.

"You know she hit on Rye Harper two days ago. Callie saw it happen." James believed Callie Shepherd. Callie had never lied to him, had no reason to. Rye had turned Ally down, but it proved beyond a shadow of a doubt that they couldn't trust her.

Noah's eyes narrowed. "That's a lie. The way I heard it, Rye hit on her. I should never have let her go into that bar alone."

"She didn't even tell you she was going." Ally didn't tell Noah much. And Noah was being disturbingly stubborn. Noah was the smartest man James knew, but he was being damn dumb when it came to Ally. How could he not see that Ally had gotten serious about him once she realized Noah had recently come into a ten-million-dollar trust fund?

"It doesn't matter. I should have protected her. She can be very naïve."

James felt his fists clench. Noah was the naïve one.

It had been six months since James had brought that gold digger into their lives, and Noah still couldn't see what was right in front of his face. For months, James had been forced to watch his brother fall under this woman's spell, and he was utterly helpless to stop it. He hadn't joined them in bed in the last three months, not since he'd caught Ally making out with a biker at Hell on Wheels. He'd overheard her telling the biker all about how she'd found two rich boys to fleece. He'd told Noah. They hadn't spoken for weeks. "Can't you see what she's doing? Why the hell won't you believe me? I heard her. She's using us for money."

Noah's face flushed. He was only a year younger, but he'd been so smart he'd managed to graduate in the same class as James. Noah had a brilliant mind, but a wickedly stubborn heart. "You're mad because for once a woman loves me more than you."

And that was the goddamn heart of the matter. Ally was smart. She'd seen the weak spot in their relationship, and like the cancer she was, she'd zeroed in and started a festering sore between them. "Noah, I don't care about her. I never really did. She was fun, but that was all she ever was to me."

Noah's face went red, his shoulders squared. "Yeah, I get that. You just wanted to fuck her."

"Don't you talk to me like that. How many women have we gotten between us? Hell, Noah, I can count on one damn hand how many times I've slept with a woman without you. Why won't you believe me?"

His younger brother's face was a mottled red as he scrubbed a hand through his scruffy hair. "She's beautiful. She's smart, and you can't handle the fact that she only wants me."

"She only wants you because I turned her down. You think she didn't try to pull this shit on me first? She came to me because she knew I'm going to inherit this ranch." The land had been in the Glen family for three generations. Before his father had formally started a relationship, he'd made sure the Circle G wouldn't pass to anyone but his son.

Of course, he'd loved Noah as his own. He'd set up a trust for Noah, and Ally knew all about it. Noah had come into his trust two months before. And that was exactly the time Ally had decided she wanted to get married.

"Fuck you, Jamie. She loves me. She only slept with you to get to me. I never told you that because I didn't want to hurt you, but it's the truth. I am sick of living in your shadow. Ally sees the real me."

"What the fuck are you talking about? My shadow? Are you insane?" Had Noah forgotten their childhood?

"You were the football star. You were the rodeo star. You were the one every girl wanted, and I went along for the ride." Noah's voice was low, as though he didn't want anyone to know how jealous he was.

But James had his own envies. "And every teacher we ever had wondered how you got all the brains in the family. I barely made Bs while you were a Merit Scholar. I didn't get to go to college."

Their stepmother had gotten sick. James could remember the day he and Noah sat down and decided that one of them had to stay behind to run the ranch while their dads cared for the woman they both loved. It had been a no-brainer. Noah was brilliant. He'd always wanted to be a vet, and there was no doubt the Circle G could use a vet.

Noah's jaw tightened. He picked up the suitcase, locking it shut with a horrible finality. "That wasn't my fault. And you never wanted to leave this ranch anyway."

"I never got the chance." He'd had everything in place. He'd been ready to go to the University of Colorado with Noah. They had picked out a place to live.

He'd been standing in the driveway as Noah had driven off.

"Well, you got the ranch, and I get the girl. I would say we're even."

"Not anywhere close, Noah." James felt his blood pressure starting to rise. "We paid for your college. All of that money came straight out of ranch funds with the agreement that you would come back here and start a practice. Doc Harris is retiring next year. We won't have a vet, much less one who can deal with large animals. You can't walk out on us."

Noah's face went a little white. "You'll find another vet. Stef Talbot will import one if you get Max or Rye to ask him. They'll need a vet, too."

"Everyone is waiting for you." Everyone in Bliss had been thrilled when Noah had returned to do his internship with Doc

Harris a year earlier than anyone had expected, but then that was Noah. He was a type A overachiever to his core.

Noah's face fell. "That's not my problem. Damn it, I can't stay here. I love her."

How was this happening? "She is using you. She wants your money."

"You don't understand. She's an actress. She needs to be in New York."

She was an actress all right. She had played them both to perfection. "And who's paying for this trip?"

He shook his head. "It's not a trip. I believe in her. We're going to live in New York while she builds her career. I can work anywhere."

"You're going to leave your family over her?"

"I love her," Noah replied simply. "And I don't have much of a family anymore. Not since Mom and Dad died."

"You still have a father." How the hell was he going to tell his father that Noah was leaving? Hadn't their father lost enough?

Noah turned away. He looked out the window. Even from where James stood, he could see what Noah was looking at. This room had a glorious view of the ranch and the mountains. They would sit for hours as kids, looking out over the country. "I love your dad. He's my dad, too, but you know as well as I do that Ally isn't cut out for ranch life. You aren't going to talk me out of this. You can make up all the crap you want about her, but I know the truth. She loves me, and we're getting married. We're going to Vegas before we head to New York."

"Don't do this. Don't leave. I need you here. I don't think Dad is going to last more than a year, and the ranch is in trouble. Please stay." He was ready to get down on his hands and knees if it meant keeping his brother away from Ally.

"I'm sorry." Noah brushed past him. "I love you, brother, but I have to do this."

He was left standing in the hall of the house where they'd grown up.

"Guess he's not going to listen to you." A voice came from down the hall. It was soft and sweet and completely poisonous.

James turned. Ally had been listening in. Most likely, she'd been laughing the whole time. "I swear to god, I will protect him from you if it's the last thing I do."

Her lips curved up in a secret smile. Ally was gorgeous, but there was a coldness to her that no man would ever thaw. He could see that now. Ally stood there in her designer jeans and a tight sweater that showed off her perfect breasts. She leaned casually against the wall, as though she owned the place. Ally always looked comfortable, as though she belonged everywhere and could take you along for the ride. "He doesn't want your protection, Jamie. He loves me. He'll do anything for me. Part of that is because of you. He wants something you can't have. That was the key to Noah. Once I realized you would never leave this ranch, I decided that Noah would suit me fine. And he was a breeze. Baby brother wants something of his own. So desperately. He wants to be the big man for once. He wants to be the winner. And don't bother telling him any of this. He won't believe you."

Unfortunately, she was right about that. "His trust fund won't last forever."

She shrugged, staying out of James's reach. "Then you can have him back in a couple of years. Bye, Jamie. It was good while it lasted. You know, a girl could get used to the whole ménage thing."

A few minutes later, he heard the car pull away. He was alone.

He walked out and saddled up. The ranch didn't care that his heart hurt. The ranch didn't care that his rage threatened to explode out of his chest. The ranch just kept going.

And the ranch was the only thing that mattered now.

* * * *

Noah's heart was in his throat as he looked back at the home he'd grown up in. He stood in the circular drive in front of the only home he could really remember. His car was packed, waiting for him to drive away. How was he leaving this place? How was this happening? The conversation he'd just had with his brother sat in his gut, guilt churning inside him.

Ally put a hand on his shoulder. "He'll be okay. James always is."

His brother was the strong one. It was what he'd heard all his life. His brother was the golden boy, ranching coming easy to him. Noah struggled with it. He'd had to work three times as hard to do things half as well as Jamie.

He was the boy. James was the man. If he stayed here, that was how it always would be.

Of course a man would stay and honor his promises. That's what his father would have said.

Ally looked at him, her gorgeous eyes shining with tears. "Are you thinking about staying? Are you thinking about leaving me?"

God, she was beautiful, and she needed him. No one ever truly needed him, not the way Ally did. Every woman they'd ever shared had wanted Jamie and taken him on because they were a packaged deal. If he let Ally go, he might be sentencing himself to a life where he was always the afterthought.

Still, he hated the way he and Jamie had just parted. He couldn't stand the thought that everyone in this town would think less of him. Was he making a terrible mistake?

He'd grown up here. He loved Bliss. Hell, he'd missed Bliss while he'd been in college. The whole time all he'd wanted to do was come home and start his life. Then it had all taken a turn when Ally had walked in. When he'd caught sight of her he'd known beyond a shadow of a doubt he'd met the most beautiful woman in the world.

And she'd wanted him. Him.

What if they could make a life here? He knew she had her dreams, but he had his, too.

"Have you thought about the fact that I can make a good living here?" It wouldn't be close to what he could make in a city, but the cost of living was low.

A single tear caressed her cheek and she seemed to shrink back. "You *are* leaving me."

There was such panic in her voice that it made him reach out, to get his hands on her to reassure her. He couldn't let her think for a second that he would leave her. She had serious abandonment issues.

"No, I promised you that I would stay with you. I love you. I'm just saying I owe this town. We could stay around and I could repay that debt. I could work as a vet until Stef finds someone else and you could work in the rep theater, get a résumé going."

It could work for both of them. She was young and so beautiful it hurt to look at her. She could stay here for a few years and hone her craft, and they could leave when the time was right.

"I can't, Noah." She backed away from him. "I've got a big audition in a couple of days. You know that."

He did. It was all she'd talked about. "I'll go with you. I'll fly us both in. First class. We can see what happens and make a decision from there."

"You don't believe in me."

He sighed. "I believe in you, baby. I believe in you so much. You're incredibly talented, but there are a lot of factors at play in every audition. Manhattan is expensive. Maybe we should stay here for a while and we can fly in and out until we're sure this is what you want to do."

She sniffled, a sure sign she was holding back tears. "I've known this was what I wanted to do since I was a child. I won't change my mind, Noah, and living here would kill my soul. I need a big city. You can do your work anywhere. There are always animals in need."

"But the people need me here."

She shook her head. "If this place is so wonderful, I'm sure they won't have any trouble finding someone to take your place. Noah, you promised me. You promised we would get married and you would come with me. I'm starting to think all my friends were right and you don't want to marry me at all. You were using me."

How could she possibly believe that? "I love you, Ally. You're the only woman I've ever loved."

He was heartsick at the thought of her not believing him.

She moved in close. "I have to be in New York. Please come with me. I can't stand the thought of not having you by my side. It's such a big city and anything could happen to me. I love you so much, Noah. I need you. Please don't leave me all alone."

He looked back at the house he'd grown up in. His choice. Love or duty? But didn't he owe his first duty to the woman who was about to be his wife? Didn't he owe her everything? They were going to have a family, build a life together.

The ranch was his past. Ally was his future. He had to choose her.

"Get in the car. It's time to go." He ached at the thought of leaving his brother, but this was the love of his life.

Ally smiled and his heart nearly broke at the relief he saw there. "You won't regret it."

Of course he wouldn't. But he would regret how he'd left James. He would make it up to him. He would find a way.

He got in the car and drove off into his bright future.

* * * *

Two years later
Dallas, TX

It was the sound of his voice that woke her up. Deep and soothing, it had been his voice that had called to her the night before. He'd been sitting at the bar when she'd walked in. It was a dive bar in a bad part of town, but it was cheap and no one would ask too many questions. The fact that it had been a block down from the crappiest motel in the world had been a plus. She'd stayed two nights at that rattrap, and she swore the first night she'd watch a chick drag a dead guy into her room. At least she'd thought he was dead. Something had woken that guy up because there had been serious noise coming from that room, and it hadn't been the two of them fighting.

The weird light she'd seen had been a figment of her imagination.

Or all the alcohol she'd drank. Yeah, she was willing to admit that, too.

But the man she'd met the night before might make up for all of it. He was gorgeous, with dark hair and the body of a linebacker.

So different from her slender demon with his genteel manners and looks.

21

She shivered despite how warm the room was.

"Yeah, I know, Ian. Everything is set up. Tell Lodge he can take down the senator tonight at the party. I'm monitoring the situation."

He was still here. He wasn't a dream. Damn it. She forced her eyes open. The guys she slept with almost never stayed the night. But then she usually went for the assholes, and from what she could remember of the night before, this one had seemed like a nice guy.

Of course she didn't have the best radar at who was nice and who was a psychotic killer, so there was that.

She tried to piece together what she could from the night before. She'd gotten to the bar early and started in on the vodka, the cheapest she could find. She'd watched him. He'd talked to some guys and seemed to be making some kind of deal. At first she'd worried he was a dealer of some kind, but then the guy sitting beside her had gotten handsy and he'd stepped in. What was his name? Andy? Adam? Aaron? Something with an A.

It was kind of a blur from there, but she could see his face looming over hers as he laid her down in bed.

Damn it. When would she stop this? When would this cycle end?

She wasn't sure there was any peace at all for her in this world, and she'd made the choices that brought her here.

"I need to go. Let me know if you want me at The Club tonight." There was a pause. "No, it's not what you think. I'll fill you in later."

Why was he still here? Hadn't they had a good time? Maybe if she stayed very still, he would get a hint and leave. She rarely had to face her good-time guys the next day.

"Hey, I know you're awake. Are you feeling okay? I went out and got you some water and aspirin."

Fuck. There was nothing for it now. She opened her eyes. Her mouth was parched and she desperately needed that aspirin.

She was still in her clothes. That was definitely new. When she got in that horrible place she seemed to visit so often since that final night in Georgia, she didn't end up all nice and neat and napping. She ended up trying to obliterate herself with a toxic mix of casual sex and as much alcohol as she could drink. It did not lead to her waking up in her clothes.

"Here you go." The big, gorgeous man with golden-brown hair and striking green eyes stood above her, offering her a bottle of water and two aspirin. "You seemed upset last night."

She swallowed the aspirin and hoped it stayed down. Her gut felt twisted. "I was just partying. Uh, thanks for getting me back to my room."

She forced herself to sit up. The clock on the bedside table read way too early. She hadn't seen that side of eight in months.

She'd used to love the mornings. They were quiet and she could pretend she was alone, the only girl in the whole world. The mornings had been her happy time.

Now she lived in the night.

"I don't think you were partying, Hope." He sank his big, muscular frame into the single chair in the room.

He knew her name? How far gone had she been the night before? She was smart enough to not give some random guy her real name. A chill went through her. What if he wasn't so random? Now that she really looked at him, he had that cop look about him. Oh, not the kind who walked the street and dealt with that level. No. This guy would be a detective or...her stomach turned...a fed.

Her hands shook as she took another drink of the water. "What do you want from me?"

His green eyes suddenly narrowed, but not in a hard way. He seemed concerned. "I don't want anything except to help you. It's obvious you're in trouble."

Maybe he didn't know. Maybe he was just some do-gooder. She could handle that. She gave him a weak smile. "I just finished up the semester at my college and I was out for a good time."

"Honey, no one goes into that bar looking for a good time. You go into a bar like that to find trouble. I'm not the cops, but I know a woman in trouble when I see one. You nearly passed out at the bar. If I hadn't been there, one of the men would have taken you god knows where and done whatever they liked with you. You weren't there with a bunch of girlfriends. You walked into that bar knowing how the evening would end. Something terrible happened to you and you'll do anything to forget it, including putting yourself in a position where you might not wake up in the morning and you're okay with that. I know because I've been there. I know a woman who understands where you are, too. I would love for you to talk to her. Her name is Eve. She's my..." He seemed to choke up for a moment. "She's the best person I know. She can help you."

There was no help for her. But she got the idea this guy was in full-on dad mode, and he might be forceful about it. "I'm okay, Mr...I'm sorry, it's Aaron?"

"Alex. Alex McKay," he replied with a sad twist of his mouth, as though he'd realized the situation was far worse than he'd imagined. "I was working last night, setting something up for the security firm I own. I would very much like to help you. If there's someone after you, my firm can look into it."

She didn't have more than a hundred bucks to her name, and the minute this so-called security firm started looking into her they would likely turn her over to the police.

Panic started to thrum through her system. How did she get out of this? There was only one door to the place. She couldn't push past him. Maybe she could play on his better instincts. He seemed to have those. "So this woman you know, she's been through some bad stuff, too?"

"Yes, some really bad stuff and she's strong. We're not through it. I don't know that we ever get through it, but we're both functional," he said. "I can bring her out here, or maybe we could meet her for breakfast."

She had no idea what his game was. He couldn't possibly be this good. If anything, her past had taught her that she was about to be sold into some kind of slavery ring. Or that the really nice guy would find out what she'd done and he would happily chuck her into a jail cell. She had to get away.

"Breakfast would be nice. Where do you want me to meet you?"

He sighed. "I'm not going to convince you, am I?"

She shook her head. "I can talk to her, but I need to take a shower and change my clothes. I can meet you."

"It's dangerous. What you're doing is dangerous, Hope. Did you know you scream out in the night? Something about a fire."

Yes, she'd definitely done something dangerous. "I have nightmares sometimes. That's all. I would rather talk about this with a woman."

That was the way to play this man. She'd gotten good at manipulations. It was so horrible to think that way. She used to be nice. She used to pride herself on how she helped other people, and now she looked for vulnerabilities to get her way. Now she didn't care about anything but her next drink.

God, she wanted a drink. A drink would make the day bearable.

He stood and there was a wealth of disappointment in his eyes. "All right, then. There's a diner a block down from here. I'll call my wife...ex-wife...and we'll be there for an hour or so. I genuinely hope you show up, Hope. You don't have to be in this place. There are ways out."

Tears pierced her eyes as he walked away and closed the door behind him.

She sniffled and wiped the tears from her eyes and got out of bed.

Fifteen minutes later she slipped behind the wheel of her crappy car and started it up. Everything she owned was in a duffel bag. She glanced over and noticed there was an envelope on the seat, her name written in a neat, masculine script.

She hesitated for a moment but opened it. Five one hundred dollar bills were wrapped in a paper that contained a note.

Don't give up on yourself. And try to find a better motel wherever you go. There were arrows in one of the doors next to this one. I'm fairly certain someone is hunting in the parking lot. Here's my number if you need me. Alex McKay

She stared at that note for the longest time, but finally took the cash and tossed the number out of the window before she drove away. She pointed her car west and didn't look back.

He was wrong. There was no peace for her.

Chapter One

"God, man, I can't believe you're leaving." James held a hand out to Logan Green.

Logan shook his hand briefly before letting it go. In the past, James would have pulled the younger man in for a big bear hug, but the last year had changed something fundamental in his friend. Logan looked far older than his years since that day when he'd been tortured and left for dead by a member of the Russian mob.

"Me, either." Logan turned back slightly to where Wolf Meyer stood by his enormous black truck. James had already said good-bye to Wolf and knew how anxious he was to get to Dallas. The former Navy SEAL had been talking to a woman online and over the phone for weeks. Wolf Meyer was going to Dallas in the hopes that things might work out between him and the woman he'd been set up with. Another friend leaving.

"I wish you didn't have to go."

"I have to do something, man. I can't keep on like this." Logan smiled slightly, a hint of the sarcastic friend James knew so well. "If I don't get my ass fixed, I'm going to end up in jail or dead."

Despite the fact that he didn't want to lose another friend, James knew Logan was right. Logan had been on the edge of something dark and nasty for months and months. Still, it seemed like everyone in the whole goddamn world was moving on, and he was standing utterly still, watching it all go by. "So you think Wolf's brother can fix you?"

Logan shrugged. "Wolf seems to think so. I don't know. He seems to either cuss his brother out or talk about him like he's some kind of saint. It's weird."

"No, it's not. That's what happens with brothers." It had certainly been that way between him and Noah before they weren't anything at all. He didn't like thinking about the last time he'd seen his brother. Noah had shown up for James's father's funeral, but he'd been a different man. Bitter and sarcastic and distant. He'd stayed a single night and then he'd gotten back on a plane for New York.

God, he missed his brother.

Logan frowned, his brow furrowing. "I hope it's normal because I'm supposed to live with them for a while. I don't think it's a good idea if I'm the sanest person in the place. Did you know they're taking me to a BDSM club?"

James laughed. He shouldn't be surprised. After all, his new partner was one of Leo Meyer's "fixes." Leo was a psychologist who specialized in men with impulse-control issues. The term "impulse-control issues" pretty much summed up Logan to a tee. "Uhm, so they think putting a collar on you is going to fix your problems?"

Logan rolled his eyes. "I'm the Dom, dummy. Apparently this Leo guy thinks training in a club will help me find some measure of control. You wouldn't believe the schedule this dude has me on. There's apparently a lot more to therapy than I thought."

James could imagine. Group therapy from nine to ten. Whips and Chains 101 from ten to noon. Break for lunch, and then on to Advanced Butt Plugging. Actually, it sounded kind of fun. How long had it been since he'd had anything but vanilla sex?

"I think this Leo guy is pretty good. According to my new partner, the man practically walks on water."

Logan's arms crossed over his chest. "McNamara? I kind of hoped to meet him. Damn, that guy was some kind of quarterback."

He felt a weird surge of emotion at the thought of his new partner. Trev McNamara was absolutely the calmest presence he'd ever been around. He'd only been on the ranch for a short time, but he was already someone James could count on. "He's some kind of man, Logan. He's been to hell and back, and apparently Leo Meyer was the guide on the 'back to reality' portion of his life. Seriously, Trev is someone I admire, and he gives Wolf's brother all the credit. I think you're going to be in good hands."

He'd been a bit disappointed when Trev had come complete with a family. When Trev had called to let him know he was coming to Bliss with a wife and a partner in tow, James had realized that he'd secretly hoped Trev could fill the void Noah had left behind. Trev, Beth, and Bo hadn't been in Bliss for long, but James was already jealous of their close-knit little family.

Logan nodded. "I know his story. I think it's one of the reasons I'm willing to go to Dallas. And I trust Wolf."

"He's a good man, too. Damn, I'm going to miss you." He'd said that far too much in his life.

Logan smiled slightly. "You, too. You've been a good friend these last couple of months when I didn't really deserve it."

"You always deserved it, Logan." If this went on much longer, James was going to embarrass himself. "Go on. Go to Dallas and get fixed up."

Logan flushed, looking like the comic-book-loving geek he'd been before that terrible day. Even a hint of that fun-loving man made James hope for the best. "Well, you're my last stop before I head out. I've already said good-bye to my moms and everyone in the department. I made sure I said good-bye to Holly and Caleb and Alexei. I said I was sorry, too. God, I wish I could look at that man and not get mad."

Alexei Markov was the reason Logan was twelve kinds of fucked up. He was also the reason Logan was alive. "You'll get there. You have to. I don't think the man is going anywhere."

Alexei Markov was madly in love with Holly Lang. He and the town doctor, Caleb Burke, had settled their differences and were happily sharing Holly. It was kind of a way of life here in Bliss.

Logan leaned against the rail of the white picket fence that wrapped around the porch. It had been a joke among his parents that they had found the American dream of one woman, two men, and a whole bunch of cattle. "I wanted to talk to you last because I have to ask a favor of you."

"Anything." For the last several years, Logan had been his closest friend. He would do almost anything for the man.

"Something's wrong with Hope."

Just like that his stomach took a nose dive. A vision of Hope McLean assaulted him. God, how could a woman who wore too-big clothes and hid behind glasses get to him the way she did? He steered clear of that girl. He made it his mission in life to not get close to her because every time she talked in that ridiculous Southern accent of hers, his cock got hard and his heart soft. It was a bad combo. "What do you mean?"

Logan sighed. "God, you have to get over whatever it is that puts you off her. I don't get it. She's so freaking nice. Why are you the only one in this damn town who can't be cool with her?"

Because every time she walked in a room, his libido went into overdrive and his brain took a nosedive. He'd cultivated an air of cool indifference around the lovely, soft, and scrumptious Hope McLean. "We don't get along, I guess."

Bullshit. You would love to get along with her, but she's not some good-time girl. She would want more than a quick fuck and you know it. You would want more. And you have no idea how to do that without your brother at your side.

Logan straightened up. "I'm asking you to look past that. I like the hell out of her. Something's up with her, and I can't get anyone to talk to me about it. She's closemouthed. She won't admit to anything. I think Nate knows something, but the bastard never tells me a goddamn thing. He's even been quiet around Callie."

Nate Wright was the sheriff of Bliss. He was also married to the worst gossip in Bliss. And his partner was Bliss's only tavern owner. Between Callie and Zane, gossip flowed freely. It said something that Nate Wright knew how to keep a secret. What the hell kind of secret could someone as sweet and harmless as Hope McLean have?

29

"What makes you think she's in trouble?"

"She's not sleeping. I can tell. I've caught her napping in the break room several times this week. She's working far more than she's scheduled to. Cam and I added up her hours for the last week, and we're pretty sure she hasn't been at home for more than a few hours a day. And she's been touchy. She's usually a rock, but she's been jumpy lately. I overheard a call two days ago. She yelled. Hope never yells. She told someone named Christian to leave her alone."

"He sounds like a douchebag." The thought that Hope had a boyfriend named Christian unnerved him.

"I need someone to figure out what's going on with her. I might not be the best cop in the world, but I know when something's wrong with one of my friends. I would feel better about this if I knew you were looking after her."

What choice did he have? Logan was in serious trouble. He needed help. It wouldn't be the friendliest thing to do to tell him that he wouldn't look into Hope's trouble because he was worried he couldn't control himself around her. "Sure."

And he would do it. He'd promised with one simple word, and that was his stupid-ass bond.

Logan sighed, his relief obvious. "Thank you. I really like Hope. I would hate to think something bad was happening and no one cared. Just figure out if it's dangerous and handle it. Okay?"

It was right there on the tip of his tongue to ask what could possibly be dangerous. He held that thought. In the last several years, Bliss had seen its share of druggie bikers, stalkers, serial killers, and the damn Russian mob. Hope could be involved in anything from white slavery to alien abduction, and it would be the norm in Bliss. "I'll check it out."

Logan reached out and slapped his shoulder. "Thanks, man. Give me a call if you find anything out. I want to know what's up with that girl. She's a sweetheart. Makes the best chocolate chip cookies ever. And she always watches out for me. She showed up at Hell on Wheels to haul my ass home one night. I owe her. Please, Jamie. Take care of her. She's a friend."

James nodded his head slowly, the true weight of what he was agreeing to coming down on him. "I will."

He would. He didn't have much in this world beyond his word. He would figure out what was making Hope not sleep at night. It was probably something like a lost library book.

He wouldn't get close to her. He wouldn't spread her legs and penetrate her. He wouldn't tie her up and have his wretched way with her. He wouldn't take those glasses off and look in her eyes while he stroked into her with his cock. Nope. He was going to figure out her problem and solve it and send her on her way.

Logan put out a hand. James shook it. He was losing another friend. It seemed to be a theme to his life.

He watched as Logan got into Wolf's truck and drove off to face his future. James knew where his future was. It was right here on the Circle G. It always had been. This land was his legacy, his burden, his destiny.

He'd given up a lot for this land.

And now he only had half of it left. He sighed as Wolf's truck drove off, churning up dirt in its wake. He still had the Circle G. He'd almost lost it.

James turned and went back in the house. He needed to head into town and see what was up with Hope. He'd made a promise, and he intended to keep it.

* * * *

Hope McLean stared out the window of the Sheriff's Department, watching the world go by. Not that there were tons of people walking down Main Street. A couple of late-season tourists walked up the steps to the Trading Post. Mel and Cassidy walked down the street, their hands tucked together. Cassidy wiped her eyes with her free hand, and Mel pulled her close, whispering something to her that got her smiling.

Cassidy had recently said good-bye to her son. And Hope had said good-bye to her friend.

She sniffled. God, she was going to miss Logan. She understood why he was leaving, but even at his worst, Logan had been a good friend to her.

Mel waved as he walked by. Hope raised a hand and prayed she

31

was smiling. She could feel her lips tugging up, but sometimes she wondered if the people around her could tell that it was all for show.

She sighed as a Bronco pulled up and Deputy Cameron Briggs slid from the driver's seat. Cam Briggs was an all-American hunk of man. He filled out his khakis with impressive style.

He was also totally taken and insanely happy with his woman. He and his partner, Rafe Kincaid, shared Laura Niles.

There was a whole lot of sharing going on in Bliss.

And Hope was alone. But then she deserved to be.

"Hey, Hope. Anything happening?" Cam asked with a smile as he walked through the inner doors. He pulled his Stetson off his head and set it on his desk.

She shook her head. "Nope. I think we're in a quiet period."

That was the way it was in Bliss. Months of lovely boredom broken up with flashes of catastrophe. It wasn't the easiest thing in the world to work for the Bliss County Sheriff's Department, but she did love her job. Sometimes it was the only thing she had.

"Nate's settled into the cabin," Cam said. "Callie seems to be recovering quite nicely. Those babies are adorable. And Stefan gave them a little present."

She could guess what the King of Bliss had given to his oldest friend. Callie had been unaware she was having twins. "A second set of everything?"

Cam grinned, sitting on the edge of his desk. "Callie was damn happy about that. So were Nate and Zane. They'd talked about putting baby Charlie in one of the dresser drawers." He sighed. "I love this town. Back where I came from no one would have cared enough to make sure those babies were comfortable. The women wouldn't have made sure that Callie didn't have to cook for a couple of weeks. They would have shrugged and moved on. Of course, the town where I came from would have driven them out. They're kind of traditional."

Most of the world was. Bliss was different. "Did Logan say good-bye?"

Cam hopped off his desk and came to stand right in front of her. He put his hands on her shoulders. She had to look up, way up, to see his face. His blue eyes were somber as he looked down at her.

"He's going to be okay. He's going to get what he needs, and then he'll come back and maybe it can work for the two of you."

Hope felt her own eyes go wide. "Logan is like my brother. I have zero interest in him in any kind of a physical way."

He dropped his hands. "Damn it. I always get that wrong. I thought you two would make a good couple. You're not seeing anyone. He's not seeing anyone."

She shook her head. "Not going to happen. But I do care about him."

They hadn't tried dating. They'd seemed to be such good friends that there was no reason to screw it up by dating. Sex screwed everything up.

So why couldn't she get her mind off James Glen? He was sex on a stick, walking around town in cowboy boots. He was too perfect, too gorgeous. With his easy smile and laid-back manner, he charmed almost every woman in a hundred-mile radius. He was flirty and playful. There wasn't a woman in the county that James Glen didn't sharpen his skills on. From babies to old ladies, he was charming with them all.

With everyone but her. It was her luck that the only man she was interested in was totally turned off by her.

Cam shook his head. "Well, it shows what I know. Laura told me I was wrong. She seems to think you have a thing for that rancher."

Her stomach twisted. The last thing she wanted was for gossip to start. "James? I don't think so."

"Well, that's good because from what I can tell, he's on top of any female who will let him climb on."

Again. Any female with the singular exception of one Hope McLean. Her skin grew hot at the thought of the one time she'd asked him if he maybe wouldn't mind having dinner with her since they had both been alone at Stella's and it seemed silly to take up a whole booth when they could sit together.

He had explained that he was done even though his burger was untouched. He'd thrown some money down and nearly run out the door.

Hope hadn't eaten that day, merely walked up the steps to her apartment, sat down, and cried.

No. James Glen wasn't for her.

"Hey," Cam said, patting her on the back. "What do you want for lunch? It's on me. We're going to be stuck together for a couple of weeks until Nate gets back or we hire another deputy. We might as well enjoy ourselves. I brought a set of checkers and some other games."

Logan had been the one to sit and play games with her. It would have been easier on her ego if she had been madly in love with Logan.

"I would love the special." She had no idea what the special was today. It could be anything from enchiladas to something utterly unpronounceable made from goat and truffle oil. It all depended on what Hal, Stella's short-order cook, had recently seen on the Food Network. Still, it was always an adventure, and Hal was nice to her.

"Brave girl. I'll go pick it up." Cam winked and then disappeared, jogging down the street.

She watched him go, her eyes trailing back toward the diner. It was the place where all the citizens of Bliss met and hung out. She'd eaten lunch with Logan there at least four times a week. Even at his surliest, he'd been company. Now he was gone.

And James was dating some actress, though dating wasn't exactly what Hope would call it. James wasn't known for his long-term relationships.

Hope caught sight of the mailman. Barney Osman was a sweet man nearing retirement age. He drove all across two towns, carrying the mail in his truck. Hope stepped outside the double doors, walking to meet him before he had to come up the steps. Barney was a nice man, but his knees weren't what they used to be according to his many health-related stories. Hope spoke to him for a moment, learned about his ongoing battle with gout, and waved him on his way. She stood outside, sorting through the mail, which included a catalog of fishing equipment, some formal-looking letters that Nate would probably toss out in favor of the fishing catalog, an ad for computer equipment, and a large flyer for the new play being presented by the Repertory Theater.

"You should come. It's going to be a great night," a confident voice said.

Hope turned, her heart sinking a little. Speak of the perfectly coiffed devil. Serena Hall stood in front of her wearing jeans, a silk blouse, and heels. She looked utterly out of place and wholly beautiful. She was also known to be a complete bitch. According to the gossip, she was sweet as pie around men but liked to play the queen bee around other women.

Still, Hope tried to get along. She nodded, clutching the mail to her chest. "I'm sure it will be."

"I have the lead this time." Serena adjusted her handbag. "It's hard to have to carry a whole play, but I've been assured that I'm doing a good job. Everyone who has seen it so far loves it."

Hope barely avoided rolling her eyes. "I'm sure you're great."

She shrugged slightly. "You know, you never can tell. James told me how good I am, but you know him. He'll say anything to get a girl in bed. You know the type."

Yep. She knew the type. "Sure. Well, good luck with the play. I should get back to the station in case anyone dies or something."

"Please, Hope. No one dies around here."

Hope stared at her.

"Well, no one important dies. It's all people from the outside." Serena's eyes narrowed. "I wanted to talk to you about James. Look, every woman in this town knows you have a thing for him. I think you should know that I understand. He's a very attractive man, but he isn't interested in you. You need to stop making a fool of yourself. It's sad the way you look at him. I'm trying to help you out."

Hope felt her eyes narrow. She might be quiet, but she wasn't an idiot. And she wasn't a doormat. "No, you're being mean. I haven't pursued him. I asked him out once. He turned me down. I stay away from him. I'm not any kind of threat to you, so why are you here throwing this in my face? There's no reason for you to do that except for the fact that you want to hurt me. Are you so insecure that you feel the need to hurt the people around you?"

Serena sputtered. "I am not."

But she was, and Hope could see plainly that she didn't like to be called on it. Well, too bad. She hadn't done anything wrong.

She'd liked a man who hadn't liked her back, so she'd left him alone. She wasn't going to take crap off this woman. "Yes, you are, and I think that makes you the pathetic one. Now, I have work to do."

Serena's lovely face hardened, losing the pseudo sympathy of before. "I'm dating him now. I'm warning you to stay away from him."

Hope sighed and actually felt a little bad for the brunette goddess. The fact that she called what she and James were doing dating meant she didn't understand James at all. James Glen didn't date. He hooked up, and he didn't tend to do it for long. Though usually he made the arrangement perfectly clear, from what Logan had told her. James was famous for the speech he gave before he slept with a woman.

She turned as quickly as she could, hoping not to get humiliated again. That was when she saw him.

A ghost from her past. Her heart nearly stopped in her chest because it couldn't be him. Not him.

It was a single glance. Golden hair and a lanky, lean build. Piercing gray eyes. Sensual lips. He stood outside the Trading Post, leaning against the huge evergreen that dominated the street. He was dressed in loose clothes and an open-necked shirt that showed off the beginnings of a cut torso. He was heartbreakingly gorgeous and evil beyond compare.

Her heart froze. She blinked, and he was gone as though he'd never been there in the first place.

And he couldn't have been. There was no way she'd seen what she thought she'd seen. No way he was here. It was a trick of her mind since that one phone call had sent her reeling back into the misery of ten years before. She could still hear it. A single sentence. "Hello, love." Then he'd hung up. And her world had turned upside down.

"I'm warning you, Hope," Serena said, her bratty voice sounding far away. Hope didn't look back. She simply stared at the place where the ghost had stood, a little smile on his face as he'd watched her. After a moment, Hope heard the click-clack of Serena's heels on the pavement as she walked off to meet her friends. Serena and her jealousy didn't mean a damn thing now.

Only one thing mattered. Christian Grady.

He couldn't have been standing in front of the Trading Post. Hope rushed down the street, but she saw nothing beyond the tourists and the women from the rep theater walking toward the diner. She hadn't seen Christian, and she was sure of it.

Because she'd killed him. She'd killed him, and he wasn't coming back.

Chapter Two

One week later

James hung up the phone with a frustrated sigh. According to Cam, Hope had ditched work this morning.

Hope was trying her damnedest to avoid him. That was what she was doing. She'd told Cam she had an emergency, but he had to wonder if Cam wasn't covering for her.

He'd spent a whole week pursuing that girl, and she was proving to be one slippery customer. He'd gone so far as to ask her out, giving her his smoothest smile and a full dose of cowboy charm. She'd turned a nice shade of green and had practically run out of Trio, leaving her BLT and fries behind and her bill unpaid.

She owed him five dollars and fifty cents. And a whole lot of explanations. Logan was right. Something was wrong, but either no one knew or no one was talking. Hope sure as hell wasn't talking. She'd started turning and walking the other way every time she saw him coming.

And she didn't look at him anymore.

It was damn frustrating. Especially since he wasn't even sure why he was pursuing her. The need to fulfill his promise to Logan was still in there, but it was more than that. Almost immediately after he'd decided to take his pledge to Logan seriously, he'd started to think.

The reason he'd stayed away from Hope was because he couldn't offer her anything past a couple of nights in bed. He couldn't offer any woman much more than that. After his father had died, it had been all he could do to keep the ranch from going into bankruptcy. When he'd finally realized there was no way to do it on his own, he'd gone to Stef, who'd put him in touch with a rancher friend of his named Jack Barnes. Barnes had taught him how a small ranch could thrive during a recession and introduced him to Trev McNamara.

The Circle G was on solid ground, and he wasn't alone. With the influx of cash Trev brought, he'd been able to hire some new hands. For the first time in five years, he might be able to have a personal life. He wasn't getting any younger. Maybe it was time to see about settling down.

He wanted Hope. But apparently he'd fucked that up.

James walked out onto the porch, needing to catch a breath. He thought better outside. The early-afternoon sun bathed the yard in light. It was starting to warm up, but they were beginning the quick slide into winter. It was already chilly at night and in the early part of the morning. Soon his fields would be covered in snow, and he would have to hunker down and survive until spring.

It got damn cold in Colorado during the winter. A man needed someone who could warm him up.

James growled and slapped his hand on the railing. His cell trilled. Finally Stef had managed to pay someone enough money to fix whatever the hell the Farley brothers had done to their cell tower. It had been months. He glanced down and grimaced. Serena. Maybe he could pay the Farley brothers to do it again. Serena was proving to be more tenacious than expected. He'd pursued her because she'd always flirted with him. It didn't hurt that she was easy on the eyes. She was only interested in her work and had told him flat out she just wanted to have a good time in bed.

Then she'd started calling him. A lot.

The cell continued to ring. He ignored it. He would have to go and talk to her. Let her down easy. He'd told her he didn't want a relationship. He would have to talk to her again, but now wasn't the time. Now he had to find Hope and pin her down.

Pin her down. Spread her out. Penetrate her with his cock. Yeah, that might be the way to get her to the heart of the matter. After she'd come five or six times, she might be willing to start talking to him.

"I sincerely hope I'm not the one who has you in such a bad mood." Bo O'Malley walked out of the main house. Bo was Trev's partner. They shared a wife.

James had to check himself, letting go of his anger. There was still a part of him that resented Bo. The big, blond cowboy had an easy smile and a manner that would help him fit in nicely on the ranch and in Bliss, but James hadn't gotten close to him. It wasn't fair, and he would get over it.

"Is old Red still giving you hell?" Bo asked, gesturing toward the barn.

Red was a horse he was trying to break. Big and powerful, the gelding would make a perfect ranch horse if he wasn't such a stubborn son of a bitch. Only yesterday, the horse had tossed him right into the dirt. His backside still ached. "He gives everyone hell."

Bo grinned. "I've worked around horses all my life, and I won't go near that one. That one is a mean son of a bitch. I bet he came out of his momma with an attitude problem. How did you end up with him?"

James rolled his eyes. "Because I'm a dumbass and a cheapskate. Now I'm going to have to either eat the money and buy another horse or even worse, admit to Max Harper that I can't break Red to a saddle."

"Max is the horse trainer? The one everyone claims is the meanest man in town?"

James laughed. "Max isn't mean. Max is an intolerant, impatient son of a bitch, but he doesn't have a mean bone in his body. I like Max, but he charges through the damn roof, and he will never let me hear the end of it. No. I am going to break that horse."

"Not if he breaks you first," Bo said, palming his keys. "Can you look in on Beth while I'm gone? I shouldn't be too long."

"What's wrong with Beth? And where's Trev?" He hadn't seen Trev this morning. If something was wrong with his wife, Trev would be climbing the walls. He was crazy about his wife. Beth McNamara-O'Malley was a sweet thing. And she was almost intimidating when it came to home improvement. She was planning to completely renovate the guest house for her family. Beth was planning a second floor and an expansion that would rival the main house.

God, he'd had to sell half his land to keep afloat. It wasn't merely Glen land anymore. It was McNamara land, too. His father would hate him for that.

Bo smiled, a secret grin. "She's all right. She's perfect, actually. Oh, she's puking her guts out, but apparently that's to be expected when she's…well, expecting."

James felt his eyes go wide. "Beth is pregnant?"

There must be something in the damn water. Everyone was pregnant lately. Rachel Harper had a baby. Callie had given birth to twins. And now Beth. Bliss was getting damn full of babies. And it didn't freak him out the way it should. He kind of liked babies. He really liked the idea of a family.

He was getting fucking old.

Bo's grin split his face and made the blond man look like a teenager. "Trev and I forced her to pee on a stick last night. Now she has to stay away from paint fumes and all sorts of things. She's real depressed about that. She loves the guesthouse, though. She says she can expand it without inhaling a single fume that might hurt the baby."

Beth had all sorts of plans for beautifying the ranch. Now those plans would include a nursery. Something weird twisted in his gut at the idea of babies running around the ranch. They wouldn't be his. The world kept moving on, and he stayed in one place.

Why was he staying away from Hope when he wanted her? Was he going to let his life slip by because he wasn't sure he could take care of a woman on his own? He could still hear his fathers joking with each other that the ranch was a second wife, that between the ranch and a woman, no single man would be able to handle them both. The ranch took so damn much time.

Every girl he'd tried to seriously date had walked away because he couldn't treat them right. He'd stopped trying. It had been different when Noah was around. Maybe he needed to be stronger. Maybe he needed to figure out a way to have the family he wanted. The one-night stands were getting old.

Of course, he might be shit out of luck. Hope wouldn't stay in the same room with him anymore. Had he been wrong about her? He'd been so sure she was interested, but maybe she'd figured out he wasn't a great catch.

"I'm headed into town. Trev went to a meeting in Alamosa, so it looks like I'm on saltine duty." Bo didn't look like a man who minded. James didn't bother to ask if Bo was disturbed by the fact that the baby in Beth's belly could be his or Trev's. It wouldn't have bothered James. It would have been his kid no matter what.

He nodded as Bo took off toward some future he was reaching for. James stood in the drive and wondered if he even had a future.

* * * *

Hope looked up into the newcomer's eyes and wondered if the universe hated her. He was gorgeous. Six and a half feet of pure sin wearing a pair of Levi's. He had dark hair and a perfect face. He was sober.

That last part was meaningful to Hope—unfortunately, he was also married.

She sighed and decided it was for the best. She shouldn't meet the future father of her children at an AA meeting. "You said your name was Trev?"

He'd introduced himself to the group for the first time this morning. She'd been affected by his story. Trev had lost everything to his disease. He'd had a promising career, money, everything a person could want, and he'd thrown it all away. Of course, the fact that he was here meant he knew how to fight his way back. She admired the hell out of that. She supposed he was from Alamosa.

Most of the group was. She was the only idiot alcoholic who had to drive in from Bliss.

She might be the only alcoholic in Bliss. Though she loved the town, its inhabitants were oddly perfect for all their troubles. She doubted Max Harper, for all his rage issues, had ever put himself in a hospital because he had to find the bottom of a bottle. She was pretty sure that even Mel could have the occasional beer without spiraling into a well of self-hatred.

Of course, she also bet neither of the men had seen what she had seen.

"Yes. It's Trev. And you're Hope, right? Is that a fake name? It's okay if it is. Trev is really my name. I can't exactly fake it, you know."

She didn't, but it didn't matter. "My name is Hope. Listen, I was moved by your story. I'm glad I came in today. It's been a hard week."

Trev took a long drink of his coffee. He'd walked in with a travel mug of coffee and had been refilling it every half an hour or so. The man seemed to like his coffee. "What's been rough?"

What hadn't been? And James Glen wasn't making it easier. He seemed to be taking up where Logan had left off. She'd thought when Logan had ridden off with Wolf that she could hide what was going on. But no, James "too hot for any one woman to handle" Glen was suddenly interested in how she was doing. Logan had set an attack dog on her. But she wasn't about to tell Trev that. She had plenty of other crappy things happening. "Well, my boss had twins a few weeks ago. He didn't have them. His wife did, but we only have one deputy now, so I'm working a lot. My car is nearly dead. It's on its last legs. I'll be surprised if I make it home. Oh, and there was a fire in the diner. I live over the diner. My apartment is now unlivable. I'm homeless. Yay!"

Trev's lips quirked up. "I can see where it's been a bad week. You need a place to stay?"

Addicts stuck together. It almost brought a tear to her eye. "Oh, I'll be fine. I live in a small town. I'll find a place to stay."

Stella had given her the bad news earlier today. It was why she'd run here. She'd basically packed up her Corolla with everything that wasn't smoke damaged and driven straight to the nearest AA meeting after teaching Cam how to work the dispatch. Not that there was anyone to dispatch. Cam was the only one working. And there was the fact that she was seeing ghosts. She was seeing ghosts everywhere. Since that day Serena had ambushed her, she thought she saw Christian more and more often. She would catch a glimpse out of the corner of her eye only to turn and realize it was nothing.

She shook her head, trying to rid herself of the thought.

She had no idea where she was going to stay. Her boss lived in a tiny cabin with his wife, twins, and Zane Hollister. Zane alone could take up all the space. Logan was gone. Cam was in the same situation as Nate. The remaining deputy lived with his girlfriend and best friend.

She was screwed. Well, she hadn't been screwed in years, and that was part of her problem.

"Are you sure? I have a big place. My wife hasn't made a lot of friends. She's a sweetheart. She's also pregnant, so you would have to deal with that."

Everyone was pregnant in Bliss. It only made sense that it would transfer outward to Alamosa and Del Norte. Everyone was starting families and moving forward in their lives, and all she seemed capable of doing was staring at James Glen. God, why was she so attracted to a manwhore? He was a manwhore. There was no other way to describe him. He slept with all the freaking ski bunnies who checked into the Elk Creek Lodge. He slept with anyone who didn't need more than one or two nights with him.

She needed a drink. It reminded her of the fact that she hadn't eaten all day. That was how she used to play. No food. Nothing to mitigate the effects of the alcohol. "How's the coffee?"

Trev smiled. "It's crap, but it does its job." He poured her some coffee into a little Styrofoam cup. "You did right, you know. Coming here. When the pressure builds, you gotta get in here. You gotta talk about it. Who's your sponsor?"

She sniffled. Kate had moved on, too. "She left a couple of months back. She moved to California. I've only been here about a year. I guess I'm a little lost without her. I could call, but it's not the same."

Trev got one of the napkins on the table and quickly wrote out a number. He passed it to her. "You need to find another sponsor. I know I can't be your official sponsor because I'm a guy, but I can still listen. I've been sober for one thousand seventy days. I know we're supposed to take it one day at a time, but I fully believe I won't take another drink for the rest of my life. I won't drink or do a drug. I love something more than myself, more than any high. If you need me, I'll be there for you. Please call me. I like to be needed."

Yes, what she needed was a gorgeous god of a man to tell her troubles to. It was hard to look at Trev and see addict. He was one of those people the universe had blessed with amazing looks and charm. And yet, despite all of that, he was here with the rest of them. Maybe everyone had a well of sadness lurking no matter how perfect their lives seemed. She took the number. "Thank you. I appreciate it. You might not. I might turn out to be the neediest thing you've met."

He laughed, the sound a deep rumble from his chest. "I doubt that. You've never met professional wide receivers. Now that is a needy class of people."

He'd mentioned something about football when he'd told his story to the group earlier. She didn't follow the sport, but it seemed Trev had been popular. She simply pushed the napkin into the pocket of her jeans. It was something to think about. She missed Kate. She couldn't talk about her past with her friends in Bliss. Keeping it all inside was starting to fester like an untended wound. Maybe if she found someone to talk to again, she would be able to sleep at night. Maybe she was seeing ghosts that weren't really there. "Thanks."

She shuffled out of the small church where Alcoholics Anonymous held daily meetings. It was a sparsely populated part of the country, but there was always someone here.

Only Nate Wright knew what she'd been through, and even he didn't know the full extent. It was a burden she was finding it difficult to bear alone even after all these years.

She got into her piece-of-crap Corolla and wondered how much Gene would charge her to stay at the Movie Motel. If it wasn't already full. There was a convention coming this week. Psychics and Wiccans were coming out to test the ley lines or something. Hope wasn't sure about any of it, but she'd overheard Nell and Henry talking about the possibility of finding the doorway to other planes. They were sure there was a doorway located somewhere in Bliss.

Hope turned on to 160 and wondered if that other plane would be better. Maybe on some alternate plane, she hadn't fucked up the way she had on this one. Of course, according to Nell, the other plane was filled with warring faeries or something. And she'd mentioned vampires, but they were corporate types. It had been a trippy conversation, but then Nell was known for those.

She let her mind drift. She was happy in Bliss, but she wondered if it wasn't time to move on. If Christian's former followers ever found her…she wouldn't think about that. Wouldn't think about him. Except it was hard. That night was always right there on the edge of her consciousness. It teased and taunted her. It had been almost ten years, and she could see it, smell it. God, she could still smell the blood. She could still feel the scream that was forever trapped in her throat.

And when she looked in the mirror, she could still see the girl she'd been at seventeen. The stupid, idiotic, wretchedly selfish girl she'd been. She wondered if her mother still cursed her name or if it had been long enough that she'd forgotten the daughter who had disappointed her.

Tears coated her eyes, making a watery mess of the road in front of her. She'd run so hard, but it was still there. It might always be there. She glanced down at the clock. She'd been driving for a while. The turn for the Great Sand Dunes National Park was to her right. She'd spent a perfect day there once. Logan had invited her along with his friends. It had been high summer, and everything had been in bloom. The dunes seemed to go on forever, as though she'd been transported to a different world. James Glen had been there. They'd brought a picnic and ate and then splashed in the creek that ran along the dunes. The sun had been hot, but the water cool. It ran off from the mountains. She'd turned her face up to the sun and for a while imagined that she was James's girl. She'd imagined that cowboy's smile was for her and that she deserved it.

She imagined a world where he would never discover what she'd done.

Yes, it was time to leave Bliss. It was time to lose herself in a city where no one cared. She loved Bliss, but sometimes it was all too much. She didn't deserve the people who tried to help her.

If only they knew.

She heard a weird popping sound, and her car swerved as if of its own volition. *Damn it.* She was still miles from Bliss, but there was no way to avoid the fact that a noxious cloud was currently billowing from beneath her car's hood. She struggled but managed to get the car off to the side of the road.

The engine died. It made a sad sighing sound, and everything went dark. No lights on the dash. No sounds from the radio.

It was the perfect end to a shitty week.

She tried her cell, but there was no reception. And probably no minutes left, either. It was almost the end of the month. She was stuck on the side of the road with no phone, no car, and everything she owned was piled in her trunk and the backseat.

She put her head down and let herself cry.

Chapter Three

Noah turned his truck to the west and wondered for the four hundredth time that day exactly what he was planning to say to his brother. Days on the road and he still hadn't figured it out. His stomach turned as he realized that the Circle G wasn't more than forty minutes away. Forty minutes and then he would have to stand in front of his brother. Noah turned to his companion, his best friend in the world.

"Hey, so the marriage thing didn't work out. You were right. She was after my money, and when she'd gone through my trust fund, she dumped me for a lawyer named Phil. Oh, but there were numerous men before that. I don't even know their names. We hadn't had sex in a couple of years, and I spent all my time vaccinating overprivileged Pomeranians. Can I come home now?"

The dog beside him whined slightly, as though moved by his words.

He doubted James would have the same sympathy for him. "You think that's going to work, Butch? I don't know. I've dug a pretty deep hole."

Butch was some weird cross of Great Dane and Rottweiler. He was an ugly, big son of a bitch, but he was as harmless as a damn fly. He'd also been the closest thing to a friend he'd found in the last several years. He'd known his marriage to Ally was utterly over when she'd told him to choose between the dog and her.

Noah shook his head. His marriage hadn't been over when she'd cheated or spent every dime he had. It hadn't been over when she'd walked out for three months and crawled home because her lover had kicked her out. It hadn't been over when she'd tried to stop him from attending his second father's funeral. It had ended over a dog. He'd told her to get out, and she'd walked straight to Phil's arms.

He'd given up his home, his honor, his family over a woman who had taken everything and given nothing in return. He was crawling home with his goddamn tail between his legs.

At least he had a job waiting for him. Stef Talbot had kept in regular contact. Even when he hadn't talked to his own brother, Noah had talked to Stef. Stef kept tabs on everything. When Noah had called to see if there was still an opening for a vet in Bliss, Stef had told him to get his ass home.

But he wasn't sure about how James was going to take it.

"Maybe he'll be satisfied that he's the rich rancher, and I'm the dipshit brother whose wife ran through ten million dollars in five years. You think so?"

The sad-sack look on Butch's face didn't hold a lot of hope.

"We might be living in a tent. Or the caves. Mel used to have a bunch of caves Jamie and I played in when we were kids. Don't drink the moonshine, though. It can make you blind." Actually, a bit of Mel's "tonic" might be exactly what the doctor ordered. Or he could get his ass abducted by aliens, and then everything would be a moot point.

At least he would get to work with large animals again. He'd missed working with horses and cattle. If he had to deal with one more hamster, he might scream. Those goddamn rodents bit him every time.

God, how had he fucked up so badly?

His hands tightened on the steering wheel. He'd spent the night before in a cheap-ass motel. He was seriously considering finding another one. Anything to put off the inevitable moment when he had to tell James what had happened with Ally.

A little resentment bubbled up. James had everything he truly wanted. He'd always loved that ranch. The Circle G was James's personal kingdom. Noah wondered briefly if there was any way his brother had gotten married and settled down. Maybe some gorgeous thing had come into town, and James had taken one look and tied her up. He liked to tie up women. God, Noah liked to tie up women, too. Maybe Noah would walk onto the ranch and see James had been the smart one who had waited for the perfect woman. The thought was depressing, and his reaction to it made guilt boil in his gut. He was the one who had left James, not the other way around. He had left everyone in Bliss behind for a gold digger who couldn't even love a dog.

He forced himself to focus on the road. He didn't need a GPS to show him the way home. He knew it by heart, but some things had changed in the last five years. And some things never changed. Inevitably, some poor sap's car broke down on the emptiest part of 160. Sure enough, there was a compact car on the side of the road. A single figure stood by the vehicle, her brunette head in her hands.

She was crying. He could see it from here. He should drive right on by. Crying women got him in trouble. Ally had been able to cry so beautifully. Her lip would tremble, and she would manage a single, crystal tear that never wrecked her artfully applied makeup. It was all fake, of course.

The woman looked up, and it was easy to see that she wasn't pretending. Tears coursed down her red face. No one could fake that. This woman was upset. Her face turned down as though she didn't want to watch him pass her by.

He was an idiot. Even as he told himself this wasn't his problem, he was pulling over. Butch stuck his big head out the window as Noah rolled it down. "You need help?"

She sniffled, and he could see warm brown eyes behind a pair of dainty glasses. She was cute. Hot-librarian cute. She had a light sweater wrapped around her waist, as though it had gotten too warm for her to keep it on. She was down to a dowdy skirt and a tank top that was too big for her frame. It wasn't so big that it hid her incredibly nice rack.

"I think I do. Uhm, my car isn't working." Her voice was raspy, a little tortured. She bit her bottom lip—a nice, plump bottom lip. She had gorgeous lips to go with that nice rack.

He'd been way too long without sex. Actually, this was the first time in a long time he'd even thought about getting down with a woman. It was kind of nice to know he could still think about sex. Maybe she would be so ridiculously grateful that he helped her that she would take pity on him and invite him back to her cabin, and he could put off the whole "prodigal brother returns" scene for another couple of days. "I'll take a look at it."

He put the truck in park. Butch seemed to like the lady just fine. Of course, he wasn't exactly discriminating. Butch pretty much begged anyone human and in the vicinity for a pet. He opened his mouth to command Butch to leave the poor woman alone, but she smiled at the big mutt and put out a hand. She didn't move away when Butch leaned forward and gave her a big, nasty kiss.

"Sorry," he muttered, sliding out of the truck. Yeah, that probably wrecked his shot at getting invited back to her place. Not that things like that ever happened to him.

He liked the way she smiled. Though her eyes were red rimmed and her skin mottled from her tears, she was kind of adorable in a soft, feminine way. "It's okay. He's a sweetie."

"He probably needs a bath. We've been on the road for days." Noah walked around to her car. It had to be ten years old. He would be surprised if it didn't have over a hundred thousand miles on it. The car looked tired, weary. The car looked a lot like Noah felt. "Can I pop the hood?"

Butch had escaped the cab, and his tail thumped against the ground as the woman knelt and petted the enormous animal. Sometimes Noah was sure Butch's tail thumps registered on the Richter scale, but Brunette Hot Librarian didn't seem to mind.

"Of course. I'm afraid I don't know how to do that. I'm clueless about cars." She leaned down and touched her cheek to the dog's head as though she was desperately in need of affection. He checked out her left hand. No wedding ring.

51

What the hell was he thinking? He reached into the car, releasing the hood. There was a click, and the hood popped open. Smoke billowed out, but he couldn't see fire. That was a plus. He wasn't going to get blown up on the side of the road. "I'm Noah, by the way."

"Where's the other dog?" There was an odd little smile on her lips. He liked it. It was slightly mysterious, with the sweetest hint of snark.

"I don't have another one." Butch had been too big for the tiny condo in Manhattan that had cost him half a million a year.

She shook her head, soft brown hair escaping from her ponytail. "Sorry. It was a dumb joke. You said your name was Noah. I immediately went to the ark and all the animals going in two by two."

He snorted. Yeah, he could do one better. "I'm a vet."

Now she laughed out loud, the sound washing over him like warm caramel. That was what she reminded him of. Soft, rich caramel. Sweet, but with a hint of tang. "That is perfect. It's nice to meet you, Noah, the vet. My name is Hope, and you're the best thing that's happened to me all week. I thought I was going to have to walk into Del Norte."

And she was local. "I like your name, Hope. It's pretty."

"I don't know how applicable it is. I seem to be hope*less* lately, hence the dead car and other various tragedies." She sighed and allowed her arm to hug Butch. Butch, the lucky bastard, rested his head on that truly fine rack. She was at least a C, maybe a D. He bet her ass was round and curvy, too. Fuck, he was getting a hard-on just looking at her.

He looked down at her engine, trying to force his eyes anywhere but on the too-tempting dish in front of him. Why was he reacting this way to her? She wasn't polished. She wasn't even wearing makeup anymore. She'd cried it all off. She looked a little lonely, a bit needy. She probably looked a whole lot like him.

He wasn't merely looking for a lay. He was starving for someone, anyone who might be able to like him. Pathetic, yes, but it was the truth. She'd said she was on her way to Del Norte. Bliss was fairly isolated. There was a good chance she'd never heard of him or his infamous flameout. He went over all her fluids, checking each carefully as he thought about the situation. Maybe he could ask her to dinner. He could use someone to talk to. He hadn't had that in years. Well, he hadn't had anyone who didn't bark or growl or whine back at him.

"I think your radiator is shot, but I also think you're leaking oil. And maybe brake fluid."

"Is that expensive?" Her eyes were round under her glasses.

He wanted to tell her no. But the truth would hit her soon enough. "Just about everything on a car is expensive, and this one is old. They might have a hard time finding parts. I think you're going to need a tow. I don't have a cable."

Why didn't he have a cable? His dads would have had his hide if they knew how little emergency equipment he had in his truck. He could hear Daddy Fred telling him that ranching required a man to always be prepared.

"Oh, uhm, it's okay. If you don't mind giving me a lift into town, I can take care of it from there."

This was all ending way too soon. "I could take you home. Do you have a shop you like to use?"

She started biting that bottom lip again. It was her tell, proclaiming loudly to Noah that she wasn't being truthful. "Oh, yes, I have a shop. I'll get into town, and they can come pick it up and fix it, no problem."

Crap. He hated it when someone lied. And Hope didn't even do it well. She was hiding something. He should shrug and move on, but he felt his eyes narrowing. "What's the name of the shop, sweetheart?"

Her bottom lip disappeared, sucked into her mouth. Yeah, she was a terrible liar. "Uhm, I don't know. It's a shop that fixes cars. I can call them when I get to Del Norte."

Curiouser and curiouser. He wasn't sure exactly why, but he didn't like Hope lying to him. "There's only one shop in Del Norte. I happen to know the owner. I'll come in with you."

She shook her head, her face flushing again. She got to her feet. Butch danced around her. "It's okay, really."

Noah let the hood drop. "No, it's not all right. I'd like to know what's going on. You're lying about calling a shop. Why?"

"It's none of your business."

Brat. He'd missed brats. He'd spent five years with a woman who was perfect on the outside and rotten on the inside. He liked the fact that this woman had no idea how to handle him. "As I'm the one standing here on the side of the road with you, I think it is."

Her chin came up. "You don't have to stand here. I thank you for stopping. I'll be fine."

Stubborn little thing. She ruined her stand by sniffling as her bottom lip quivered.

"You want me to go?" He had no intention of going.

"I want you to take me into town and not ask a lot of questions."

Yes, that would be the easiest thing to do. He could satisfy his conscience and move on. Except he didn't want to. For the first time in forever, he felt like he might be able to help someone, to make another person's life better even if it was only for a few moments.

"Are you going to call your husband? Your boyfriend?"

She took a quick step back. "Are you some kind of weird serial killer? Someone knows where I am."

Another lie. "So let me get this straight. You don't have a husband or a boyfriend, and you didn't tell anyone where you were going. And from all the stuff in the backseat of this car, it looks like you're living out of it."

Tears filled her eyes. "It's none of your business."

So many things fell into place. She was in trouble. She *was* trouble. Big trouble. And he was a masochist. It wasn't the role he usually liked to play. "You don't have enough money to fix this car, do you?"

"It's none of your business."

"You don't even have enough for a tow."

Tears coursed down her face. "It's none…"

He didn't let her get any further. It was stupid, but he had to reach out to her. "I'm making it my business."

She shook her head but didn't fight him at all as he pulled her into his arms. So sweet and naïve. Damn, she needed a keeper. She shuddered a little, and then her head sank to his shoulder.

"You should let me go." Her words came out in little gasps.

"Shhh." It felt so damn good to be the one in charge. "It's going to be all right, Hope."

He held her, tilting his hips back so he didn't scare the crap out of her. She would probably notice his massive hard-on if he got too close. In the distance, he could see a truck pulling up.

Drive on by. Please keep going.

But the truck obviously wasn't telepathic. The large vehicle pulled over, its wheels driving up dirt and crunching gravel. Hope pulled away, wiping at her eyes. Their moment was over, and Noah was the slightest bit pissed at the man who'd broken it up. He stepped back from Hope, Butch's tail thumping at his feet.

"You folks need help?"

Noah took a look at the newcomer—and did a major double take. He recognized that ridiculously handsome face. Trevor McNamara—the former king of pro football's bad boys. He'd been a tabloid favorite before he'd gone into rehab and dropped off the face of the earth. What the hell was he doing in Colorado on the side of the road helping out a broken-down motorist?

"Hi," Hope said, giving him a wave. "I think I mentioned I might not make it home."

McNamara's face split into a high-wattage smile. "You did, indeed. And I offered a little help." He turned to Noah, holding out a hand. "Trev McNamara."

Noah nodded and took the proffered hand. McNamara had been a hell of a quarterback. And he'd walked away from it all. "Noah Bennett. You and Hope know each other?"

"We met today." Hope sniffled a bit, but she moved closer to Noah.

He could feel himself stand a little straighter. What was she doing to him? "Her car is trashed. Do you happen to have a tow cable?"

Trev smiled. "I certainly do. We can get her out of here. No problem. Where am I going?"

Noah could see the hesitation on her face. He took over. "She said something about Del Norte."

She shook her head. "If you don't mind, I should probably go to

Bliss. It's a little town between Del Norte and Creede. I have some friends there."

She was from Bliss. His heart constricted at the word.

Trev's smile was practically a mile wide. "You're from Bliss? My ranch is right outside of Bliss."

Noah felt his eyes widen. What the fuck was that? There was only one ranch anywhere close to Bliss. The Circle G. The Circle G was pretty damn big. There wasn't any room for another spread. "Really? I thought the Circle G was outside of Bliss."

"You've heard of it?" The former football player looked entirely pleased with himself.

Noah's stomach rolled. "James Glen owns the Circle G."

Trev settled his cowboy hat on his head with a satisfied air. "He's owns half of it. I own the other half."

"He sold our fucking land?" He hadn't meant to yell, but he was pretty sure his voice echoed through the valley.

Trev's mouth dropped open. "Holy shit. Are you Noah? James's brother?"

"Yes." His head was reeling. "I'm Jamie's brother, and I really want to figure out why he would sell our land."

He would have gone on, but Hope stopped him. She didn't say a thing, merely turned stark white and then started to fall, her every muscle seeming to lose control. Her body twisted and gravity began to do its work.

He closed the distance between them as quickly as he could, his arms coming up to catch her as she fell. "Hope?"

Trev shook his head. "She's out." He sighed. "We'll have to call the doc once we get her to the ranch."

Noah checked her pulse. It was strong and steady. "I'm a doctor."

Trev shook his head. "No way. You're a vet. If I don't call the people doc, he'll have my head. I haven't been in Bliss for long, but I've heard what Doc Burke does to the men who piss him off. He's very thorough with the prostate exam. She's probably dehydrated. I've seen it plenty of times. Get her into my truck. I've got air conditioning."

"I do, too. I'll take care of her." Noah held her, lifting her up.

Her eyes fluttered open.

"Don't tell James." She went limp again.

Fuck. She knew his brother. They all knew his brother.

And his brother had a lot to answer for.

* * * *

James looked out over the front porch. It looked to be a damn busy day at the Circle G. First they find out Beth is pregnant, and now they had visitors. The drive from the highway to the house was fairly flat so he could see cars coming from a mile away. And there was a long line of them. What the hell was going on?

The first SUV pulled into the circular drive, and Caleb Burke hopped out.

"Hello, Doc." James was a bit surprised to see him. Apparently Bo was more worried about Beth than he'd claimed. Doc wasn't known for his love of socializing, so this had to be business. Caleb Burke was known for being a bit taciturn, though that had changed slightly since Alexei Markov had come back to Bliss and forced Doc to acknowledge his feelings for Holly Lang. The lovely redhead got out of the truck following Alexei, who handed her down.

"James. Is my patient here?" Doc was all business.

"I think Beth is in the guesthouse." He pointed toward the back.

Doc frowned his way. "Not Beth. Wait. What's wrong with Beth?"

"She's pregnant."

Caleb slapped his hand against his forehead. "Goddamn it."

"Doc doesn't like pregnant women?" James asked, looking at Holly.

Holly grinned while Alexei patted his partner's shoulder in what seemed like a sign of solidarity. "Doc is horrible at reading sonograms. I made him promise to take a continuing education class. I can see him now with a bunch of bright-eyed tech students."

Caleb sighed. "I'm going to start preaching birth control. None of this tells me where my patient is."

"Uh, if you're talking about the calves I have coming this spring, I don't think you're going to be much help. Unless you're going to be more than the people doc." James had dealt with his own calving for a couple of years now since the vet had retired and they had no one to take his place.

Doc's eyebrows climbed up his forehead. "I'm talking about Hope."

His heart clenched. Hope was in trouble. *Damn it.* She was in trouble, and she wouldn't talk to him. Now she needed a damn doctor. "What? What's wrong with Hope?"

Doc shrugged. "No idea until I see her. Your partner called me. He said she passed out. He's bringing her back here because it's closer than my office."

James was surprised at the shot of panic that went through him. "What happened to Hope? What made her pass out? Why the hell was she with Trev?"

As far as he knew, Hope hadn't even met Trev. Trev, Bo, and Beth had kept to the ranch in the weeks since they'd gotten here. There had been an enormous amount of work to be done. With Wolf's help, the men had completely reposted the fence along the east pasture. They'd worked their butts off because Wolf was leaving.

Doc merely shook his head. "No idea. And I won't know until I see her. Where can I set up?"

Holly moved beside the doctor, shaking her head Noah's way. "Don't mind Caleb. He's got the worst bedside manner ever. I'll show him to the guest room. We'll set up in there. Don't worry. I'm sure she's fine. Trev told Caleb that her heart rate is steady, and she didn't hit her head when she fell."

She'd fallen. Why had she fallen? Caleb's voice cut through James's thoughts.

"Hey, you didn't mind my bedside manner last night." It was said without a hint of leering playfulness.

Alexei sighed, a long-suffering sound. "He's also got no good manners when it come to being discreet." He leaned in toward Caleb. "I don't think we should be talking about how many times we make her scream last night. We must to be discreet about how good we become with the double penetration."

Holly's eyes rolled. "Yeah, Alexei's the one to teach Caleb how to be discreet. Both of you take a left at the first hallway. Second door on the left. Set up there." Holly's men walked in the house. Her face suddenly turned serious. "Trev called about ten minutes ago. I think that was his truck about a quarter mile behind us. There's something else he told me, Jamie."

Oh, god, how much worse could it be? In the distance, he could see another truck coming up the drive. Trev's. There was a second truck behind the first. It was Grand Central Station at the Circle G. He started down the steps. He wanted to see Hope. He wanted to put a hand on her and make sure she was fine. After all, he'd promised Logan he would take care of her.

No. He'd promised Logan he'd figure out what was wrong with her. That didn't mean he had to care for her. But what if this was his chance? What if this was his way in? He wanted her. He wasn't getting any younger. Maybe it really was time to think about settling down.

Trev got out of his truck—alone. A dark Chevy pulled up behind him.

"Where's Hope?" He wanted to carry her to Doc Burke and to let her know it was going to be okay. It had to be okay.

Holly followed behind. "Jamie, I need to talk to you."

But he could already see what she wanted to talk about.

Noah.

Five years older, looking a bit worse for the wear. His little brother had obviously decided that working out was a good hobby. All of the boy in Noah seemed to have burned away, leaving nothing but a hardened man in his place. He easily lifted Hope into his arms as he pulled her out of the cab. A massive dog lumbered out after them.

"I can walk," Hope protested.

"And risk you taking another header? No way, sweetheart. You're going to be a good, obedient girl and let the doctor look at you." Was that rough command really coming out of his brother's voice? Noah had always been the soft one.

James had to take a deep breath. What the hell was his brother doing here? And why was he holding Hope like he had the right to do it?

"I don't need a doctor." Hope looked pale and somewhat frail in Noah's arms. James didn't like the tight feeling in his gut.

He stepped up. "I'll take her. Doc's already here."

Noah's arms tightened around her. "I have her."

James wasn't going away. His brother couldn't waltz in here and think he was going to take charge. Hope had been left in James's care. Logan was the closest man to Hope. He'd asked James to watch out for her. In his caveman brain, that made her his. "I know her. Give her to me."

But then it looked like Noah had gotten to know his inner caveman, too. "And I saved her. Let me through."

Holly got in between them. "Hey, you two are fighting over her like two dogs over a bone."

The huge mutt thumped his tail. It was a monstrous thing. Holly looked down at the dog. "Actually, the dog here is better behaved than the two of you. Trev, would you mind carrying Hope in so Caleb can do his overly thorough exam? Sorry, sweetie. He's planning on taking blood and everything. If he could haul you to an MRI, he would. He lives to run tests."

Trev hoisted Hope's body out of Noah's arms before he could complain. The former pro quarterback didn't even seem to notice her weight as he hauled her up.

"I really can walk." Hope let her arms drift up around Trev's neck.

Trev's mouth was curved up in that perpetually mysterious smile he had. Trev always seemed amused with the world around him. He handled everything with an odd calm, from untangling a terrified calf from barbed wire to dealing with buyers. Trev was always in control. "I think I should do what Holly tells me to. I make it my goal to never argue with a pretty lady."

He strode into the house, the screen door swinging behind him.

Holly looked from him to Noah. Her eyes narrowed. "I know your momma is no longer with us, but I remember her, and we mommas stick together. You two boys behave."

She stalked off, the screen slamming shut again, but with an irritated sound this time.

He was alone with Noah. And Noah's enormous dog.

He needed to breathe. He needed to calm down. Something had happened or Noah wouldn't be standing here. He would still be in New York with his wife. Ally wasn't with him. *Fuck*. What had happened? And why was he driving that piece-of-shit truck? The last time he'd spoken to him, Noah had bragged about his new Benz. Something was up with Noah, and he owed it to him to listen. He was the big brother. He had to be patient.

Noah's hands went to his hips, his self-righteousness apparent. "You want to tell me what the fuck you think you're doing selling off this ranch?"

And there went his patience. "It's my fucking ranch. You got your goddamn money. You want to tell me how you spent that? If you have a problem with me, then you should feel damn free to take your ass right back off my land. Get back to New York, city boy."

He turned and started back in the house, not waiting for Noah or issuing an invitation. His head was spinning. How dare that little shit walk back in here after five long years and start questioning his business decisions?

Noah was hard on his heels. "Don't you walk away from me. This used to be my home. My father worked here. My parents helped build this ranch."

Now he remembered their childhood? James turned and stalked into the kitchen. It was one of the biggest rooms in the house. He didn't remember much about his biological mom. She died long before he could truly know her, but when he thought about his adoptive mom, he saw her in here. His mom would cook for hours, and he and Noah would sit at barstools hoping for a taste.

He needed to talk to Beth about redecorating. There were so many ghosts here.

"You were so interested in this ranch that you walked away from it."

"I got married, Jamie."

His brother was missing the point, but then he always had. "And left this whole town high and dry. You can't walk back in and start questioning me. You haven't been here."

Trev walked in and went straight for the coffeepot. It was always on these days. Beth or Bo came through every couple of hours and put on a fresh pot. What must that feel like? To have not one but two people who cared enough to check on a coffeepot? All James had was a wayward brother who started harping on him the minute he rolled his ass back into town.

"Well, I have to start questioning you when you make such dumbass decisions." Noah pointed toward Trev, who was refilling the travel mug he almost always carried with him. "Do you know who he is?"

Trev McNamara had been a tabloid favorite. The bad boy of football. He'd been fired from his pro contract after he'd failed one too many drug tests. "I'm not stupid. I know exactly who he is."

"Maybe y'all should leave me out of this." Trev suddenly looked like he wanted to be anywhere but here.

"You sold off part of the ranch to a guy who spends all his time with strippers," Noah said with an ugly twist of his lips.

Trev shook his head. "I have been stripper free for one thousand eighty-seven days. Certified. Well, professional stripping. Beth has gotten really good. She tends to like hard rock."

"I'm glad you're amused, man." James was actually kind of glad Trev was here.

Trev sighed. "I'm not really. I'm actually getting a little pissed off at your brother. I don't like getting pissed off."

Noah turned to Trev. "Sorry you're pissed off, but I want to know what exactly you did to get my brother to sell part of the ranch."

"Half." The word dropped like a rock.

Trev tipped back his mug, but James could tell he was getting riled. His fingers tightened around the mug. *Damn it.* The last thing in the world he wanted was to cause Trev hell.

"Half?" Noah fairly screamed the word. "You gave away half the ranch our fathers worked to build to some ex-athlete addict? What the hell were you thinking, Jamie?"

He stared at his brother, anger rising. "I was thinking I needed the fucking goddamn money. I was thinking if I didn't find a partner, I would go into bankruptcy. I was thinking I couldn't hire hands or buy new stock, and damn straight couldn't pay the vet when my stock got sick. I was thinking I had to save our fathers' hard work, and I was thinking it all a-fucking-lone."

Noah backed down, his face turning ashen. "I didn't know the ranch was in trouble."

"Yeah, well, you never asked. You weren't here after Dad died. You weren't here during the drought or the wildfire that burned five thousand acres or the sickness that took half my herd a few years back. You weren't here when my bills got so high I seriously considered bankruptcy. You weren't here. Trev was."

Noah took a deep breath, visibly swallowing. "How much?"

God, as pissed as he was with his brother, he didn't have the heart to tell him. "It doesn't matter now."

Noah turned to Trev. "How much?"

"Ten million," Trev replied with hard eyes. "Ten million, and we both formed a loose partnership with a man who knows how to make money in this market. The Circle G is still considered small. We've gone all grass fed and all organic. We're selling to specialty markets and upscale restaurants, and it's going to pay off. Now, if you don't mind, I'll take my ex-addict ass elsewhere."

James felt so fucking tired all of a sudden. "Trev."

Trev shook his dark head. "No, he needed to know. He needs to know what a little prick he's being if he's going to stand half a shot at healing the breach between you. And you tell him to keep a civil tongue in his head when he talks to my wife or Bo or we're going to have some trouble. I'm going to go check on Hope. Doc should know something by now."

The room went quiet, a weird, eerie silence that seemed to permeate the walls. He turned and looked at his brother who had gone stock-still. "What are you doing here?"

There was a grimness in Noah's stare. "I lost everything. I wanted to come home."

The silence was back because James had no idea what to say.

The front screen squeaked. "Hello to the house!"

James sighed. Nate. That figured. Oh, well, saved by the bell. "We're in the kitchen."

Sheriff Nathan Wright walked in, dressed in casual clothes for once. He was in jeans and a T-shirt that looked worse for the wear. James's eyes went to a large, nasty-looking spot on Nate's shirt.

Nate waved it off. "Spit-up. Charlie likes to vomit. A lot. It's his hobby."

Charlie Hollister-Wright was one of Nate, Callie, and Zane's newborn twins. "Can a baby have a hobby?"

Nate nodded. "Yep. The twins' hobbies are spitting up, hanging on their momma's boobs just before spitting up, and doing this real cute thing with their legs that makes me not care that I'm covered in baby vomit. Now I heard Hope was murdered by a sand-dune monster."

Despite the previous drama, James bit back a laugh. "It's gone through Mel, then?"

"Yep. Apparently the aliens have taken to the dunes. Now, before it got to Mel, Hope had passed out on the side of the road, been kidnapped in Del Norte, and will be sold for her body parts—someone's been letting the Farley twins watch horror movies—and, my favorite, she's pregnant with your secret love child. That's why she passed out."

"Oh, god, no." People were talking about them? Of course people were talking about them. Everyone gossiped in Bliss. It was the town's pastime. "It's the first one. She passed out. Doc is with her now in the guest room. Uhm, my brother found her."

Noah looked like he might be the next human to vomit all over Nate Wright. "Her car broke down. I think she's fine. Definitely no sand monsters."

"I didn't know you had a brother." Nate's eyes moved between them, assessing.

He didn't want to go into it. "Ask Callie. She'll tell you the whole story."

"Callie?" Noah asked. "Callie's still in town?"

Noah had a lot of catching up to do. James gestured to the sheriff. "You're looking at her husband. Sheriff Nathan Wright, this is my brother, Noah Bennett. Different last name. Different fathers. Different mothers. Our dads shared our stepmom."

Nate's whole face broke open in a smile. "I love that we're carrying on Bliss traditions. I'll have to have Callie tell the whole story to me and Zane. He'll find it amusing, too. I'm going back to check on Hope."

Nate walked away, and he was left alone with Noah again.

Noah looked out the big kitchen window into the backyard and out over the seemingly endless spread they had grown up on. "Everything's changed."

"Yes. That's what happens."

Everything changed. The people of the town had changed. The land had changed. Bliss had moved on without Noah in it. Bliss might not have missed Noah, but James had, even though his anger still burned bright. There was no way to stop the march of time or to see mistakes coming before he made them. James stood beside his brother.

Bliss had changed. James had changed. Noah had changed.

Had they changed for the better?

He let the silence sit between them as he contemplated the question.

Chapter Four

Hope hissed as the doc took some blood. Some more blood. He was on his third vial. Hope was pretty certain Caleb Burke was a vampire.

And she was in such deep shit.

She lay back on James's guest bed, closing her eyes. How had this happened? How was the man she'd met at AA James's new partner? She'd worked hard to keep this part of her past quiet. Quiet? Silent. She'd tried to make sure no one in Bliss knew she was an addict. She and Nate had made a deal a long time ago on a lonely road, and she was happy with it.

Now she had to leave. No question about it. She had to get out of Bliss and fast.

"Well, you're dehydrated at the very least." Caleb held her hand in his, tracing the lines of her veins. "These should stand out. They're sunken in. When was the last time you ate or had some water?"

"I had some coffee earlier in the day." She hadn't felt like eating or drinking. All she could think about was that glimpse of a man she thought she'd left behind long ago.

Caleb looked down on her, sympathy in his eyes. "You're exhausted, Hope. And your blood pressure is on the high side. Are you under some sort of stress?"

She felt those damn tears start again. Yeah, she had some stress. "My car is dead. My apartment is unlivable."

I'm seeing a ghost, and he's not the happy, Casper-the-friendly kind. He's a killer.

What she'd thought she'd seen the week before haunted her. She'd written it off in her waking brain, but the dreams had come again. He came to her each night, his hair golden and his lips turned up in a gorgeous smile. He'd had that charming smile on his face when he'd slit her best friend's throat.

"I need you to calm down." Caleb was looking at her, a serious expression on his ruggedly handsome face. "Your pulse shot up. Maybe we should get you to a hospital."

"Oh, god, no." If she couldn't afford to fix her car, she really couldn't afford a hospital. "I'm fine. Nothing rest and food can't fix."

And running. Lots of running.

Holly walked in the room, a glass of orange juice in her hand. "Here you go. This should help. And avoid the kitchen if you can. Those boys are staring at each other like two rattlesnakes waiting to strike."

Noah. Noah was James's brother. "I didn't know James had any family left."

Holly frowned, a sad look in her green eyes. "They haven't talked in years. I moved to Bliss after they were grown, but before Noah moved away. They were close back then. They had an odd family. Not odd for Bliss now, but at the time it was odd. They were the first threesome. Jamie's dad and Noah's dad were best friends. After Jamie's mom died and Noah's walked out, Noah's dad moved them to the Circle G and helped out on the ranch. A couple of years later, they hired a housekeeper and both fell in love with her. Noah and Jamie were raised by their dads and a stepmom. They were raised as brothers, and just like their dads, they preferred to share a woman. Until Ally walked in."

Hope sat up, interested in this story. James Glen was everything she wanted in a man. He was loyal and kind. He worked hard. Of course, he was also a ladies' man. And he never noticed her. His brother…god, his brother…had her panting over him two minutes after he'd gotten out of his truck. She'd been attracted to the tall, dark, and handsome cowboy the minute she'd met him. Noah and James were dangerous, and her brain was already going to crazy places. "Did this Ally person only want one of them?"

Holly sighed and sat down on the bed. "Drink your juice and I keep talking."

Caleb winked at her. "You're a good nurse, baby."

She smiled brightly. "Thanks. Maybe I'll go back to school with Alexei. Now, Ally spent time with them both, but Jamie caught on to her. She was looking for a man with money. Jamie broke it off with her."

"But Noah didn't." Hope drank her juice, the cool sweetness sinking into her veins.

"Not at all," Holly confirmed. "Noah married her and left for New York."

Caleb grimaced. "He's the vet. He's the one who was supposed to replace Doc Harris."

"Yes. Noah was supposed to take his place. We haven't been able to find a local vet since he retired. Now Noah's back and I do not see Ally with him. And he seems interested in you. He and Jamie squared off in the driveway." Holly turned to Caleb with a frown on her face. "I had to ask Trev to take her so I could keep them from fighting."

Caleb shrugged. "Well, you always said James had a thing for her. Sometimes jealousy makes a man move."

Her lips turned up in a sultry grin. The heat between the doctor and Holly was palpable. "It made you move fast enough."

"I have to keep up with that damn Russian bear." But there was a happy smile on his face. Caleb Burke was a changed man. He was still gruff, but he smiled more. He was a man in love and happy to be sharing with his friend. Hope envied them.

There was a knock and Nate Wright's big frame filled the doorway. "Hey, you. You look good for a woman who's been attacked by a sand monster."

God, she was going to miss Bliss. "Just a little tired, boss."

"She's going to be fine, but she needs sleep and rest, and she definitely needs less stress. I'm going to take the blood samples in for testing, but I think I'm right. I think she needs to eat and put her feet up." Caleb took Holly's hand and led her out, leaving her alone with her boss.

Nate waited until the door closed. "Talk to me."

She didn't want to do this. He was overburdened as it was. He'd recently had twins with his wife. He should be perfectly happy, not dealing with her shit. "I'm tired, Nate. I was stressed because my apartment is unlivable. I went to a meeting and my car died. I guess I haven't eaten enough. I'm fine."

Nate Wright's sharp blue eyes stared through her with the intensity of a longtime lawman on a case. "Not according to Caleb. And I don't buy any of this. Tell me what's happening."

"Nate, let it go. You need to be with Callie."

"The twins are sleeping. They like to do that during the day so they can keep us up all night. Now what's going on?" He was tenacious when he wanted to be. He wouldn't let up until she was honest with him.

"I thought I saw him the other day."

Nate's shoulders straightened, his eyes flaring. "Christian Grady? I thought he was dead. The police report said they found his body. I knew that report was shoddy."

Christian *was* dead. He'd died in a fire—a fire Hope herself had accidently set. "Nate, don't overreact. I'm sure he's dead. I saw someone who looked like him."

"Or one of his followers who figured out where you are." Nate crossed his arms over his chest. "Could that have happened?"

God, she loved this man. Since she'd started wandering ten years before, Nate Wright had been the only man to believe she was anything more than a drunk, idiot kid. Nate had found her at her lowest point. He was the reason she was still alive. "I hope not. I would have thought the group would break up after Christian died, though I'm sure some of them view him as a martyr."

"It wouldn't be the first time. And you were the last one to see him alive. Have you considered that his followers might wonder if you had something to do with the fire?" Nate leaned over, his eyes going soft. "I know you don't want to talk about it, but if you had something to do with that fire, I wouldn't turn you in. If I'd been there, I would have handed you the match." Nate was a lawman, but he understood that justice and the law didn't always go hand in hand.

She nodded, but she couldn't tell him. She knew he had an idea, but she couldn't verify the fact that she'd killed a man. It didn't matter that the man had been a monster. She still felt the guilt.

Nate sighed, obviously willing to let it go for now. "I have a favor to ask."

"Anything." She would do almost anything for this man. He'd found her one night roughly a year before. She'd been far too drunk to drive. She'd walked out of the Hell on Wheels and fallen asleep in her car. Nate had knocked on her windshield and talked to her. He'd taken her home with him. Callie and Zane had opened their tiny cabin. Zane had cooked for her. Callie had held her hand.

And they'd found a meeting for her. She'd walked into an AA meeting with Nate at her side. She'd walked out a different human being. He'd given her a job and a new lease on life. He'd been the father she'd never had. Her own had walked out before she'd been born, but Nate Wright understood the meaning of responsibility.

"Don't run," Nate said, his voice steady and true.

Damn it. He was also a meddling, magnificent bastard who could see straight through her. "Leaving might be for the best."

"No. It's not. Unless you're ready to call your mother. I could handle you going home, but outside of that, this is where you belong."

She sighed. "It's not. I love Bliss. I really do, but I don't belong the way the others do."

Nate's eyes rolled. "I don't think James is feeling that way right now. He's finally coming around. I don't think he'll let you leave. No one else will, either. Come with me. You need to see something. You've been here for about an hour now. Come and see how little the people of Bliss think of you."

She took his outstretched hand and let him help her up. She

didn't bother to put on her shoes. She liked the feel of the carpet beneath her feet. She felt better, but her stomach was starting to rumble. She had to admit that she felt safer here on the Circle G than she had all week. Then she remembered her problem. "I don't want to, Nate. Trev…"

She closed her mouth. What happened at AA stayed at AA. At least it did with her. She couldn't be sure about Trev. He might tell, but she wasn't going to out him.

Nate's eyes widened slightly. "Oh, shit. You met Trev at a meeting?"

Oh, no. She'd outted Trev, and he'd been so nice to her. "How did you know? Nate, you can't tell anyone that."

Nate snorted. "Trev can't hide, honey. Everyone who has ever watched ESPN knows Trev's story. He's famous. And I doubt he'll mention how the two of you met to anyone. He's a solid guy. Come on."

She followed. She didn't want to see the look in James Glen's eyes when he realized she was a drunk, and if he ever learned about the rest of her past…that wasn't even worth thinking about. She would leave. She wouldn't be able to handle that no matter what she owed to Nate.

She heard the chatter the minute she walked into the hall. Lots of voices. Lots.

"Who's here?"

Nate smiled. "Everyone. Well, not everyone, but the ones who aren't here are being kept up to date."

She walked into the living room and was shocked to see so many familiar faces. Rachel Harper stood talking to Laura Niles and Nell Flanders. Their men, Max and Rye Harper, Rafe Kincaid and Cameron Briggs, and Henry Flanders stood talking in a group. Alexei and Holly were helping Caleb pack up. No sign of James.

Rachel turned and frowned. "You're supposed to be in bed, girl. Doc told us you need stress relief. Nate, do you have a plan to give her a break?"

Rachel could be a bit bossy, but she was a sweetheart. "No need. I'm fine."

"No, she's not," Caleb called out. "She needs rest."

Nate nodded toward Laura. "Laura and I already worked something out."

Laura was a gorgeous blonde. She'd always looked slightly out of place in town, but there was no doubt Bliss was her home. "I'm going to cover for you for a week. I've done it before. We all used to take turns giving Callie time off. And we've solved the deputy problem, too."

"That's good because I had to work damn hard to get paternity leave," Nate said with a frown.

Nell's hands fluttered as she spoke. "It was wrong. If the sheriff had been a woman, he would have gotten eight weeks paid leave. Just because he has a penis doesn't mean he shouldn't bond with his children."

Nate grinned, his eyes lighting with mirth. "I sicced Nell on the town council. Two days of listening to her sing "We Shall Overcome" and Hiram wilted like a hothouse flower. I get a whole month paid. I'm taking it. So Cam is acting sheriff. Who's going to be his deputy?"

"I am not his deputy," Rafe said with a frown. "I'm co-sheriff."

Cam had a shit-eating grin on his face. "No such thing, buddy. I'm the boss. But think about how much fun we can have with our receptionist."

"Oh, god. I'm going to need more Lysol." Nate groaned. "Why does everyone have sex on my desk?"

Rye Harper shrugged. "It's on the official Bliss bucket list. Ask your partner. He's the one who made it. 'One hundred things to do in Bliss before you die.' Number eleven is fucking on Sheriff Nate Wright's desk."

Nate laughed and shook her head. "Asshole. I'm going to beat him when I get home."

He wouldn't. Nate loved Zane. It was one of the things she'd adored about being close to the threesome. Their relationship wasn't merely about Callie. Zane and Nate would never touch sexually, but the love between them was plain. They were committed to their friendship and their family.

Rachel walked up and put a hand on her shoulder. "Hope, we're all worried about you."

"Yes. We're worried." James's voice cut through the talking. Hope's eyes went straight to where he stood in the doorway between the kitchen and living room. "Doc wouldn't let me back to see you."

He'd wanted to see her? "I'm fine."

"Stubborn. I can respect that," Rachel said. "We've all brought casseroles. Mine's a lasagna. Laura sent some enchiladas, and Nell has stir-fried something granola."

"It's black beans and rice," Nell said with a smile. "Totally vegan. Cruelty-free."

Hope liked meat, so she wasn't sure about the "cruelty-free" part, but she smiled anyway. It was tradition in Bliss for the women of the town—and some of the men who liked to cook—to keep casseroles on hand. There was always someone in need, and Bliss came out to support. Of course, she wasn't sure how she was supposed to cook the things. "I appreciate it, but my apartment is unlivable right now. I don't have a fridge."

"You can stay here." Noah joined his brother. Hope could hear a collective intake of breath from the longtime Bliss residents. Max and Rye both turned, their jaws coming open.

"Noah?" Max and Rye asked, their voices one.

Noah's face flushed. Noah was a gorgeous slab of man, only slightly shorter than his brother. Noah was tall, dark, and handsome, and James was an all-American hunk with broad shoulders and golden-brown hair. But there was a hesitancy in Noah's eyes that let her know he was worried about his welcome. She knew that feeling. It made her heart go out to him.

Noah cleared his throat before talking. She loved the deep timbre of his voice. She'd gotten a little hot when he'd turned that dark voice on her out on the highway. "Hey. It's good to see you guys. Been a while. Are you two still the bane of women all over the valley? I remember when no woman could resist the two of you."

James snorted, obviously enjoying the fact that his brother had no clue. Rachel turned, frowning.

"They better not. Really, you two? The bane of women? I can probably buy that. I have no idea who you are, Noah, but any woman looking at those two will have to deal with me and our baby girl. Married. They're married."

"Max and Rye got married?" Noah asked, looking like the world had changed.

James huffed and started pointing around the room. "Callie's married with two kids. Max and Rye are married and have a baby. Logan's gone out of his damn mind. He's in Dallas where someone thinks BDSM is going to save him. Mel has a girlfriend he apparently met during an alien abduction. Stella married Stef's dad. Stef married an artist. You remember the pretty blonde lady who came to town a couple of months before you left? Laura Niles? Turns out Laura was on the run from a serial killer, and she's now with her two former partners who managed to kill the serial killer. Holly is getting it on with an ex-Russian mobster and the gruffest people doc any of us has ever met."

Caleb looked up. "That's fair."

"It more than fair, Caleb. You are far too interested in prostate exams," Alexei said with a frown.

Noah looked poleaxed. "Max got married? I get Rye, but Max?"

Rachel threw her head back and laughed. "Okay, I like him. Someone tell me who he is."

Rye sidled up to his wife, his hand tracing the curve of her hips. "Jamie's brother."

Rachel's eyes widened. "The one Max curses every time he has to call in the animal doc from Del Norte?"

"I curse everyone," Max admitted, coming up on the other side of his wife. "Except you, baby."

Rye shook his head. "I have tapes. I'll play them when I need to."

Noah stepped forward. "I think Hope should stay here. She doesn't have anywhere else to go."

"I came to take her back to our place." Rachel hugged each hubby and then turned to Hope. "She needs someplace quiet."

"And your baby is quiet?" James asked. "Not to mention Max. I've heard he even growls in his sleep. You have people coming in and out of that place all the time." He frowned her way, his brows forming a *V* over his handsome face. "I might be pissed at my brother and wondering why he's inviting women to stay at my ranch, but he's right. This is the best place for Hope. People Doc says she needs rest and to be less stressed. She can do that here."

That was a terrible idea. She needed to leave Bliss, not sit around and stare at James Glen and his impossibly gorgeous brother. "I can go to the Movie Motel."

"No." James and Noah managed to say it at the same time and with the same inflection.

She had to make them see reason. She couldn't stay here. Watching James with all his conquests would kill her. Being close to Noah and knowing she couldn't have him would make her crazy. "You have too many guests already. You have your brother and Trev and his family. They haven't moved out of the big house, have they?"

James smirked. There was no other word for it. "They took over the guesthouse. I have three free rooms, darlin'. You want to bring a friend? And I haven't decided if I'll let that one back in."

Noah's jaw tensed. "I can always leave."

This Noah didn't match the one she'd met on the highway. He'd been so kind to her before. She wasn't sure what his whole story was, but she liked him. It was easy to see these were two brothers who had a lot to work out. "I think you should talk to your brother. And it would be easier for you to work out your differences without another person in the house. I'll be fine. I have a little money saved. I can stay at the motel."

"I hear Gene say motel is all booked," Alexei said, dashing her hopes. "Many witches come to town."

She'd forgotten about the annual psychic festival. It wasn't organized by anyone in Bliss, but it was a nice way for the businesses to make a little money in between the end-of-summer hiking crowd and the snow bunnies who would be out in full force in a few weeks.

"God, I hate Woo Woo Fest." Max put his head in his hand and groaned.

"I don't think that's the proper name," Laura pointed out.

Nate seemed to agree with Max. "I'm planning on getting Callie pregnant and having the baby every year at this time so I don't have to work through Woo Woo Fest. Congrats, Cam. You're going to get to be sheriff to the freakiest people in the world."

"I am disappointed by your intolerance, Sheriff," Nell said with a frown. Her husband stood behind her. It was obvious Henry was ready to protest the sheriff of Bliss's attitude.

"Well, you should be used to it," Nate replied.

The argument started fast and furious. Caleb zipped up his bag and then looked at James and Noah, pointing to the kitchen. He crooked his finger, an obvious order for her to follow. She walked out of the living room as Nell accused Nate of trying to start another Salem witch trials.

Caleb leaned against the countertop, frustration evident in his stance. "Hope, you need a place to stay. I would offer to take you in, but Holly's cabin is small and the guest room is now my stepson's room. This is the best place for you. James has already offered. Why aren't you accepting?"

For a multitude of reasons that Caleb didn't need to hear. The worst reason was that she wanted to. She wanted to stay right here and play house with James and his brother. "It doesn't seem right."

"I don't get it. Why don't you want to stay here? Why would you rather stay at a motel where no one can look after you?" James asked.

She couldn't tell him the real reason, but she had a handy one. "I think you and your brother have some things to work out. You two don't need me hanging around when you obviously need to talk."

Noah and James had the same look of startled disgust on their faces. They might not be blood relations, but they were so alike it hurt.

"We're not talking," James said with a dismissive shake of his head.

"She makes it sound like we need therapy or something." Noah's boot tapped on the floor.

She'd never seen people who needed therapy more. Well, until she looked in the mirror.

Caleb laughed a little. "Hope, you don't understand how men work. Alexei and I don't talk when we have problems. We growl at each other. He threatens to shoot me. I threaten to punch his kidneys. We get over it and watch whatever game happens to be on the TV that night. I suggest James and Noah do the same thing. And take care of Hope. Did someone call and have her car towed?"

"I called," Noah said. "Trev was going to tow it, but then Hope passed out and we wanted to get her back here as quickly as possible. Long-Haired Roger is going out to get it."

More money was flying away. "I don't think that's a good idea."

"I'll pay for it." James looked to his brother. "She doesn't have a lot of money. She's always worried about it, and she'll lie when you ask her."

Maybe James knew her better than she thought.

Noah's eyes swung toward her. "Yeah, she already did that with me. I told her I didn't like lies."

James's eyes were on her, too. She got the feeling if these brothers ever got their crap together, they could be an intimidating team. "Nate's the only one she really talks to. If I wasn't so sure Nate was in love with his wife, I would think she and Nate were a couple."

"What?" She practically screeched out the word.

Caleb's cool green eyes rolled. "Guys, she needs rest. And some stress relief. We've gone over eating and drinking water, but let's talk about sex. How long has it been?"

Caleb Burke was not going there. "That is none of your business, Doc."

"Your health is my business. Sex is a great stress reliever. Get some. You'll feel better." Caleb smiled broadly. "I know I do. James here has slept with everyone else in the valley. He's got to be pretty good at it by now. Give him a try."

James's head fell to his hand. "Doc, you're a bastard."

Caleb shrugged as though that was a foregone conclusion. "It's true. But your blood work shows you're healthy. Hope's healthy. Look, if you don't want to sleep with James, I advise you to masturbate. It's good stress relief, too. I mean, you could jog or something, but no one likes to do that. Okay, my work is done. Hope, take some time off, let the men help you out, eat, and drink a lot of water. I'll run your blood work to the lab and call you later."

Caleb strode out of the room.

"Your people doc is crazy," Noah said as he watched the door swing shut.

"Well, we don't have much to compare him to. We haven't had an animal doc in four years," James said, accusation plain in his tone.

They squared off again. Noah's fists clenched. "Well, you have one now. I'm back, brother. I can stay here on the ranch our parents built together, or I can head off into town and find a place. Either way, you're going to have to deal with me." There was a long moment of silence. The air filled with the distinct possibility of violence. Then Noah turned. "Fine. Be that way. Hope, get your things. You're coming with me."

"I don't have any 'things.'" She nearly rolled her eyes. She could see what was happening now. James ignored her until it was brutally obvious that his brother was interested. Noah didn't know enough about her to know whether he really liked her. He was reacting because his brother suddenly seemed like he gave a damn.

Caleb thought this would be relaxing?

"She's not going anywhere. Doc said she had to stay here," James insisted.

Noah leaned in, his jaw a hard line. "Doc said she needed someone to make sure she was eating and drinking enough water and getting enough sleep. He didn't say it had to be here. Doc also talked about your insanely active social life. We wouldn't want to disrupt that now."

Hope was grateful that neither mentioned the other thing Doc had told her to do. "It's obvious you've got enough to deal with. I'll go talk to Nell and Henry."

She would be in for days of tofu and long discussions of global poverty and the evils of gas wells, but it was for the best. She couldn't run without a car. She didn't really want to. The fact that half of Bliss was currently in the Circle G's living room because they gave a damn about her made her want to stay. She didn't want to lose another family.

She was about to walk out of the kitchen when strong male arms lifted her up. She was off her feet before she could protest.

"You aren't going anywhere," James said, his arms going under her knees and around her back. "Except back to bed."

She felt so small against him. It took a lot to make her feel small. She threw her arms around James's neck. Sometimes it felt like she'd wanted him forever. It seemed unfair that the only way to get him to take her to bed was to pass out and need medical attention.

James walked her through the house, not paying a lick of attention to the calls from the peanut gallery.

"'Bout damn time, James!" Max shouted.

"Give him hell, Hope!" a feminine voice called. She thought it was either Laura or Holly.

"Don't listen to them. You give me hell and you'll feel the flat of my hand on your pretty backside." James's face looked like it was made of granite.

He was a spanker? She should have seen that coming. Why did the thought of James Glen's big hand smacking her backside make her pussy hot and wet? She could feel it. Her girl parts were softening and getting ready to sing a hallelujah chorus. "Neanderthal."

She had to at least put up a good fight.

"You've spent too much time with Nell, baby." He used the flat of his boot to kick the door open and entered the guest room. At least he hadn't taken her to his room. "I think a nice spanking would do you a world of good."

A lot of things about James Glen could do her a world of good. It had been forever since she'd had the solace of another body against hers. She'd practically forgotten how good it felt to hold a man, his cock sliding in and out of her pussy, rocking them both to perfection. Forgotten? Had she ever really known? Her past threatened to rush in. She closed her eyes. *Don't think about it. Don't think about it.*

"Hope? What's wrong? Goddamn it, you're shaking." He set her on the bed.

She opened her eyes to see him looking down, staring at her with a singular purpose. She flexed her hands. She shouldn't think about that time. Usually she was really good about not thinking about it, but the last few weeks had turned her carefully held-together world upside down. "I'm just cold."

"No. You went white. You're scared. Are you afraid of me?" He said it like the entire idea horrified him.

She sat up. As much as she worried about James finding out about her past, she couldn't let him think she was afraid of him. He might break her heart, but he would never harm her physically. Hell, he wouldn't allow anyone else to harm her. It wasn't her in particular. It was simply James Glen's way. "I'm not afraid of you. I told you, I'm cold."

Except she suddenly wasn't. She wasn't cold at all. He loomed over her, his body so close to hers that she could feel the heat coming off of him. James was a big man. Six feet three inches, with corded muscles that covered a big-framed body. His broad shoulders blocked out the early-afternoon light streaming in from the window.

"I can think of some ways to warm you up." His voice had gone deep, cajoling.

She'd rarely seen him without his ever-present Stetson on his head, but now his golden-brown hair curled over the tops of his ears and brushed his eyebrows. It was messy and overly long, as though James hadn't wanted to be bothered with a haircut. It was shaggy, and she thought he looked utterly perfect.

"Don't." But even as she said the words, her hands found their way to his shoulders as though her body wanted something her mind knew was a spectacularly bad idea.

"Why not?" He hovered over her, his chest nearly touching hers.

"You don't like me." The words made sense. They were logical and sound. Her hands curled around the muscles of his shoulders. She could feel her nipples tightening.

His blue eyes flared. "Is that what you think?"

She wasn't an idiot. She pulled her hands back. She wasn't going to play his fool. "I asked you out once and you practically turned green and ran. Don't pretend you've changed your mind."

He shook his head, his body still far, far too close for her comfort. "No. I haven't changed my mind, but my circumstances *have* changed. Hope, baby, you're not like the other women I've dated. You're not looking for a good time."

"You don't know that." He'd never asked her what she wanted. A good time would have been nice. Maybe. Any time would have been better than the utter loneliness of the last eight years. She'd never fooled herself that James would want her for the long term. But a night of pleasure would have been nice, a night she didn't spend alone.

Who was she kidding? She could have gotten that if she wanted it. For the last year, she'd stayed away from men altogether, with the singular exception of James. She only wanted James. The only other man who had sparked her deep interest was Noah.

Yeah, she wasn't very smart.

"I do know that. And if you're telling yourself that we could spend a night in bed and get up and walk away in the morning, then you are fooling yourself. I feel a connection to you, and that scares the crap out of me. I don't know if I want it. My parents had it, and it destroyed them when it was broken. After my mom died, it didn't take long at all for both of my fathers to follow her. I don't know if I want to love someone like that."

Her heart seized at the idea that James could honestly care for her. But if it wasn't something he wanted, then it couldn't work out. She needed to move on. Despite what Nate had said, and perhaps because of all the wonderful people who'd shown up to check on her, she needed to leave Bliss. Even if Christian's former followers hadn't caught up to her, it was only a matter of time before someone did. It could be the Followers of the Light or the law, but sooner or later her time was going to be up.

"I'm not asking you to love me." She wouldn't. Loving her was a bad idea.

And still he leaned closer. He was so close their noses touched. "Well, lately I've been thinking that I should just find someone I like. I'm not getting any younger, girl. And neither are you."

It was a horrible reason to date someone. Indignation rose inside her like a tidal wave. No way was she going to be his convenience. She opened her mouth to tell him he could take his "like" for her and go straight to hell when he pressed his lips to hers. In a single heartbeat, all her righteous anger turned to lust. James stopped trying to hold his weight off her and sank, his big body covering hers, pressing her into the mattress. His lips played. His tongue seduced.

This wasn't a soft opening volley. It was a full-on assault, and everything feminine in her responded. James dominated her mouth. His tongue found hers and glided over and around, his lips fused to hers. His chest nestled against her breasts, and his legs gently pressed at her knees. Before she knew it, her legs were splayed wide, and he'd made a place for himself at the center of her body. As he kissed her, she could feel his cock pushing against her pussy, lengthening and hardening. His hips moved as though they were dancing, but the only music Hope could hear was the mingled sounds of their breath and the soft moan that was forced from her throat.

So good. He felt so good. She could let him take over, and she would feel better. It wouldn't be like the other times. This time would be different. She wouldn't strive and work and not find satisfaction. James ground against her as he started to kiss her neck, and already she could feel pleasure. Her pussy was warm, and she was already wet. She wanted to move against him. She didn't want to lie there. She wanted to sink her nails into the skin of his back and force him to shove his cock inside.

She didn't recognize herself, and that felt good, too.

"James." His name was a breathy plea coming out of her mouth.

"Yeah, baby. Yes. I knew it could be like this." His lips turned up in a sensual smile as his hand claimed her breast. "Let's get you out of these clothes, and we can have a real good time."

She froze. A real good time. Good-time girl. That was what she'd been before Nate had found her. She'd been a good time—except she hadn't had one. She'd been looking for a way to obliterate herself, and she'd used booze and sex to try to do it.

"Hope?" James had stopped, his body going still on top of hers. His baby blues were wide with concern.

"I thought she was supposed to be resting, not getting pawed by her host," a deep voice said.

Hope pushed at James. Noah's harsh words saved her from complete embarrassment. He stood looking into the room, his eyes on his brother's back. Butch sat beside his master, his massive tail thumping as though he didn't understand the whole simmering tension thing going on between the humans.

James stared at her for a moment even as she pushed at him. It was as though he needed her to realize he was stronger, and he'd stop the encounter when he decided to. "I'll let this go. But not forever."

He pressed his lips swiftly to hers before she could protest and then he was up and off her, leaving her feeling very much alone. She'd been warm with James on top of her, but now she felt the chill.

"You take a nap. I'm going to see if I can manage to herd these people out of here." James turned back when he reached the doorway, his eyes carefully avoiding Noah's, but seeking hers out. "We'll talk at dinner."

That sounded ominous. "I might need to rest."

She might need to run, but, damn it, she didn't have a car.

"Then I'll come back and carry you to the dinner table," James promised. "We eat at six, and I will be watching everything you eat. Doc made me responsible for you, and he's not the only one. Logan asked me to look out for you, too. I take those promises damn seriously. We're going to talk about what's bothering you, and we're going to talk about what we, and I do mean we, are going to do about it. I'll see you at six, and if I find out you're trying to leave this ranch, I won't hesitate to put you over my knee."

With that, he turned and left. That was the second time in twenty minutes that he'd threaten to spank her and the second time all of her girl parts had responded to the totally off-the-wall, outrageously insulting threat by softening and practically purring.

She hated to do it, but she looked up at Noah. He had to think she was some kind of slut. Surely he'd figured out that she wasn't his brother's girl, but she'd been caught wrapping her arms around his neck and panting. She steeled herself to meet his judgment, but there was a little smile on his face as he looked at her.

"He really will spank you, darlin'. You should watch out for him." Noah's dark hair shook slightly as he walked into the room and started to open drawers. He pulled a thick quilt from the bottom of the dresser, turned, and then walked toward her. "And he's an awful host. You're obviously cold, and he didn't even offer you a blanket."

No, he'd offered her the warmth of that big body of his, every inch of it corded with hard-earned muscle. James worked for a living, and he worked hard. When James's hands had touched her skin she could feel the harsh calluses on them. So different from Christian's soft skin.

"Now, see, I'm beginning to think my brother is right, and there's something awful going on in your head. Every now and then, your eyes tense up, and it's like you're somewhere else. Somewhere bad." He pulled the blanket up over her, covering her to her chin. "I don't like that look you get in your eyes. It makes me worry."

"Don't. You don't know me, and the truth of the matter is, I'll be leaving town soon." She decided to be honest with him. It was better to get it all out there.

His handsome face didn't even frown. His grin widened as though he knew something she didn't. "Well, I think I'll have to do something about that, Miss Hope. I don't think I'm ready for you to leave, not when I so recently came home. We'll have to make the most of our time together. Lunch tomorrow?"

That was a horrible idea. "No. No. I have to go into town tomorrow and see about my car."

If he was offended by her turning him down flat, he didn't show it. He simply put his hands under the covers and pulled off her leopard-print ballet flats. "You don't need these. I'll find you some warm socks. Until then, Butch can help you out." He whistled, and the dog bounded onto the bed, covering her feet with his enormous body. He stared at her, his tongue lolling out, begging for a little praise.

"Thanks, Butch." It was odd. There was a dog warming her feet. It was also rather sweet. Butch put his head down, as though utterly willing to have her feet poking his belly for as long as she needed him.

Noah winked down at her. He was stunningly gorgeous with forest-green eyes and hair so black she would swear there were shades of blue in it. "As for tomorrow, how exactly were you going to get into town? It's a long walk for a woman who's supposed to be resting. I happen to have a little time built into my schedule, so I already called Long-Haired Roger, and we have an appointment at eleven. My stomach starts crying right around eleven thirty, and it's been five long years since I had some of Stella's butterscotch pie. Do you want to make me drive all the way back here weak with hunger? I saved you on the side of the road. I'm willing to drive you all over town. I've offered up my very own dog in order to keep your feet warm. Are you sure you won't allow me to feed you a decent meal so I don't worry about it all day?"

Asshole. He'd made his whole heartfelt speech with the smile of a man who knew he'd put a woman in a corner. "Fine, but don't think you can use me to make your brother jealous."

He flushed slightly but didn't back down. "It's not that, although we always have been competitive. We also have the same taste in women. I'm attracted to you. Terribly attracted to you, and it's been a long time since I wanted a woman. It feels damn good, and I won't back off because Jamie wants you. He doesn't have you yet, and that makes you perfectly fair game. And I'm the smarter one this time. I get the feeling he's fucked up with you. I don't intend to do that. So you should know I'm going to treat you right. Now you rest. I'll be back to take you to dinner at five forty-five."

"James said six."

"Yes, he did, didn't he? The early bird catches the worm. You rest well, darlin'."

Noah strode out the door, and she was left with a foot-warming dog and about two million questions.

As she drifted to sleep, her mind was filled with two cowboys. She smiled as sleep claimed her because there wasn't room in her brain for anything else.

Chapter Five

James walked through the house, carefully avoiding the crowd in the living area. His cock was still righteously hard, and his brain was in a damn tailspin.

She'd been soft and sweet underneath him. She'd flowered open, her whole body blooming under his. He'd gotten a hand on her breast, and as he'd suspected, they were real and perfect, the nipples pointing beneath his palm. If they'd been skin to skin, they would have pressed against his chest until he wouldn't have been able to handle it, and he would have been forced to drag his mouth to her breasts and suck those nipples inside.

He strode through the kitchen, cursing his brother's name. He slammed through the back screen door and dragged cool air into his lungs. This was what he needed. He needed to be outside, where every wall of the house didn't press at him with some memory of his childhood.

Sometimes he thought he'd tear the fucker down and rebuild. Every room contained a memory. He couldn't walk into the parlor without seeing his mom putting up a Christmas tree. She'd never had one of those Martha Stewart perfect trees he'd seen on TV. She'd said that having a theme for a Christmas tree went against the spirit. Their tree was decorated in a wild kaleidoscope of color. In the attic, there were boxes and boxes of ornaments his dads had thought would please her and pieces of crap that he and Noah had made. Every one she'd treasured and displayed despite the fact they weren't her blood. They were more than blood, she'd told him once. Ellen Glen-Bennett had looked down at him, tears filling her brown eyes, and told him that she'd chosen to be his mom. She'd picked him and Noah as surely as she'd picked their fathers.

Fuck, he missed his mom.

Hope reminded him of her. Not in any physical way. It was there in her sweetness. It was in the way she took care of the people around her. She made sure Logan got his lunch. She baked cookies for everyone on their birthdays. She'd brought salad to Nell and Henry when their protests lasted longer than expected, and when Mel and Cassidy had taken to their bunker, she'd made sure Cassidy got her favorite mystery novels to keep her entertained.

Hope McLean knew how to take care of a person. She knew how to love.

And that scared the fuck out of him.

He strode toward the stable. What was he doing? Hope was too close to perfect. Hope was the type of woman who could help on a ranch because she would understand. She would get that it was a team effort, and she would throw herself into it.

And that was perfectly fine. He wanted and needed that in a wife. What he didn't need was a wife who made his heart pound at the very thought of her. He couldn't do it. He didn't want what his parents had. He didn't want to fade away when his love was gone. His father had only been sixty-seven, and after his wife and friend were gone, he'd faded. There wasn't another word for it. Fred Glen had been a walking ghost after their deaths.

James didn't want that.

And yet he wasn't sure he could walk away from her.

He found himself standing at the fence of the training area. It was a large, round, three-tiered wooden fence. It was where he trained his horses, but lately it was where he got his ass kicked. Red had been brought out for his daily exercise. James nodded at Kirk, one of his newly hired hands. Kirk nodded back. He was standing far from Red, who snorted and put up a good front. Red was a magnificent horse with amazing lines and a sturdy frame, but he snorted and bit at everybody who got close. The minute he felt a man's weight on him, he bucked and went crazy.

Red was a good summation of his life for the last couple of years. Harsh. Rough. Brutal.

He should find a wife who wouldn't disrupt his life and be done with it. He should find a wife and have some kids and move on.

But now Noah was back, and James wasn't sure what the fuck that meant.

"Pretty boy." Rye Harper put a booted foot on the second ring of the fence and stared out at Red.

James sighed. At least they hadn't sent Max out. He had no delusions that the group hadn't decided to "talk" to him. Not a single person in town understood what it meant to stay out of other people's business. "He's a pain in my ass."

"The good ones always are." Rye tipped his hat back. "In horses and women."

Yep. He should have known. "Are you here to talk to me about Hope? You're wasting your time because she's told me she isn't interested."

But she had been. He'd felt her nipples and smelled the lovely scent of her arousal. If that fucker Noah hadn't interrupted, he would have been balls deep inside her and groaning out his orgasm more than once. He knew that was true because once wouldn't be enough. He'd need her over and over again. He would fucking imprint himself on her.

"I doubt that. But you have ignored her for nearly a year. You must suspect that would make an impression on her," Rye replied.

If only he'd been able to ignore her. He'd always known the minute she walked in a room. "I haven't had time to really date. This ranch took up every minute of the day until Trev and Bo got here."

It wasn't merely having two more sets of hands around that made a difference. It was the cash infusion they'd brought with them that had turned things around. For the last year, it had been him and

Wolf and the hands he could hire for what little he could pay. Now he had some experienced hands, and it made a huge difference. He could breathe again. He could have a life again.

Rye leaned against the fence, looking every bit like a slightly disapproving older brother. "But you have something going with that woman, right? The one with the dark-brown hair?"

Dark brown? That wasn't the way he would describe Hope's hair. Her hair was a rich brown threaded with gold, and when the light hit it right, some red. It was a soft color, and there was so damn much of it that he wanted to thrust his hands in and pull on it. He could braid rope into it and make it so it was a gorgeous testament to D/s, the rope hanging lower than her hair, ready for her Master's tug. "What are you talking about?"

"The woman from the rep theater?" Rye's mouth flattened. "She's telling every girl in town that she's your girlfriend and they better back off. I was surprised. I was pretty sure you had a no-dating policy."

Fuck a goddamn duck. "No. We went out a couple of times."

"By going out, I assume you mean you fucked her a couple of times."

He felt himself flush. Rye Harper was only a couple of years older than he was, but he'd been like a big brother to him and Noah. Max, Rye, and Stef Talbot had been the older boys they'd looked up to. "Yeah. But, I made it clear I wasn't looking for anything serious. I never lie to a woman. I want a good time and that's all. You know how much time this ranch costs me? It isn't exactly an eight-hour-a-day job."

Even with his breathing room, he still didn't have a ton of time. It would be years before the Circle G attained the kind of wealth that would allow him some real free time.

Rye's face softened. "I know. It's twenty-four-seven and only because that's all there is to give. It's blood and sweat and tears, and never think for a single minute that your dads wouldn't be proud of you."

He hated the tears that threatened. "I don't think so. I sold half our land."

"Fred and Brian would have done the same damn thing. Don't

you dare think otherwise. They would have done anything it took to keep this place afloat. Your dads understood the meaning of compromise and partnership. Now, they would have wanted Noah to step in, but in his absence, they would be proud of everything you did to keep their legacy alive."

James found the words comforting even though he wasn't sure he believed them. "I had friends who helped me."

Max and Rye had supplied unpaid labor in bringing the herd in when the winter proved too much. The owner of the Feed Store Church had given him credit when he couldn't pay. Mel sat up with him during calving season, pulling each calf free of his momma and pronouncing them all free of alien influence. Nell and Holly had brought him food and sat with him while his father was dying. He loved this town. It was home. It was his heart. He would never be able to understand how Noah had left.

"And you always will. I know you'll do right by Hope. Oh, you're going to fight it and make some dumbass mistakes that you'll pay for. If I could stop you, I would, but this is your path, and you'll walk down it as you will. We all know Hope is going to be good for you. You'll wise up. They didn't send me out here to talk about Hope. I'm here to talk to you about Noah."

That was worse. He'd had months to think about Hope. He hadn't had more than an hour to process the fact that Noah was back. "I don't want to talk about Noah."

"He's your brother," Rye pointed out.

"He left me."

"And now he's back, and you have to deal with him. The question is are you going to make him pay or are you going to be the magnanimous brother who welcomes him home?"

There was no question about that. "Make his ass pay."

Rye laughed, the sound filling the air.

"I told you he was more like you than me." Max sidled up to his brother. Their identical faces settled into grins.

"You did, indeed, brother." Rye slapped his brother on the back.

It was what people who didn't know them always got wrong. James had known the brothers all of his life, and despite Max's outer shell, he was actually the softer of the two. Max could growl all he liked, but when it came down to it, he found it difficult to maintain a true grudge. He would scratch and claw when he thought he was being rejected, but the minute someone needed something, he would quietly help.

Rather like Noah.

Just because he understood Noah didn't mean he was willing to forgive him yet. "He leaves for five years with barely a phone call and then waltzes in and expects me to welcome him with open arms? When he left, it didn't just hurt me. It hurt this whole town. We were all counting on him."

Max frowned. "You won't get an argument out of me. We haven't had a vet for four years because your brother is a dumbass, but we all knew he would be back. I can curse his name and will continue to do so for the foreseeable future, but damn, that boy's been through something hard."

"He's not the same Noah who left here," Rye added. "Talking to him for ten minutes proved that to me. He's harder, and he's waiting for you to reject him. I think there might be a piece of him that wants you to reject him."

"Are y'all talking about that kid with the chip on his shoulder?" Nate walked up with Rafe, Cam, and Henry following behind him. It looked like all the men of Bliss had decided to descend. "That boy is in some kind of trouble."

James rolled his eyes. "He's not in trouble. He's out of money. His wife divorced him."

Henry looked slightly out of place among the ruggedly dressed men. He wore loose cotton pants and a sweater made out of something that didn't involve an animal or manmade fibers. And the dude always rocked the Birkenstocks. Still, he had his unassailable place among these men. "Yes, and now he needs his family."

"What about when I needed him? I'm supposed to forgive him and say, 'hey, no problem. You weren't here when I needed you most. You weren't here when our dad was dying. You didn't have to watch him fade away. You didn't have to answer the questions he asked.' I'm supposed to forget?" It wasn't fucking fair. All of his life he'd had to watch out for his little brother. Noah was smart, but that didn't matter because James was stronger. Well, Noah had filled out. Maybe it was time for baby brother to stand on his own damn feet.

"Jamie, I've known you for a very long time," Henry said, adjusting his glasses. "If I know one thing about you, it's that you're one of the kindest men I know. You won't be able to hold out for long. All you do by being angry now is delay the inevitable. Do both of you a favor and sit down and talk to your brother. Don't start a war, because that's what this could turn into."

"And I don't want to see Hope get hurt," Cam said. "If you and your brother are going to fight, then maybe she should come back with us."

Rafe nodded in agreement. "She's going to be stuck in the middle, and not in a good way. You're both looking at her like two dogs about to go into battle over a particularly juicy steak. She doesn't need that."

James felt his rage simmering just below the surface. "I'm not going to hurt Hope, and by god, you're not taking her out of here. Doc left her care to me. Logan asked me to look after her. So all of you can leave it be. She steps foot off this ranch and there's going to be hell to pay."

Max snorted. "Well, I guess that answers that question. Someone needs to tell that actress chick to lay off."

He was going to have to deal with Serena. What had happened to his formerly peaceful life? Oh, it had been full of backbreaking work and loneliness, but damn, he'd forgotten how obnoxious people could be. "I'll handle her, and I'll deal with Hope. Something's up with her. I want everyone watching out for her."

"Will do," Nate replied with a smile. "We watch after our own."

"Be careful what you promise, Jamie," Henry said, his eyes lighting a little. "She's going to help me and Nell run our booth at the Festival of Spiritual Renewal."

Everyone groaned.

"Woo Woo Fest," Cam said.

"Yep." Nate slapped the acting sheriff on the back. "Don't let Nell hear you call it that."

James shook his head. "Hope needs to rest, not sell stuff to people who come looking for Bigfoot."

"Sasquatch," Henry corrected. "They genuinely prefer Sasquatch. Nell and I can handle it, but Hope is a bit stubborn. I'm merely giving you a heads-up. I think you and your brother could greatly benefit from some of the psychic healing that goes on at these things. I believe someone is putting up a sweat lodge. After a couple of hours sweating out your inner turmoil, I think you and Noah will be fine. Max and Rye could use it, too. They fight too much. I'll make sure to set appointments for all of you."

"Yeah," Max replied, his eyes on his brother. "Brotherhood can be a rough thing."

Rye snorted. "Damn straight. Especially when you're tied to someone like him."

Max came off the fence, his shoulders squaring. "Tied? Brother, you are lucky to have me."

Rye's face lit up. He took a step back. "Lucky? You're the lucky one. You would spend every night in the doghouse if it wasn't for me. You're lucky our baby girl has my sweet temperament."

Max attacked, his fist flying. Both brothers laughed. James sighed. That was Max and Rye. They fought, punching each other until one cried uncle or Rachel put her foot down.

"See, that wouldn't happen in the sweat lodge," Henry said with a long sigh.

"Why is Nell talking to your cattle?" Rafe asked, pointing toward the field where Henry's wife stood, whispering into a cow's ear.

Max and Rye continued pounding on each other. Max said something about Nate and a duck, and Nate joined in with a yell.

"She's trying to talk the cows into passive resistance," James explained.

"She's such a beautiful soul," Henry said with a happy grin as he watched his wife. "One day she'll get through to them."

She was insane. But James loved her. Max, Rye, and Nate tried taunting Rafe and Cam to join them in their fist-flying free-for-all. Nell started to sing to the cows in his field. He heard Rachel slam out the back door and all of the women ran out, yelling at the men to stop acting like boys.

And Noah stood in the background of the gleeful chaos. He

stood by the back door looking like the same sad five-year-old who had first come to live on the Circle G. Out of place. Small. Vulnerable.

He wasn't small anymore, but his brother looked pretty damn vulnerable without even his dog at his side. Noah watched the fight from afar and then walked to his truck and grabbed a single bag.

That was all he had? One small gym bag? He'd left Bliss with a trunk packed full and ten million in the bank. He'd come back with nothing.

"Don't even bother trying," Henry said as Rachel passed off her baby to Laura and threw herself in between Max and Rye. "He's your brother. He's home. Start over. That's what families do."

A hard lump formed in his throat. His family was gone. And he wasn't sure he would ever get that feeling back.

* * * *

Christian Grady liked Bliss. It was one of those sleepy towns that stuck together and had a can-do attitude. It was utterly ripe for the plucking.

Like Hope had been at one point in time.

Why was she wearing those ridiculous glasses and hiding her body under voluminous clothes? She was a goddess, but now she looked rather like some sad-sack housewife. She put her glorious hair in a bun and wore no makeup. It was wrong. When he had her back in his arms, he would make sure she showed herself off to perfection.

He walked into some place called Trio. She hadn't been at the station today. Nor had she been at her tiny apartment. She'd left for somewhere. He needed to find out where. Though it was still early in the game, it was time to show his face around town a bit. The festival started soon. He could easily blend in with the idiots pouring into town. He'd made a careful practice of standing out, but he knew when to blend in as well.

"Hi, welcome to Trio." A pretty woman with black hair greeted him. He was excellent at reading body language, and hers screamed out anxiety. Her smile was forced, her eyes slightly red. She was upset, emotional. He loved emotional women. They were easy to manipulate. Of course, they could also go a bit insane if not properly handled. His Hope was proof of that. She'd tried to murder him, but he could forgive her. He had murdered her friend, after all.

"Lovely town you have here." He followed the pretty waitress to a booth.

"Oh, yes, I've always loved Bliss." Now her smile was genuine. "I grew up a couple of towns over, and I swore when I could I would move here. It took me more years than I would like, but I finally made it. It's the best town in the world."

He pegged her age at roughly twenty-five to twenty-seven, but she sounded like a teenager. And she blushed like one when he smiled at her and held out a hand. "I'm Chris."

No need to give away everything if he didn't have to. Hope would have to deal with him soon enough.

"Lucy." She shook his hand. "Nice to meet you."

The door opened and a big man walked through. He was enormous, with broad shoulders and dark hair. Lucy's whole face tightened again. She passed him a menu and promised to be back soon before scurrying behind the big man, calling out, "Alexei."

The man named Alexei turned and smiled down at the waitress. It was a warm smile, but not intimate. The big guy might like Lucy, but he wasn't interested in her sexually. Lucy spoke rapidly, her hands twisting around the towel she carried. Alexei's hand came on to her shoulder in an almost brotherly gesture. He was trying to calm her down. He couldn't see Lucy's face, but the big guy was on full display, and Christian heard the one word he'd been dying to hear.

Hope.

He heard her name from the big man's lips. Though he was across the room, the music in the tavern wasn't loud, and Christian could make out a little. Alexei had obviously come from somewhere, and he'd seen Hope. Lucy was worried about her.

Well, that wasn't surprising. His Hope had made friends so easily. She was smart and soft mannered, truly the perfect mate for a man of his stature.

Of course, she'd taken his stature down when she'd left him, but she was the one who could bring it all back, too.

Lucy returned, her shoulders relaxed. There was a flush on her face. "I'm so sorry. I didn't get your order. Do you want a beer?"

He never drank. He would never allow himself to be out of control. No alcohol and no drugs, though he found drugs very useful when it came to dealing with weaker minds. Drugs were a lovely way to keep his minions in line. "No. I'd like some hot tea if you have it."

She nodded. "All kinds. Earl Grey. Jasmine. Oolong. Pretty much you name it and we got it. It's an odd crowd. We have to be ready."

He smiled, giving her his smoothest grin. "I'll take green tea, please."

He was patient as she nodded and turned. No need to push her. He was supremely confident in his ability to charm a woman into giving him the information he needed. He watched the slow roll of people as they came in and out of the establishment. He would almost bet his life on which ones were the locals and which were coming into town for the festival. The ones in the cowboy hats and sensible clothes were almost certainly locals. The ones who appeared to have watched far too much science-fiction television were the tourists. He could manipulate both. It was all about figuring out what a person needed and giving it to them. For a price, of course.

He ordered off the menu. A salad and a bowl of soup. Too much meat wasn't good for his digestion. He sipped his tea and contemplated how to handle Hope.

He'd known what she'd needed once. She'd wanted a lover and a father figure all rolled into one. Her own father had left at an early age, and she'd had a rough time with her mother. He'd met her at the tender age of seventeen, so lovely and malleable that he was sure he'd found his perfect match. He was strong. She was sweet.

She'd played her part beautifully for eighteen months. She'd been his perfect angel, fully buying into everything he was selling. She was the embodiment of the "light" he'd preached.

Too bad she'd figured out that the whole religion thing was a front for selling drugs and women and other various sordid things. He'd never intended for her to discover the actual paying side of the business. It was a shame since it had worked beautifully up until the moment his lovely bride had decided to light him on fire.

"Here you go." Lucy set the soup and salad in front of him.

He had to admit it smelled halfway decent, and given the fact that he'd spent the last several years in various shitholes trying to hide from the mob boss he owed money to, halfway decent was right up his alley. "Thanks. I appreciate it. You seemed upset when I first walked in. I'm glad you're better now."

She flushed under his words. She was a lovely girl and obviously in desperate need of attention. "I was worried about a friend. I heard a whole bunch of crazy stuff about her today, but it turns out she's just a little under the weather. You never can tell around here. You know we're like the murder capital of the world, right?"

This nothing town? "Seriously?"

"Oh, yeah, per capita, we're terrible. *Time Magazine* did an article a while back, and then the serial killer came through and that assassin who tried to kill my shift manager. Alexei seems okay, but now we have this guy named Michael who lives in a cabin on the mountain and scares everyone. That's a long story, but a good one. You see Michael was in love with his partner, and Holly had to kill her because she was trying to kill one of Holly's lovers…"

If he let her go on, she wouldn't talk about Hope for an hour. "I would rather hear about your friend."

"Hope? Oh, she's just overworked according to our doc. She needs rest, though I wonder if she's going to get it out at the Circle G. She's got a crazy crush on the rancher who owns it, but maybe it will finally work out for her. I'm relieved she didn't get eaten by Sasquatch or the sand monster, and she's not pregnant. She really shouldn't be pregnant since she hasn't had sex, you know."

Oh, Lucy was a ball of snark. She had a saucy smile on her face that bespoke an intelligence he actually liked. He appreciated smarts and innocence. It was what he'd found in Hope. And he was damn happy to discover she wasn't sleeping around.

It meant he had less people to kill.

"I think it's nice you care about your friend."

Her smile widened. "Hope is the best. She's such a sweetheart. I hate the fact that I can't go out there and see her, but my boss's wife is the other waitress, and she recently pumped out twins. I'm taking doubles to make up for her absence. Alexei is working overtime, too. We're supposed to get some relief, but the new waitress isn't coming until next week. I was supposed to have dinner with Hope, but now she's stuck out on the G, and I hope she gets well soon. She's been acting a little weird."

He bet she had. He knew she'd seen him standing there before. He'd stood under a big evergreen and watched as she talked to some overblown woman with plastic breasts. Hope had been shocked when she saw him. He'd slinked away, but he wouldn't soon. Soon he would approach her, and she would be his again. She would fall into his arms because they were meant to be together. She couldn't let a little thing like bourgeoisie morality keep them apart. Surely in the years that they had been alone, she'd been able to see what a mistake she'd made.

That dumb bitch Elaine couldn't be the thing that broke up two soul mates.

"She sounds like a great friend." He looked at Lucy's chest. Her breasts were large and round. Pretty and perfect. Rather like his Hope's. She might be a nice way to keep track of his girl. "She's lucky to have you."

Lucy blushed again. "I don't know about that." She sighed, her chest moving up and down. "Can I get you anything else?"

Your best friend on a silver platter? "I'm great. Thank you. But I'm alone in this town. I would appreciate it if you could point me the way to a guide."

She hesitated only for a second. "I could show you around."

He was in. She would lead him straight to Hope. "I would appreciate that."

They made plans to meet later in the evening, but his mind was already on Hope. He would get her back. Or bury her.

Chapter Six

Noah noticed that his brother managed to look everywhere but his direction. He had to hand it to James. He hadn't thrown a punch yet, and that was kind of what Noah had expected after he stole Hope right out from under his nose.

But he couldn't help it. He wanted her. It felt so damn good to want someone after all these years that he was willing to risk his brother's wrath. Of course, another thought played at the edges of his consciousness as he watched Hope laugh at something the sweet-faced brunette named Beth said. Share her. Sharing her would bring James back into his life. Sharing her might set his own life back on track. It was what had gone wrong with Ally. He should never have tried it alone. It had been a compromise, and he didn't want to compromise his future anymore.

But he damn straight couldn't convince his brother to share Hope if James wouldn't even look at him.

"Doc says I'm not very far along," Beth said, digging into the meal she'd heated up. There were now a ton of casseroles in the freezer. Rachel Harper made a mean lasagna. How long had it been since a woman had cooked for him? Ally hadn't even wanted to order takeout. She'd been dedicated to keeping herself as slender as possible, even going so far as to nag him about his weight because he wasn't being supportive.

Hope didn't seem to have the same problem. She took a healthy portion of lasagna. "I don't know how much I'd trust Doc. He's amazing if you get shot and need emergency field surgery. Don't laugh, James. You know it comes up more than you would think."

James smiled her way. "I wasn't arguing with you. I totally agree. Bliss should be declared a hazard zone. Doc's had to stitch up Alexei more than once. And he saved Logan's life a few weeks back."

"What the hell?" Noah felt like he'd been dropped onto a different planet. "What's going on? Bliss has never been violent."

James finally looked his way. "You've forgotten a lot of our childhood then. What about the time when Marie shot Teeny's ex-husband after he tried to kidnap Logan? Or the bank robbers who tried to hide out on Mel's land and found themselves taken out one by one?"

Yeah, maybe it hadn't been the bastion of safety and peace he remembered it to be. "Or the bear who tried to mate with old Hiram. Hi did not take kindly to his near molestation. Does he still have that bear's head over his mantel?"

James's lips curved into a smile. "He still curses it every day. Says it's part of his daily ritual. We should be glad we have a people doc at all. Even if he can't read a sonogram."

Trev took a long drink of his coffee. "I'm grateful. I would be nervous knowing that something could go wrong with Beth or the baby and the nearest doc is thirty miles away."

"The ski lodge has a nurse and a couple of guys who are trained paramedics," Hope pointed out. "We've used them before."

Beth grinned. "Are you talking about Ty? I met him in town a few days back when I was ordering some curtains."

Hope flushed slightly, nodding. "God, that man is hot."

"Who the hell is Ty?" Bo asked.

Hope shrugged, a secret smile on her face. "He's a guy from the ski lodge. He grew up in Creede with Lucy and their friend, River. Apparently she's the one who convinced him to take the ski lodge job. He's also working as the county EMT. So Bliss hasn't changed in all these years, huh?"

She'd turned to Noah, her big brown eyes pulling at him. He would do anything to keep her staring at him like that. "Apparently not. Although having a people doc makes a difference. Back when Jamie and I were growing up, we had to take care of ourselves."

James groaned. "There's a reason he's a vet."

"Hey, you're still alive."

"No thanks to you." James shook his head, obviously lost in memory a bit. "When we were kids, we would stay out at the east cabin for weeks and weeks during the summer."

Noah felt his face light up. He hadn't been there in forever. "The Man Cave. No girls allowed."

"Except for Callie," James pointed out.

"Callie wasn't a girl. She was a Callie, and if I recall the incident you're discussing, she was just as responsible as I was." It felt so good to talk to him. Noah had known he'd been lonely for a while, but sitting and talking to his brother, reminiscing, made him achingly aware of how lonely he'd been. He'd been without family, without anyone who truly understood the forces that had created him. He'd been utterly adrift without his roots. "We were lucky Mom let us go back out after that incident."

"What happened?" Hope asked, leaning forward. That deep anxiety that had plagued her seemed to flee as she listened to them.

"Yeah," Bo said eagerly. "I love a good 'broken bones' story."

Trev's eyes rolled, but even he seemed to want to hear the tale.

James put his fork down. "Our dads bought us this dirt bike when I was thirteen, and Noah was barely twelve. You've got to understand. We come from an incredibly frugal family."

"Two bikes would have been an extravagance." Noah could still remember how he'd felt when he'd seen that shiny dirt bike.

James took up the story. "So we're up in the Man Cave, had been for about a week. We kept in touch with our mom and dads with walkies, and the hands would check on us from time to time. Mom came up once, walked in and nearly gagged. She said the

101

whole place smelled like feet. She never came back."

They hadn't exactly been concerned with cleanliness. "We were kids. We didn't have discerning noses."

"So I took the bike out," James continued. "Max told me I couldn't get the bike up the mountain."

Bo laughed. "You tried to take a little dirt bike up that huge damn mountain?"

James's smile spread across his face like the Cheshire Cat's grin. "Oh, I did. I got to the top. It was getting back down that proved troublesome."

Noah let his head fall to his hand. "He got down that mountain a hell of a lot faster than he got up."

His brother grimaced. "And the bike came down with me. I was torn up and bleeding. That mountain shaved off layers of skin, I tell you. It was awful."

Hope gasped. "Is that why you have those scars on your chest?"

James winked her way. "It sure is. It's why I have scars on my chest, back, shoulders. Everywhere. It took my Indiana Jones T-shirt, too. I loved that T-shirt. So I'm half-dead, but I manage to walk two miles back to the cabin, pushing that bike along. And would you like to know what my dear brother said as I walked in bleeding?"

"I ran to get you," Noah said, knowing where James was going.

His brother shook his head. "He yelled, 'What did you do to the bike!' He grabbed the bike, and Callie had to come out and help me into the cabin. Asshole. Then he and Callie cleaned me up with alcohol and put gauze over all my wounds so we wouldn't have to go home. Well, you can imagine what happened."

Noah winced. "He scabbed over the gauze. It was horrible. It really is why I became a vet. Dogs don't howl the way Jamie did that day. Mel was there, luckily. He said the same thing had happened to him during an abduction. I guess the aliens aren't any better at first aid than Callie and I were. He took Jamie back to his cabin, made him soak in a hot tub, and the gauze sloughed off. Mel was a pretty damn good medic."

James laughed. "Hey, I didn't get an infection, and no alien death rays have come for me."

"Damn, I miss the Man Cave. I want to go up there." He wanted to see it again. Maybe if he could touch that place that had meant so much to him, he could start to feel right again. It was why he'd come home. He wanted to find the boy he'd been so that maybe the man he was could start healing.

His brother's face shut down, all his joy fleeing in an instant. The rest of the table got quiet.

"What?" He wasn't sure what he'd said wrong.

"The east cabin burned down when a wildfire burned off near five thousand acres. I got scars from fighting that, too." James went back to eating.

"I didn't know." How could it be gone?

James shrugged. "You wouldn't. You would have to have called or given a damn in order to know. Trev, do we have a feed shipment tomorrow?"

Noah sat back, his appetite gone. The conversation flowed around him, but he simply sat there. The cabin was gone. His brother was further away than ever.

It had been a mistake to come back. He should have found a job in some other town and started over.

"Give him some time." Hope smiled at him, her voice low as Trev and James and Bo discussed the feed shipment.

"I don't know if there's enough time in the world," he replied in a whisper. He'd really hurt his brother. He hadn't meant to. James seemed harder than before, but then it appeared life had kicked him in the crotch more than once since he'd left. Noah had thought he'd had the rougher road, but James's hadn't been easy.

"He'll come around. You're his brother." Hope patted his hand.

And James noticed that. His gaze sharpened on the spot where Hope's hand touched his. James frowned, his fork suspended in midair.

Noah smiled warmly at Hope, well aware that his brother was watching their every move. "Thanks, Hope. I'm looking forward to our date tomorrow."

"Date?" James ground the word out.

Hope's gorgeous eyes rolled. "He's taking me to see Long-Haired Roger so I can find out how much I owe in order to get my car back. It's not a date."

"We're having lunch afterward." He knew he was stabbing his brother in the back, but it was the only attention he could get. And once he had Hope in his arms, maybe he could find a way to ease James into the relationship. He knew damn straight that if James got her first, he would be left in the damn cold, and he didn't want that to happen. He felt a connection to Hope. For the first time in forever, his brain and his dick were on the same page.

"Only because you guilted me into it," Hope complained.

He shrugged. He was fine with that. He'd been guilted into many things himself. It was sometimes the way the world worked. He'd listened in a bit earlier to the talk in the living room. It was obvious she was in some kind of trouble. She needed someone to look after her. Noah couldn't see why that shouldn't be him. James hadn't claimed her. She was alone by her own admission. She might actually need him. She might be the only fucking person in the world who needed him.

"I'll take you," James pronounced.

Trev, Beth, and Bo watched, their heads going back and forth as though they were watching a tennis match. Or a fight between two dogs over a bone. He wasn't giving up his bone.

"She already agreed to go with me," Noah said, willing to fight.

"You two stop." Hope slapped at the table. "Both of you. You are acting like toddlers. I don't know what is going on here, but you're brothers. Don't you talk, James. I know he left, but he's back." She looked to Noah. "And you, stop baiting him. Do you want to start a fight? I am not Rachel. I will not throw my body between the two of you and proceed to allow you to molest me. I will get a hose and cool you both down. Do you understand?"

James's eyes dropped to his plate, but there was the faintest hint of a grin on his face. "Yes, ma'am."

Hope turned to him, a stern expression on her face. She was in charge. For now.

"Yes, ma'am." Noah didn't try to hide his smile. She was pretty when she was mad. And she could obviously handle unruly men.

"Excellent." She sighed and picked up her iced tea. "Then we can finish a pleasant meal."

She began to talk to Beth, but Noah watched her. He was well aware his brother was doing the same damn thing.

* * * *

Hope sat up in bed when the door opened. Long lines of moonlight transformed the guest room, washing it with silvery light, making the whole space romantic and surreal.

When had she changed into a white gown? She was sure she'd gone to bed wearing a T-shirt and pajama bottoms, but the silky white gown felt right on her skin. It was luxurious, like she was wrapped in a soft cloud. She pushed the quilt back. The fall air was already cold at night, but she was a little hot. She kicked the covers away, aware of the way the change in temperature caused her body to react. Her nipples tightened, and a thrill of gooseflesh raced along her skin. Aware. She was so aware of her body. She stretched, feeling a little like a cat waking up from a nap, and that was when she felt his eyes on her.

James.

He stood in the doorway, his long, lean body covered by nothing but a pair of jeans. The moonlight caressed his flesh like an admiring lover. His chest was perfect despite the scars there. No amount of silvery scars could take away from how perfectly cut his torso was. His shoulders were broad, sculpted by an artistic hand. His arms were muscular but not bulky. He was a cowboy god. Sin walking on two legs.

"What are you doing here?" Hope asked. Was that throaty voice really her own? She knew she should cover herself, but she couldn't quite make her hands work.

"I wanted to make sure you were okay." He stalked into the room. His voice was a deep, velvety caress. He stood over her, his blue eyes staring down. "Do you have everything you need?"

Nope. Not even close. She needed him. She held a hand out.

His smiled warmed her. "I want you, Hope."

Music to her ears. How long had she wanted to hear that from him? But she was leaving. "I can't stay in Bliss."

His handsome face tightened. "I'll take whatever time we have.

Come on, girl. Don't keep me waiting."

He'd kept her waiting, but she didn't want payback. She wanted him. Years she'd gone without wanting anyone. She'd wanted solace. She'd wanted to disappear. She'd wanted to forget. But she hadn't wanted a person for who they were, for their beauty and body and soul. James Glen was a manwhore. She knew it, but he was also honest and forthright and a gentleman. He was smart and funny, and he made her heart pound.

Her hands went to the silky straps of her gown, gently pushing them down. She showed him her breasts, praying he wouldn't reject her. He'd been with so many beautiful women. What if he didn't want her once he'd truly seen her?

His eyes went to her chest, a sensual smile playing on his lips. His golden-brown hair fell forward. He was almost never without his hat, but the shaggy hair made him look younger, freer than he normally looked.

She caught her breath as his fingers came up to play with her nipples. The buds tightened, and her arousal started to flow.

He palmed her breasts and leaned forward, his mouth close to hers. "Tell me you want me."

Oh, so much. She was drugged with desire. "I want you."

He brushed their lips together, a caress that left her wanting so much more. He stood back up. "Then show me everything. I want to see you. I want to see the hips I'll hold, the legs that will wrap around me, and I definitely want to see the pussy I finally get to fuck. Show me."

His words were fuel for her movement. With a languid sigh, she got to her knees and let the gown slip off her body. It seemed to almost evaporate, as though it knew it was no longer needed. She knelt there, naked before James Glen.

He studied her for a long moment, his eyes caressing her. She let her insecurity go. She breathed and let the moment stretch between them. Finally, his hand came out. The tips of his fingers barely touched the notch of her collarbone. She was sure he could feel her pulse pounding. He let his fingers float along her skin, skimming between her breasts, down her belly, across her navel. He stopped just shy of her mound.

"Are you wet?" His voice sounded like it came from all directions. It filled the room until it was all she could hear.

Her pussy flooded with arousal. It was his to command. "Yes."

His hand moved quickly, tangling in her hair, pulling it back with a nice bite of pain. "Yes, what?"

"Yes, James."

"That's right. You call me by my name." He whispered the command in her ear.

She shivered at the dominant tone. "James."

"That's right." He slipped in behind her and cupped her breasts.

"My James." He was hers. For now.

His fingers tightened on her nipples, rolling them between his thumbs and forefingers. He tugged and rolled and played her like a finely tuned instrument. "You're lovely, Hope. You hide under all those clothes."

She had her reasons for wearing her dowdy, sensible clothes. They reminded her that once she hadn't been sensible at all, and it had cost someone her life.

She banished him. Christian had no place here. But Noah did.

"Hello, darlin'."

James didn't stop his slow exploration of her breasts even as his brother's voice filled the room.

"You are one gorgeous woman," Noah said.

Like his brother, he was half-naked, showing off a phenomenally built chest. He was bulkier than his brother. He obviously spent a lot of time in the gym. He was darker, more brooding. He was completely sexy. She could still hear his dark voice telling her to not lie to him. He'd taken control when he'd found her on the side of the road. He'd been commanding, and everything deep inside her had responded to his take-charge attitude.

She liked the fact that he was a little rough. He hadn't tried to charm her. He'd told her what he wanted. Charm could be deceptive. There he was again. Christian was always there trying to fuck everything up. But this was her time, and he wasn't welcome.

"She's gorgeous, brother." James lowered his head as he gently pushed her back into the pillows. When had he gotten in front of her? He seemed to move like a wraith. One minute he was behind her, his denims making contact with the soft flesh of her ass, and then next he was easing her down to the bed.

Noah stood beside them, looking down on Hope with a satisfied smile. "I knew we would be here."

She wasn't sure why they weren't fighting, but she was willing to go with it. The idea of both James and Noah wanting her made her heart soar. So different and yet sweetly alike. Their shared history was incredibly interesting to her. She'd never had a sibling. Her mom had one child, and that had proven way too much for her to handle. Hope had dreamed of a family and one that didn't consist of mere duty. Her mother had shoved a plate of food in front of her at dinnertime and then turned on the TV. And when she was sixteen, her mom had screamed at her to get out because Hope hadn't gotten along with her new boyfriend. She wanted a family like James and Noah had had. It was as alluring as their hard bodies and gorgeous faces. It was sexier than anything.

She imagined herself between them. Warmth and strength would surround her. She would feel small even though she wasn't. She would feel safe, engulfed by their power.

"Could someone kiss me?"

Something was wrong. She could feel it. There was something she was missing, but James leaned forward and sucked her nipple into his mouth. Noah climbed on the bed behind her, turning her head gently so he could take her mouth. His tongue surged inside, playing against hers. She loved the way he tasted and how James sucked her nipples. This was what she'd longed for—to be the center of their attention. She'd only known Noah for a day, but she longed for him.

She hissed at the nip James gave her.

"Oh, he's a bad man, Hope." Noah chuckled against her lips. "He's going to leave marks."

She would take them. She didn't mind rough. She liked it. She would like to walk around knowing her flesh bore a little bit of James Glen's discipline. Damn. She was a freak, but it was fine.

"I'm going to leave a mark, too, darlin'." Noah pressed kisses all over her face. "I'm going to spank that pretty ass of yours right before I fuck it. I'm going to open up your asshole and shove my cock in."

She shuddered a bit. Dark and forbidden. He would take her to places she'd never been before.

"This is mine." James's fingers slid through her pussy. "I'm going to eat this like a ripe peach."

That sounded perfect.

James kissed his way down her torso, dipping his tongue into her navel before rubbing his nose right in her pussy. "You smell good, Hope."

"He likes to eat pussy," Noah said. "I do, too, but I can wait my turn."

She gasped as James's tongue slid over her clit. It felt so good. Her whole body was languid and soft. She was their pretty plaything.

"You'll be waiting a while, brother. This is my treat for now," James said before shoving his tongue right up her pussy.

"He never liked to share our toys." Noah frowned. "I'm going to tell Mom."

"Are not." James's head came up.

"Are, too." Noah was frowning like a mad toddler.

"Are not."

"Are, too."

Hope sat straight up in bed. "What is wrong with you two?"

"It's his fault." Noah pointed at James.

James rolled his eyes. "Is not."

"Is, too."

"You'll have to forgive them," a very cultured British voice said. Hope looked down, and Butch sat at the end of the bed dressed in a crisp doggy tuxedo. "They really have no manners. But that one does. His manners are practically perfect."

She followed the dog's line of vision.

James and Noah were gone. Christian Grady stood over the bed, the golden halo of his hair shining in the moonlight.

"Did you think I would let you get away from me? There's no leaving me, Hope. You're mine. Forever." He smiled down at her, and that was when she noticed the long silver knife in his hand. It dripped with blood. "I can keep you with me forever."

She woke up screaming.

Her heart raced as she clutched the quilt. The dream hung over her like cobwebs, muddling her mind. She was at the Circle G. She was in the guest bedroom.

And she suddenly wasn't alone. The door slammed open and James stood there, his hair wild, wearing nothing beyond a pair of boxers. He had a baseball bat in his hand, his every muscle ready for a fight. "What's happening? Is someone in here?"

James held up the bat as he walked around the room. He threw open the closet door.

Her hands were still shaking. She looked down to make sure she was still in her pajamas. It was stupid, but she was still foggy. Everything was in place. Before she could answer, Noah and Butch were in the doorway. Noah had on flannel pajama bottoms, and Butch was just a dog. His tongue lolled out, and his tail thumped. He looked excited about the potential of some late-night play.

"Are you okay?" Noah asked, his eyes wide.

She was now. And she felt a little dumb. "I am sorry. It was a bad dream. I take it I screamed?"

"Like someone was trying to kill you." James's chest moved up and down as he finally let the bat drop. He eyed his brother. "Were you going to have Butch lick the intruder to death?"

Noah absently ran a hand across his dog's head. "Were you going to use someone's head for batting practice? Let me point out that your batting average was under two hundred."

James shot his brother the finger before turning back to her. "Would you like to tell me what the dream was about?"

God, no. *Let's see, it was about having some hot sex with both you and your brother, and then Noah's dog turns out to be the voice of reason and oh, yeah, my criminally insane ex showed back up, and he was holding the knife that he used to kill my best friend.* Yeah, no way was she telling him any of that.

Hope shook her head. "I can't remember. It's all foggy."

Butch hopped on the bed, obviously giving up on a late-night romp. He put his head down and closed his eyes. Definitely not a guard dog.

"Can't remember?" James asked, crossing his arms over his

sculpted chest. Despite the fact that her hands were still shaking, she couldn't help but notice that both men looked even better than they had in her dream. James's chest was perfectly cut and tapered from broad shoulders to a lean waist. Noah's pajama bottoms rode low on his muscled hips, revealing the glorious notches that pointed straight toward what she suspected was a really nice man part.

She didn't have to suspect anything about James's man part. His poked out of the hole of his boxers. She knew she shouldn't look but couldn't turn away. James was built on big lines, and his cock wasn't any different. Her voice came out in a breathy whisper. "I don't remember."

"Dude, how can she remember a damn thing when your junk is practically pointing her way?" Noah asked.

James flushed, his tan skin turning the sweetest shade of pink. He tucked himself back in. "Sorry. I was having a dream of my own."

"Yeah, I bet." Noah's mouth formed a flat line. "Do you know what I was dreaming about? I was dreaming about being warm because my own damn brother didn't bother to give me a blanket. He told me to sleep on the couch and then he turned off the heater."

James had a shit-eating grin on his face. "Well, you didn't exactly call to let me know I needed to set up another guest bedroom."

"If you two are going to fight, go to another room." She was pleased that her voice sounded halfway steady. She could still see Christian standing there. She wouldn't sleep the rest of the night. She would lie in bed and wait for dawn. It was the way it had been for a solid week. She thought about asking Noah to let Butch stay with her.

"We're not going to fight." James strode right to the bed and pulled back her quilt.

"What are you doing?" Hope asked as she scooted to the middle of the bed.

James climbed in, crowding her. "If I leave you alone, you won't sleep a wink. I'm not naïve. You remember everything about that dream. It's going to haunt you all night, and I would bet this ranch that you've been having the dream or something like it for weeks. You're tired, baby. You have to get some rest. Noah, turn the light off as you leave. You can take my bed."

Noah snorted. "Not happening."

The light went out as James pulled her close. She could feel his heat. He was better than any electric blanket. She knew it was a dumb idea, but her arms wound around his body, and she laid her head on his chest. The strong rhythm of his heart beat against her ear, a safe sound.

"I have to protect Hope. God only knows what you would do to her." Noah climbed in on the other side. "Besides it's way warmer in here."

"Well, if you're going to stay, you better stop complaining and go to sleep." James sounded sleepy. His arms curled around her shoulders.

Noah's arm draped over her waist. He sighed as he settled in behind her, pulling the quilt up. "I'll stop complaining. Now I'm happy."

She should protest. She should force them both out, but her eyes were already closing as though her body knew to be grateful even when her brain held on to stubbornness. Her body was winning. Noah cuddled up against her backside. She was surrounded by warmth.

She slept for the first time in weeks, safe in between them.

Chapter Seven

James drove into town, a frown on his face. "Do we have to take that dog with us everywhere we go?"

"I think he's sweet," Hope said, grinning as she turned slightly to acknowledge Butch's presence.

"He's not kissing you." He was going to need a shower after this trip into town.

"He likes you," Noah said. "He's just a big old lover, aren't you?"

"He needs a bath." James sighed as the damn dog's head came to rest on his shoulder. Butch was sitting in the back of the cab, and since they'd taken off for Bliss about twenty minutes before, Butch had shown him a whole hell of a lot of doggy affection. Noah had always had a heart for big, ugly mutts. Ever since they were kids, he'd been a stray magnet.

The trouble was James didn't want doggy affection. He wanted Hope affection. He'd woken up with a wretched hard-on, and for the barest moment in the minutes between waking and full consciousness, he'd thought about rolling over on top of her and kissing her. He could make them both happy. He could make love to

113

her while they were both still sleepy, before all the reasons they shouldn't took over, and by the time he'd slid inside her and she'd wrapped herself around him, there wouldn't be any going back. He wouldn't have a choice if he made love to her. If he made love to Hope, it would be a commitment, and while he was still half-asleep, that had seemed like a fine idea.

And then his goddamn, interfering brother had sat up and started talking about plans for the day. Plans. All of James's plans were blown, and now the only kisses he was getting came from a mutt with doggy breath.

And to top it all off, there was traffic. Traffic. He was stuck at one of the two damn stoplights in town behind a dilapidated RV. James hung his head out the window, trying to get a sense of what was going on. There was a line of vehicles but not what he was used to seeing. People in Bliss tended to drive trucks, SUVs, and Jeeps. These were what he would term city cars. Outside of the RV, there was a Volkswagen Beetle that had seen way better days, and several sedans. The Beetle had a sign on the top of its dome proclaiming that someone named Madame Delphine provided expert palm readings.

God, it was starting. The crazies were coming to town, and given where he lived, that was saying a lot. When Mel was one of the saner people in the area, he preferred to hunker down. By the time the first snow fell, Bliss would be back to normal. Apparently snow killed the "vibes." He'd also noticed a lot of the psychics, warlocks, or whatever they called themselves tended to prefer warmer climates.

The light changed, and he was finally able to move.

"You guys can drop me off. I know you're busy." Hope spoke briskly as she looked out the window, carefully avoiding glancing at either James or Noah.

James turned to her. He noted Noah did the same thing. They were both simply staring her way.

She looked between the two of them. "Fine. But don't complain later when you're bored waiting around for me."

What exactly did she think he was going to do? Did she think he was going to wait in the truck? "I'll handle it."

Noah laughed.

"What?" James asked.

"Good luck with that, brother," Noah muttered.

"Handle what?" Hope asked, her voice tight. She was back in her dowdy clothes this morning. He'd preferred the pajamas. She'd looked young and sweet with her hair around her shoulders and her eyes soft with sleep. He wanted to take her hair out of that ponytail. He sort of wished Trev hadn't retrieved her clothes from her car. Then he could find something pretty for her to wear. He liked the idea of buying her nice clothes, things as pretty as she was, clothes that would make her feel as gorgeous as she truly was. But since he hadn't had the chance to buy her clothes, the least he could do was take care of her car.

"I'll handle Long-Haired Roger. I know a little something about cars. I also know Long-Haired Roger will try to keep the cost to a minimum by using crap-ass recycled parts." He knew that because Roger had fixed his truck more than once in the last couple of years, and he'd worked hard to make sure James could afford his bill. Roger was a fine man, but he didn't want Hope driving around in a car that had been fixed with parts someone had found at a junkyard. In fact, he intended to see if Roger wouldn't just tell her to get a new one. He hated the way her car always shuddered when it started or stopped.

"Uhm, that's exactly what I want him to do," Hope said, her hands on her lap like they hadn't clutched him all night long as she'd slept. "I don't have a lot of money. I need my car."

"I told you I would handle it." She didn't seem to be understanding. Stubborn. She was awfully stubborn.

Noah groaned.

"Do you mind?" He didn't need the peanut gallery's opinion.

"Nope. I'm finding this intensely entertaining." Noah craned his neck and looked around. "The place still looks the same. Wow, I missed Stella's."

"You are not taking charge, James." Hope turned to him, a stubborn gleam in her eyes. "You're not my husband, and you're not my dad."

It was good that she understood the last part of that statement.

"I'm damn straight not your dad, but I'm the man responsible for you."

"What century are you in?" Hope asked, indignation evident in her tone.

He pulled his patience around him. This was why he didn't do relationships. He was shitty at them. Cows. He understood cows. Cows didn't yell at him when he tried to take care of them. "Logan talked to me before he left. He asked me to look out for you. I agreed. That makes me responsible for you."

A brow rose over her right eye. "And Logan was responsible for me how?"

How was he supposed to answer that one? "Because he cares about you, Hope."

Noah stayed silent, but he didn't miss his brother's shit-eating grin. Asshole probably knew exactly what to say to get her to understand, but he remained frustratingly silent.

"Well, I care about him, too." Hope took a deep breath and went quiet.

James drove past Stella's and Trio. He found the road that led to the Feed Store Church and went north before turning onto the side street that housed the garage, beauty parlor, a ski shop, and the post office.

"Whoa, when did Polly decide to light up the world?" Noah asked, staring at the enormous neon flashing lips that marked the site of Polly's Cut and Curl. He watched in obvious awe as the lips blinked on and off, opening and closing in a kissing motion. "I think you can see it from space. Does Mel know that Polly's putting out the astral equivalent of a request for an escort?"

James couldn't help but laugh. His brother was always quick with a joke or an observation. "It was brought up at a town hall, but Mel assures everyone that aliens are far more interested in probing than kissing." He pulled into the parking lot and had a sudden plan. If Hope wasn't around, she couldn't cause trouble. "Hey, why don't you go on over to Polly's and get your nails done? I'll talk to Roger."

She smacked him on the arm—and not a girly slap. "Jerk."

Noah let her out, holding her hand to help her down. She didn't look back as she strode into the office, her sensible bag on her shoulder.

"What did I do?" His arm still stung. She had not gone easy on him.

Noah laughed as James got out of the truck. "Man, you don't get how to handle her at all. How long have you known her?"

"About a year. I thought she would like getting her nails done. She works a lot of overtime. I thought it would be relaxing." Yeah, he would hide behind that.

Noah obviously wasn't buying his excuse. "No, you thought it would get her out of the way, and then you could make sure her car got fixed properly and maybe make it take longer than it normally would because that means she has to stay out at the G while she's getting it fixed. You were thinking it might make her dependent on you, and then you'd have a better shot at her."

His brother knew him way too well. "I thought it was a good plan."

"It is. I agree wholeheartedly, but you're going about it all wrong. You're expecting her to be compliant, and that little filly is anything but compliant. We have to be sneaky."

"You have a plan?" James hated to ask, but Noah was always good with a plan. Noah had been the brains behind their operation.

"Yep. Follow my lead. When the time comes, distract her while I explain to Roger that we'll handle the bill, and he should take his time and do it up right."

Tag team. Damn it, it made sense. "Fine. Our dads never had this trouble with Mom. When did you get so sneaky?"

Noah frowned, a line appearing between his brows. "I learned from the best."

Ally. They were going to have to talk about Ally. Noah wasn't going away. Hell, he couldn't even get away from his brother when he was in bed. Though it had been nice when Noah made coffee. "Sorry about the divorce. Is it final?"

They started walking toward the office after Noah gave Butch the command to stay. "It's final. We divorced six months ago, but the marriage has been over for years. You were right about her. I was a fool."

He didn't like the defeat in his brother's voice. Despite his anger at Noah, he was still his kid brother. Hope was right. Noah was his family. "So you decided to come back to Bliss because Stef gave you a job? I assume it was Stef who said you could have a job. Or did you show up and hope for the best?"

Noah's jaw straightened. "Stef hired me. And I can find a place to stay. Even if I have to live in Creede."

James pushed through the doors of the shop. "It's your home, too."

"Are you sure?" The question came out of Noah's mouth in a flat monotone that told James his brother wasn't at all sure what his answer would be.

His mother would have his ass if he told his baby brother he couldn't stay in his childhood home. But that didn't mean he had to like it. "Just stay away from Hope."

Noah huffed. "Not going to happen. She needs me. Bitch all you like, but you need me, too."

They turned the corner. James was about to explain that he needed Noah like he needed a damn hole in his head when he stopped at the sight in front of him. Oh, he needed something all right.

He needed his baseball bat. That was what he needed. He was shocked by the flare of righteous indignation that shot through his system. Hope stood in the middle of the garage floor, but she wasn't anywhere close to being alone. She was surrounded by two large men, both flirting outrageously with her.

Yeah, he would need his brother because he was about to start a fight.

"Who the fuck are they?" Noah asked, his voice low. "Wasn't Roger's mechanic a big old hefty dude with a mullet?"

The new mechanics weren't close to hefty. They were both well over six feet and probably didn't have an ounce of fat between them. One had longish brown hair and a scruffy beard, while the other's black hair was shorter and his face clean. But Clean-Shaven Dude had a problem with shirts. He'd taken his off. Hope smiled up at the guy, a softness on her face James hadn't seen in a long time.

"We're going to have to find another shop," Noah said.

118

"So you think it's fixable?" Hope asked, her eyes spending too much time on Scruffy Guy's shoulders.

"Absolutely, love. Me and Cade here can fix almost anything with wheels."

"He's being humble." Cade winked down at her. "We can fix anything. We've got a gentle touch."

They were about to have two busted lips. "Hope, you want to introduce us to your friends?"

There was no way to mistake the mischief in Hope's eyes. "Friends? These are the mechanics working on my car. Jesse McCann and Cade Sinclair. We were discussing how long it might take to get it back."

"Hey," a new voice said. Long-Haired Roger walked in, his coveralls coated in oil. "No one told me we had company. Cade? Where the hell is your shirt, son?"

Cade grinned, but picked up his T-shirt and shrugged into it. "Anything you say, boss. We were just telling Miss Hope here that her electrical system is shot."

"Not that it was all that great in the first place," Jesse admitted. "This car is ten years old. I can tell you that if the electric hadn't blown, the engine was going to go soon. That tuna can has a hundred and fifty thousand miles on it." He turned judgmental blue eyes on both he and Noah. "Which one of you is her man? Why would you let her drive around in a death trap like that?"

"Neither one is my man," Hope replied, and James was damn happy to see her frown at the scruffy mechanic. "And I couldn't afford anything else."

"Now, Hope," Roger said with a conciliatory pat to her back. "We're going to work something out. I promise. Don't you listen to those boys. They like to make everything sound worse than it is. We'll fix your car, or I'll help you find another one."

Cade smiled down at her. "Jesse and I are working on a real sweet ride. We can get it to you for a good price."

"Where the hell did you find these guys?" James asked, his eyes on Long-Haired Roger and his perfectly bald head.

Roger turned back to them. "I was real lucky. After I had to turn down that nice Russian fellow because he scared the crap out of me,

I was worried I would have to cut back on taking on new work, but Cade and Jesse showed up one day on their motorcycles and said they would work for one paycheck."

Cade smiled, his eyes never leaving Hope's chest. *Fucker.* "We knew we wanted to live here. We've been looking for a place to call home for a long time. When we heard about Bliss, we knew we had to come here."

Roger leaned in, whispering James's way. "I think they heard about our low cost of living."

Nope. They'd found out how easy it was to share in Bliss. James knew all the fucking moves. They were crowding her, one on each side. Cade would play the hard-ass while Jesse would be the sweet one. They wouldn't leave any exits for the girl they wanted to get in between them. They would form a plan, and each would have a role to play. He knew damn well how that game went because he'd practically invented it with his brother.

"When the hell did Long-Haired Roger go bald?" Noah asked, his mouth hanging open.

Roger turned, and his eyes widened as he looked at Noah for the first time. "Noah Bennett?"

"Yeah, hi, Roger." Noah turned sheepish again, his face falling a little.

Roger's face went red. "My dog died. How do you like that, Mr. Vet? Did you like New York City? I hope you did because my Princess paid the price."

Long-Haired Roger stomped into his office and slammed the door.

"Is he talking about that ancient Chihuahua he used to have?" Noah asked, staring after him.

James couldn't help but shake his head. "Yep. She died about two years ago."

Noah sent him a what-the-hell look. "That dog was eleven hundred years old. I remember her. She was blind and had arthritis in every joint, and he had to feed her baby food because her digestive tract was shot. She was hypoglycemic and had hydrocephalus, which was why the poor thing could barely raise her head. I won't even go into the problems with her patellas. And yet that dog lived years longer than anyone would have expected. How is that my fault?"

"What did he say?" Jesse asked.

It was nice to know at least they weren't the brainiest of men. Score one for the brothers. *Fuck*. He was not thinking like that. He was mad at Noah. He couldn't trust Noah. "What my brother is trying to say is that dog was a miracle on four legs."

"She wasn't on four legs. She couldn't walk. Roger walked her around in a baby carriage. Once I even saw him chewing up food and feeding it to her like a momma bird. He's the crazy one." Noah seemed ready to continue the argument when Hope put a hand on his arm.

"He and Liz never had kids. Princess was their baby," Hope explained. "I'm sure he still misses her. You wouldn't have been able to do anything if you had been here. But you can start repairing your reputation. You can apologize."

"I didn't do anything wrong," Noah insisted.

Hope obviously wasn't listening to any excuses. "From what I understand, you walked away and left everyone in the lurch. Until you acknowledge that, how can you expect them to trust you?"

Noah's shoulders sagged. "I'll go talk to him."

She'd gotten to Noah in a way James never could have. She'd stated the problem simply and with no real judgment that would have sent his brother into a tailspin of defensiveness. He listened as Noah rapped on Roger's door and began to make his first real headway in coming home for good.

Hope had done that. Sweet Hope, who was also practical and plainspoken and kind.

Why did he find that so damn sexy?

"Hope, we haven't seen you around town. Why don't we remedy that? Let us take you out to dinner tonight." Jesse sidled up to her, getting way too close for James's comfort.

"She's not going out with you." James held off picking up the nearest wrench and bashing Scruffy's head in. Hope already thought he was some form of lesser man. Violence would be something she would likely take exception to. So he put an arm around her shoulder and went for compromise. She wanted him to get along

121

with Noah? He could give in this once. "She's going out with me and my brother."

She shook her head but didn't move out from under his arm. "Playing it that way, huh, James? Fine. I'm going out with them because it's relaxing. I love to listen to them argue."

He wasn't having a fight with her in front of them. "We do it all for you, baby. Now show me what's going on with her car. You might have to use little words because I know horses better than cars. Hope here knows everything so don't worry about her."

She elbowed him, but there was a happy light in her eyes. "Jerk."

He kept his arm around her while they got the full tour of how fucked up her vehicle was.

* * * *

Noah walked out of Long-Haired Roger's office with a feeling that something had finally fallen into place. Roger was insane, for sure, but he was also right in a way. He hadn't merely moved when he'd followed Ally to New York. He'd walked out on a bunch of people who needed him. Noah had left his home behind. He should have talked to people, explained why he was doing what he was doing. He should have worked hard to arrange for another vet. He should have called and checked up on the people who had been his family.

He hadn't acted like a friend or a brother or a son. He hadn't acted like a neighbor. He'd been an obsessed asshole.

He looked across the garage at Hope. Damn, he was getting obsessed again, but this time it was over the right type of woman. Ally would have turned her nose up and rolled her eyes and told Noah that he didn't need Long-Haired Roger. Hell, Ally would never have walked into this garage in the first place. If her car had gotten so much as a scratch, she would have whined until he bought her a new one.

Ally had no idea what it meant to be truly loved. But Noah was starting to remember.

"Where did the other one go?" Noah asked. The douchebag

with the beard was talking to Hope. The one who liked to strip was nowhere to be seen. He kind of wanted to punch them both, but Hope would have his ass.

Why did he like that idea? It had been an awfully long time since someone cared about what he did.

"I don't know," James muttered, his gaze firmly on Hope. "He walked out the back door about ten minutes ago. But they've backed off. I made sure of it."

At least James was doing one thing right when it came to Hope. "Good. I talked to Roger. We're going to take care of the repairs to her car. If the estimate goes over five grand, then Roger is going to sell us a car for that much. He's going to take at least a week before he can give her a firm estimate. He's busy, you see."

He'd had to smooth talk the hell out of Roger to get him to agree. And he'd had to promise to stay in Bliss until he died and to help Roger find a new dog. Both promises were fairly easy. He was a stray magnet and damn good at matching pets to owners. His last brilliant move in Bliss had been to match a nasty mutt named Quigley and a set of twins with equal personality problems. He could find Roger a baby, no problem.

And he was never leaving Bliss again. He'd learned his damn lesson.

"Good." James settled his hat back on his head. "I think Hope's planning on leaving, but she can't without a car."

Noah didn't like the idea of Hope leaving, so he was mighty happy he'd made the deal he had. He was going to have to make them all over the county. He had to go out tomorrow and talk to Max and Rye. He wasn't looking forward to it. He might have to work for free for a year or two. Hope turned her head toward him, and his breath just about stopped. Yeah, he didn't give a shit about the cash.

James stared at him.

"Dude, you're looking at her like she's got a halo on her head. Didn't you learn your lesson with Ally?" James asked.

"She isn't Ally."

James threw his head back and laughed.

"What?"

"I'm realizing a few things."

"Well, hell, brother, fill me in."

James pointed straight at him. "Ally damn near broke you. She turned your whole fucking world upside down. She lied to you and used you, and here you are six months later back for more."

It made him sound like a fool. Maybe he should back off. Maybe he should think about this more.

"Don't frown like that," James admonished. "I wasn't saying it was a bad thing. I was just thinking that five years with a greedy bitch didn't wipe out your childhood. I was thinking it was a good thing."

Noah froze because his brother was right. Five years of being abused emotionally didn't erase all the decades of watching real love. Watching his dads and his mom had merely made the longing sharper, less avoidable. He knew what he wanted. He'd gone about it all wrong. He'd allowed childish jealousies to lead him, but he wanted real love now. He wanted what his parents had. "I'm not a kid anymore. I want a family. I want what our dads had. I want the same thing you want."

James took a step back. "I don't want anything close to what they had."

"How can you say that?"

James turned his face down. "I don't want to fucking fade away. Look, I want a family, but what we had growing up isn't going to work for me. I watched my dad die because your dad and their wife were gone. He sat down and waited for it."

And that seemed like a beautiful fucking thing to Noah. "What's wrong with that? I think they're together again."

"And if they aren't? If this is all there is?"

His brother's low words struck a chord in Noah. How much had being alone affected his brother? "Then at least they had each other. At least they really loved someone and someone loved them."

"You weren't here. You didn't watch it."

"I watched Momma die. I watched our dads have to live through it. I know I wasn't here for Dad, but watching Papa was bad enough. And I know damn well he wouldn't have taken back a moment of it. Not even the end." He'd watched his fathers both die inside the day his mother had passed, but they'd found comfort in each other. "You remember what they did the night before her funeral?"

"They sat up all night and talked. They talked about her. I think they went through every picture we had." James's face was red, and Noah could tell he was trying to hold it together. How hard had it been to have to live in that house every day and know what he'd lost? To have to live with the ghosts of his family? Would the burden have been easier if Noah had stayed?

They'd been raised differently. Other brothers were raised to know they would leave one day and that their relationship would be at best friendly—a congenial friendship made up of seeing each other on holidays and birthdays and the occasional backyard barbecue. That wasn't how he and James had been raised. Their role models had been two men sharing a wife, sharing the burdens and joys, knowing always that they weren't alone. They had their dads to look up to, and hanging out with Max and Rye hadn't helped. Max and Rye Harper had always known they were halves of a whole and incomplete without the other. He and James weren't twins, weren't even blood, but their childhood had made promises that Noah had broken.

And it looked like James was paying the price.

"Are you two okay?" Hope asked, walking up to them. "Are you fighting again?"

"No," Noah said. "We were talking about our dads."

Hope's face went soft, and without a moment's hesitation, she walked up to James and wrapped her arms around him. For the barest second, Noah worried James would simply stand there. He'd never been one to show his emotions. He was a stoic cowboy to the end. Except now his brother's arms clutched at Hope. He pressed her close, and his face became buried in her hair. They stood that way for a long moment, James seeming to take comfort from the petite woman.

"She's taken then, huh?" The scruffy one sighed. "All the pretty ones seem to be taken."

"Yes, she's taken. She belongs to me and my brother." He said it quietly because he was pretty damn sure both his brother and

Hope would disagree with him. It didn't matter. He could be stubborn, too.

Jesse shrugged. "One of these days. Where did Cade slip off to?"

Hope's eyes were suspiciously bright as she and James let go, but his brother seemed much more in control. "Okay, someone promised me lunch. I am totally letting the two of you pay since it seems like I'll need every dime to get a new car. Oh, and afterward I need to stop by and help Nell at the festival. I think she's selling bread and some kind of dream catcher. But it could be tofu and cruelty-free undies for all I know. It doesn't matter since I promised I would help her set up. I have a schedule to keep, after all. Just because I'm not working right now doesn't mean I don't have plans. Oh, god. I was supposed to have dinner with Lucy and River last night. I'm a horrible person."

"Lucy called the house." James put an arm around her shoulder. She didn't move away. "She was worried, but I told her you were all right." He looked over at Noah. "Lucy is one of the new folks in town. She moved here from Creede recently. She's working at the tavern that Callie's husband runs. River took over Mountain Adventures."

"Is she Pat's kid? I vaguely remember her," Noah said, a vision of a dark-hair kid whispering along his brain. He hadn't known the Creede kids well, but Patrick Lee had been a nice guy.

James nodded. "Yep. She recently got married, but Hope doesn't like the guy. I don't think Lucy does either."

"I think he's sketchy, but River seems happy," Hope said with a wrinkle of her nose. "Thanks for explaining what's going on the Lucy. She worries."

They started walking toward the door, James and Hope, side by side. One day he was going to be on the other side. That would be his place. He would prove he belonged there.

"Are you coming?" Hope asked, a hint of a smile on her face.

He caught up as fast as he could. Maybe it wouldn't take so long. Hope was stuck with them for a while. Anything could happen as long as James didn't kick him out. He certainly hadn't expected to sleep with her cuddled between them last night. He felt surprisingly optimistic for the first time in a long time. He was back at the G. He was making headway with his family. He'd met a woman he really liked.

Things could work out.

He pushed through the doors as he felt his stomach growl. "I am ready for some lunch."

Hope gasped as she looked at the truck.

"What the hell?" James asked.

There was a single flower on the hood of James's truck. It was perfectly white and wholly incongruous. "I think someone likes you, James."

James rolled his eyes. "I have to have a talk with someone. It seems like a girl I was dating has taken the whole two times we went out way too seriously."

"Serena?" Hope asked. Noah couldn't help but notice her face had gone utterly white.

James sighed. "Yeah. Hope, you gotta believe me. I never promised her a thing. It was two dates, but on one of them I brought her some gardenias because it was the opening night of her play. I kinda slept through most of it. She must have thought she was being cute. I'm going to talk to her."

Hope shut down, her face going blank. "What you do about Serena is none of my business. Could you get rid of that thing, please?"

She opened the door of the truck and got inside without another word.

"Fuck." James grabbed the flower off the hood.

"Don't beat yourself up. I don't think she's upset about Serena. She freaked out when she saw that flower. Why would she be afraid of a flower?" He was certain of it. Her skin had turned pale, and he'd worried for a moment that she was going to pass out again. Hope was deathly afraid of something or someone, and that flower was a clue.

"Are you sure?" James tossed the flower into the garbage bin against the side of the building. "I haven't always treated her right. I don't have the best reputation."

Noah shook his head. "I'm sure."

"Why would a single flower put that look on her face?" James asked.

Noah had no idea. But he was going to find out.

* * * *

Christian watched from across the way. He could see Hope's face plainly, though she could not see him from behind the tinted windows of the beauty parlor. His new friend, Lucy, had been extremely talkative on their date the night before. He'd kept his hands to himself and focused on her. He was a perfect gentleman. He knew exactly how to deal with someone like Lucy. She was looking for some combination of boyfriend and father figure.

Rather like his Hope.

"I'll have a place for you in a minute, sir." The woman who had introduced herself as Polly winked at him. She was pure small town with her helmet of bleached-blonde hair and a face that bore far too much makeup. Still, all women could prove useful, and small-town women lived to gossip.

He thanked Polly but kept his eyes firmly on Hope. Her eyes widened as she walked toward the truck and caught sight of the flower. He knew that look. He'd seen it before on many faces.

Fear.

He'd hoped there would be a bit of nostalgia in her eyes when she saw his gift, but he was willing to settle for fear. He'd covered their marital bed with gardenias the first night of their honeymoon. The very smell of gardenias made him think of Hope.

"I'm ready for you. Come this way, please. Oh my god, is that Noah Bennett?" Polly asked.

"Who is he?" It was good to have a name. Lucy had mentioned someone named James Glen, who apparently spent an enormous amount of time with cattle, but she hadn't mentioned a second man. He wondered briefly which one had walked out with his arm around Hope. Christian meant to cut that arm off.

Polly took off on a wave of gossip. "Noah Bennett is the prodigal son. He left Bliss over five years ago. Took off for the big city. I never thought I would see him in these parts again. Hell, I'm sure surprised he had the guts to go in there and talk to Long-Haired Roger. He blames Noah for the death of his dog, and let me tell you, Long-Haired Roger takes that seriously. Now not regular Roger. He has a dog or two, but he mostly trains them to protect him when the feds come after him. He thinks he's going to secede from the US and set up his own kingdom, so he's probably right about the feds coming in one day. Although I don't think they should take him too serious now. The man can't boil water. I doubt he can run his own government, even if it's only him and his wife and possibly a Sasquatch. He claims he sees one all the time and that he's real friendly-like."

Christian took a deep breath. She was going to prove tiresome, but necessary. She was obviously a talker, and he could use some information before he finally made his intentions very plain to Hope. He had to know what he was getting into and how much he could plan on getting away with.

The truck that Hope was in started to pull away.

Years he'd waited, and his patience was starting to wear thin. She thought she could bring other men into their game? "Perhaps he's come back for that woman."

"Hope?" Polly laughed. "Oh, that girl never dates. She's practically a nun. I'm surprised she's staying out at the G. James is a bit of a ladies' man. Maybe he's thinking about settling down now that his brother is back. He's not getting any younger and that ranch needs a mistress. They could do worse than Hope. She's a sweet little thing. I wish she'd let me do something about that hair. I would love to put some highlights in it."

Christian remembered the way her hair would hang in waves down her back. He liked the fact that she was living like a nun. She'd been so pure and innocent. It was the thing he'd loved most about her. She'd been a virgin when she'd come to him. She'd been his sweet child bride and the best cover of his life. No one would suspect the quiet preacher with the soft, submissive wife was doing anything criminal. He needed that again. Everything had gone right when Hope had been at his side.

As for her nearly killing him, what marriage didn't have a few problems? He took a deep breath and smiled at Polly. "Lead on, ma'am. I'm happy to find such a nice salon in a small town."

"And I find it nice to have such a gentleman for a customer. What is it you do?"

Christian sat down. "I'm a preacher, ma'am."

And he wasn't going to let any man come between him and his god-given wife.

Chapter Eight

Hope stared at the menu, but her mind was somewhere else. Specifically it was back in Georgia. She could smell gardenias, and it was starting to upset her stomach.

How could that one flower ruin her whole day? This morning she'd felt better than she had in weeks. She'd felt close to James after seeing how talking about his dads had made him feel. When he'd put his arms around her, she'd seriously thought about whether something could work between them.

And Noah. Noah with his sad eyes and gorgeous face just called to her. If he'd handled Roger differently, she might have been able to keep her distance, but he'd been gentle and kind to the man. And he'd been kind to her.

So why did Christian have to invade her brain and ruin everything?

When she smelled gardenias, she could feel his soft hands on her. She could hear him telling her how sweet and pure she was. She could hear him apologize for what he had to do, but it was a husband's duty, after all.

Christian had been incredibly gentle when he'd had sex with her—the few times he'd done it. She'd been a virgin and completely ignorant, but she'd known something was wrong. She'd thought her love could conquer all.

She'd been an idiot.

"Do you know what you want, hon?" Stella asked, her eyes looking down from under a pair of rhinestone-decorated glasses. Stella must have seen some question in her eyes. "Sebastian made me get glasses. That old man is going to drive me crazy. He's on me like honey on a bear, I tell you."

"He's making up for lost time, Miss Stella," James said, handing her his menu. "You know that man loves you. And the glasses make you look highly intellectual."

Stella beamed. "I think they do, too. Maybe the men of this town will see me as more than just a beauty queen now. Hope?"

If she didn't eat, her two self-appointed keepers were going to throw a hissy fit. "I'll have the soup and salad. Thank you."

"I would like a burger, medium with all the fixings, please. And some fries. Definitely fries." Noah sighed as though he could already taste the burger.

Stella frowned his way. "I'd like to not have to drive fifty miles to get my cat vaccinated. I suppose we can't all get what we want now, can we?"

James laughed, but Noah seemed to understand this was serious.

"I will make house calls, Miss Stella," Noah offered, tripping over the words. "You won't have to drive anywhere at all from now on."

Stella humphed. "See that you do. She needs her yearly next week." She turned on her boots and walked off.

"I have to admit, it is fun watching you trying to get out of the dog house. I think Stella was willing to feed Butch there before she fed you." James needled his brother.

"This job gets harder and harder." Noah's frown was so adorable she wanted to kiss him right between his eyebrows.

And then she thought about that damn flower. Had it been Serena or someone else? Was she going crazy? She'd even wondered about Cade and Jesse. They had shown up in town right around the time she'd started to see signs of Christian. Christian always had a few attractive male followers. She hadn't thought about it before, but now she could see that those men had most likely been in on Christian's criminal activities. The men who surrounded Christian were always strong and good at bringing in dumb, unsuspecting females. The new mechanics fit the bill. It would have been easy for one of them to slip out the door and leave the flower.

She shook her head. But how would they know what the gardenia meant? Christian was dead. If one of his followers wanted revenge on her, they wouldn't do it by reminding her of the intimate moments of her marriage.

"Hope, you with us?" James asked.

She forced herself to focus. "Of course. I was thinking about how we're going to rehab Noah's image without giving away his income for the next twenty years."

Noah practically pouted. "I could run through town and let everyone throw shit at me."

"Or you could take a booth at the festival and offer free vaccinations." Hope warmed to the idea. "It would give everyone a chance to talk to you again in a professional way. Oh, and I can bake homemade dog treats."

Noah shuddered. "You want me to work Woo Woo Fest? Damn, you drive a hard bargain."

"I want you to work the Festival of Spiritual Renewal. And you know I'm right. We'll print up some business cards, and Butch can be our mascot. I'll help out." She'd never worked with animals before. It sounded like fun. She'd lived in an apartment throughout her childhood, and her mother hadn't wanted to pay a pet deposit. Christian hadn't liked animals. He preferred a pristinely clean environment, and dog hair was on his "no" list.

There he was again.

"I'll do it." Noah gave in with a frown that did nothing to take away from his masculine beauty. "But I draw the line at trying to psychically speak to dogs. I've been to Woo Woo Fest before, and some of those people think they can talk to their pets. One year a woman tried to convince me her dog was the reincarnated spirit of Marie Antoinette and that was why she had to be fed cake. That woman understood neither history nor the dietary requirements of a Maltese. I swear, Jamie, if I catch you laughing at me, we're going to have a knock-down, drag-out."

"Get ready then because I intend to laugh my ass off," James promised.

They continued to talk, but she was lost in dark thoughts.

She could hear Christian telling her how fragile she was, how pure and innocent. She could smell the incense he would burn at his gatherings when he would talk about God and how man had been cut off from the divine by all his technology.

She'd been barely seventeen and she'd thought she'd understood everything. She'd joined Christian's commune because it seemed happy and safe, and Christian Grady had been the kindest, most spiritual man she'd ever met. She'd been over the moon when he'd looked her way. How could a man who was so smart, so beautiful and wise, ever want her?

She wanted a drink. It would be easy to walk over to Trio and order a vodka and cranberry juice. No one knew she had a problem. She'd kept it hidden. Trev was the only person besides the Wright-Hollister clan who knew, and he was back at the ranch. Zane wasn't working today. He was at home with his babies. Alexei would be tending bar, and he would merely garble some English as he passed her whatever she wanted. She could get up and walk out of Stella's, and Noah and James would probably follow her and join her. They wouldn't question it. They would enjoy the party. She could maybe have both of them if they had enough alcohol to overcome all the obstacles.

She could forget for a while. The liquor would turn off the images and voices in her head.

She clenched her fists. She couldn't even go to a meeting now. She didn't have a car. Her sponsor was gone. She could call Trev, but that seemed like a bad idea. He was James's partner. He was too close to her real life.

Real life? Hah. She didn't have one. She had a bunch of crap she'd made up because she didn't want all these nice people to know who she was deep down.

"Hope, snap out of it." Noah's voice broke through her inner monologue. He was using that same deep voice he'd used when he'd found her crying on the side of the road.

"What?" She forced herself to focus on him.

Noah's fingers drummed impatiently along the tabletop. "I've asked you the same question three times now."

"I'm sorry. What did you ask?" How long had she been sitting here thinking about a drink?

"I no longer care about whether you've seen the movie that's on at the motel. I now care about what's bothering you. You didn't even notice when Jamie got up and left the table."

James was gone? She hadn't even noticed when James had slid out of the booth. "Where did he go?"

"He caught sight of the preacher from the Feed Store Church. He wanted to ask him about how he can get organic alfalfa and how many sermons he's going to have to sit through to get a ten percent discount." Noah leaned forward. "Now start talking."

It was too much. The flower. Seeing someone who looked like Christian. The phone calls. It was too much. The walls were closing in on her.

"I'm still tired. Maybe I should go and see Caleb again." Anything to get out from under Noah's suspicious eyes. She could already feel her skin flush with heat. She would start to sweat soon. Her heart rate was speeding up as she felt the walls closing in. Anxiety attack. She hadn't had one in almost a year, but it was creeping up on her now.

She couldn't do this here. She couldn't freak out. She needed to get someplace quiet where she could ride it out.

She stood up abruptly, her knees hitting the table with a painful thud. "I'll be back."

She wouldn't. She would find someplace else to stay. She couldn't handle them. She could stay with Lucy. Lucy wouldn't ask too many questions. Lucy would be happy for the company. Lucy wouldn't push and probe and try to figure her out. She wouldn't watch her every minute of the day. Yes, she would call Lucy.

Hope pushed out of the doors of Stella's and walked past Butch, who was sitting on the sidewalk waiting patiently for his master. Tears blurred her eyes. She liked the dog. She liked his master. She'd loved the way it had felt to sleep between Noah and James, but she couldn't do it again. She'd felt safe, and she wasn't. She wasn't safe because she didn't deserve safety. Not after the things she'd done.

Without truly thinking about where she was going, she found the stairs that led to her small efficiency. She pulled her keys out of her purse, ignoring the smell of smoke. It wasn't that bad. Maybe she could stay here. It wasn't much. The furniture had been here when she'd moved in. Jennifer Waters had left everything behind, including the dishes and cookware, when she'd left for Dallas. When she'd returned to Bliss, she'd married Stefan Talbot and had no interest in her former apartment.

All she really owned were her clothes, some books, and a framed picture of her and Nate and Logan taken a year before.

She had nothing. She was twenty-seven years old, and she had nothing. And she never would.

"Hope."

She should have locked the door. Noah stood in the doorway, his big body blocking out the sun. "Go away, Noah."

"That is not going to happen. You're going to talk, and you're going to do it now."

"I am not talking to you. I want to be alone." Tears coursed down her face, but she was filled with anger. At herself. At Christian. At Noah for standing there and looking perfect.

His jaw squared, and he walked into her tiny room. "I'm not going to do that. I'm done playing around. You can hate me later, but you're coming with me now. We're going to walk back downstairs and pick up our lunch, and then you and me and Jamie are all going back to the ranch. You're not leaving the house again until you explain to us what's wrong."

"You can't force me to go with you."

"Sure, I can. I'm bigger and stronger and quite frankly, I think I'm meaner than you."

She believed him. "I'll call the sheriff."

"I'm sure you will if you can get to a phone. I think you might find that hard to do after I tie you up."

Oddly, she wasn't afraid of him. Not physically. "You think you can kidnap me and make me talk? What if there isn't anything to talk about, Noah? What if I just don't like you? What if I don't want to be around you?"

She'd struck a direct hit. She could see that plainly in the way his eyes flared. He wasn't as confident as he seemed, but he simply crossed his arms over his chest and continued. "I don't think so. You might not like me, but I sure as hell feel something for you. And I know you're in trouble. So yes, I will do whatever it takes to get through all this stubborn crap and make sure you're safe. If I end up in jail, then at least I'll know I did what I had to do."

Tears welled again, though this time it was pure frustration. "Get out of my house."

He looked around. "This isn't much of a house. It's more of a hole-in-the-wall that it looks like you're hiding in. And it reeks of smoke. You can't stay here."

He wasn't going to let it go. He wasn't going to leave her alone. How did she get him to drop it? "So you're going to fix me? You? You can't fix yourself, Noah. Everyone in this town hates you. You're the last person who can help me."

It was horrible, and she wanted to call back the words the minute they left her mouth. Had she sunk this low that she'd become cruel to the people who tried to help her? At least when she was drinking she was only horrible to herself. She was about to ask for forgiveness when he moved into her space. She was forced to look up, and there wasn't a bit of forgiveness in his eyes. His lips were turned up in a cruel smirk that was so far from his normal sweet grin that she wondered if she hadn't truly woken a beast inside Noah Bennett.

"Is that what I am? The most hated man in Bliss County? Well, then I guess it won't matter that one more person hates me." He practically spat the words from his mouth, and he gripped her shoulders. "I lived for years with a woman who knew how to cut me down to size. You've got nothing on her. Why don't you tell me how useless I am? How bad I am in bed? How perverse I am? Do you want to know why I'm perverted in my ex-wife's eyes? Let me tell you. I made the mistake of telling her some of my fantasies because I thought it could save our marriage. I told her I wanted to tie her up and spank her ass. I wanted to bend her to my will in the bedroom. I wanted to fuck her in some fairly kinky ways. You know something, Hope. I never wanted to do the things to her that I want to do to you. A little over twenty-four hours after meeting you and I want to shove my cock up your ass while you're trussed up like a sacrifice to my pleasure. So if you want to hurt me, you tell me how pathetic I am for wanting those things. That's what will get to me. Don't give me some crap about how everyone hates me. They couldn't hate me any more than I hate myself."

"I'm sorry." She whispered the words because she couldn't speak them out loud. She really saw into Noah Bennett, and she understood him. He might not have earned his self-loathing the way she had, but it was there, mirroring her own. He didn't deserve it.

"Goddamn it, girl, don't you cry. Don't you cry." His hands moved from her shoulders to her face, cupping her cheeks and turning her chin up. "Don't cry, Hope."

He leaned in and brushed his lips to hers, and it was like a wildfire went through her. This was what she needed. She needed connection. She needed to lose herself in Noah. She went on her tiptoes and wrapped her arms around him. She touched her tongue to those plump, sensual lips of his, and he went wild.

His fingers moved up, tangling in her hair, holding her still as he pillaged her mouth. His tongue surged in, dominating her own. She softened, ceding control. How long had she wanted this? A man who could take control. A man with whom she could relax and let him pleasure her, show her how to pleasure him. She'd found plenty of men who would take from her, but none who would give back. She thought it would be different with this man.

She rode the wave, holding on to Noah as he pushed her against the wall, pinning her there with his body. She was caught between the wall and his solid chest as he kissed her until she was breathless.

"I want to do nasty things to you, Hope. I meant it. You should run from me."

But she was interested in all those nasty things he wanted to do. "I'm not running."

She might later, but she needed him now. Now, all the dark thoughts were replaced with desire. She wanted to get to her knees and take him in her mouth. She wanted his hands in her hair, pulling as he worked his cock in and out of her pussy. She wanted him to lube up her ass and make her feel the burn.

She would be his for a while. She would belong if only for a few moments.

"Take off that shirt. I want to see your breasts."

He kept close, giving her very little room. He stared down at her, his eyes warm again, that terrible darkness banished. She was nervous, but he needed this, too. His ex-wife had obviously done a number on him, making him feel like a freak. But she wanted what he could give her. She craved it.

With shaking hands, she undid the top button on her shirt. It was bulky and cheap, but it didn't matter. He didn't care about the shirt. He wanted to see what was under it. That was what she was nervous about. She'd put on a few pounds. She wasn't seventeen anymore.

"Stop it. Stop questioning yourself and show me your breasts."

She picked up the pace, the dark command in his voice breaking through her self-consciousness. She let the shirt hang open and unhooked the front clasp of her bra before she could think twice about it. Her nipples peaked in the slightly chilly air. Her breasts were heavy, but those nipples perked up as though wanting Noah's attention.

He hissed slightly, and his hands covered her breasts. "Fuck, you're beautiful."

He dropped to his knees, and she could feel the roughness of his five-o'clock shadow on her skin. It gave her an edgy, restless feeling. She let her hands drift up to the silky darkness of Noah's hair. His tongue flicked out, teasing at her nipple.

She whimpered and tried to get him to take more.

He pulled her hands into his own, gripping them on just the right side of pain. "You don't control this. I meant what I said. I'm going to be in control of this. If you can't handle it, all you have to do is tell me to stop. You say no and this ends."

She didn't want that. Not when she was so close to maybe

getting what she needed. "Please, Noah."

"I'll tie you up if I have to," he swore before leaning forward again and sucking a nipple into his mouth.

Fire shot straight from her nipple to her pussy. She forced her hands to stay at her sides. Noah's arm circled her waist, pulling her into the heat of his mouth. He sucked and bit at her nipple, making her squirm and moan until he released the first and moved to the second. His teeth grazed her.

"Fuck all, Hope. You're a sub."

She'd rather suspected it. When Jen Talbot talked about some of the things Stef did to her, it always made her restless. Jen would talk to Rachel and Callie, making them laugh, but it seemed serious to Hope. Discipline didn't seem like a thing to joke about. It seemed like a way to get what she needed.

"I can smell what this is doing to you. It's so fucking hot." His hands ran down her legs and up her skirt, skimming along her skin until he got to her panties. "But these have to go. You're not to wear them. I don't like them. Do you understand me?"

Noah didn't like panties. She could do that. "Commando it is then." She remembered what Jen had said some subs liked to call their dominant lovers. "Sir."

Noah groaned. "You have no idea what that does to me."

He dragged her cotton whites off her hips and down her legs. When he'd pulled them free, he put them right to his nose and breathed deep. "You smell perfect."

She knew she should think a man smelling her panties was a bad thing, but it really turned her on. The idea of Noah putting his nose to her pussy was even better.

He shoved the white bikinis into his pocket and went right back to her nipples, lashing them with his tongue and teeth as his fingers teased their way back up her thighs.

"You spread your legs for me," he ordered, lips moving against the flesh of her breast.

She widened her stance, leaning against the wall for support.

"That's what I want." Noah's fingertips brushed her pussy.

Hope dragged oxygen in as he opened her labia and pressed a single digit to her opening. She could feel the muscles of her pussy quivering in anticipation. She hadn't even used a vibrator in years. She hadn't had a man touch her in more than eighteen months, but she already knew this experience would be utterly different. She wouldn't have alcohol to dull her. She was only drunk on the experience of having Noah dominate her.

But she could easily become addicted.

"You're tight, darlin'. So tight. You're going to squeeze the hell out of my cock." He turned his face toward her. He was a work of art with a square jaw and a perfectly masculine brow. He could be on the cover of a magazine, but he was talking about fucking her. He was talking about shoving his cock inside and riding. "It's going to be good between us. I'm going to make it good."

It sounded like a vow.

His thumb brushed her clit, and she had to bite her lip to keep from begging.

"You like that. Tell me what you like, Hope. Tell me what you want. I need to hear it."

He growled the words at her, his finger working its way deep in her cunt. She tightened her muscles around it, trying to keep him inside, but he fucked in and out with that one finger.

"I want you." She'd wanted him from practically the moment she'd seen him, the attraction instant. It had only grown as she had heard his story and gotten to know the man. She liked him. She liked how kind he was to his dog and how much he wanted to make things right with his brother and the town. He wasn't sure how to do it, but she rather liked that, too. He needed her, and that felt heavenly.

"What part of me do you want?" His finger pressed up and pulled back, his thumb barely caressing her clit. It wasn't enough. Not nearly enough. Something was building, something lovely and amazing and elusive with just that one finger inside her. More. She needed more.

"I want your cock, Sir." She wanted him filling her up. She was so empty with only that single finger inside her. She needed more.

"You want cock? I can give it to you." He stood up abruptly.

"I want your cock." He needed to understand that. She only wanted his cock and James's. She wanted James. God, what would James think? She forced that thought from her mind because Noah looked down at her with wonder on his face.

"You won't regret it, darlin'. You won't fucking regret it." He kissed her again, though he'd lost some measure of his control. It didn't matter. She was out of control, too. For the first time in her life, she wasn't thinking about anything but where this feeling went. She had to know. She'd been frustrated for years seeking this magical connection, and it was close. So fucking close.

Noah pressed her against the wall. He ground his cock against her pussy. He felt so big, so hard. He rubbed against her, and she felt the first stirrings of something amazing. She nearly screamed in frustration, but she was far too busy watching as Noah opened the fly of his jeans. He shoved the denims down, fishing his wallet out of his pocket. He tossed the wallet aside but came up with a condom.

"What can I say? I'm optimistic. No, I'm really not, but you seem to bring out the best in me." He shoved down his boxers, and his cock bounced free.

Big, with a bulbous head, Noah's cock was gorgeous. Perfectly formed and thick, there was a small drop of cream on the head. She wanted to suck it off, but Noah tore open the condom and started to roll it over his cock. She couldn't breathe, but it didn't matter. It was all deliciously out of control, and she liked it that way. He pulled at her skirt, and she found herself pinned to the wall.

"You hold on to me." Noah reached between them and fitted the head of that glorious cock to her pussy. "Wrap your legs around me."

She did as he asked, leaving the safety of balancing herself and relying on Noah. She was caught between Noah's hard body and the wall as he started to thrust up.

"That's what I want, darlin'. Wrap yourself around me. You feel so tight, so fucking good."

He felt good. His cock stretched her, inching in as Noah pressed up. The stretch burned, but it was so, so good. It was connection and need. It was everything she'd been missing. She wrapped her legs around his waist and held on for dear life. He took his time. His hands were firmly on her ass, guiding his cock in a controlled fashion. She could see the way he gritted his teeth as he took care of

142

her.

But she wanted that burn. She wanted that bite of pain. "Fuck me, Sir. Fuck me hard."

"Your wish," he growled. He pulled down on her hips and shoved his cock up.

She whimpered at the hard stretch that took over her pussy. It burned as his cock filled her, pushing in all the way until she could feel his balls against the cheeks of her ass. He groaned as he leaned in and kissed her.

"It feels good," Hope whispered against his lips. She moved her hands back to his hair. "Fuck me, Sir."

"I'm going to spank your ass red for topping from the bottom. And don't think I won't find out what's going on, but for now, you win." He pulled out almost to the tip and then fucked in again.

Hope tightened her arms around him. She was a mess. Her shirt was hanging off her arms. Her panties were in the pocket of Noah's jeans. Her skirt was jacked up around her waist. She was sure she had mascara running down her face, and her hair was crazy. And none of it mattered because Noah was fucking her. He ground his pelvis against hers and shoved his cock deep inside. Over and over he fucked into her, bringing her closer to the edge. He pressed up as he ground on her clit, and she slipped over. The orgasm was an earthquake that started in her pussy and ricocheted outward, lighting up every inch of her skin from the inside out.

He pumped into her, his beautiful face tight with desire. His teeth were clenched as he raised her up with his arms and then let her fall back, impaled on the hot length of his dick. He hit a magic place inside her, and she screamed, the orgasm doubling.

Noah groaned as he held on to her hips and ground himself against her. He buried his face in the crook of her shoulder as he rode out the last of his orgasm.

He held her up. She'd never felt so connected, so happy and satisfied. She could feel the blood thrumming through her system as she draped her body around Noah's, trusting him to keep her up. She loved how his heart beat against her chest, and she could feel his breath on her neck. She inhaled his masculine scent.

"Thank you." Noah's voice was ragged. He clutched at her like he would never let her go.

"Thank you, Sir," she whispered. She could go back to calling him Noah later, but here she would give him exactly what he needed. She felt him smile against her shoulder.

"Well, I guess I'm not fucking needed here," a dark voice said.

Hope's feet hit the ground. She barely missed falling on her ass as Noah turned suddenly. She was breathless, but not with desire this time.

James stood in the doorway that they hadn't even bothered to close, Butch at his side. She'd fucked Noah. Oh, god, she hadn't even thought about James.

Noah pulled his pants up with an awkward tug. "Hey, brother, I just came up here to talk to her."

"I can see you did a lot of talking." James didn't move, didn't turn his head to spare her. He stared right at her, a frown on his face, judgment in those gloriously blue eyes of his. Butch seemed to stare at her, too.

With shaking hands, she started to button up her shirt.

"Look, Jamie, I'm sorry it happened this way, but it was inevitable. I've wanted her since the moment I saw her," Noah began, his voice unsteady.

"Yeah, and we all know that you go after what you want with absolutely no thought to anyone else. You've been that way since you were a kid."

"Jamie, I want to talk about this." Noah ran a hand through his hair.

She'd made things worse between the two of them. Noah had made some progress earlier, and now she'd screwed everything up because she hadn't thought at all. She had no real illusions that James wanted her, per se. He was mad at Noah. Noah wanted her, therefore James wanted her, too. She wasn't going to stand here and believe for a second that James Glen was jealous. He simply wanted to punish his brother, and she was the tool.

"I think you both should leave." Her heart ached. She'd loved being with them. She had no real idea where she was going to go. It had seemed like a good idea to go to Lucy's before, but now she wanted to be alone. She screwed things up so often that maybe it was better for her to be alone. She was right to hold herself apart. She could be kind to people, but not truly close to them. She was poison. "I'll have someone drive me out to the ranch tomorrow so I can get my things."

She mentally counted her money. She might have enough for a bus ticket.

Noah turned, his brows drawn together. "What the hell is that supposed to mean?"

"I think you two should talk without me around. I'm going to mess this up. You're brothers. You need to talk."

James stalked in the room. "I'm not talking to him, but I am going to lay down a few rules for you. You are going to go to the bathroom and clean yourself up. If this place still has running water. What the hell happened in here?"

"There was a fire in Stella's kitchen," she explained. "The smoke drifted up here. It's nothing dangerous. Just a bad smell. I can stay here."

"You're not staying here." Noah tucked his shirt in.

"Shut the fuck up, Noah." James snarled his brother's way before turning back to her. "I wasn't finished with the rules. You're going to clean up, and then you're going to get in the truck. I have work to do. I talked to Nell while the two of you were fucking. She needs you this afternoon. I made her promise she won't overwork you. I'm going to drop you off at the fairgrounds, and I'll pick you up at two. If you give me any more hell, I'll put you over my knee right now."

"Any more hell?" His tone was starting to push past her guilt. "When have I caused you hell?"

Those lips of his turned slightly cruel. "Every second of every day since I met you. I've thought about you every minute."

Bullshit. "You could have had me any time you wanted me, James. You didn't give me a second glance until Noah wanted me. You're like a child who doesn't want a toy until his brother has it. Did you two fight over all your girlfriends?"

He slapped the wall behind her. "The fact that you asked that question proves that you don't know me at all. Until the day my brother walked away, I shared everything with him. I had rarely slept with a woman without my brother because in my family, that was the way it was. Brothers shared because that's how we made a family. Ranching is rough. It's rough on a woman. I never wanted my wife to be lonely, and that's damn straight what she would be if she married me. And I would be lonely because all my life I didn't have someone to rely on. Don't you dare tell me I'm a spoiled brat who can't share. You just fucked the brat, baby. He walked away. He chose to leave me and our family over a woman. And then walks right back into town and takes the only one I actually care about."

She wanted to reach out to him. He sounded like he meant what he said. "James, I don't understand. I asked you out. Do you know how hard that was for me?"

He reached out, and his fingers touched the buttons of her shirt. She had buttoned up so quickly she'd missed one. She stood there while he corrected the problem with a tender twist of his hand.

"I didn't date you because I didn't date," James explained, his eyes pinning her. "I didn't have anything to offer you until Trev brought some money back into the ranch. I only had work and worry to offer anyone, so I kept my relationships physical. If I'd known you only wanted a good throwdown every now and then, well, I would have stayed away from you because I wanted more. It doesn't matter now. You're my responsibility no matter what mistakes you make or what terrible taste in men you have. I take care of my responsibilities. I don't walk away from them because they become difficult. Now, do as I told you or I will spank you. I'll be waiting in the truck."

He turned and walked away.

Noah looked ashen.

She felt sick. What had she done? It seemed she was always doing the wrong thing, and it cost everyone around her. "Noah, you should go talk to him."

"He won't listen. He won't... Damn it, go and get cleaned up. Do what Jamie told you to do."

She felt her eyes go wide and her gut churn. "What?"

Noah's stance hardened. "Jamie gave you an order. Do you expect me to go against him? Do you think you can play the two of us off each other? I can be indulgent, but this isn't going to work if you put us at each other's throats."

"Have you gone insane?" Hope asked, her voice shrill even to her own ears. "You need to see what's going on here. He's mad at you. He's using me to get to you. I get that what happened here doesn't mean anything. I do. I am not an idiot. Your loyalty is and should be to your brother, not some chick you banged. So go. He can't make me do what he wants."

He grabbed her wrist gently and pulled her along, sitting down on the couch and pulling her over his lap. Before she could think twice, he shoved her skirt up, the cool air hitting her skin. She was shocked to find herself staring at her floor. She turned her head slightly. James hadn't bothered to close the door. It was still standing open. She was damn happy that she lived on the second story or she would have probably had an audience. She opened her mouth to protest, and the flat of his hand smacked her ass.

He'd spanked her. It hurt, but it also did something for her. God, she was such a freak. She wasn't about to let him know she was affected by him.

"Are you done?" She was pleased with how even her voice was when all she wanted to do was ask him to try again.

"Not even close. Jamie's right. You need rules. You are not to talk about yourself that way again." His hand smacked against her other cheek. He wasn't playing. Hope groaned at the sharp, stinging pain.

Noah continued. "You're not some chick I banged. You're Hope. You're my girl. Maybe sex is some easy exchange of bodily fluids for you, but it isn't that way for me. You're the only woman I've slept with in years. I do not take what happened lightly." Another smack, this one to the center of her ass.

Hope whimpered but didn't complain. The pain bit into her flesh, but his words were a balm.

Two more righteous slaps. "And I am not willing to give up. Jamie might be pissed, but if we play this right, he'll also be in. He can be mad as hell at me and still want you. I want you. He wants you. You can bring us all together. You're the piece of the puzzle that's been missing."

He spanked her until she'd counted ten slaps, every one a hot reminder that he wasn't going to allow her to go anywhere. He wasn't going to let her disappear.

He finally stood, picking her up and setting her on her feet. His face was flushed, and she could see through his jeans that he was hard again. "Now go and do what you were told."

She turned toward her bathroom, her hands shaking, but not with anxiety this time. With a little bit of wonder. Noah was showing her a whole world she'd only dreamt of. "I won't let you bully me."

She felt the need to put in some rules of her own.

"I'm sure you'll let me know when I cross the line."

She closed the bathroom door with a quiet snick and took a deep breath.

She wasn't going anywhere.

Chapter Nine

"He left Noah there?" Nell asked, smoothing out the canvas that covered one of four tables inside her small, newly erected tent.

Hope picked up the next canvas and began covering the table to Nell's left. The tables were set up in some weird feng shui that Nell said would bring happiness to her customers and reasonable, economically kind profits to the business. Nell believed in fair trade. "He did. I got into the truck and before Noah could follow, James took off. I barely managed to get the door closed."

At least James had waited until Butch was safely in the backseat. The poor boy had whined as he'd watched his master being left behind, but when James had dropped her off, Butch had followed him back to the truck and jumped inside.

Nell crossed her arms over her chest, and her Birkenstocks tapped against the grass. "Well, that seems rude. It's bad enough that Jamie drives that gas-guzzling truck, but as long as he's doing it, he should take as many passengers as he can."

Henry chuckled as he walked in behind them. "I don't think Jamie is concerned with his fuel emissions right now."

Nell looked up at her husband. Nell wasn't that much older than she was, but there was such innocence about her. "Well, he should be. I left him a pamphlet and everything."

Henry dropped a quick kiss on his wife's cheek. "I would bet that Jamie is realizing that Noah is going to be competition for him."

"Competition?" Nell asked.

Damn Henry. He was too smart for Hope's own good. She did not want to talk about this. "Henry means they're brothers, and they have a lot to work out."

"And they want the same woman." Henry regarded her with a sunny smile. For all his intellectualism, Henry was kind of a hunk. He was leaner than most of the men in Bliss, but there was a strength to his frame. "I have long suspected that Jamie thought you would simply hang out and be waiting for him when he was ready to get married."

"That's ridiculous." Except that was what she'd kind of been doing. She hadn't gone out with Logan when he'd asked. That had worked out for the best because they had been really good friends. There had been a couple of men over the months who had asked, and she'd turned them all down. She'd told herself she wasn't ready to date, but the truth was she hadn't been ready to give up on James even while he screwed his way through half the females in Colorado.

"And it's not very romantic of him," Nell protested. She took the end of the canvas and started to help Hope lay it out. "I think I prefer Noah's version of courtship. He couldn't take his eyes off you yesterday."

"And Jamie couldn't help but stare holes through Noah," Henry pointed out.

"He's mad because Noah left," Hope explained.

Henry sighed and leaned against the table that was meant for environmentally friendly blankets. "I wasn't here when Noah was in town. I came to Bliss a couple of months later, but I remember how the town was reeling. It was hard. They were counting on him. No one more than his brother."

Hope was interested in any insights about the way James and Noah worked. "I guess I don't understand. I mean, I get that Zane and Nate were friends and fell for the same woman and decided to share her rather than fight. I get that. But they didn't go out looking to share a woman."

"Oh, I don't think you understand Nate and Zane at all," Henry said. "I actually envy them in some ways."

Nell smiled brightly. "He says that but he wouldn't share me."

He practically ate his wife up with his eyes. "Not at all, my love. But that's because the relationships in this town aren't about fantasies or sex. If I'd had a brother I was close to or if I'd had a friend who felt like the other half of me, I would have been happy to share you because you can be trouble."

Nell didn't seem at all offended by Henry's statement. Her eyes sparkled with mirth. "I have no idea what you're talking about."

Henry leaned over and touched his nose to hers. "So much trouble." He turned back to Hope. "If I could have a partner I trusted, I would share her. Look, I'm hetero. I was born that way. So were Nate and Zane, but they love each other, too. The relationships Zane and Nate and Rafe and Cam and even the Doc and Alexei have are deeply intimate. They don't simply share a woman. They share a life. They share a family and their problems and their worries. They take comfort in the presence of the other. It's a beautiful thing."

Nell took a long breath. "It is. You explain it so well, Henry. I'm going to go write that down." She turned back, her eyes wide. "Not for any reason other than the fact that it's lovely. I'm not writing a book or anything. I'll bring back the dream catchers."

Nell scurried away.

Henry laughed and started to move boxes onto the tables. "You take a seat, Hope. You're supposed to be resting. I told Nell we could handle this, but she seemed to think you would need a break."

Nell understood her. She needed this time away from both of them. "Yeah, I'm not finding the Circle G to be the most relaxing place in the world."

Except she'd had the sweetest sleep in years the night before because she'd slept between them.

"You could come back with us," Henry offered.

"No." The word came out of her mouth before she could call it back. Despite all the crap, she didn't want to leave the ranch. She knew she'd thought about running, but now that she could breathe for two seconds, she understood that she wouldn't. The idea of not seeing them again cut through her like a knife.

Henry smiled. "Then there's your answer."

Yep. There was her dumbass answer. She should be on a bus to god knew where, but she would get back in the truck when James came in a few hours. She would just have to pray that someone picked Noah up and gave him a ride back.

Noah. She could still feel his hands on her, his deep voice commanding her. He had made her forget everything except him. In that moment, there had been nothing except the two of them. What would it have been like if James had been there?

"You talked about friends. Zane and Nate were partners and friends. So were Rafe and Cam. But is it any different for Max and Rye?" She couldn't help but think about what James had said.

"You should talk to them. Well, maybe you should talk to Rye. I think Noah and James have a slightly different story, but they do have a lot in common with the twins. By the time I got here and met and married my Nell, Ellen and Noah's dad were gone, but I heard the stories. They were a lovely family. Very tight-knit. They had to be. The Circle G is big and requires a lot from a man. The way I understood it, Fred and Brian always made sure Ellen had what she needed. It would have been harder on their own. When she got sick, one of them was always with her. James grew up believing in that lifestyle, and then his brother was gone. The last couple of years, he's tried to replace Noah. He's shared women with Logan and Wolf, but I don't think it was the same. And then Logan and Wolf left. James is in a bad place, but I think he has what he needs to come back."

"I don't know. Noah seems to think he can get his brother back. I don't know what he wants me to do."

"I want you to do whatever comes naturally." Noah walked into the tent.

"Spy much?" How long had he been standing there?

"Had to catch my breath. Not used to walking a mile at nine thousand plus feet anymore." Noah took a seat in one of the chairs Henry had set up. "My asshole brother stole my dog, didn't he?"

Henry laughed. "Well, the word is you stole his girl."

Noah shrugged. "That was fast. I take it they can still hear things from the kitchen?"

"What?" Hope asked, praying they didn't mean what she thought they meant.

"Everyone knows that the pipes at Stella's carry sound," Noah admitted. "If you're standing in the kitchen, you can hear what's going on in the upstairs apartment. When Stella lived there, she used to yell down at the kitchen staff."

"And it never occurred to you to mention that to me?" Now she really wished she didn't sing when she cleaned.

Noah shrugged, his hair falling over his forehead. "I was busy at the time. I also wished I'd closed and locked the damn door, but you were way too tempting, darlin'. I wasn't thinking about anything but you."

"Does everyone know?" The Bliss grapevine worked quickly.

"Hey." Rachel Harper walked in carrying three white bags. "I stopped in at the diner to pick up a coffee, and Stella asked me to drop these off here. She said something about Hope ordering takeout, and then she laughed about you calling someone Sir. I take it that's you, Noah."

Noah didn't have the decency to blush. He simply grabbed one of the bags. "Thank god. I'm starving."

He had the burger halfway down his throat before Rachel could pass Hope her lunch.

The strawberry blonde's lips quirked up. "Stella said you didn't specify a dressing, so she gave you ranch since it's obvious you really like being out on the ranch, and she said you should watch out because cowboys like to lasso pretty little fillies. I have no idea what she meant."

Noah grinned as he grabbed some fries. "I do."

Rachel laughed because she obviously did, too.

Hope huffed. "Damn you, Noah. Now everyone knows."

"Well, I was going to tell everyone anyway," Noah admitted. "I wasn't going to hide it. Jamie told those two new guys at the shop that you were taken. Why does he get to stake a claim but I don't?"

"Stake a claim?" Nell asked as she walked in. "Noah Bennett.

Are you talking about Hope? She's a person, not a piece of land. And it would be offensive even if you were talking about land. And are you eating meat in my tent?"

"No, ma'am," he lied as he swallowed the last of his burger.

Nell eyed him. "Well, I have to believe you because I give all of the universe's children the benefit of the doubt. Now, you can finish up those fries that better have been fried in vegan oil and then you can give us a hand. We already have people walking around and shopping. I met some nice squatchers who would love some zucchini bread."

Noah groaned. "I hate squatchers. They make all kinds of noise, and they set up those cameras all over the forest, and then Mel sees the infrared and thinks the aliens are watching him. I've had to tromp through the woods more than once to make sure Mel didn't take one out."

"I forgot about that," Nell admitted. "Maybe we should go warn them."

Noah winked as he walked out with Nell.

"I'll go get the bread and the price tags," Henry said. "You sit down and eat. Rest. Or Jamie will have my hide, and I like my hide."

"What on earth is a squatcher?" Rachel asked. "I missed Woo Woo Fest last year."

Hope had worked this particular festival last year. Nate had growled for four days straight. Hope wondered how Cam was coping. "It's like a ghost hunter except they hunt Sasquatch."

Rachel sank down into the chair Noah had vacated. "Bigfoot? They really think Bigfoot is here? I thought that was just Mel."

"I think they think Bigfoot is everywhere. We get a lot of Sasquatch sightings. Mel showed me on his computer once. He also showed me that ninety percent of the sightings align with the nudist nature walks. He's pretty sure that Carl from the community is responsible. He needs to wax, apparently. They're harmless. They'll hike out into the woods and make all sorts of Sasquatch mating calls. I have no idea why they think they know what a Sasquatch sounds like when he's in the mood for love. Really, the only thing annoying about them is the fact that they try to work the word squatching into every sentence."

Hope pulled out her salad and the cup of soup. She was hungry. Apparently good sex made her hungry. She had to smile. Despite the fact that she'd slept with his brother, James had taken her hand and made sure she got out of the truck okay. He'd insisted on walking her to the Flanders's tent and having a man-to-man with Henry about what she could and couldn't do. He was acting like a Neanderthal, and she thought it was sexy.

Was she honestly thinking about it? Was she thinking about trying to have a relationship with two brothers?

"I take it this one is James's lunch?" Rachel asked.

Hope waved a hand. "Go for it. He fled the scene. You can eat his lunch."

"Good. I'm trying to diet, but it doesn't work. Today is the first day in months I don't have my baby girl on my hip. It would be nice to have lunch and talk to someone. Jen and Stef might have come back, but I swear they've barely left the playroom." She dug into James's turkey sandwich. "And Callie is up to her ears in diapers and men. She's going to breathe a sigh of relief when those men finally go back to work."

Hope took a spoonful of Stella's truly excellent tortilla soup, grateful that Rachel had brought it to her. "Stef might not have come out of his playroom in a while, but he apparently managed to arrange for Noah to return."

Rachel took a drag off James's Coke. "That's the King of Bliss for you. He's always got his hands in whatever pie is cooking."

"Why would he bring Noah back here if everyone's so mad at him?" Everyone they had met had been rough on Noah, including Rachel's hubbies. They had both given Noah hell.

"I think Stef knows that after a while, everyone will calm down. Since Noah showed up yesterday, he's been just about all Max and Rye can talk about. I've heard a bunch of stories about their childhood. I didn't grow up in a small town. I grew up in Dallas. Kids played with kids their own age and ignored anyone younger or older, but it wasn't that way here. There were so few kids around that they all hung out even though Noah and James were younger. I had no idea how close they used to be. Apparently after Noah left town, James retreated. I know he had the ranch to deal with, but I never knew that Max and Rye missed him. And I had no idea Noah existed at all. But yesterday I heard some of the craziest stories. Stef always knows what he's doing. Max might growl at Noah for a month or two, but he'll come around. Noah is family."

Family. It was a sweet word, but one Hope didn't understand the way Rachel obviously did. "Well, I'm glad Max sees him that way. In my family, it was always fighting. My mom had two sisters, and she didn't talk to either one. She didn't talk to her parents either."

Rachel's eyes went soft. "My mom and dad were great. I miss them every day. I wish…I wish things had been different. I can only imagine my dad taking on Max. Let me tell you, my father would have both of those boys in line."

"Come on, Rachel. You really think your parents wouldn't have a problem with the whole ménage thing?" It worked in Bliss, but the outside world was different.

"They loved me. They would have accepted it. And after a while, they wouldn't be able to help but love my guys. They're thoroughly lovable. And they would have adored Paige. Come to think of it, my parents would have probably loved Bliss. You never mention your folks. Are they alive?"

This was where a helpful lie usually worked, and yet Hope found herself wanting to talk for the first time in a long time. "I ran away when I was sixteen."

"I ran away when I was twenty-eight," Rachel said softly. "It's nice we both found our way here."

Hope shook her head. "Not the same. Well, maybe a little." She knew the story. Rachel had run from a stalker. She'd had a date go bad, and the man had obsessed about her. She certainly hadn't been as stupid as Hope. She hadn't decided she was in love with a man who turned out to be a killer. Rachel hadn't facilitated her stalker's crimes. She certainly hadn't brought in girls for her stalker to torment. It didn't matter to Hope that she hadn't known it at the time. It only mattered that it had happened. "You were older, but you didn't have anyone to help you either. I left my mom's apartment with nothing but the clothes on my back."

Rachel leaned forward, the sandwich forgotten. "Why did you leave?"

"My mom had a new boyfriend. He was interested in me." And brutal and rough looking. Christian had been the utter opposite. Christian had been gentle with her and polite. Christian had been gorgeous. And his masculine beauty had been a perfectly laid trap. She shook it off. "So I left and I stayed with friends, and I wound up here. It's a boring story."

"Ten years explained away in a sentence. Nice. You're good."

Hope felt like Rachel's green eyes were staring right through her. "Sometimes these things are boring."

"I sincerely doubt that. We all have secrets. Some of us are lucky enough to be able to find a family who can handle our secrets."

A little bitterness welled up in Hope. She hadn't drawn the high card when it came to families. "Yeah, well, I wasn't lucky. Like I said, I had my mom, and she was happy to see the back of me."

Rachel sighed as though Hope had missed the whole point of this conversation. "I wasn't talking about your mom. I was talking about Bliss. Look, you're not that much younger than me, but I'm wiser than you in this. Family isn't just blood. Blood is a crapshoot of biology. I love my daughter, but I expect to have to earn her affection. A child isn't something that a mom can shoot out and ignore and then expect that child to adore her. But family, real family, is something we make ourselves. It's this weird, amazing fusion of people we share our lives with. I loved my parents, but I've told Callie and Jen things I would never have shared with them. Never. But I can tell those two women anything and they accept it. I can tell my husbands anything. Oh, I'm not stupid enough to do that, but I could."

Good for Rachel. "I think it's nice that you have such good friends."

"Family," Rachel insisted. "It goes beyond friends. I'm not terrifically close to Marie or Teeny or Mel, but I love them. I've learned more in the time I've been in Bliss than in all the years before. I would never have given someone like Mel a second glance back in Dallas. But living here forces a person to be tolerant, and once you're tolerant, you can see past a person's oddities and get to know how truly amazing they are. But you can only do that if they're honest with you."

Hope didn't like where this was going. She felt restless again. "Don't play around, Rachel. Say what you mean to say."

Rachel sighed. "See, I told Jen that was the way to go, but no, she said I should be gentle. Fine. You're in trouble. I can see it plainly. Whatever you're running from is starting to catch up to you, and it's eating you alive. You can tell us because there's nothing you can say that will make us turn away from you."

But Hope knew the truth. Rachel was being naïve. "You would be surprised what I can say."

She shook her head. "No, I wouldn't. But I'm willing to wait. I just want you to know that you have a family here, and we're all sitting and waiting for the time that you trust us enough to come out of whatever closet you're hiding in."

A lovely thought. Maybe. But she had to think about it. And she would have to talk to Noah and James first. God, she didn't know if she could do that. "I'll consider it."

Rachel picked up her sandwich again. "See that you do. Now, what are we going to do about Noah and Max because we have a horse with a lame leg, and Max can't figure out what's wrong."

That was a much easier task than dealing with her past.

"Tell Max we'll give him twenty percent off house calls," Hope said. "But he has to pay full price on all meds."

Noah was going to kick her ass. And he'd give Max the discount, too.

Rachel's brows went up in surprise. "Rumors are true then. Well, Noah moves fast. Excellent. It's so much easier to work with the woman. You have no idea how much the people of this town celebrated after Caleb finally fell into Holly's bed. Alexei is a damn town hero for making that happen. Now we don't have to call Doc. We call Holly. So much easier that way. I'll let everyone know to go through you. And let's make it fifty percent."

Rachel drove a hard bargain. But her husband was a hard case. "Nope. Dealing with Max comes with a price tag. Can you guarantee me that Noah will only have to deal with Rye?"

"Damn it, forty percent."

"Thirty-five and Noah will personally apologize."

Rachel sighed. "And I promise Max won't throw him into the horse trough. Deal?"

They shook on it.

Hope sat back, a happy feeling overtaking her. She was going to get Noah on track, and if he didn't like it, well, he could always spank her again.

"So what are you going to do about James?" Rachel asked.

Happy feeling gone. She had no idea. But she was going to come up with something because all of the sudden she knew this was one problem she couldn't walk away from.

* * * *

James slammed out of the truck and then remembered he wasn't alone. Damn dog. He took a deep breath. The dog wasn't at fault here. His brother was. He turned and opened the door, and Butch bounded out.

The big ugly mutt scampered around like a puppy. He ran in a huge circle as fast as his legs could take him.

It was obvious the big guy had been cooped up in an apartment for way too long without a place to run.

Had it been that way for Noah, too?

Well, at least the dog handled it properly. The dog ran around chasing its own tail, not Hope's.

Chase? Noah had caught it. And he'd fucked it. James had stood there listening as his brother had screwed Hope against the wall of that tiny, piece-of-shit apartment. Hope's skirt had been tossed up, and those shapely legs of hers had been wrapped around Noah's waist as his brother pumped into her.

His first thought had been to tell Noah to hurry the fuck up so he could have a turn.

His second had been to kill his brother.

Well, it was done now. She'd made her choice.

How had things gone to shit in a day? And what the hell was he going to do about it?

He thought about going into the house and doing the paperwork sitting on his desk, but he couldn't stand the thought of being cooped up. His eyes trailed to the corral. Trev stood there talking to two unfamiliar men.

Damn it. He'd forgotten about the interviews. Late last night, he'd gotten a call about a couple of hands looking for work. He still needed three or four more men, but the thought of conducting an interview right now made his stomach churn. He could only think of the questions he would ask.

Do you intend to waltz in and throw my girl up against a wall and fuck her?

Do you intend to stay on for a couple of years, let me rely on you, and then head off the first time something shiny catches your eye?

He had problems, and they all came back to his brother.

What he needed was some seriously rough work. He had a few hours before he needed to pick up Hope, and by then he had to decide if he was going to force his brother to walk back to the G. He had no doubt Noah would have made his way to Hope's side by then.

"Hey! James, this is Brad and Jay." Trev tipped his hat toward the two newcomers. "They're answering the ad we put out last week."

Brad was a solidly built guy, but something about the other one was off. Jay was awfully skinny for someone who worked with cattle. Even a lean cowboy had a lot of muscle. And his jeans looked brand new and pressed. He didn't know a single cowboy who pressed his damn jeans before he went to work, but maybe the kid was nervous.

And it wasn't like there was a lot of choice. The ad had run for a week, and this was the first time anyone had answered.

"Good. Nice to meet you." He jerked his head a bit to indicate he'd like to talk to Trev alone.

Trev asked the men to wait on the porch, and they ambled off toward the house. "If I weren't so desperate, I would send both of them packing. I don't know why, but something's off with those boys. They said they're best friends, but they don't fit to me. I don't know."

James waved him off. He was mired in his own misery. "Give 'em a shot. We can always fire them later. We have to move the herd in before first snowfall. You have no idea what a winter here is like. We're going to need them since you're going to want to spend time with Beth."

Trev's face fell. "I'm not going to let you down. Bo and I can take turns watching out for her. Are you all right?"

"I'm fine." He wasn't going to force his new partner into a heart-to-heart, huggy damn discussion about the fucked-up state of his life.

Was Noah planning on running off with Hope?

"I was asking because I heard about what happened with Hope."

James turned. "God, what now?" His hands were in his pockets reaching for his keys when Trev responded.

"Uhm, you know, the stuff with Noah in her apartment. Lucy called the house and talked to Beth because she wanted to talk to Hope, but Beth grew up in a small town, too. She knows the sound of a woman with gossip to tell. She got the story out of Lucy who heard it from the fry cook at Stella's. Are you okay?"

Goddamn grapevine. A man couldn't take a crap without someone in this town commenting on it. "I'm fine. Hope wants to screw Noah, more power to her."

"Really? I thought you were interested in her." Trev put a booted foot on the railing.

"I was doing a favor for a friend." No point in talking about it now. He hadn't really wanted Hope. He hadn't dreamed about her last night. He hadn't liked taking care of her this morning. He hadn't enjoyed looking at her across the breakfast table and talking about stuff. No. He liked being the odd man out because it meant he was free.

Freedom sucked ass.

"Well, that's good then," Trev said with a sigh. "I would think you would be happy for your brother. Maybe this will settle him down. If things work out with Hope, he could find his place back here. A family settles a man. I should know. I know I'm odd, but I like the responsibility. Damn, I can't wait to see that kid. You know what else? I can't wait to see how Bo and Beth handle it. And if your brother works as fast as I think he will, we might have a whole bunch of kids running around the ranch."

A red mist swam in front of James's face, and then his hand throbbed.

Trev shook his head. "Damn. We're going to have to fix that."

He'd put his fist through the railing. Right through. He was damn lucky he hadn't broken his hand. The very thought of Hope pregnant with his brother's baby had made him insane.

He'd had a vision of her pregnant, his and Noah's hands on her belly as she lay between them.

But she'd made her damn choice. And Noah had made his.

"So, not so happy about that idea," Trev commented.

Trev McNamara was a manipulative bastard who had known exactly what putting that image into his head would do to him. "It's none of your business."

"Oh, partner, you'll find one of my great flaws is sticking my nose where it doesn't belong. I can't drink anymore, and I swore off strippers, so giving advice is my pastime now."

James shook his hand out. Trev was also a great guy in addition to being a nosy asshole. "Fine. What's your amazing advice?"

"Well, the way I see it, you have two choices, the first one being infinitely preferable to the second. You can make up with your brother. You can convince him to share Hope with you."

"Hope might have something to say about that," he pointed out.

Trev chuckled. "I doubt it. I saw the way she looked at both of you. Let me tell you, there aren't many women who will turn down a chance to be in the middle of two men they want. They might say it's only for a night or two but soon enough if the men are smart and talented, she's got two rings on her finger and a baby in her belly and she's all—'what happened, where did all this laundry come from?'"

The idea of Hope surrounded by dirty laundry amused him greatly. Most likely, he would end up doing hers. But he wasn't ready to try option number one. "I don't want to talk to him. I don't know if I can even be in the same room with him."

"Then you move to option two. Tell her to choose again."

"What?"

Trev shrugged. "You think your brother stole her? Steal her back, man. The way I understand it, I don't know that Hope truly understood there was a choice to be made."

He was never going to hear the end of this. "I asked her out."

"That might have been your mistake," Trev said. "Noah didn't ask her out. Not really. He went at her on a desk or something."

Ah, the flaws in the gossip mill. "It was a wall."

Trev frowned, shaking his head in a disapproving fashion. "Sounds uncomfortable. And quick. You could do better. And that girl's a sub if I ever saw one. If I were in your shoes and I couldn't stomach sharing with my brother, I would tie that pretty lady up, smack her ass 'til it was a nice shade of pink, and show her who's boss. A couple of hours of that and she might change her mind."

Not the worst idea in the world.

"But seriously, the first option is best," Trev insisted. "I think in the end you're going to want to have a relationship with your brother."

He couldn't stand the thought of a heart-to-heart with Noah right now. "My fist would like to have a relationship with his gut."

Trev seemed to give in to the inevitable. "Or you could be a stubborn ass. That's a way to go. You know, you could always suck it up and step back. I didn't offer that as an option because I see the way you look at that girl. You've waited a long time for her."

"I didn't have anything to offer her before. I don't know how much I have to offer her now. I fucking don't know. Goddamn Noah has to come back and fuck everything up. Now I have some timetable, and I don't like that."

Trev laughed out loud. "You and Bo should get together some time." He sobered up. "Thank your brother. Bo thanks me every day. If I hadn't come along, he and Beth would both be alone. Sometimes we need that third part to get the machine moving. But you try it your way. I think it'll all work out in the end. Are you going to kick his ass to the curb or are you going to make him watch?"

He had the definite feeling that Trev was, once again, butting in. He'd thought about not allowing Noah back on the ranch. But Trev just put that idea in his head. Probably because he thought proximity would bring him and Noah closer.

But proximity might give him a little revenge.

"Can I use your playroom?" James had known that they would get along when the first thing Trev had set up in the guesthouse had been a playroom complete with everything a Dom needed to torture a sexy sub.

"Of course." Trev pushed off the fence. "It's prepped and ready to go, and since Beth is feeling a little green now, it might be a while before we use it again. I'll go get our two new hands set up."

"I'm going to have a session with Red." Getting his ass kicked by a mean old horse might take the edge off. He wanted to let Hope know he could handle her, not scare the crap out of her.

"Your funeral, man." But Trev was smiling as he walked away. He looked like a man who had done everything he had planned.

Trev was going to be damn disappointed because he wasn't making up with his brother.

He wasn't.

Chapter Ten

By the time James drove up, Hope knew more about Sasquatch than any woman should know. The "squatchers" were nice enough, if utterly obsessed.

"You know from a biological standpoint, it's hard to believe that there's a whole species of superpredator out there and the only evidence we have is a video filmed in the sixties and some footprints."

Hope slapped at his arm. "Stop baiting them."

Noah's green eyes rolled. "Well, I do have a doctorate. Do they have doctorates?"

"Look, Doc, I dropped out of college to squatch. I am an expert on the big guy. He's real, and just because you don't believe in him doesn't mean he won't take your head off one day," Trey, the leader of this intrepid group of squatchers, said. He was a thin man who obviously didn't believe in a razor. Unfortunately, unlike his favored mythical beast, Trey didn't grow a beard well. It was kind of in patches across his face.

"I have a master's in philosophy," a bright-eyed girl who couldn't be more than twenty-two said. Like her brethren, she could be mistaken for a sweet-looking homeless person.

"I graduated with a degree in English," another young man admitted. "It was this or work at fast food. I'm not that big on hydrogenated oils."

"And you, Dr. Bennett, need to keep an open mind," Nell said, giving him a frown. She was in her element, holding court in front of her tent. She'd invited the Bigfoot hunters to give her bread a try and then plied them all with her organic apple cider. They'd been sitting around for an hour talking about mythical creatures. Noah had sat on the ground beside Hope, a mug of cider in his hand. It hadn't been too long until he'd managed to get his head in her lap, an arm wrapped possessively around her legs.

It occurred to Hope that this whole festival thing was like a temporary commune for supernatural geeks. She bet a whole bunch of these people had *Star Trek* costumes somewhere in their closets.

"And you're all wrong. Sasquatch isn't from this plane. He probably wandered in from another plane. My own mother fell through a door from her plane. She was a faery, but she really liked it here." Nell sat back in her chair, knitting as she spoke.

Henry merely looked on indulgently as his wife explained her native origins.

Trey leaned over, his voice low. "That lady is crazy, but she makes good bread."

James honked his horn.

Hope stood, forcing Noah to stand as well. They said good-bye and started to walk toward the truck.

"At least he doesn't have a gun." Noah walked beside her. He tried to reach down and hold her hand.

That seemed like waving a red flag in front of a bull. She took a step away. "We should talk. When we get back, I think we should have a discussion about what's going on between us."

And she would have to decide how much to tell them about her past. In the hours she'd spent with Nell and Henry and Rachel, she'd decided that she would have to tell the brothers about her problem with alcohol. It wasn't fair to hide it from them if she was going to have even a short, meaningless relationship with one of them.

"Damn straight we're going to talk. I told you I wasn't going to hide this." Noah kept walking beside her. She could see the tight line of his jaw.

James got out and walked around the truck, opening the passenger side door for her.

"Are you going to make me walk back to the ranch?" Noah asked.

James simply closed the door behind Hope and walked right past his brother to the driver's side.

"You can't make him walk. This is ridiculous." Hope started to open the door, but the lock clicked into place. "Damn it, James."

James gunned the engine. "He knows what to do."

There was a thump, and when Hope looked back, Noah was in the truck bed. He tapped on the glass. Hope reached back and slid the small window open.

Noah pressed his face in. "Jamie, I swear to god, if you kill me, I will haunt your ass for the rest of time."

James grinned as he took off, proving his truck had a serious engine.

"Asshole!" Noah screamed, his hand clutching the window, his body sliding as the truck moved.

"You're trying to hurt him," Hope accused.

James kept his eyes on the road. "Nah, he's had worse. He was the worst truck surfer in the county. Max really did damn near kill him that time he stopped because there was a bunny in the road. Saved the bunny, nearly decapitated Noah."

"I was younger then and way stupider," Noah yelled. He seemed to have found his balance. He'd managed to sit back up.

"Well, you were younger." James stopped at the stop sign, gleefully applying the brakes.

"Can we talk about this?" Hope asked. "I don't want to come between the two of you."

She did. She really, really did, but not like this.

"We'll talk, baby. We'll talk when we get to the ranch," James replied.

"Don't trust him, Hope," Noah interjected. "That's his 'I got a plan' voice. His previous plans included bow hunting a bear, setting off fireworks as a way of getting the herd to move, and don't forget tractor wars. Who ended up in the hospital every damn time you had a plan, Jamie?"

James shrugged. "I can't help it that I was faster than you."

"Well, you weren't this time, were you, brother?"

James gunned it, his foot hitting the floor.

Hope crossed her arms across her chest and thought about calling Doc Burke. He carried a tranquilizer gun with his med kit. She'd like to shoot them both. James slammed on the brakes as the light turned yellow, and a small bit of white fabric flew past the windshield.

"Oh, my god. Were those my panties?" Hope asked, horror dawning.

The Farley brothers were standing in front of the Trading Post, their arms filled with bags of stuff they were probably planning to use in an attempt to bring about the apocalypse. But they were way more fascinated by the pair of feminine delicates that landed in one of the bags.

Noah talked rapidly, his hand reaching toward her. "Hope, I am so sorry. They came loose, and when I grabbed them, my asshole sibling-killing brother stopped at a yellow goddamn light. It's Jamie's fault."

"You kept her panties?" James nearly yelled.

One of the Farley brothers, Bobby, she suspected, held up the underwear like it was a foreign object meant for study.

"She's not allowed to wear panties. I took them into custody," Noah explained as though stealing underwear was an everyday affair.

James took off before the light turned green, his tires squealing. Noah's hand was back to gripping the windowsill.

Hope had had enough. "James Glen, you will slow this truck down, and you will obey all traffic laws or I swear to god I will get out of this truck the next time I can and nothing you do will force me back in."

"Don't worry. I'll take care of her," Noah said, his face pressed against the glass.

She was going to murder them both. "You stop, too. When we get home, we're going to have a civilized discussion."

"When we get home, it's my turn." James turned toward the valley.

A sudden silence descended.

"What do you mean by 'your turn'?" Hope asked after James's words sank in. He couldn't possibly mean what she thought he meant.

"He thinks he can do better than me. That's what he means," Noah said through the window.

Now that James seemed to be taking her threats seriously, Noah was able to get on his knees and try to inject himself into the cab.

"Do you two think this is some sort of competition?" Hope asked.

She didn't know whether to be horrified or a little aroused. She was kind of both. Now that she'd actually reached a real honest-to-goodness, man-given orgasm, she was wondering if she could manage another. The idea that she could have them both played around the edges of her mind.

"I think that you can't make an informed decision without letting us both try." James never looked at her, simply stared at the road ahead.

She couldn't do it. She couldn't just have sex with James because he wanted a turn. And Noah was going to throw a fit.

Except he wasn't. He was staring at his brother. "You got to watch me. I should get to watch."

"Feel free." James didn't sound like that would bother him at all.

"Well, it's good to know how much it meant to you, Noah." There was her answer. She was nothing more than a toy they would use and discard. She was a ploy in their competition, and the minute they were fine again, she would most likely be told it was over. "Drop me off at the Movie Motel. I'll call Lucy, and she can come get me."

James blew right by the motel.

Frustration threatened to swamp her. "I meant what I said. I am not going to be used like this. I'll call Cam when we get to the G, and he will come get me. Do you want to deal with the law?"

James's hands had a death grip on the steering wheel. "Tell me you don't want me and I'll turn the truck around and take you and Noah wherever you want to go. Maybe in a couple of years I'll be able to think about letting Noah back on the ranch, but you can't expect me to stay in the same house while the two of you sleep together."

"She wasn't saying that," Noah said, his voice much smoother than Hope would have expected. "She's pissed off that you weren't romantic. I was romantic."

"You were not romantic. You didn't even take your damn pants off." James slapped at the steering wheel. "Where do you want to go, Hope?"

She stopped and realized she was missing something. Why was Noah trying to soothe his brother? Why did James look like he was holding on for dear life? There was a tightness to his eyes. He only got that when he was upset. She'd been around him enough to know that.

What was happening? Was she the bone they would tear up in their effort to hurt each other? Or the drop of glue that might, just might, hold them together? Was Noah offering her up because he didn't care about what happened to her? Or because he thought they wouldn't work without James?

What if James had told her the truth? What if he'd stayed away because he had thought he had nothing to offer her? What if a relationship with her had only seemed possible because his brother had returned? James could complain about Noah all he liked, but according to everyone in town, they had been close once before and likely would be again.

Henry's words made sense. Deep down, they both only knew one way of life. They wanted what their parents had. They wanted a woman to share and a brother to rely on.

Could she be that woman? Maybe not, but could she live for the rest of her life knowing she hadn't even tried?

"I haven't heard an answer." James stopped the truck before the entrance to the ranch. There was a huge wrought-iron arch that covered the road. *The Circle G. Established 1898.*

The Glens had been in Bliss before there had even been a Bliss. Generations had held this land and passed it down to James. His parents had passed this land down along with their legacy of love and companionship. Now he was fighting his instincts. What if she could show him it was all right to have what his parents had? Could she bring him back to the life he'd hoped for?

She took full hold of her courage. She wasn't some wilting flower. She'd done a lot of things she wasn't proud of. This wouldn't be one of them.

"Noah is right. You got to watch. So should he." If Noah was there, it would almost be like he was with them.

She watched James swallow, his breath slow and methodical as though he was steeling himself.

"Then he should get ready because I don't intend to toss you against the wall and get my rocks off. And I don't want you to call me Sir. My name is James. You can shout it when you come."

James was back to his overly confident self. She stared at him while he made the long drive to the house. He wasn't as hard as his exterior might suggest, and he wasn't as distant. But he had his pride. James's pride was a mighty thing since it seemed it was the only thing he had left.

She would have to break through it if they were going to have a chance at anything beyond a little sex.

And she wanted more.

Noah's hand came through the tiny window, awkwardly patting her shoulder. When she looked up, there was encouragement in his green eyes.

The first man she'd slept with in a year and a half was silently promising that everything would be okay if she would just sleep with his brother. She wasn't so sure, but she knew one thing.

It would change everything.

* * * *

Christian had watched her all day—from a safe distance, of course. It was easy with all the tents and booths going up in what appeared to be a huge park. He'd been able to watch from the safety of a psychic's booth. Someone named Delphine Dellacourt Guidry had promised him he would get everything he deserved. Of course he would. He would make sure of it. Then he'd had his tarot cards read, and all the while he'd been watching her. Charlatans, every one of them. And he should know. He'd been a "preacher" for ten years, and he didn't even believe in God, much less that he was embodied in nature.

Hope was still beautiful. She couldn't hide her radiant innocence. He could still remember how it felt to lie on top of her and fill her. She'd been an obedient girl, as she should have been. Unlike the whores he'd known, she had been a virgin and perfectly shy that first night.

When he closed his eyes, he could see her pale skin and the way her hands had shaken. Careful. He'd had to be incredibly careful with her. Unlike the other women in his group. They had been whores who had given themselves to him in degrading ways. Oh, they had served their purposes. He'd used them, and when he'd been done, he'd prostituted them out. Women like that were good for a quick fuck or a quick buck.

"Can I help you?"

Christian focused on the woman in front of him. She was obviously Hope's friend since Hope had spent the afternoon sitting with her and talking. Her laughter had been a soft wind through the grounds. "I was just prowling around. The festival isn't supposed to start until tomorrow, but I see it's already going strong."

The woman with straight brown hair smiled, her whole face alight. She was actually quite beautiful when she smiled. "I'm afraid most of these people don't believe in schedules. You know Sasquatches don't have timepieces."

He smiled his most charming smile. Here was another sweet, innocent little lamb. He liked his lamb rare. "I'm Chris. I would love some of that cider if you have any left."

"I'm Nell. It's nice to meet you." She reached behind her and grabbed a cup. With a practiced hand, she poured a measure of cider into a mug. "Here you go. If you like, you can take the mug with you. Just leave it at one of the other shops. Everyone knows to send them back this way. I can't do disposables, I'm afraid."

Christian practically salivated. The little idiot spoke a language he knew well. "I admire you for that, Nell. I travel across the country trying to educate people about the cost of our disposable society. I like your setup here. It's very earth friendly."

Her brown eyes lit up. She was a true believer. "Everything is reusable. I lose a few mugs every year, but you would be surprised at how many people bring them back. People are inherently good."

He wasn't, but he knew some who were. And lucky for him, they usually proved to be the ones with no protections. If he had time, he would think about charming the lady. She was older than his usual. He preferred them in their teens, and this woman was likely pushing thirty. But then Hope wasn't seventeen anymore, and he was still obsessed with her. Perhaps he was maturing. Alas, he had a wife to reclaim. And his own almost murder to avenge. He wasn't sure if he intended to make love to Hope or bury her.

Maybe both.

He shook his head and tried to flush a little. "I have to ask you something embarrassing."

Her eyes widened. "Oh, you can ask me anything. I'm very open."

"Uhm, there was a wo..woman here earlier." He made sure to stutter, happy with the sympathetic gleam in her eyes. "She was so lovely. She was a brunette wearing a skirt and a button-down. Look, I don't want to come off as some creepy stalker..."

"Then don't." A man came out of the tent, his eyes hard behind what looked to be relatively thick glasses.

"Henry, don't be rude," Nell admonished.

"Never, my love." But the man didn't take his eyes off Christian. He stood there like a Bohemian guard watching over a prize.

Nell winked at Henry and turned back to Christian. "Don't mind him. He wouldn't hurt a fly. He likes to play jealous sometimes."

It seemed this innocent lamb wasn't unprotected after all. Though this Henry person wasn't the tallest man or bulky, there was strength in his frame. But the eyes were what gave him away. He might have his wife fooled, but somewhere in the past this Henry had hurt far more than a fly. Christian would bet Henry hadn't

173

always been a peddler of apple cider.

"It's all right," Christian said, taking a step back.

"I have to admit, sometimes his caveman tendencies come in handy. But you were talking about Hope," Nell began.

"Her name is Hope? That's beautiful." He'd always loved her name. It was the perfect name for the child bride of a preacher who made his way in the world by suckering in the hopeless.

"Oh, Hope is wonderful," Nell said and then laughed a bit. "We're very happy to have her in our community."

"She's lovely." He'd also always liked that his wife had an understated beauty that most men would miss. She wasn't the showy, glamorous kind. She was modest, and that was important to him. Her beauty was meant for her husband and her husband alone. "I was thinking of asking if she might be willing to have dinner with me."

He wouldn't ask at all, but this Nell's answer might tell him something. He didn't have to ask. Hope belonged to him and he would reclaim her.

Nell smiled, but she'd turned distinctly wistful. "That's so sweet of you, but I'm afraid you're too late."

"Late?"

Nell blushed. "Uhm, she's taken. She might not know it, but her men do."

Christian's brain caught on that one simple noun. "Men?"

Henry nodded, those steely eyes steady on him. "Yeah, welcome to Bliss. We're pretty tolerant. We have some very happy polyamorous trios. Just trios though. If you want something crazy like a six-way, you have to go to Wilde, but I've heard it's lovely there this time of year."

Christian prayed the smile he gave Nell didn't hint at what he was feeling inside. Fury rolled in his gut. He'd seen that man sitting at Hope's feet, her fingers patting his head. He hadn't thought much about it. Hope had always been a tactile person. She'd always hugged her friends and held their hands.

What if Hope had been doing something she shouldn't? He'd been so sure she wouldn't even look at another man. She'd been in his thrall. Hope would have done anything for him. She'd looked at him like he was the sun in the sky. The truth of the matter was she hadn't seemed to like sex. It was one of the things he'd found attractive about her. She was a lady. He would never have married a whore.

Perhaps sometimes ladies turned into whores.

"You really liked her, huh?" Nell asked, her face lined with sympathy.

He had a sudden vision of slitting Nell's throat. He could do it easily. She would be a soft, sweet gazelle in a lion's jaws. She wouldn't have time to scream before his knife cut through her throat and started spilling her blood on the ground. That would make him happy. That would calm his beast. She looked enough like Hope that he could pretend Nell was her.

Christian took a deep breath. He wasn't going to do that. Well, not now anyway. He had to keep his eyes on the prize. Eight years and he'd almost put his group back together. He had everything in place. He was ready to start a new website and to begin building his followers. It had taken the millions he'd fleeced out of his previous followers to clean up the mess Hope had left when she'd started that fire, but he'd built himself back up over the years he'd been in hiding.

And he'd fucking done it for her while she'd been finding another man.

Christian shrugged. "She reminded me of someone I knew. My wife."

"I am so sorry. Did you lose her?" Nell asked.

Yes, he'd lost her. He'd lost her to her own feminine weakness. Without a strong man around to keep her in line, she'd given in to her proclivities. "She died eight years ago in a fire."

Nell's sympathy was a palpable thing. "That's terrible."

What was even worse was that her body had lived on even after her soul had given in to darkness. Christian's brain was reeling. He'd never thought for a single second that she wouldn't be at his side when he reemerged like a phoenix rising from the ashes. She would be with him. One way or another, but perhaps the time had come to change tactics. He'd come here to watch her, to find out just how easy it would be to convince her to come with him, to forgive him for not hiding his masculine tempers.

He knew he'd made mistakes, but never had he allowed another woman into his heart.

"Thank you for your time, Miss Nell."

"Mrs. Flanders." The man named Henry corrected him with a flat tone.

Nell rolled her eyes and giggled a bit. "He's so possessive."

Any real man was. No real man would allow his property to be violated.

Christian nodded, left the mug, and walked off. It was time to move this plan forward. He pulled out his cell phone. He wasn't an idiot. He had men in place. He was never without his followers. He explained what he wanted and then turned back toward the town.

It was time to talk to the sheriff.

* * * *

James had to force his hands to stop shaking. Control. He was in control. He had to be.

Hope had said yes. Well, not yes, exactly, but she'd assented. Now if only he'd managed to keep Noah out of it everything would be perfect, but the bastard had managed to insert himself into the situation.

It had been a natural thing once. Before they'd slept with their first woman, an adventurous college student from Boulder on spring break, he and Noah had made a game plan. They had sat up the night before deciding who would handle what and how to bring her the most pleasure they could. They'd been invited to spend four days in her bed before she'd gone back to school.

They'd shared almost every woman until Ally had come along and started playing her games with Noah.

He wasn't sharing Hope. James was going to show Hope that he was the man for her, and his brother could go to hell. If Noah wanted to watch his own downfall, then that simply made him more of a masochist than James ever dreamed.

James pulled the truck up in front of the guesthouse.

"We're not going home?" Hope asked.

James put the truck in park, and it shuddered as Noah hopped out of the bed. James unbuckled his seat belt and tried not to think about how much he liked the way she said the word home. "Trev has a room set up."

Noah opened Hope's door. "Trev McNamara, the ex-number one pick in the draft, has a playroom?"

"He's a man of many talents." James inwardly cursed. He should have been faster. He should have been the one to help Hope out.

Hope took Noah's hand and let him help her out of the truck. "Trev used to play football? Nate said something about ESPN."

He bit back a groan. Hope was going to need an education in way more than BDSM. "Baby, you don't want much TV, do you? Trev was the quarterback for the San Antonio Bandits. He was considered the best QB in the last decade but…"

"He got involved with drugs." Hope's eyes trailed toward the house.

"So you have heard the story?"

Hope's whole body seemed to sag. "More times than you know."

"We don't have to play here if you don't want to." Why was this so hard? He was smooth as glass with women, but now he felt like an idiot. He had no idea how to handle Hope, not really. He thought she would be submissive when it came to sex, but she damn straight wasn't out of bed. She was prickly and too smart. He thought she saw straight through him, but she was opaque, something he could almost understand, but her truth was elusive.

She turned her face up, her hand skimming his cheek. "You like Trev, right? It doesn't bother you that he had a problem?"

James was confused. "No. I think the world of him. And if you want to judge him for his past…"

She put a hand on his lips, stopping him from talking. "I think what he's managed to do is amazing. I admire him greatly."

Thank god. For a minute he thought he'd been wrong about her. Hope had always seemed like a woman who wouldn't judge those around her for their pasts. "I do, too. I trust him. Hell, he's my partner."

She went on her tiptoes. She hesitated for the briefest of moments before brushing her lips across his. "I would love to play with you, but you'll have to be patient. Everything I know comes from eavesdropping on Jen and Rachel and Callie."

"Hey, I taught you a little something." Noah had taken a step back, his face closed off.

Hope laughed. "Sweetie, you threw me against a wall. I did learn to call you Sir, and that sex can be way more than I thought it was, but I didn't get a lesson in being a sub. That's what it's called, right?"

She was interested. That was all he could ask for. "Yes, baby. There's a Dominant partner and a submissive partner. The Dominant partner is responsible for the submissive's safety and pleasure. Noah is way out of the game if he thinks that taking care of you includes screwing you against a wall where everyone in town can hear you."

"She needed it." Noah stepped up now, his face flushed. "You weren't there at the beginning. You don't know. She was panicking, and I couldn't get her to talk."

So Noah thought fucking her would solve all her problems?

Hope stepped between the two of them. "Stop. You two need to stop, or I'll walk out of here."

She meant it. It was right there in the stubborn way she held her jaw. She put herself right between him and Noah, her petite, five-foot-three-inch body tiny compared to theirs. She had a hand on both of their chests, as though she could actually stop them if they decided to throw down.

"I don't want to fight." Noah sighed, and his hand went over hers as though keeping it over his heart.

Fuck. It was obvious that his brother was in deep. But James couldn't let it go. He knew damn well he should, but the thought of not knowing what it felt like to sink into Hope McLean's softness, to hear her calling out his name the way she'd called Noah's, wouldn't let him go.

"We're not going to fight," he promised. "But we are going to have a serious discussion about topping from the bottom."

Hope's lips curved up. "See, that sounds like fun."

"Oh, she's going to get in so much trouble," a new voice said.

James looked up and noticed that at some point, Bo had walked out onto the porch. The guesthouse already had a new coat of paint and now boasted a cozy porch swing. James had seen Bo and Trev sitting there in the late afternoon after work was done for the day. They would sit and swing with Beth in between them, each man holding her hand or touching her hair.

"Trev is still dealing with the new guys. He asked me to show you around." Bo tilted his blond head toward the door. "Unless you're going to fight first."

Hope dropped her hands and walked up the steps. "No fighting. But it is weird that we get a guide."

Bo laughed. "Oh, honey, you haven't seen weird yet. Look, I love my partner, and I've gotten used to play, but these fellas take all this stuff very seriously."

"Protocol," Noah said.

Bo pointed. "See, they use all sorts of big words, but it all comes down to the fact that they like spanking a pretty ass and they're control freaks. So come on in. The dungeon's wide open."

God, he was going to have to talk to Trev about his partner's sarcasm. James followed Bo up the steps with Noah following behind him.

"Do you even remember how to behave in a dungeon?" James asked. Noah had been vanilla for years. He couldn't see it any other way. Ally wouldn't have allowed him to top her. No way.

"I've gone to a dungeon at least twice a week for the last three years. I probably know more than you now."

He stopped his brother before they got to the hall that led to the dungeon. He was completely floored by the admission. "You cheated?"

He shouldn't be shocked. He knew he shouldn't. From what little he'd heard, Ally had given Noah hell and had several lovers. Still. He was shocked. His brother had always been adamant. When they were dating someone, Noah never even looked at another woman. The thought of Noah cheating hurt.

Noah shook his head. "No. I haven't touched another woman with my cock until earlier today. And I only did that because I care about Hope. Hell, man, I think I'm falling for her. I took vows. Just

179

because Ally didn't honor hers didn't give me a free pass to let mine go. About two years in, I knew how fucked up my marriage was. I found a club. I became friends with the owner, and he let me work a couple of nights a week as a Dom. I never got off. I took care of subs. It was the only thing that made me feel needed."

How hard had it been for Noah? He forced the question away. That wasn't his problem. Noah had made his bed. But he couldn't help the fact that his heart hurt at the thought of Noah all alone in the city. Noah's words really penetrated, leaving him with another question. "You knew two years in but it was another three before you came home."

"Yeah," Noah admitted, his voice low.

Noah couldn't have been too lonely if he was willing to spend three years in hell. If he had been willing to stay away until the money had finally dried up. "I'm letting you watch because Hope wants it, but you better obey the rules, brother."

Noah's face shut down, but he followed James down the hall.

Hope's eyes were wide, and there was a bit of fear in her stance when James entered the McNamara dungeon. Trev had done a damn fine job turning what used to be an office and spare bedroom into a Dom's pleasure palace. The Berber carpet had been replaced with gleaming hardwoods and the walls painted a decadent, rich red. There was a large St. Andrew's Cross adorning the wall. It accompanied a spanking bench, a padded sawhorse, and in the middle of it all, a huge bed.

The fact that everything came in singles told James a lot. Beth was the sub. Bo was not. He'd wondered because Bo tended to defer to Trev's authority, but it seemed he probably topped Beth in the bedroom.

Hope would have had two Masters if Noah hadn't been such an asshole.

He had to get that out of his head. Noah was talking to Hope, and here he was thinking about how mad he was at his brother.

"Don't let this place fool you. There's nothing but pleasure for you here," Noah was saying, his voice soothing her.

And that was James's damn job. He hadn't even kissed her yet, and his brother was already pushing him out. James took Hope's hand and gently pulled her to him. He sighed as he put his arms around her and smoothed back her hair. "I think you're going to like this, baby, but if you're scared, we can go back to the house and sit and have a nice dinner and then we'll go to bed and I'll treat you like a lady."

She shivered. "Don't. I'm a woman, and I would rather be treated that way."

What the hell had he done? She tried to pull away, but he had the worst feeling that if he didn't take control she would, and everything would be over. He hardened his voice. "I'll treat you like a sub. Now calm down, Hope. In this room, you obey me or you say no and this is over. Bo, does Trev keep paraphernalia for guests?"

Bo's face went blank. "Are you talking about toys?"

He'd been trying to be discreet. "Yeah. Sometimes Doms keep a small supply of toys for visitors."

Bo grinned and opened a panel. The custom-made door slid open. "Beth got cheeky. She's been having fun with this room."

He heard Hope gasp at the wall of perversion Bo had uncovered. There was a neat assortment of floggers, whips, paddles, spreader bars, and restraints of all types. There were handcuffs and long lengths of rope. There was a whole row of various types of lube.

"I take back everything I said about Trev," Noah said, his eyes wide. "He's a perfect addition to this ranch."

"He's a complete pervert is what he is. You want it, he probably has it in various colors, shapes, and sizes. Oh, and he told me to tell you that he has a whole training set of plugs still in their boxes," Bo explained.

James was grateful for his partner's years of formal training. His own training had been rather informal. He'd gone to clubs with Stef, Max, and Rye over the years. Stef had taught him a lot, allowing James and Noah to practice on his own submissives before he'd finally settled down with Jennifer. But Trev had actually been a full-time Dom for several years.

"What does he mean by 'plug'?" Hope had turned her face up to his, looking at him like he would protect her.

She didn't realize she needed protection *from* him in this case.

His cock tightened at the soft, sweet look on her face. "Anal plugs, baby."

"He keeps boxes of anal plugs for guests?" Hope asked.

Bo shrugged. "Apparently it's the BDSM equivalent of a party favor."

Hope shuddered a little. "I think I might prefer those things you blow on and they make noise."

Oh, she would be blowing on something, and James was definitely going to make a little noise. "Thank you, Bo. We can take it from here."

Bo smiled. "You're going to be all right, Hope. If you have any questions later, you just talk to Beth. She's going to be excited about having another girl around the place."

He gave them a salute and then shut the door behind him.

"Clothes off, Hope."

Begin as you mean to go. He was in control. He was in charge.

And she was practically shaking she was so nervous. He sighed and hauled her close. He hadn't kissed her. He needed to get his head in this damn game. He softened as he looked down at her. "Do you know how long I've wanted to kiss you, baby? That one taste wasn't enough. I want to kiss you again and again."

Her anxiety seemed to flee in favor of an awed wonder. "You really want to kiss me, James?"

He thought about rubbing his rock-hard cock all over her so she couldn't doubt it but decided on a sweeter approach. Words. Women liked words. "I wanted to kiss you the first time I saw you. You were sitting with Logan and you turned your face up to me, and all I could see were big eyes and the softest lips. I love how the bottom one plumps out when you're thinking. I always want to suck at it and kiss you until you can't breathe."

She leaned into him. "Are you serious? Because I couldn't handle it if you weren't."

Serious? He was seriously in trouble, but he couldn't find the will to back out. He had used all the words he was going to for now. He leaned forward and kissed her the way he'd wanted to that first day. She'd been sitting on the bench next to Logan, the afternoon sun hitting her hair. Logan had been talking about some game he was playing online, but James had been watching Hope wondering where Logan had found her.

He pressed his lips to hers and tilted her head back. She opened underneath him, her mouth ceding control. His tongue surged in. That first day had scared the crap out of him because she wasn't his type, but he hadn't been able to stop thinking about her.

Now he knew. All the other women hadn't been his type. He only had one type. Hope.

Her arms wound around his neck, and she clung to him. Her soft tongue played against his.

If he didn't take control soon, he would do exactly what Noah had done. He would toss up her skirts and throw her against the first surface he could find and sink his cock in. He wouldn't even have to dispense with her panties. They were probably being scientifically studied by the Farley boys at this very minute. He broke off the kiss.

"I want you. I want you so bad it hurts, but we do this my way. Now take off your clothes." His voice was breathless, but she seemed to respond properly this time.

Her face flushed, and her hands went to the buttons of her shirt. Her voice was shaky as she spoke. "I don't see what the two of you have against these clothes."

"She's damn sarcastic, Jamie. I already spanked her once today for that mouth of hers." Noah leaned against the wall, staying as far away as he possibly could.

"Is that right?" James wished he'd seen that. "Did Noah spank you?"

Her shirt hung open, leaving a tantalizing line of skin on display. He could see the curves of her breasts against the cups of her plain white bra.

"Yes." The word came out on a breathy little sigh.

Well, his brother had gotten further with her than James had thought. "Did it scare you?"

She was here, so he was betting on a no.

"I liked it."

And he liked honesty. He touched the half-moon at the top of her breastbone and then let his finger trail down. He toyed with the front clasp of her bra. "Did it get you hot?"

She nodded. "It did."

"Thank you, baby. It means a lot to me that you're honest. That's what this is all about."

A cloud passed over her face, but she turned her eyes down and shrugged out of her shirt. He flicked the clasp of her bra open and pushed the straps off.

Hope might be petite, but she had curves. Pretty curves. Curves that made his dick throb. She had perfectly perky nipples. They tightened under his gaze. Her skin was a lovely shade of cream, with dustings of freckles here and there. Later he would explore every inch of her, kissing each little spot and marking her as his. But for now he wanted to see more.

"Get rid of the skirt, baby."

She took a deep breath before pushing the skirt off her hips.

"God, Hope, you're beautiful." James couldn't take his eyes off her. She was damn near perfect. Her hourglass figure was made for a man's hands. While she was short, she wasn't tiny. She had hips he wanted to grip and shapely legs that would look good wrapped around his waist. "Turn around."

She turned on shaky feet.

Her ass was glorious. Round and juicy. Yeah, he would be using one of those plugs on her. He pulled her hair out of her ponytail, and soft brown silk fell like a waterfall over her shoulders. She was beautiful, and she hid it behind dowdy clothes and a boring hairdo. But it wouldn't matter now. She could wear whatever the hell she wanted. He would see her like this. He would see her with soft skin and sexy curves and those dark eyes that kicked him in the gut. She could gain or lose weight. She could wear sexy clothes or a potato sack. She could get old and gray, and he would see her like this.

"Face me."

Hope turned back. She was biting that sexy lower lip of hers. She pushed her glasses up. Damn, he even thought those were cute. "Do you really think I'm okay?"

"I think you're gorgeous. Look what you're doing to me." His cock was just about to push through his jeans. She smiled, a shy expression that made him understand something. She didn't think she was beautiful. He would use every tool he had to make sure Hope came out of this experience knowing that she was the sexiest woman in the world. He pointed to his brother. "Noah's not any better. Look at that thing in his jeans. Though he's not going to get a damn bit of relief for his."

He didn't want to remind her that Noah was even here, but she needed to know how beautiful she was.

Noah grinned and pointed toward his erection like a game show hostess showing off a brand-new car. He was dippy and stupid and dumbass, and James felt his heart twist because Noah was acting like the brother he remembered. Noah had been a goofball. A brilliant mind with a goofy, funny soul. Hope was bringing him back.

Again. Not his problem. This wasn't about Noah. This was about him and Hope. And it was time to get started. "Eyes on me, Hope."

She turned obediently, but he could see that his play had worked. She was far more confident than before.

"I want you to take my clothes off, baby."

Her breath hitched.

"Your reply should be a 'yes, James.'"

"Yes, James." No hesitation now. She moved forward, and her hands were on his shirt. She smoothed it down before moving to the pearl snaps. Carefully, she unsnapped the buttons one by one. It was torture. He could feel those small hands moving down his torso. She pulled the shirt free of his jeans. "Can I touch you? I don't know how this works."

"This is for fun, baby. It's a way of life for Trev and Beth and Bo, but this is just fun for us. If you're not tied up and we haven't agreed on a scene, then you can touch me all you want."

She closed her eyes and placed both hands on his chest. He was pretty sure she could feel his heart pounding. He held still, letting her explore him. She ran her palms over his pecs and down to his abs, those small fingers making him shake on the inside.

"You're killing me, baby. Finish what you started. Undress me."

"I wouldn't want to kill you." The shy girl seemed to be gone, and a playful siren was in her place. Yeah, she was going to give him hell, and he would enjoy every minute.

She undid the buckle of his belt. She dropped to her knees, and he couldn't help but hiss a little as she undid his fly and brought down the zipper. She unwrapped him like she was unwrapping a Christmas package. She licked her lips as his cock bounced free.

It was definitely time to start taking control or she would unman him.

"That's enough, Hope. Let's start this scene of ours."

She frowned but sat back on her heels.

James kicked out of his boots and got out of his jeans and boxers, grateful to be free of the confines.

"Have you ever been tied up, baby?" He needed to assess how much she knew. Hope seemed awfully innocent.

"No."

He was grateful. He wanted to be the first. He wanted to introduce her to how much fun it could be. "I want to tie you up. I want to restrain you so I have total control over your body. I don't want to do this for me, although I will enjoy it deeply. I want to do it to bring you pleasure. If it scares you or makes you upset, then it isn't doing what it's supposed to. Do you understand?"

She nodded.

"I need a verbal answer." He would have to ease her into play. He might not be a full-time Dom like Trev, but when they were playing, he wanted respect.

"Yes, James."

"Good. Then put your hands behind your back, lace the fingers together."

She caught her breath but did as she was asked. She was beautiful sitting there, her breasts thrust out, her chest rising and falling with each breath. He walked to the wall Beth had cleverly hidden and pulled out some thin rope made of jute. Trev, it seemed, was a practitioner of Shibari, or as James liked to call it, the fine art of tying up a lady.

He caught sight of his brother staring at Hope like he wanted to get to his knees and worship her. But it was James's turn. He wasn't going to call his brother in. He wasn't going to have Noah hold her wrists as he bound her. He wasn't going to have her suck his cock while his brother worked a plug in her ass.

He wasn't going to do any of that.

He forced himself to get to his knees and bind her hands behind her back. He wrapped the rope around her wrists, forming a bowline knot. He tied it off, testing it to make sure it couldn't cut off her circulation, and then leaned back, admiring the arch of her back and how it flowed to the globes of her ass.

"Spread your knees a little more, baby."

Hope pressed her knees out. The dimples above her ass deepened. James couldn't help but run his hand down the length of her spine. "Have you ever had a cock in your ass?"

She was quiet for a moment and then a hesitant, "Yes."

He was a bit surprised, but he didn't know everything about her. She was twenty-seven years old. She wasn't a kid. "Did you like it?"

Her hair shook. "It hurt."

"It's not supposed to. How long did you wear a plug?"

"I didn't. It…was a mistake."

There it was. A tiny shake of her shoulders. She got upset when she talked about certain things, and this seemed to be one of them. Hope's past was starting to be a mystery he had to solve. Someone had hurt her. The thought made him want to find that someone and beat him to death, but he needed to deal with her now. "I want to play with you today. I want to show you that it doesn't have to hurt."

"Had many cocks shoved up your ass?"

He stifled a laugh as he grabbed the small footstool Trev likely kept for the purpose James was about to use it for. She was a smart-ass, and she'd given him a very good reason to put his hands on her. He set the footstool in front of her. "No sarcasm. Lean forward. Put your ass in the air."

"I already got a spanking today." Her bottom lip quivered sweetly.

"Well, you're getting another one because you didn't learn your lesson. It's a count of twenty right now. Would you like to make it thirty?"

She huffed and leaned forward, settling her torso on the padded stool. It was perfectly sized and suddenly her ass was on display.

"Well, hell, baby. Noah didn't even leave a mark."

"I was trying to be careful with her," Noah said, his voice a low growl.

"Well, now, there's careful and then there's perfection." He pulled his hand back and smacked that gorgeous ass.

Hope whimpered as her flesh flushed to a nice shade of pink. He struck three times in rapid succession, varying the strength of his hand.

"This is what we call an erotic spanking, baby. And before you ask me, yes, I have had this done to me. Noah and I met a nice Dominatrix who taught us a few tricks, but she used the other one as an example. Oddly enough, I think we were better at the techniques we had applied to us. I took the spanking, and I'm awfully good at giving them." He went in for another round, the sound of his hand on her flesh filling the room, accompanied with her breathy cries. "This spanking should heighten your arousal. The pain blends with heat until you can't tell the two apart and it's all one long sensual experience."

He struck the center of her ass. There was a fine sheen to her backside as he continued on, but he could smell the sweet scent of her arousal starting to flow. She'd stopped tensing at each blow as he hit seventeen and eighteen. She relaxed down and took the last two with a breathy sigh.

Later, he could introduce her to the pleasure of a single tail. Hope was perfect.

"What was Noah good at?" The question came out on a sensual gasp.

James snorted. He couldn't help it. "You want to tell her?"

Noah's face was as red as Hope's ass. "I...well, I...I lost at cards and I...I'm really good at anal sex."

Hope's laughter filled the dungeon. James joined in.

Different. It was different than his other experiences. Hope made him laugh. The sound of her laughing made him feel buoyant and young.

"What Noah doesn't know, baby, is that I cheated at cards. There was no way I was taking that plug." He grinned at Noah's offended huff. "But if you want me to try it, I will. I'm a little older and a lot more open."

"It sounds like Noah's the one who's more open."

God, he was crazy about her smart mouth. He leaned over and kissed the cheeks of her ass. "Let's see how open we can get you. Stay in this position."

He got to his feet and found the offered plug set. As Bo had said, they were neat, clean, and sterilized for use. Trev was a perfect host. He thought briefly about the ginger lube but decided he wanted to keep his head on his body. *Later.* A simple water-based lube would work today. And a small plug. He didn't want to scare her. He needed to make her love this. Noah might be better at anal than he was, but it couldn't be by much. He loved the way a perky asshole opened to take his cock. Sharing that with Hope would be so good.

He got back to his knees, well aware that Noah was looking on, his face back to being grim and dark. He wanted to be involved. Well, he should have thought about that before he'd fucked Hope earlier.

James gently pulled apart the cheeks of her ass. Damn, that was pretty. Her asshole was pink and looked tighter than any fist. She was small, and he would have to be careful.

"I'm going to use some lube first, and then we'll settle this plug in. Are you all right, Hope?"

"I'm nervous," she admitted.

But she was still aroused. He let his hand slide down to her pussy. She was soaking wet. Every inch of that pussy was swollen and wanting. He split her labia, pulling the petals aside and delving into her with a single finger. Heat surrounded him. She was blazing hot. Whatever anxiety she had, she still wanted him. He slid the pad of his finger over her clit. Pleasure. That was what she needed. A starter orgasm would make everything easier.

"Relax." He made it an order. He was starting to understand her.

Her shoulders lost their tension. Her eyes closed, and her knees spread a little wider.

That was what he wanted. Trust. He worked his thumb into her cunt, allowing two fingers to slide over her clit. Cream coated his fingers. So fucking wet. She started to move, to try to take him deeper.

He smacked her already-sensitive ass. "You stay still. Take what I give you."

"It's hard. It feels so good."

"Has you taking control worked before?" He would bet his life the answer to that would be no.

"No," she murmured. "Nothing worked until this morning."

Noah wouldn't have allowed her to control the sex. He might have been Ally's lapdog, but he seemed to want more from Hope. Noah seemed a bit harder than before.

"Then you do as I tell you, and I promise I won't stop until you're satisfied. I'll give you what you need."

She stilled beneath him.

James went to work. He pressed his thumb in, rotating and opening her up. He caught her clit between his two fingers and pressed, pinching at it as he hooked his thumb and rubbed her G-spot.

Hope's mouth opened, and a cry let him know he'd hit the perfect spot. Her body shuddered as she rode out the orgasm. Arousal poured out of her, coating his hand and permeating the air. Her scent was like a drug, making his cock jump.

How long was he going to be able to hold out?

When the shudders stopped, he pulled his hand out and, without a single self-conscious thought, licked his fingers, tasting her for the first time. Tangy and sweet. Like Hope herself. He sucked her cream off his fingers.

"You taste like heaven, baby. I can't wait to get my tongue on you."

Her breathy sigh told him she was interested in that prospect. But he had something to do first.

"This is going to be cold in the beginning." He dribbled the lube right over her asshole. She whimpered. Those sounds she made were killing him. How would she sound when he had her on a cross counting out lashes in that sweet Southern voice of hers?

He picked up the plug and fitted it to her asshole. The small hole was closed, but he knew it wouldn't stay that way. He rimmed her with the plug, opening her in tiny increments. He could see his cock there. When he fucked her ass, he would take it slow, and he would watch as his cock sank in, disappearing into the hot recess of her ass. He would push in until his balls caressed her flesh, and then he would watch as he pulled out. He would watch that same asshole that had tried to keep him out, fight to keep him in. He would watch and memorize every moment. It would be a beautiful thing, the ultimate trust.

He pressed in, the plug finally gaining ground. Hope moaned, her ass twitching.

"Almost there, baby."

"It feels weird." A fine shiver went across Hope's skin.

"But it doesn't hurt, does it?"

"No," she admitted. Her voice was tight. "It's odd, but it doesn't hurt. I don't know. But don't stop."

He wasn't about to stop. He slid the plug home, seating it deep in her ass. He looked at it for a minute. The flat base was neatly pressed between the cheeks of her ass.

His cock throbbed. She was absolutely perfect. Never in all his thoughts about her had he imagined he would get her in a dungeon. He'd thought about fucking her and cuddling her and sharing a life with her, but not this. When he'd thought about getting married, he'd figured he would have to give up this part of his life, but now he wondered why.

His wife should know all of him. His wife should love all of him. If Hope could accept him, the dark and the light, maybe they could be happy. Maybe they could be more.

He helped her to her knees, her eyes slightly dreamy. He'd given her that. A whole fucking year wasted because he'd thought he had nothing to offer her. This. He could offer her this.

He leaned forward and kissed her, a sweet brushing of lips, ignoring the desperate calls of his cock. He took a moment to hold her, her bound arms forcing her nipples out to poke at his chest.

"Are you all right, baby?"

There was a soft smile on her face. "I'm lovely. James, you said I tasted good."

He kissed her again, opening her mouth under his and letting her taste herself on his tongue. "You taste like heaven, baby."

Her nose nuzzled his. "I want to taste you, James. Please."

His cock finally took over. She'd asked so sweetly. He wasn't about to refuse her.

Chapter Eleven

Hope's head was still reeling as James moved the footstool aside and took that gorgeous cock in hand. She looked at it. It was really a work of art. Long and thick and the nicest shade of purple. The crown of his cock was perfectly shaped, and there was a drop of pearly fluid seeping from the head.

He wanted her. She couldn't pretend he didn't. The evidence was right there in front of her.

She wanted to touch him, but her bound hands wouldn't allow it. It was probably better that way. If she could, she would caress him, selfishly exploring every inch of that bronzed skin covering muscled flesh. He was one amazing cowboy. Lean and tight, he'd earned his physique through grueling daily work. She wanted to run her tongue over the notches at his hips.

But more than anything, she wanted to please him as he'd pleased her.

Her body still hummed from the orgasm he'd given her. And he'd been right. Tying her up and forcing her to remain still had helped enormously. She hadn't been able to think about anything but what he was doing to her. He'd forced out her self-consciousness and her doubt. Without the use of her hands or the ability to move, she'd had to be in the moment. There hadn't been a thought in her head beyond James, his touch, his voice, the heat of his skin.

She didn't even mind the plug. She hadn't told James, but her only experience with anal sex had been horrible. She'd been drunk and stupid, trying to obliterate herself. So dangerous, but with James she felt safe. She was safe. At least her body was safe. Her heart was in serious damn jeopardy, and from more than one source.

Noah was watching. Noah was here, but he couldn't touch her. And she wanted him to.

"You want to taste me? I want that, too, baby. But I'm not coming in your mouth. Not this time." He stroked that hard cock, his balls tight against his body. "This first time I want to be deep inside your pussy."

She couldn't imagine anything better. Until she caught sight of Noah. Being between them would be perfect, but she would have to work to bring them together. James was still far away from that.

Noah gave her an encouraging wink. He wanted this, too.

Hope took a deep breath, uncertainty crowding her again. Christian had never wanted a blow job. When she'd offered, he'd told her only whores did that. "I don't know that I'm very good at this."

James's hand found her hair. Noah would have tightened his hands and told her not to talk bad about herself, but James smiled down, his face soft, his hand smoothing over her hair. "That doesn't matter, baby. All that matters is that you want to. And how would you know? You've never given yourself a blow job. Hell, I bet you're really good at it. And it doesn't take much to please me. I promise it's going to be okay."

Tears pricked at her eyes. He was gentle when she needed it, as though he could read her emotions and cared enough to give her what she needed. Somehow, these two brothers who could barely stand to be in a room together managed to give her exactly what she needed, when she needed it. Earlier it had been Noah's outrageous dominance that had pulled her from the edge. Now James's understanding made it easy to lean forward and let her tongue find his cock. She swiped the drop of pearly cream up, tasting his essence. Salty. Savory. James.

He groaned, thrusting forward. "See, that is working, baby."

It was. Another drop leaked from the slit of his cock. His cockhead seemed to pulse her way like a compass pointing north. She sucked the head into her mouth and whirled her tongue around.

So good. She was so aware. Aware of her own body and not merely the task at hand. She was aware of the hard wood under her knees and the rope that held her wrists together. She was aware of the soft tickling of her hair caressing her back and the hard thrust of the plug that claimed her ass. Every inch of her body seemed awake and alive.

James buried his hands in her hair as he started to thrust lightly in and out of her mouth. She opened her jaw, trying to take him deeper. He was so big. She groaned as he forced another inch or so in. Her mouth was full, and she didn't think she had half of him. She worked her tongue, trying to suckle every bit of soft skin she could.

His hips pivoted. "Damn, girl, you're killing me."

He pulled out and then slowly thrust back in. Hope lapped at the head before sucking him inside, hollowing out her cheeks. She tried to relax and take more than before. Another hot inch and then another. He filled her, tickling the back of her throat. His cock pulsed inside her mouth. She could guess what that meant, and she wanted it. She wanted him coating her tongue, shooting down her throat.

James pulled out abruptly, a curse on his lips.

She looked up, doubt flooding her again. "Did I do something wrong?"

His breath sawed in and out of his chest. "We're going to have to work on your self-esteem." He palmed his cock, though he held his hand still. "No, Hope, you almost unmanned me. One more suck from that sweet mouth and I was going to blow, and I promised not to do that until I'm inside you."

He took a long breath and disappeared from view. She felt a flick across her skin, and her hands came undone. James picked her up like she weighed nothing, one arm around her back and the other under her knees. He cradled her to his chest.

"I want you to hold on to me this first time. Later, I'll fuck you with your arms and legs tied down, but now I want you wrapped around me." He placed her on the bed, following her, covering her body with his.

The sweetness of being skin to skin with James pierced her. She'd dreamed of it, but it was better. He was so much more tender than she'd imagined, his lips tracing a line from her forehead to her nose, stopping briefly at her lips before lightly touching her chin. In her dreams, she'd imagined him as demanding and overwhelming. She'd longed to pleasure him, but never dreamed she would get so much back. He held her, kissing her over and over as though he couldn't get enough.

This wasn't the "wham, bam, thank you ma'am" of his legend, tearing his way through most of Southern Colorado. This wasn't crazy sex, despite the bondage and the butt plug. This was making love. James was making love to her, and the only thing missing was Noah. She looked his way, and the longing in his eyes cut through her. She was about to open her mouth to beg James, but Noah shook his head.

This was James's time.

She closed her eyes and concentrated on the man in her arms. James kissed his way down, stopping to suckle her breasts and play with her navel. He took his time as though he wanted to learn every inch of her. She was in a near frenzy by the time his mouth finally hovered over her pussy. She could feel his heat and his control. Such control. She knew his cock must be aching, but he remained disciplined.

"This is what I've been waiting for. I missed my lunch, baby. This will make up for it." His tongue danced a slow stroke down her pussy, delving into her juices. Hope nearly came off the bed. She spread her legs wide as James settled between them, his head buried in her pussy. He teased and licked and speared her with his tongue. Every inch of her female flesh lit up and went on high alert. She had to clutch the silky comforter beneath her or she would have sunk her hands in his hair to force him to fuck her harder.

Over and over he licked and sucked, keeping her on the thin edge of orgasm. She held on to the comforter, giving over to him. He wouldn't leave her like this. He wouldn't torture her with no hope of release, but he would push her. And she would let him because she trusted him. It was stupid, but she did, and she would lie here underneath him, giving him everything he requested.

"Such a good girl," he murmured. "A good girl like you deserves a treat, baby."

She loved the way he called her "baby" in that dirty, decadent way. He might call her baby, but he treated her like a woman. He'd used her mouth, allowing her to pleasure him. He'd made her a part of their lovemaking rather than treating her like a china doll. Even as he held her down, his big hands clamping on her thighs, she felt sexier and more like a woman than ever before.

James pressed two fingers up into her and sucked her clit hard. Her vision swam as the orgasm took her. Before she could even process the feeling, James was moving up, covering her with his big body. He found her lips, their chests rubbing together. She tasted her tangy essence, but this time it was mingled with his. She opened her mouth, allowing him to dominate her. She loved his weight on top of her, pressing her into the silky softness of the bed.

He moved briefly to his knees, and Hope watched with a pleasant lethargy as he reached over to the small nightstand and grabbed one of the condoms that had been thoughtfully left there. James opened the condom and sheathed his dick. His bright blue eyes found hers as he lined his cock up to her pussy and started to press in.

"So tight. God, baby, I can feel the plug. When Noah…" He stopped himself, shaking his head as though to rid himself of the thought. He twisted his hips, working his way in. "I love the way the plug feels. When the time is right, I'm going to take your ass. I'm going to fuck you every way I can. There's not going to be an inch of you I don't cover because you're mine, Hope. You're fucking mine."

But she knew what he'd been thinking. He'd been thinking about Noah. He'd been thinking about sharing her with his brother. Noah had been right. James might not be willing to share now, but he wouldn't be able to help himself in the long run. If she opened herself, and if Noah continued to make amends, she might have what she wanted.

She wrapped herself around James. "I need you. I need you so much."

She did. She couldn't imagine leaving now. She held James close as he finally worked his way all the way in. Between the plug and James's cock, she could barely breathe she was so full. She held him. He'd given her so much pleasure she didn't expect she could handle more. She would let him take his pleasure and be perfectly satisfied.

But James wanted more.

"Give it to me, Hope."

"I can't." It was almost too much. He ground his hips down on her clit, as though he sought to fuse them together. Hope shook her head, but there was no denying it. There was no stopping it. James's cock slid inside as he thrust deep, and she screamed as she came. This orgasm caused her body to shake. It started in her pussy in that perfect place that James's cock had found, and it drove outward like an earthquake. Her vision blurred, and she held on to James for dear life.

He groaned, gritting his teeth above her as he came.

He thrust into her one last time and then allowed his body to drop on top of hers. His chest heaved, and his body shuddered. He buried his face in her neck, his breath hot on her skin. She let her legs fall from around his waist, but she couldn't bring herself to let him go.

His head came up slightly, his blue eyes sleepy but content. "See, that wasn't all that bad. We're going to play, Hope. We're going to play a lot."

"She needs aftercare." Noah's soft voice cut through the afterglow. Noah. He was still here, still watching.

James's eyes hardened. He rolled off her, and she missed his warmth. "You think I don't know what I owe her?"

"I don't know how much you've played lately. You could be out of practice." Noah's face was flushed, his breath heavy. He turned his eyes away from her.

James didn't seem to have a problem with nudity, but Hope suddenly felt hers. She pulled the comforter around her.

"I haven't had a lot of time to play," James said, his voice sharp and biting. "I had to take care of the ranch, and I had to take care of my father, so no, I haven't been trolling clubs the way you have. But I still know damn well how to take care of my sub."

Noah flinched slightly but didn't back down. "Her backside is probably aching. That's all I'm saying."

She forced herself to sit up and wished that Noah hadn't said anything. "I'm fine. It's sore, but not painful."

She actually liked the ache. Every muscle in her body felt pleasantly used. Her blood was still humming through her system, but the amazingly sweet fog that had encompassed her brain was fleeing.

"Okay, then. I was just worried about you." Noah pushed off the wall. "I'm going to go back to the main house. Am I still allowed to stay at the house or should I go into town?"

James shook his head, his hand scrubbing his scalp. "Take the guest room."

Noah walked out without looking behind him. The door closed with a quiet snick.

James stared at it for a moment, his shoulders set. He was silent.

"James," Hope began.

He turned, and for just a moment, she saw the look of naked pain on his face, but he wiped it away in favor of a devilish smile that didn't quite meet his eyes. "Alone at last. I think he has the picture now, baby."

Noah was walking away. She couldn't stop the panic that welled inside her. "You should go talk to him."

He huffed and crawled back on the bed. "I'm not going after him when I just got rid of him. Don't worry. Noah always bounces back. He's the smart one, after all. He'll get over this, too."

She wasn't sure Noah was going to get over being estranged from his brother, and James was only putting up a good front. "Please, I don't want to come between the two of you."

James crowded her, climbing up her body after he dragged the comforter away. "You won't. I'll make sure of it. This is not your problem. And this is my time. I don't want to talk about Noah. I want to concentrate on you and me."

He lowered his lips to hers, and Hope stopped thinking.

* * * *

Noah took a deep breath of the rapidly cooling Colorado air. It filled his lungs with a sweet ache. He wasn't used to the altitude. It wouldn't take him long. He'd been born in these mountains. When he'd sat in his tiny Manhattan apartment, he'd dreamed of them. He would close his eyes and feel the wind that rushed from the mountains into the valley, caressing his face. He would hear the aspens shake and smell the dirt.

He'd made a mistake. More than one. And now he had to wonder if coming home had been the biggest one of all.

Noah walked out of the guesthouse. Everything had changed. The guesthouse had been a place for friends to stay, and now there were plans to make it bigger than the main house. His childhood playground was gone, burned down in a fire he hadn't even known about.

Maybe he'd burned down his whole connection to James when he'd walked out. Maybe he didn't deserve to come home.

Maybe he owed it to his brother to walk away.

With a heavy sigh, he walked into the house. He walked through the living room and into the kitchen, wondering if James still kept a bottle of whiskey under the counter like their fathers had for years before. He and James had found it and gotten into some serious trouble for giving it a try.

Noah walked in the kitchen and was assaulted once again by the fact that everything changed.

Beth sat in Trev's lap, her head on his shoulder as he sipped a cup of coffee and looked through some paperwork. It was an intimate scene. It cut through Noah like a knife.

"Sorry." He started to step out. One more place where he wouldn't be welcome. There seemed to be a lot of those.

Trev's eyes came up. "I thought you were with James and Hope."

"They need time alone. I was going to get a drink and go to my room. Don't mind me," Noah said.

Beth sighed and slid off her husband's lap. She pressed her lips to his. "I have to go. Bo is going to drive me out to the valley. I'll be home before supper."

Trev smiled at her. "You tell Bo to take good care of you. And you tell Nate that I'm not going to let him work you into the ground."

Beth's eyes rolled. "I'll be sure to tell him." Beth winked at Noah as she walked by. "Don't you worry about him. His bark is worse than his bite. His bite is actually quite nice."

Trev watched his wife walk away with a smile on his face. Noah started to back out of the kitchen. Maybe he would go for a ride. It had been forever since he'd been on a horse. He needed to figure out what to do now.

"The sheriff found out Beth is damn good at home renovations. He and Zane are going to add to their cabin, and they want to consult with Beth. If I know my Beth, she'll figure out how to make a mansion out of that cabin. Hey, why don't you sit down? I'm going over some records for Red, but it's all in vet speak, so I don't understand much of it. There's a whole lot of Latin in here. I would love to know if any of this explains why he's such a difficult horse."

Noah hesitated. "I don't know. I'll be honest, I don't think I'm going to be here for long. I think I might head out tomorrow."

Why not now? A voice inside pestered him. *Why wait? It would be for the best if you just never saw Hope again.*

"Please sit down, Noah," Trev asked politely, but there was a hardness to his eyes that let him know the man wasn't going to take no for an answer.

He pulled a chair out and sat. He'd been an asshole to Trev. If Trev wanted a piece of his hide, maybe he should give it to him. "Say what you need to say."

Trev let the papers in his hand fall. "I'm not going to insult you. I'm going to tell you that you made a mistake by walking out of that playroom. You did exactly what James thought you would do."

Noah leaned forward. The last thing he needed was yet another busybody sticking his nose in. "What the hell do you know about this?"

If Trev was upset by Noah's show of temper, he didn't show it. "I know way more than you think. Bo and I didn't just meet and decide to share Beth. We had a past, and I was the one in your shoes. I had hurt the hell out of him, and I had to make amends. You hurt your brother."

He hadn't meant to. "I was in love."

"And that gave you the right to walk out on your obligations?"

"At the time, it felt more important than anything." God, he felt old. Weariness began to settle into his bones.

Trev sighed and took a sip of his coffee. "I do know what you mean. But you have to understand James's perspective. I think he's going to make a horrible mistake, and you're the only one who can stop it."

"He's going to force Hope to choose." It had been there in James's eyes. This was going to be his revenge. He was going to take Hope. "I won't let that happen. I'm not going to put her in the middle of this. I think Jamie loves her, and I know she's crazy about him. I'm going to make it easy. I'm going to let them be."

Trev clapped his hands and pointed briefly Noah's way. "Ah, so you're going to go the martyr route."

"I'm trying to help my brother," Noah explained.

"No, you're running away and trying to ease the guilt in your gut. I know this sounds awful, but you're still being a selfish shit. If you walk out, Hope and James will fracture. There's a reason they weren't together before you came home, and it's not about the ranch. He's fooling himself. This was about you."

"I don't understand." James wanted him gone. He'd stated it plainly.

Trev shook his head, leaning forward and obviously warming to his subject. "Can't you see? Do you know that James has spent the last couple of years sharing women with his friends? Not for more than a night or two, but I know for a fact that he's shared women with both the deputy and Wolf Meyer. He's been trying to replace you for years because he's scared that he won't have the life he was promised."

Their parents. Their family. Their childhood. Every moment of their upbringing had taught them to share, and Noah had walked out on that. He should have known. How could he have a relationship with a woman when he'd left half of himself behind in Colorado?

He'd been so damn lonely, and he'd missed James. "I don't think he wants me here."

"Oh, I assure you he doesn't want you here. But he damn well needs you, and it's time to man up and do what you need to do. He's your big brother. Did he stand by you? Did he protect you?"

So many times. James was his big brother, his hero. Noah nodded, not trusting himself to speak.

"Then you better pay him back," Trev proclaimed.

That was so much easier said than done. Noah felt frustration well up inside him. "I don't know how. I thought Hope could bring us together, but she's tearing us apart, and I don't know how to stop it. When I try to talk to Jamie, he says he doesn't want to. I've tried to apologize, and he just looks through me. I thought I could give him some time, but he's going to push this. He's going to hurt Hope."

Trev's eyes went sympathetic. "He's going to hurt everyone because he can't see past the nose on his face. So he doesn't want to sit down and talk about the past, you make him fight for the future. Hope is a big girl. I don't know her well, but I bet she's been through more than you think. I bet she can handle a bit of a fight."

"I don't even know how to start," Noah admitted. But Trev was getting through to him. What if James didn't know what he wanted because he was too angry? Was Noah willing to leave him because it was easier than fighting?

Trev slapped at the table, causing the paperwork he'd been reading to jump. "You have to break through that wall surrounding James. You can't do that if you walk away. You can't do that if you take a step back. You can only do that if you make him believe that you're not leaving again, and that you're here for the long haul."

Noah was starting to like Trev McNamara. "I want that. I want to try this thing with Hope."

"Then you're going to have to figure out how to break James down. Look, I care about James. He's my business partner, but he's also my friend. We clicked the minute we met, so I think I understand him. You're going to have to get him emotional about this. It's going to be way easier to get him mad than it will be to get him to discuss the real issue. Get him talking. Let him beat on you.

You shouldn't mind. You're doing that martyr thing."

Noah wasn't sure about that. James could hit hard. But if he could get his brother back, it would be worth it. "I am an expert at making him mad."

Trev nodded. "Then all you have to do now is wait."

Wait for his brother to finish fucking Hope. He could wait for a good long while. He could sit here and think about all the horrible things he could say in order to get his brother good and mad. Or he could go through a bunch of paperwork and make his brother's life a little easier.

Trev's hand tapped against the stack of papers on the table. His brows arched as he waited.

"Fine." Noah grabbed the paperwork.

There was a loud banging on the door.

Trev's eyes narrowed. "Saved by the bell. I wonder who that could be. I thought we would be isolated out here, but there are always people coming in and out. I hope the new hands didn't screw up. Ranch hands aren't what they used to be."

Trev got up and walked toward the door.

Noah picked up the paperwork and tried to focus, but a vision of Hope swam before his eyes. She'd been so damn beautiful when she'd submitted to James. Watching his brother spank Hope had gotten him hard as hell. For a moment, it was almost like it used to be. He'd been with his brother sharing a woman—except better because this time it was the right woman. He knew it deep down to his soul. Hope was the woman who could make them complete. Hope was the woman they could share a life with.

She was strong enough to handle them and sweet enough to love for an eternity. Noah wasn't afraid the way James was. He wanted that connection, longed for it. He wanted everything his parents had had, but he was terrified he'd thrown it all away.

"Uh, Noah, Henry is here." Trev walked in followed by Henry Flanders.

"I need to talk to Jamie," Henry announced.

James would kill his ass if Noah allowed his first time with Hope to be interrupted. "He's busy right now. Is there anything I can do for you?"

More than likely, he would be forced to listen to how the ranch could make its practices more earth friendly. Yes. This was his punishment.

"I need to talk to you both. It's about Hope. I'm afraid she's in trouble." Henry's brows creased over his glasses.

"Talk to me." Noah stood up, his heart hitching. He'd known there was something up with Hope, but it had been easy to forget about her trouble in the midst of his own misery. Now all of his instincts were screaming again that something was going wrong.

Henry crossed his arms over his chest and a hard look came into his eyes. "Someone walked up to our shop today and started asking questions about Hope. I didn't like him. He was lying about something."

"What did he want to know?" God, how much trouble was Hope in? Ever since Noah was a kid, Bliss had attracted people on the run and down on their luck. Which one was Hope?

Henry adjusted his glasses. "He claimed to be interested in her, but I'm suspicious. He had a reaction when he found out she was involved with the two of you, and it wasn't the one he tried to portray. He was angry. Volcanically angry."

"Does he know her?" Noah searched his brain trying to remember everyone he'd seen at the fairgrounds today.

"He claimed not to, but again, I would say yes."

"Fed?" Was the law after Hope? He clenched his fist to make sure it didn't shake. No matter what she'd done, he was going to protect her. He wouldn't let anyone take her.

Henry shook his head. "Not a chance. He doesn't move well. He isn't trained, at least not formally. He's manipulative. Highly intelligent but perhaps sociopathic."

Noah stared at Henry for a moment. "You got all that off a short conversation with him?"

Henry frowned, looking a little fierce. "I wasn't always a pacifist, Noah. I had a life before Bliss like everyone else. I would like to remain exactly the man my wife loves, but if you don't handle this guy, I will. He's dangerous. I would bet a lot on it, and Nell is on his radar. I don't like that. I won't handle it well if he tries to use her to get to Hope again. I'll be forced to do something I rather wouldn't."

Noah was the tiniest bit afraid of Henry Flanders in that moment. What the hell had Henry done before he came to Bliss? One thing was sure. Noah believed him.

"Did you call the sheriff?" Noah asked.

Henry sighed. "I thought it best to talk to you two and Hope first. I don't want to put Cam in a situation where he has to compromise his badge. I wanted to feel out the situation. If Hope's in some sort of trouble with the law, then you boys need to get your ducks in a row before you go to Cam. If she needs something, like a new identity or some records changed somewhere, I might know a couple of men who could help with that."

Henry Flanders knew hackers? What the hell had the world come to? The idea of Hope needing to hide her identity and flee terrified Noah. What would he do? If Hope needed to run, how could he let her go? The answer was easy. He couldn't. He would go with her, but James couldn't. His brother couldn't leave the Circle G behind.

And, damn it, Noah didn't want to leave it either. He'd just gotten home.

"Knock, knock, James. Are you here, baby?" A soft feminine voice echoed through the hall.

That was not Hope walking in. And whoever it was had called James baby. He sent Trev a look, silently requesting information. He hated the fact, but Trev knew what was going on in James's life and Noah didn't.

Trev shrugged. "No idea. He's had more than a couple of girlfriends."

Trev used air quotes around the word "girlfriends."

A willowy brunette with glossy, long hair sauntered into the kitchen. "You can try to hide, but I found you!"

She was dressed in a long trench coat and what appeared to be five-inch heels. A bottle of champagne was gripped in her hand. Her hair was perfectly mussed in a way that had probably taken her hours to achieve. She was stunning.

Noah wasn't impressed. He knew this type. He'd been married to her for five damn years. "No, you didn't. You found me."

"Who the hell are you?" the brunette asked, her face losing its previous sweet expression.

Trev leaned back against the counter having refilled his coffee mug. He had an amused look on his face as he watched the scene in front of him. "Serena, this is James's brother, Noah."

Serena frowned, looking him up and down. "Really? He doesn't look like James." She shrugged as if he didn't matter. "Where is my boyfriend?"

Dear god, he didn't need this. He had a sneaking suspicion that she wasn't wearing much under that trench coat. She didn't know James at all. He wasn't a lawyer or a businessman who sat in an office all day. If he had been, then sneaking in for an impromptu afternoon delight might make sense, but James was a rancher. This Serena girl could walk in all dressed up and ready for sex only to find the object of her desire knee-deep in cow shit or lost on the east range.

Or, in this case, balls deep in Hope McLean. What the hell had James been doing? Noah was going to have to have a sit-down family meeting because this was not going to work.

"The way I heard it, she's gone out with James exactly twice." Trev's eyes found Noah's as though reassuring him. "And not at all in the last couple of weeks."

"He's been busy. And we worked fast. We clicked. Maybe you don't know what that means. Now someone tell me where James is." Serena set the champagne on the counter.

Henry was right back to being his normal, laid-back self. He sighed. "See, I told Jamie this kind of activity would come back to haunt him. Sex is sacred. It should be taken seriously."

Noah was pretty damn sure his brother was learning that lesson even as they spoke.

Well, there was no way he was putting Hope in the same room as this Serena person. He had to get her out of here and fast.

It was far past time to protect his woman and his brother. First, he would protect James by getting rid of his good-time girl, and then they would all sit down and deal with Hope.

And she was going to talk. Noah would make sure of it.

Chapter Twelve

James looked up at Hope and promised himself he would get her naked again soon. She was dressed, all buttoned up and proper looking, but he knew the truth. He'd seen the real Hope, the sexy, amazing, beautiful Hope who had just ruined him for all other women.

It had been absolutely perfect.

So why was his heart aching? Why was he wondering where Noah was and how he was doing? He was being a complete idiot. Noah was going to get what he deserved. Noah was going to have to deal with the fact that Hope would choose him. Noah was going to have to watch as he and Hope started a life together. Noah was going to have to be the one on the outside.

What the hell was he doing?

"Are you coming?" Hope asked, smoothing down her hair. "Shouldn't you put on your pants?"

He didn't see a need for pants when she was around. They did nothing but get in the way of his dick. He'd fucked her so hard he shouldn't be able to use the damn thing for a while, but it looked like Hope was the ultimate cure for erectile problems. His well-used cock stirred at the thought of flipping that skirt up again. Noah had been right about one thing. She didn't need panties. He would make sure all of her panties mysteriously disappeared.

God, he didn't want to leave this room. Leaving this room meant deciding things he wasn't ready to decide.

Noah was in love with Hope. He'd forced Noah to watch as he made love to the woman Noah was crazy about, and he hadn't offered to share. He was feeling a little dirty. Not because of what he'd done with Hope but because he knew damn well she wanted Noah, too, and he'd kept them apart. He hadn't done what he'd wanted to do. He hadn't held her breasts up and offered his brother a taste. He hadn't asked Noah to hold her down while he tongue fucked her. He hadn't placed her between him and Noah so she knew damn well she was protected on all sides.

It was counter to everything he believed, but he wasn't ready to let Noah back in. The wound was too deep, and Noah walking back in the way he had was like ripping the scab off. James was bleeding again, and he wasn't sure how to stop.

"I'm coming." He grabbed his jeans. "How does that pretty ass of yours feel?"

She flushed. After all the nasty stuff he'd done to her, she could still look so innocent. "It's fine."

"You liked your massage." After he'd wrung several more orgasms out of her, he'd laid her down on the massage table and taken care of her the way he should. He'd enjoyed rubbing every inch of her skin and listening to her purr.

"I liked everything. You know I did, but now I'm hungry, and it's almost dinnertime. Did you plan to feed me?"

Dinner. Damn. He actually hadn't thought of that. After the way she'd sweetly submitted, he owed her a nice dinner and some serious cuddling. He owed her his care. He scrambled. "We'll go into town. We can go to Trio and have a couple of beers."

There was no way to miss the change that came over her. Her whole body stiffened, the joy leaving her eyes. What had he said?

"Or wine. I could get us a bottle of wine. I don't know much about it, but Alexei probably does. He spent all that time in Europe and those people supposedly know their stuff."

She smiled, but it didn't reach her eyes. "I don't think Alexei was a very cosmopolitan European. He spent most of his time with the mob. He probably knows his vodka better than wine."

"Then he can make you one of those fruity martinis, like the apple ones." He would buy her drinks all night if it got her to relax. Maybe she would start talking if he got her tipsy. A little liquor might loosen her up and give him a hint of the stress she was under. He would get her all relaxed and make love to her again, and then he would gently bring up the subject of what was giving her nightmares.

She shook her head. "No. I can't go out tonight. I...I need to go check on Noah. He looked upset when he left."

She started out the door. James stared, his mouth hanging open. Was she serious? He'd spent hours making love to her and she was going to check on Noah?

He reached for his shirt, hauling it over his head. "Hope, you stay right here."

She stopped at the doorway. "I'm only going next door. I need to rest. It's been a long day."

Yeah, it had been a long damn month. He'd lost his best friends, had to deal with the fact that his brother was back, and he'd finally acknowledged that he was in love. *Fuck.* He was in love with Hope. It had to be love since he'd never had this sinking feeling in the pit of his stomach simply because a woman was leaving the room.

Usually it was a bit of a relief. He'd had female friends. He loved the women of the town, but not a one of them, not a single lover in his background, made him feel the way Hope did.

"We're going to talk about it. You can walk away right now, but we're going to talk about whatever it is that's bothering you. Tonight." He was past done. He could feel walls going up between them. She had been completely open with him in bed, but now she was shutting down again, and he wasn't going to let that happen. No way. "And don't think you can bring Noah into this. I'm not going to let you use my brother to manipulate me."

Hope's eyes flared, a spark coming into them. "Me? You think I'm using Noah to manipulate you?"

A flare of guilt gnawed at his gut, but he powered through it. "Why else would you get out of bed with me to go see him? We just settled this. You made your choice."

"Choice?" Hope asked. "I had a choice?"

He wasn't going to back down. "Yes. Me or Noah. Me, who you've known for over a year, or a man who walked into your life a couple of days ago and has a bad reputation for walking right back out."

Those warm brown eyes pinned him. "Is that right? Well, it seems to me this amazing choice you're giving me is between a man who ignored me for a year and a man who wanted me the minute he saw me. And he didn't know I even lived in Bliss. Noah didn't run away from me."

"Yeah, well you haven't given him enough time." Bitterness welled. She was going to choose Noah. She was going to choose Noah because he was smarter, more educated, more urbane. He'd gone to college and lived in New York City. He hadn't spent his whole life dirty and sweaty.

Hope softened. "James, can we all sit down and talk?"

Yeah, Noah could talk a blue streak, and all James could do was sit there and be the idiot cowboy. "Ain't no reason to talk, baby. You want Noah, have at it."

Her fists clenched at her sides. "I didn't say that. I said I wanted to talk to him. James, he's your brother."

"He's no blood of mine." Noah wanted to walk off with the girl. It was what he'd always done. "My family is buried on the north hill, and it's going to stay that way. This ranch is the only thing that matters."

He'd always known it deep down. It was the truth of his life. He'd had a vision of clarity years ago as he'd stood in the driveway and watched Noah drive off toward a future they should have shared. God, had he not forgiven his brother for that, either? Had he not forgiven him for going off to college?

And why should he? If the shoe had been on the other foot, he wouldn't have left. He would have stayed and worked the ranch with Noah.

"James, that's not true." Her face had softened and she stepped a bit closer.

He backed away. "What do you know about it? Do you have any sisters? You ever had one of them betray you?"

Her hand fluttered up as though she wanted to touch him, but she drew it back. "That's not what happened. He was young and stupid. He made a terrible mistake but it doesn't mean he didn't love you."

That simply proved she didn't know a damn thing. "You weren't here. And I don't care how young and stupid he was. He can't expect to let the fact that he was a dumb kid excuse his behavior. I was a year older, and I did the right thing. I didn't run away from my obligations. That kind of thing can't be made right."

Hope went stark white, the color and sympathy leaving her face in an instant. "I guess you're right. You can never fix some mistakes."

She turned and walked out.

James picked up his boots and followed her. "Don't you walk away from me."

She didn't turn, but he saw her head shake. "I'm leaving. I'll call Lucy to come get me."

God, they were back to that again? "You will not."

She reached the front door and finally looked at him. Tears streaked down her face and his heart twisted at the sight.

"I will," she replied. "I'm not going to let you use me to punish Noah. And you're right. I don't know him. I'm an idiot. Sometimes I think I never learn, but I will this time. You go on and find your perfect woman who never did anything wrong and doesn't have a past. The rest of us aren't good enough for you."

And he deserved that, why? "I was talking about Noah, baby. I wasn't talking about you. Hell, you *are* perfect. Come on. Come back to bed and we can talk. Just you and me. Tell me what's going on, and I'll take care of it. I'll take care of you. I won't let anything or anyone hurt you."

He would wrap her in his care. He would make damn sure nothing ever made her sad again.

Except losing Noah. If he did this, would she always miss Noah? Would she come to hate him for forcing her to choose?

She shook her head, tears falling. "No. If you really knew me, you wouldn't want me anymore. I can see that now. It's better to walk away."

She opened the door and walked out.

James followed. How had everything gone so damn wrong? What could Hope have done? "If you think I'm going to let you go, you're wrong."

Hope stopped on the porch, her shoulders squared. "I think you're going to have to. It looks like you have company."

James followed her line of sight. Noah was walking out of the house followed by Trev, Henry Flanders, and a woman. *Fuck. Fuck. Fuck.*

Serena walked with them, a bottle of champagne in her hand and a smile on her face. He was screwed.

"Not serious, huh?" Hope asked.

"No. It is not serious. We went on exactly two dates. I have been utterly open and honest with you. I slept with her, yes, but I didn't promise her anything." He was starting to panic. What the hell was he going to do if Hope walked out? He'd spent so much time running from her, but now the thought of not knowing where she was made him nauseous. Hope was his. She had to be because he couldn't imagine his life without her.

"You didn't make any promises to me, either, James." Her face was flat, without a lick of emotion past the tears.

Fine. He could do that. Finally something he had control over. He reached for her hand, covering it with his own. She was cold. "You want a promise. I'll make you a promise. We're going to get married, Hope. Do you want to go to Vegas tonight? Or we can file for a license and have a big party."

Hope dragged her hand out of his, a look of horror dawning on her face. "I can't marry you. Oh, god, James, you don't even know me."

His head was reeling. "What is that supposed to mean?"

"James!" Serena tottered on her ridiculously high heels as she pushed past Noah on the lawn. "James, I came all the way out here to bring you a surprise."

Hope sighed. "It's not a surprise, Serena. Your coat's open.

Everyone can see your boobs."

It was said without a hint of venom. Hope seemed to just be pointing out a fact of life, but Serena's face went up in flames, and she turned her attention to Hope as she retied her coat.

"I didn't look, baby." James didn't even want to. Serena was a lovely woman, and he had nothing at all against her, but Hope was it for him. He wouldn't look at the Serenas of the world ever again.

Serena's eyes narrowed on Hope. "What are you doing here? God, Hope, you're pathetic. You couldn't get Logan. Wolf wouldn't look twice at you. So now you're going after James. Again."

Okay. Now he had something against Serena. He wasn't about to let anyone talk to his woman that way. He stepped close to Hope, but she held out a hand.

"Don't even bother. I can handle this." She leaned against the porch rail. "Logan was my friend, Serena. I know it shocks you that I could have a male who's only a friend because a woman like you needs to believe every man in the world wants to sleep with her. I love Logan because of the man he is and not because he has a dick that I can control him with. As for Wolf Meyer, he's a friend, too. I knew he was going to leave soon. I don't start short-term relationships with men who won't stick around. And I sure as hell don't show up naked at a man's home in the desperate hope that I might keep him. Go away. He's not going to get serious with you. And the truth is, you don't really want him to."

"How the fuck do you know what I want?" Serena fairly vibrated with rage.

James had wanted to save Hope, but it looked like she was going to save him.

"Take a deep whiff, Serena. Give it a minute for the wind to pick up." Hope breathed deeply. "There it is."

James nearly laughed out loud at the look of horror that crossed Serena's face.

"What is that?" Serena asked, gagging a little.

"That would be animal feces." Hope didn't even hold her nose.

"Sorry, the herd is close in today," Trev explained in his deep, Texas accent. "Doc here is going to check them all out tomorrow."

"I am?" Noah asked.

"Yep," Trev replied.

At least someone was properly handling Noah.

Hope gestured at the pasture in the distance, her eyes still on Serena. "This is ranch life. You look around here and see wealth, but the truth of the matter is everything is going back into the business. All of James's money is tied up in the land. He's not going to take you on fabulous vacations. Do you know what a great vacation is for a rancher? Heading to another ranch to check out bulls. So as James's beloved wife, you're going to get to watch a whole lot of bulls performing. Sexy."

"Are you ready to run a house?" Noah asked Serena. "Because our momma worked hard every day to keep this place up."

"He doesn't have a housekeeper?" Serena asked, her eyes uncertain for the first time.

"He barely has ranch hands. Some asshole took the cash he needed and left him to deal with everything alone, so all he can offer you is hard work." Noah stared at James while he explained ranch life. "It's why he didn't go after the woman he wanted all this time. It's why he stayed away from Hope. He didn't have anything to offer her."

"Uhm, I can offer incredible sex." James felt a little hot under the collar listening to Hope and Noah explain how crappy his life was. It was all true, but it made him sound pathetic. "And I have some money now. And I was planning a trip to Montana. Hope, it's beautiful up there. I think you'll love it."

"The purpose of this trip?" Hope asked.

Damn it. "I have to go look at a bull."

Hope whipped her finger in the air. "See, cow porn. Woo-hoo."

He felt himself blush. "Well, there was going to be more to it. Trust me, there will be a lot of human porn going on, too."

Yeah, that was romantic.

"Montana? You were going to take me to Montana?" Serena sounded offended at the thought.

James sighed. "No. I wasn't going to take you anywhere. I'm taking my fiancée."

Noah's mouth dropped open. "You asked Hope to marry you?"

"Not really. He kind of told me, and then his ex showed up

wearing a trench coat and a smile." Hope's lower lip sort of pouted out.

Yep. He was in trouble. He always screwed up the romantic stuff. Noah was better at it. "We are getting married."

"And apparently we're going to spend our honeymoon measuring bull penises." She turned back to Serena. "You should run as fast as those heels will take you."

Henry frowned at the whole group. "I think I'm going to talk to Stef about bringing in a therapist. Maybe we could get a group rate."

"You're not marrying Hope," Noah shouted.

"I am, too." James squared off with his brother.

"I think I had this dream already," Hope muttered under her breath. She stopped and walked down the steps toward Serena, who now clutched at her trench coat. "Did you leave a flower on James's truck earlier today?"

She was back on that? James thought they had cleared that up. "I told you it was Serena. But I doubt now that you and Noah have explained to her what a crap-ass catch I am that she's going to be leaving me any more flowers. She gets it. Hope is the only woman in the world who wants to put up with my shit."

Serena ignored him for once. She shook her head. "No. I didn't leave anything for him. I was at rehearsal earlier today. I'll be honest, I only pulled this dumb stunt because I heard a rumor that he was hanging around you. I kind of thought he was loaded. Now that I know the truth, uhm, you can have him. I mean he's hot and all, but he talks way too much about cows and feed and stuff."

Would his humiliation never end? "Well, you talked about stuff I didn't know anything about either."

"James," Serena protested. "I talked about the news and art."

Bingo. City talk.

"Hope, are you all right?" Henry moved forward. "Do I need to call Doc again?"

"No. I'm fine, but I need to leave. Henry, will you give me a ride out to Nate's place?" She didn't look at James.

Noah walked straight up to her and took her hand, feeling her pulse. "You're anxious. You need to sit down and you need to talk. Henry said a man was in town asking questions about you."

"What the hell?" James forgot about Serena. He stared at his brother. "Why didn't anyone tell me?"

"You were busy," Noah shot back. "You were too busy screwing her to take care of her."

James's blood was pounding through his system. "Someone should have come to get me. I'm her man. I'm the one who's marrying her."

"You're not marrying her," Noah insisted.

Hope turned away from both of them. "I'm not marrying anyone. I'm leaving."

Noah nodded as though making a decision. "I'll take you, darlin'. I'll grab my stuff, and we can get out of here."

She shook her head. "No. I am not going anywhere with either one of you. I will not be the toy you two fight over one minute more."

"I told you I want to marry you." James couldn't let her walk away. He definitely couldn't let her walk away with Noah. He would lose his woman and his brother because Hope wouldn't fuck it all up. She would be a good wife, and Noah would be gone.

He would lose everything.

Hope wouldn't look at him. "It doesn't matter now. In a couple of hours, you'll be very happy I left."

"Why don't we move this into the house?" Trev said, his face closing off. "We're not alone out here, and I think Hope needs to talk."

"I do not need to talk, Trev," Hope insisted.

Trev took a step forward, his mouth a grim line. He seemed to be trying to keep the conversation between him and Hope. Like they had a secret or something. Despite how low Trev's voice got, James could still make out his words. "Oh, I think you do. Do you understand what you're risking? Tell me you don't want it right now. I see the way your hands are shaking. If you need me to, I'll take you into Alamosa. There's a meeting at five o'clock. We can make most of it."

Serena looked around at the group. "These people are all crazy. Damn, Hope, come with me. We can go back to my place in Creede. I think we both need a good long drink."

"That is the last fucking thing she needs," Trev said, his voice harsh.

It was all out of control. Hope looked pale and fragile. What had happened to put that look on her face? And why was Trev McNamara, the poster boy for drug rehab, talking like he was Hope's sponsor? The only meetings Trev went to in Alamosa were AA meetings.

Hope? An addict?

Was that what she was covering up?

He was going about this all wrong. He was letting Noah get him riled up when he needed to be focused on Hope.

He took her hand and pulled her into his arms, something inside him relaxing when she laid her head on his chest. "Baby, if you need to go to some meeting, I'll take you. I'll take you into Alamosa, and I'll come in with you or I'll wait outside. It's going to be okay. Noah can come with us if you want."

If she was this close to the edge, he damn sure wasn't going to put more pressure on her.

"I want to go to Nate's. I want to see Nate." Even as she insisted, her arms wound around him.

Nate Wright. What the hell did she have going on with Nathan Wright, and why did the sheriff know more about Hope than her own lover? Jealousy burned in his gut. He'd watched Noah make love to Hope and he'd been irritated, but Nate Wright knowing her secret pissed him off.

"Why do you need to talk to Wright?" Noah's voice was a hard growl. He must be feeling the same brutal jealousy.

"It looks like the sheriff's already on his way." Henry pointed to the long drive that led from the highway to the house.

Sure enough, there was the Bronco charging up the drive, dust flying behind its wheels. The lights weren't on, but there was zero doubt that whoever was driving was in a hurry.

Hope shrank back, coming out of his arms.

Cameron Briggs, the acting sheriff of Bliss County, got out of the car, his face set in deep lines. This wasn't the Cam that James drank with on occasion. This Cam was a lawman, and he'd come to do a job.

A deep fear settled in James's heart. Something very bad was about to happen. He stepped in front of Hope only to find his brother was already standing there. They formed a phalanx, attempting to hide Hope.

Cam wasn't fooled. "Hope, I need you to come to the station with me."

"She's not going anywhere." He said the words before he thought them.

"What's going on?" Noah asked.

Cam stared through them as though he could see Hope. "I need you to come with me, Hope. Your husband is here."

James felt the world tilt out of place.

Husband.

"All right." Hope stepped around them. "I'd like to talk to Nate before I go in."

Cam nodded. "You can talk to Nate on the radio in the car, but Hope, this man who claims to be your husband has some mighty nasty accusations against you. And he has the paperwork to back it up. If you want to head out, I could always say I couldn't find you."

James still couldn't get that one word out of his brain. The only woman he'd ever loved was married to another man. His head was reeling. His stomach felt sick. Hope was married. She hadn't argued with the accusation. She'd asked to talk to Nate.

"She's not going anywhere." Noah reached for her, but she moved toward Cam.

"I am. I have to know if it's really him. I have to see it for myself. Good-bye." Hope turned toward the Bronco.

"Good-bye? All you can say is good-bye?" Noah practically screamed at her. He slapped James across the chest. "Are you going to let her walk out?"

He wasn't sure of anything anymore. He took a step back, his feet stumbling. Hope had lied. Hope was married. She belonged to another man.

He watched as the Bronco took her away toward her husband and wondered if he would ever feel whole again.

Chapter Thirteen

Noah wasn't quite sure what had happened. He only knew that his brother was sitting on his ass while their woman was being driven away in a goddamn cop car.

She was gone. She'd walked away, a hollow look on her face, like everything was already over.

"Why are you sitting here?" Noah asked, the words grinding out of his mouth. James wasn't supposed to sit on his ass. James was the guy on the white horse who rode through hell to save everyone.

"She's married."

Yeah, James seemed pretty damn caught on that.

"I'm going to call Callie in case Nate is fishing. It seems like he knows more about this than the rest of us. Callie will let everyone in town know what's going on." Henry walked back toward the main house, Serena following.

"You two need to get your shit together or that girl is going to be in trouble." Trev stalked off, too, leaving him alone with his brother.

"Get off your ass, Jamie. We have to go into town." He would rather have had the chance to talk to her before she'd left. Given what the acting sheriff had said, something very bad was going on.

"She's married. She's not yours and she's not mine. She's fucking married." There was a red rim to James's eyes that spoke of his emotion. James never cried. Never even came close. He could almost lose a fucking limb and the most he would say was "ow." The last time James had cried had been the day he'd buried their father.

Noah softened his voice. "Yes, she's married. And she's scared of him. She's terrified. This is what she was afraid of."

"She didn't tell me. She let me make love to her and let me ask her to marry me and never once did she bother to tell me she was already married."

Stubborn. His brother had always been stubborn. "She was afraid, still is. And from what I can tell, you didn't ask her to marry you. You told her you were getting married. Where is the romance in that? She needed to hear how you felt, not some order. You fucked this up. Now get off your ass and come into town with me, or I'll leave you here and I won't look back."

He would leave. He would go after Hope, but he was lying about never looking back. If James wouldn't be swayed, Noah would go, but he'd miss his brother forever. He'd miss the ranch.

James sat there, his head hung. Noah thought about what Trev had said. James had a big wall around him, and nothing he'd done so far had even started to bring it down.

"I'll do it, Jamie. I'll walk into the house, and I'll pack a bag for me and a bag for Hope. I'll drive into town and I will get her out of there one way or another, and then we're going to run. You won't see us again. You can stay here on your precious ranch and rot. You'll have the cows to keep you company. Are you so fucking scared that you're going to let her go into god knows what alone?"

James didn't even look up. "She's going to see her husband. Are you going to take her away from her husband?"

"I damn well am," he shot back. "If she loved him so much, what is she doing out here? Shouldn't you listen to the story before you judge her?"

"She lied."

Noah was ready to pull his own hair out. James was sitting here while Hope was getting farther and farther away. "We all fucking lie. You know what, brother, maybe Hope was right. You were using her to pay me back. What does that make you? Do you realize what our parents would think of you right now? Fuck you, Jamie. I'm going to get my woman and figure out what the hell is going on."

He turned his back. He was done. He owed his brother, but Hope was in immediate danger, and he'd meant what he'd said. He was going to get her. If he could bring her back to the ranch, he would. If he couldn't, then he would take her and run.

He didn't get past the end of the porch before he was tackled from behind. James hit him with the power of a locomotive. Noah groaned as he hit the dirt, the breath knocking out of him. He tasted grass. He felt a hand on his collar and then damn near choked as he was hauled bodily off the ground.

"You motherfucker," James yelled, his face red with rage. "You think you can walk back in and I'll just act like nothing happened? You think she can lie to my face and I'll just be fine with it?"

His brother's fist flew straight at his face, and Noah wished that the breakthrough Trev had promised him James would have wasn't about to come at the cost of his face. He took the first punch, his head snapping back, and then a certain mad pleasure took over.

Pain. Feeling. How long since he'd felt truly alive and connected to his brother? He'd fallen hard for Hope, and he'd thought she could bring them together, but he finally genuinely understood what his parents had found. It wasn't simply a woman who held his dads together. They had cared about each other, too. They had needed each other. They couldn't have a chance with Hope until they got their shit together.

His whole face lit up with shock and sharp, biting pain as James struck again.

"You fucking left. She's leaving. Why don't you both leave together, and don't you fucking come back this time."

There was the heart of the problem. He'd left, and James thought he hadn't looked back because Noah hadn't told him. His brother had no idea how often he'd sat and stared at the phone and prayed for the courage to pick it up. "Jamie, come on, man. I'm not going to leave again."

James's eyes flared, and for a moment, Noah thought he might have gotten through to him, but then he pushed Noah away with a disdainful huff. "I don't give a shit what you do."

He turned his back, and Noah couldn't take that. For all the mistakes he'd made, he didn't deserve his brother treating him like a piece of dirt. With a low growl, Noah attacked. He plowed into his brother, his fist flying. He didn't speak. If James didn't want to listen to him talk, then they could do it this way.

He grunted as his fist met hard muscle. He was grateful for all those hours he'd spent in the gym, lifting weights and running on a treadmill for so long and so hard that he almost could run from his trouble. James rolled, kicking out, and Noah tasted dirt again.

There was a sad whining as Butch showed up. He moved restlessly as Noah and James rolled in the dirt, grunting and kicking and punching.

If he'd properly trained that damn dog, he could force him to kill his brother. But no, Noah had to treat the dog right and turn him into a huge teddy bear who whined and howled at a little violence.

"You're such a shit, Noah." James kicked up, his face bleeding from a cut on his cheek.

"Yeah, well, you're a stubborn asshole." He punched his brother straight in the gut.

James groaned, his breath huffing out of his chest. "Go. Get the fuck off my land."

"You would like that, wouldn't you, you coward?" Noah got to his knees as his brother stood back up. They circled each other like two animals waiting to attack.

"I don't need you. That's what you don't seem to understand. I have a partner."

Noah was sick of being told how unnecessary he was. "No, you have Trev. Trev already has a partner. You have a friend who you own a business with. It's not the same thing."

"Well, I don't need anything else," James argued.

"Really? Then why have you spent the last several years sharing women with Logan and that Wolf guy? You've spent years trying to replace me. It's not going to work. There's only one me. I might be an asshole, but no one else is your brother."

"You are no blood of mine." James stopped and stared at Noah, his eyes dark.

Noah shook his head. The words hurt, but they weren't a lie. "No. I'm not your blood. But I am the other fucking half of your soul, and no amount of blood will ever trump that."

James's whole body sagged. He slumped to the ground, his ass hitting the dirt. He wiped his hand across his face, coming away with sweat and blood. "It doesn't matter. Stay or go. It doesn't matter."

Noah understood the underlying words. It didn't matter now because she was gone. How had the last several years affected his brother? James had had to scratch and claw to keep the ranch afloat only to watch a fire take a good portion of his acreage. He'd had to watch their dad fade away. He'd had to make the difficult decision to sell half his land. Noah looked at his brother. He didn't not care about Hope. He simply believed that everything would go wrong in the end.

Noah dragged a deep breath into his body. "I'm not going anywhere. I made a mistake by leaving in the first place. I knew it three days after I got married. I realized it wouldn't work because she didn't want me. She wanted someone she'd made up in her head."

"She wanted your ten million dollars," James pointed out.

"Yeah, well, she got it."

There was a long pause before James finally spoke again. "Why the fuck should I believe you?"

He sank down to the dirt beside his brother. He might not be a Glen by blood, but now he realized this land was his birthright, too. He touched the grass beneath him. It was cool against his skin, but in the summer, sometimes the very ground radiated the heat of the sun. In the winter, it would be blanketed with snow and the world would look pristine and perfect for miles. The Circle G. His father had bled for this land. His father had found a home here and love. He'd found his other half, and then he'd been lucky enough to discover the woman who could complete him. He'd found it here. On this land.

"I won't leave again because this is my home." He felt it deep down. He was connected to this piece of earth. He was connected to his brother. "Because every minute I was away, I ached."

"Then why the fuck did you leave? It seemed to me that you were always looking for a way out."

Noah stared at his brother. "That's not true."

"You went to college fast enough."

Fuck. They were back to that? "And I got through five years of school in three. I worked my ass off. I didn't do anything but study. You seem to think I had some wild time in college while you were stuck here. I worked. I became a vet because this ranch needed one. Do you have any idea how hard it was to be your brother? I had to make a place for myself or I would be incidental. I wanted to matter to this place, to our family."

"What the hell are you talking about?" James ran a frustrated hand through his hair. "You were the smart one. I was the one who couldn't do anything but work a herd of cows."

"Yes, that's why there's a shelf full of medals and trophies with your name on it. That's why our parents kept a whole cabinet to show off the buckles you won."

James frowned. "Great. I can keep my ass on a bull for a whole eight seconds. You got through college."

He'd never dreamed his brother was jealous. "You would have, too."

James shook his head. "Nah. It was for the best. I don't need a damn degree to haul cow shit."

Noah was at a loss. James did way more than shovel cow crap. "You run this whole ranch. That takes talent. You can still go to college if you want to. You could get a business degree. Hell, you could do a bunch of it online. You don't even have to stop working."

James shook his head. "I can't. I'm too old for that now. Just go away. I don't need you hanging out around here."

His brother was stubborn to the end. In the distance, he could hear a loud huff as one of the hands let Red out. The horse bucked, and the man took a step back. He'd had a couple of carrots, but he tossed them away, probably because he didn't want to get his fingers bitten off.

"You're like that horse, Jamie. You're so scared that you won't let anyone touch you anymore, and I did that. I can't tell you how sorry I am."

James stared off in the distance, watching as Red snorted and kicked. "Why didn't you call? You sit here and tell me how sorry you are and how sad you were at the time, but you never called me. Not once. I had to call you to tell you our dad died."

Noah's heart hurt because this was the part he didn't want to admit. "I was ashamed. I didn't love Ally. I loved the fact that she picked me. I was out of college, but I was still a jealous little boy. I was still trying to prove to someone, anyone, that I was as good as you."

James looked at him, his mouth twisted in a frown. "No one ever did a damn thing to make you feel that way. I loved you. You were my brother."

"And you were the mountain I never could climb." Noah sighed. "It wasn't you. You didn't make me feel that way. You were the best damn brother I could have had. I did it. I was a jealous little shit, and when I woke up and realized what I had done, I couldn't come home because I was too ashamed to face you."

"Why now?"

"Because somewhere along the way I grew up," Noah said, his words quiet. His muscles ached from the beating he'd taken, but there was a certain contentment that came with finally getting to explain himself. "I can't let the mistake I made in the past keep me from what I want. I can't let it keep me away from my home. And I won't let it keep me away from Hope."

"How could she lie like that?"

"How could you let her walk away?"

James took a long breath. "Because I guess I expected it."

"Yes. Because it's what I did. Because our parents died. Damn it, the world can't stay the same. We can wish for it, but it still burns down all around us. It still goes to shit, but isn't it better to have someone to hold on to? You talk about how bad the last years of our parents' lives were, but I don't think they would have changed a minute of it. I don't know what happens when we die, but I believe somehow, someway, they found their way back together. He wasn't fading. He was waiting. He was waiting to see them again. I swear I'll do the same if I'm the last one of us left. I'll be true. I'll wait to see you and Hope again."

James's head hit his hands and a strangled sound came out of his throat. "I love her. I tried not to, but I love her. I don't think I can be enough."

Noah put a hand on his brother's shoulder. "You aren't. Don't even try to be. Jamie, we started down this path a long time ago. I derailed us. I'm trying to get us back on track. I'm not enough for her. She deserves us both. We deserve the family we always wanted, but we're going to have to fight to get it."

"You don't deserve shit, brother." But it was said with a chuckle. James's face came up. His eyes were red rimmed. "She didn't tell me because she was afraid. If she's married and she ran from him, then he's bad. He's going to try to hurt her. She's scared of him."

Finally, Noah could breathe again. "Yeah. I think we know why she's been anxious. And I think he's been stalking her. If Serena didn't leave the flower, then it was him. Hope freaked out when she saw it."

"Why go through the sheriff?"

Noah thought about what Cam Briggs had said. "He said this guy was making some serious accusations about her. He's had a plan about how he can get her back. He'll use those accusations to scare her to come back to him. We have to go after her. We can't let this man take our woman."

James got to his feet, offering Noah a hand. "You still know how to shoot?"

"Yeah, but I hope it doesn't come to that. We need to talk to her, find out what's going on."

His brother's jaw hardened, forming that stubborn line he knew so well. When James's face went cold and his eyes settled into a predatory gaze, he was locked in. Nothing would stand in his way, Noah knew.

"You talk, brother. I'll do what I do best. I'll plow my way through."

Noah had to run to keep up with him.

* * * *

Hope forced herself not to look back. She was driving away from the Circle G. She was driving away from Noah and James and back into a nightmare.

Had she ever really left the nightmare? Weren't James and Noah simply a dream?

She could still see the look on James's handsome face when Cam had said the word "husband."

She was a liar, a coward, an addict. She didn't deserve either one of them.

"You want to tell me what's going on?" Cam asked.

"What did he say his name was?" He probably wasn't using Christian Grady anymore.

"He said his name is Christopher Jones. He has a marriage certificate."

Hope laughed a bit. "It's a fake. I married a man named Christian Grady, though who knows what his real name is."

"I bet I can find out." Cam's steely gaze remained on the road ahead of him.

"You should stay out of it." It would be safer for him.

Cam's eyes narrowed as he turned his head slightly. "Not on your life. You might have known Logan longer, but I care about you, too. And Nate would damn straight have my hide if I kept my nose out of it. Now, this man is obviously dangerous."

"Really? He's usually quite charming." Cam wasn't responding the way she'd thought he would. Everyone who met Christian liked him. It was one of the ways he'd managed to do what he did. He charmed people out of their life savings and stole their identities while they were far too busy listening to his lines of bullshit to realize he was robbing them blind.

And when someone found out, he simply slit a throat and no one talked.

Not even Hope.

"I was BAU for a long time," Cam reminded her. "Rafe and Laura were better profilers than me, but I know a dangerous asshole when I see one. Did he hit you?"

"Never." Christian had been the perfect husband. Gentle. Kind. Never uttering a foul word in her presence. Unfortunately, he was also completely insane and a master criminal. "He never hurt me."

"Who then? Because I don't believe a word he's saying. He says you escaped from a private mental institution."

She wondered how Christian intended to get her out of here without causing too much of a fuss. It was a nice play. If the local authorities thought she was insane, they wouldn't listen to a word she said about Christian. And she was sure he could produce the paperwork to prove it. If he'd survived the fire, then he would have built his network back up. He would have had some cash at his disposal. "No. I was insane when I married him. I was perfectly sane when I tried to kill him. I just wasn't very good at it."

How was he alive? How had he survived? She'd been so sure when she'd walked away from the house they had shared that he was gone. She'd felt the heat, heard the sirens, and she'd walked away with a suitcase full of clothes and some cash. She'd gotten into the small car her husband had bought her and driven away. Years had passed, and she'd waited for the police to catch up to her. No one had ever come after her. She'd waited, and when she'd realized no one was going to storm in to take her to jail, she'd begun punishing herself. After she'd found Bliss, Nate had run a check and discovered no one was looking for her at all.

Cam turned brilliant blue eyes on her. "The report from the Atlanta police department shows no sign of foul play. The police explained it as a fire started by a faulty heater."

She turned in the seat. She'd made damn sure the heater got kicked over on to a pile of rags. "How do you know about that?"

Cam sighed. "All anyone ever sees is this body. Really, I have a brain, too. The minute that man walked in, I rifled through Nate's files. The boss wouldn't leave anything to chance. He has a file on you. You married Christian Grady at the age of seventeen. You lied on your marriage license. It's not a valid marriage. You lived with him for almost two years and helped him build his conservancy business."

She felt herself flush, but she wasn't going to sugarcoat this.

"Call it what it is, Cam. No pussyfooting around."

Cam shrugged but gave her what she wanted. "You helped him build his cult. Did you know he was a con artist?"

She snorted a little. "No, Cam. I didn't. I was stupid, and I bought into everything he said. He brought people in with his talk about god or the universe dwelling in nature. He went after anyone with a love for the environment and a slightly liberal bent. He knew where to hit. He knew what to say."

"He's a con artist. That's what they do. But I think he's something more."

"Are you going to go? The light turned green a while back." Hope stared at the light. It was a luminous green, but the Bronco sat there.

Cam's fingers drummed on the steering wheel. "We have some time. I would rather go back knowing what I'm getting into. Don't worry. Laura and Rafe have everything under control."

"Did they see what you saw?" She felt a certain peace and vindication that Cam hadn't fallen under Christian's spell. She'd been dumb, but that didn't mean everyone was. When she'd fled Georgia, she'd believed the law was after her. Having someone on her side meant the world.

A vision of James and Noah assailed her. She'd had both of them on her side—until they knew the truth. She couldn't get the look on James's face out of her head. He'd gone hot, like a fever had taken him, and then so, so cold. She would never be able to look him in the face again. Never. But she would feel his hands on her body for the rest of her life.

She loved Noah and James, and she'd lost them over mistakes she'd made at seventeen. The past never went away. It merely hid until the time was right to pounce.

"What does he look like?" Hope asked, ignoring the fact that the light had changed and Cam still hadn't moved.

Maybe it was one of his followers. She'd left with money. Oh, she'd run through it. There wasn't a dime left of the fifty thousand she'd taken. Seven years had handily taken care of that. She'd spent the last several years dirt poor, but they might think she knew where more was.

"Blond. He had light blond hair. It's past his shoulders."

Her vision narrowed. Christian. Her heart raced. How had he survived? She felt her whole body start to tremble.

"Thank god. They took long enough." Cam breathed a huge sigh of relief as he looked in the rearview mirror. A big Chevy was barreling up the road. James's truck.

Oh, god, what was he doing?

"You should move, Cam. Why don't you turn on the lights and get going?" The last thing she needed was a scene with her ex-lovers. Could she even call them that? She'd had one moment with each, but she feared she would never forget them. "We should get to the station."

Cam still wasn't moving. "Not on your life, sweetheart. See, I've been in this position before. If someone had been smart enough and kind enough to delay Laura, then I wouldn't have lost five goddamn years of my life. I knew they would come around. I just needed to give them time."

Them. The Chevy stopped behind the Bronco. She could hear the brakes slam into place. Two doors opened as James and Noah jumped out. James had a shotgun in his hand. He looked like the hero of an old Western, charging in to save his woman. Noah had a shotgun, too, but he also had a dog. It did soften him a bit.

"Cam, I'm going to have to ask that you let Hope go." James held the shotgun at his side, but there was no question he was willing to use it. Caveman.

Cam rolled his eyes. "Well, I gave you the out before, but you were too dumb to use it."

"That's fair," James admitted. "Damn, man, how did we catch up to you?"

"I drove really fucking slow." Cam put the Bronco in park. "I need you involved in this, but you have to understand that she needs to see this guy, to make sure it's him and not someone else. We need to know what we're up against."

"Maybe she just needs to run," Noah said.

She couldn't. Not now. If Christian was alive, then she needed to figure out what he was truly after.

"No," James said, his voice firm. "We handle it, no matter what it is. This is Bliss. This is the last stop. You find your way here, and you stay here. I'm not letting some asshole take our wife."

Our? Tears blurred her eyes. He didn't know the truth. He wouldn't want her when he knew, but the idea that he'd come after her made her heart pound. She loved James. She loved Noah. She would give anything to change the past so she could be worthy of them.

She realized in that moment that she was so much more heartbroken than afraid. Losing them would be worse than losing her life.

"Hope, you should get out of the car." Cam pointed to the door.

"Why?"

"Uhm, because this is what we call a jailbreak, and I would prefer to not make it look good. I can just say I couldn't find you rather than James shooting me." Cam held out his hands as though to ask what she was waiting for. "I'll figure out a way for you to ID this guy from afar."

It was a sweet gesture, but she couldn't take it. "I'd rather face him."

It was past time to deal with Christian. If he really was alive, she needed to take the situation in hand. She thought she'd avenged Elaine, but if she hadn't, she would bring the law in—no matter what.

"Get out of the car, Hope. If you want to go into the station, you go in with your men, not the law." Noah opened her door. "That way this guy knows you're protected."

"Please, go." She didn't want to beg, but it was better than them hearing her story. She might walk in with them, but there was no way she would walk out with them. They would leave once they heard her story.

"Not a chance, baby. Cam's a big boy. He can take one for the team if he has to. It's your choice." James pulled the shotgun up, getting Cam squarely in his sights.

"Oh, you're going to pay for that, Glen. The next bar fight we have, I won't hold back. Your ass is mine." Cam swore revenge with a smile on his face, obviously not terribly worried that James would actually shoot.

Hope shook her head. She'd steeled herself. She wasn't backing away now. "I have to go with Cam. I have to see him. I have to know it's him."

She couldn't stay in this odd limbo of not knowing. She couldn't handle it. She'd fooled herself for weeks, but now she had to be sure. She had to know if he'd caught her. She had to know if it was time to fight.

Noah looked at his brother, and they appeared to have an entire conversation via facial tics and short, sharp hand gestures. Finally, Noah unsnapped her seat belt and took her in hand. "You're coming with us, darlin'."

"No," she protested even as her arms went around his neck. He hauled her close to his chest. She felt better than she had in an hour, feeling his warmth and strength around her, but she knew it was a lie.

"You keep quiet or I will spank that sweet ass right here on Main Street, and they won't do a damn thing to save you." James pointed up the road.

Hope turned her head and saw what he was referencing.

A mob stood outside the sheriff's office. Hope checked the sob that caught in her throat. Max and Rye stood there with Rachel. Callie and Zane were holding hands, each with a stroller in front of them. Stef was showing Jen how to load a shotgun. She knew Rafe and Laura were inside. Alexei and Holly and Caleb were talking to Nell and Mel and Cassie. Stella had a pitcher in her hand, pouring her famous lemonade as her husband, Sebastian, gave everyone a glass. Teeny, Logan's mom, followed behind with a plate of what looked to be fudge. Teeny firmly believed that fudge was required at all tragic events. Marie, her partner, her wife, stood behind, shotgun in hand. Lucy, sweet Lucy, turned her head and saw the Bronco had stopped. Bliss had come out to protect its own—her.

Tears streamed down her face. Twenty-seven years she'd longed for a family only to find one in the backwoods of Colorado.

She was going to let them all down.

But Noah wasn't allowing her to go. He leaned close. "It's going to be all right. Trust us. We trust you."

"You shouldn't," she whispered.

He shook his head. "I'm a deeply forgiving man."

"I'm not," James said with a wink. "But I think you'll find I'm different when it comes to you. We'll go in there with you, but then we're taking you back to the G, and the three of us are going to talk. Noah and I aren't going to let you run the show anymore."

That one statement was enough to bring her out of her misery for a moment. "Since when have I run anything?"

James winked at her before turning back to Cam. "Sheriff, I'm carrying this gun in case I need to go hunting. You know how it is. A man never can tell when he's going to get hungry."

Cam snorted. "Yeah, that seems to be going around. Every man in the county seems to be hunting today. It should send a message to this guy when he leaves the station. I think Nate already put the fear of god into him."

"Nate's in there?" Hope asked.

"Oh, baby, we're going to have such a talk about Nate. You're not going to be running to Nate anymore. You're going to run to your men. Is that understood?" James's mouth was a grim line as he nodded to Cam. "We'll see you in a minute."

Before she could protest, Noah hauled her back to the truck, Butch in tow. She settled between them, and James took off.

* * * *

Christian stared at the blonde. She was smiling and saying all the right things, but something was wrong. Something was wrong with all of them.

He glanced up at the clock. An hour. It had already taken that damn cop an hour, and he wasn't back with Hope yet.

Yes, something was terribly wrong.

"Don't worry," the blonde who had introduced herself as Laura said. "Cam will find her. He thinks she's probably on the mountain. It's pretty remote out there, but he'll find her."

He kept his mouth shut when he wanted to tell the dumb bitch that his wife wasn't on the mountain. She was at her lovers' ranch. He'd learned a lot about the ranch where his wife was staying, including the fact that she was screwing at least one, probably both, of the brothers who lived there.

But he forced his mouth closed. The deputy, a large, dark-haired man, stared at him from behind his desk. Not ten minutes before another man had walked in, apparently the actual sheriff. He'd closed himself in an office after Acting Sheriff Briggs had gone in search of Hope.

There was an awful lot of activity in this sleepy little mountain sheriff's station.

"I'm sorry," he said, attempting to look as wistful as possible. "It's been a long time since I saw my wife. I've been horribly worried about her. She can be...unstable."

"So you've told me. She's bipolar?" Laura asked.

"Yes. She's very sweet, but when she gets into a depressive cycle, she's terribly violent toward herself." He wanted to work on the woman's obvious sympathy. If Laura thought Hope would harm herself, she might be more willing to easily turn her over to a man who could take care of her.

"Interesting."

She didn't believe him. It was there in her eyes. He could hear the sheriff in his office. He distinctly heard the words "Atlanta" and "district attorney."

Fuck. Someone knew. He'd counted on Hope hiding her past. It seemed she'd told at least one person, and he doubted Sheriff Wright was going to come down on his side.

His paperwork wouldn't hold up under deep scrutiny. He'd get through a few layers, but if they really dug, he would be found out. He had a couple of his men waiting to help with getting Hope out of here. One was ready to pose as a doctor, the other an orderly. He had plenty of sedatives to keep her nice and compliant.

But if these rubes wouldn't let him out the door, he wasn't sure what he would do.

He'd caught sight of a small mob gathering. What the hell was that about?

Nothing was going as planned.

But he wasn't without his resources. He had other men in town. He'd placed them here after he'd discovered her whereabouts. If he couldn't waltz out on his own, he would have to find another way.

"Laura," Christian began, a plan coming to mind. "I have some paperwork in my car. Would you mind sending someone to get it?"

He wasn't about to walk through that crowd. He'd already spied the back exit.

The deputy, who looked slightly uncomfortable in his khaki uniform, strode forward. "Of course."

"It's on the passenger seat. It's her full psychological profile." He'd had one invented a couple of weeks back when he'd decided to come after her.

He handed Deputy Kincaid the keys with what he hoped was an honest-looking smile. The deputy, who looked far too hard to have spent all of his life in a small town, took the keys. He winked at Laura and started out the door, turning back before it closed. "Cam's here. He's having some trouble with the boys, though. Looks like they're coming in, too."

He smiled back at Christian, but there was no humor to it. "Your wife is coming in. You get to meet her men. I think she's going to want a divorce. If you're telling the truth in the first place."

He walked out, his feet carrying him quickly away. From behind the door to the sheriff's office, he could hear Sheriff Wright mention the name Grady.

Christian knew when he was fucked. He'd been pulling long cons since he was twenty years old. He understood when an operation wasn't going to fly. Hope had these people in the palm of her hand. She was going to win this particular battle. If he was going to win the war, it was time for a retreat.

Laura walked to the door, opening it and saying something to a woman standing outside. He could hear them laughing.

Christian decided it was time to be what he'd been for the last several years—a ghost.

He quietly slipped out the back and retreated to wait for a more proper time.

Chapter Fourteen

James parked the truck and decided he could probably leave the shotgun in the car. It looked like the whole damn town had come out. The only thing they were missing were torches and pitchforks.

His stomach was in knots, and yet he wanted to get in there. He wanted to look at this guy, size him up, and figure out just how bad the situation was. Then he could pick up Hope, throw her back in the truck, take her home, and force her to tell him everything. He would get to the goddamn bottom of this, and Hope would be filing for divorce. He would have to look outside of town to find a lawyer. Stef probably knew someone.

He slid his brother a long look. Noah was out of the truck, holding his hand out for Hope. Hope took it, but there was no masking the anxiety on her face. Her shoulders squared. He wanted to tell Noah to keep her here, that he would handle everything, but that wasn't fair to Hope. This was her fight. He couldn't take it from her. He'd simply make sure she survived it.

He and Noah would make damn sure.

He gave his brother a nod as Noah walked Hope toward him.

Noah's smile was grim, but he felt a deep solidarity with his brother. His brother would lay down his life for Hope.

Would he stay in Bliss?

James wasn't sure, but he had to believe Noah had learned his lesson. He had to try.

They walked through the throng at the front of the building.

"Nate's inside. He wouldn't let the rest of us in, so we're tailgating," Max explained.

"You're tailgating my interrogation?" Hope's lips quirked up, the first smile he'd seen on her in hours.

Zane Hollister stepped forward. "It's not an interrogation. You know that. Nate's making some calls. You go on in there and see if you can identify the bastard. We have to know for sure it's him before Nate can do anything."

Zane knew about Hope's trouble. That information twisted in James's gut. He looked at Callie, and it was written all over her face. She knew, too. Whatever was happening, the Hollister-Wright clan was on the inside. Hope had trusted them with her secrets.

James took a step back, allowing Hope to speak to Zane. His brother immediately moved in.

"Don't," Noah said, his mouth a flat line.

"Don't what?" James asked, but he was pretty sure what his brother was going to say.

Noah kept his voice low. "Don't you pull away from her just because someone else knows what we don't. You can't expect her to open up and lay herself bare. We have to earn that. Apparently Callie and her husbands earned Hope's trust. We're going to earn it by loving her and not making a fight out of this."

Noah had always been the logical one. James felt his doubts start to ebb. His brother was right. He couldn't expect her to tell him some deep, dark secret because he'd fucked her once. He'd screwed up when he'd let her walk away. He wouldn't make the same mistake again.

He reached out and grabbed Hope's hand. "Come on, baby. Let's get this over with so we can get you home."

"James," she started.

The woman wasn't going to listen to reason. He pulled her close and had his lips on hers in a heartbeat. He kissed her, gently forcing her mouth open until he felt her sigh and submit. Her hands found his waist, and her tongue slid against his. He pressed her close to his body, her chest against his.

"Took you long enough, Glen," someone shouted.

There were hoots and hollers, and someone asked if he was planning on sharing.

James decided to make his intentions plain. He dragged his mouth away from hers, pleased at the glazed look in Hope's eyes. Noah stood behind her, his front to her back. James gently turned her around. "You know a Bliss boy always shares with his brother."

Noah didn't hesitate or pay a bit of attention to the catcalls. He put both hands on Hope's backside and dragged her in, molding her lips to his. Hope stood in his arms, a sweet, soft treat.

Their woman.

"You better be glad you decided to share, James Eugene Glen." Teeny shook her small, birdlike head his way as her life partner Marie backed her up. The pair had been like second mothers to him and Noah.

"Your momma would have spanked your bottom red for not sharing with your brother. She taught you better than that," Marie said with a shake of her hand.

Noah finally came up for air. He hugged Hope to him. "She did indeed, Miss Marie. You'll be happy to know that Jamie and I intend to make our parents proud. We're going to marry Hope as soon as we figure out who this fellow is."

"Noah," Hope began.

His brother simply kissed her again. When she came up for air, she tried to push away.

"You can't kiss me every time I protest."

Noah kissed her again.

"Damn it," Hope managed after a moment.

James turned her around. It was his turn. He pulled her close and thrust his tongue in before another word could pass those lips.

She sighed when he finally let her go. "Fine. You're both stubborn. I won't deny you. I won't pretend I don't care. I won't try to leave you, but just know this—I'll let you both go when you want to go. I won't try to hold you to your promises."

She was scared of more than just the man in the station house. She was scared that whatever they heard would cause them to turn from her. Suspicion tried to worm its way in, but he knew Hope. He knew her deep down, and she was beautiful. If she'd done something ugly, it was because she'd had to. He felt a sudden certainty.

Whatever she told him, it wouldn't make a difference. He controlled that. Whatever Hope told him, he would hold on to her because that's what people in love did.

That was what his parents had done. They had clung to each other even after they passed from the earth into whatever happened next.

"It's going to be all right, girl. You don't believe me, but I'll show you." He slapped a hand on his brother's back. "We'll show you."

The doors to the station opened, and Nate Wright stood there, an authoritative glare in his eyes. "Max, Rye, we have a missing man."

Max cursed. "Did he get out the back?"

"He slipped out when Rafe went to his car, so he's on foot." Nate looked up and down the street. "I can't arrest him, but I would like to know where the little fucker is. I'm talking to Atlanta PD right now, but it's going to take time to get anything going. This was a closed case."

James took her hand as Max and Rye stepped away from the crowd and started to strategize about how to find the man. James led her up the steps because now that he knew Hope's husband was on the loose, he wanted to get her inside. He hustled her through the double doors. "You want to tell me what's going on, Nate? Seems to me you know a hell of a lot about my woman."

Nate's eyes rolled. "Well, let me get up to speed because she's been your woman for like an hour. She's been my employee for a whole lot longer, and through most of that time, you stayed clear of her."

"Well he's not staying clear anymore. Now I can't keep him off me," Hope complained.

"Welcome to Bliss, sweetie. Two men means four hands on you almost all the time." Laura patted Hope on the back. Her face went grim. "I'm sorry. It's my fault he got away. I was anxious to see what kind of report he had on you, and I was watching for Rafe. Hope's ex slipped out the back."

"We didn't have an armed posse guarding the back," Rafe admitted. There was a thick file on his desk. "Well, we'll do better next time."

Noah stepped inside. "Who is this man?"

Hope's eyes slid to the floor. "His name, if it's really him, is Christian Grady, though I'm sure that wasn't his real name."

"Cam is going to work on finding that out," Nate said.

"And this Christian guy is your husband?" James forced himself to ask the question in a calm tone. It didn't matter. She was meant for him and Noah. She was the glue that would hold them together, that would move them all forward. The very fact that this man had run solidified his stance. Whoever this asshole was, he wasn't getting close to Hope.

"Yes." The word dripped with shame. Hope's eyes slid to the floor.

"Not in a legal sense." Nate stared at James and Noah. "She was seventeen. The age of consent in Georgia is eighteen. She didn't have her mother's consent. She lied about her age, and her husband managed to produce a fake birth certificate."

Excellent. No divorce required. "Good, then he doesn't have any kind of legal hold on her."

Laura frowned and tapped the folder on Rafe's desk. "If he'd brought this paperwork into any of a hundred police stations, he might have been able to walk out of here with Hope."

"And by walk, Laura means drag you kicking and screaming in a straitjacket. According to all of this paperwork, the state of Georgia had you legally committed to a mental hospital seven years ago. You were given a day pass to go to lunch with him and you escaped," Rafe explained.

Hope's face flushed. "All lies."

"We figured that," Laura said. "I briefly went through this record, and none of this applies to you. I've known you for a year.

You've never once had a manic episode. I could buy depression, but not bipolar disorder, and certainly not a history of violence. According to this file, you attacked a woman named Elaine Reeves because you thought she was after your husband. You only got off because Elaine Reeves left town."

"Elaine is dead," Hope said in a dry monotone.

Fuck, what was she involved in? How much danger was she in? Was this man willing to kill her? There was no way his Hope had hurt anyone. If this Elaine had died, it was more than likely Christian Grady's fault.

"So he's covering up his crimes?" Cam asked as he walked in, echoing James's thoughts. He tossed his hat on his desk. "Zane brought me up to speed."

"He's in the wind," Rafe confirmed.

"Jamie, I want you and Noah to take her back to the ranch. It's the safest place for her. You have everyone watching out for her. Don't let her leave." Nate walked up to Hope and put his hands on her shoulders. He looked down at her, his eyes holding hers. "I told Laura and Rafe and Cam the whole story."

She nodded, tears pooling in her eyes.

"They reacted the same way I did when you told it to me."

"Honey, we're going to stand by you. You didn't do anything wrong," Laura said.

"Of course she didn't," Noah said, reaching for her hand. "She's the victim."

"You might not think so when I tell you the whole story," Hope said.

"I will," James promised. "I won't be going anywhere after you tell me the tale, so you should get used to the ranch. I know you don't think much of ranch life, but it's going to be yours. I promise you that I will try to take you places that don't involve cows or bulls, but I—we'll want you with us wherever we go because that's what marriage is about. Being together. Sharing this life and whatever the hell comes after it. I'm not good with words, baby, that's Noah's thing, but I'll show you."

Her eyes were wide and filled with tears, and for a moment, he was afraid he'd completely fucked up. "I think you did really well with words, James. Really well."

"I didn't get all the brains, brother," Noah said, a smile of deep approval on his face.

"Take me home." Hope put her hand in his. "I'll tell you everything."

James nodded, emotion threatening to take over. Once he had her home, he would never let her go. Once he had her back on the ranch, he and Noah would show her that she was theirs.

* * * *

Hope felt sick as the truck rolled up to the main house. Noah and James had been quiet on the trip home.

Home. She shouldn't think that way, but already the rambling ranch house that had seen better days felt like home. She'd lived in her small apartment for over a year, and not once had it felt like home. She'd never seen the stairs to her apartment and felt tears well at the thought of being inside, safe and warm and happy. But the Circle G felt that way after the briefest of times.

The thought of losing them churned her gut, but it was past time to pay the piper.

She had to hope that one of them would be kind enough to drive her back into Bliss when all of this was over. She knew she should have done this back at the sheriff's office, but she'd wanted to be alone. She'd wanted to be here one more time.

"I love this place," she said, her voice wooden because if she gave way to the emotion inside her, she would never get through the next hour. "No matter what I said to Serena, I love this ranch. I love this life. I wandered for years and never found anything as amazing as this. I would have been happy here."

Noah groaned. "God, did you know she was this overdramatic?"

James's lips curved up. "Never. Up until now, she's been a practical sort of woman. We're going to have to work on that."

"You don't get it." Frustration was beginning to well. They weren't listening to her. "You seem to think that I'm going to tell you I was innocent in all of this."

James opened the truck door and looked back at her, his face so heartbreakingly handsome she caught her breath. "No, I think you're going to tell me this overwrought story about how you screwed everything up and it's all your fault."

"And you're wrong." Noah slid out of the passenger seat. His green eyes pierced through her. "I don't care what you did. You must have had a good reason."

"You're not going to see it until I tell you." Why did they have to make this harder? She knew what the outcome would be, but they insisted on playing it out to the end.

Noah didn't let her feet hit the ground. He put an arm under her knees and hauled her close. They seemed to like to carry her around. She gave in and put her arms around his neck, inhaling his clean, masculine scent. She wanted to kiss him, to feel his tongue against hers until he turned her toward his brother and it was James's mouth on hers. She wanted that one moment when she was trapped between them, surrounded and coveted. Beloved.

One moment.

"Make love to me," she said to Noah. She could have them together once before it was all over and she was alone again. She could make it last. She could hold on to it for as long as she needed to. Tomorrow she would go back to Atlanta and begin to make things right again.

"Oh, baby," James said as Noah walked them up the porch steps. "We're going to make love to you. All night long. I told Nate that unless it was an emergency, I better not see another goddamn Bronco coming up my drive. The Circle G is closed for the night to anyone who doesn't live here."

She relaxed slightly. She was safe here. No one could sneak up or in. She'd have one perfect night.

Butch walked in from the porch, his tail wagging. Hope looked down at the dog. She would miss the mutt.

Noah sat her on her feet and kissed her long and hard. When he pulled away, there was a soft smile on his face. "We're going to show you what it means to be our woman tonight, darlin'."

"Yes." She wanted to experience it once.

"After you talk," James said flatly, sitting down on the overstuffed sofa in the living room. He sat back and crossed one booted foot over his knee. "So talk."

Noah joined him, their solidarity evident. Even Butch sat, thumping his tail as though waiting for something to begin.

"Now?" She didn't want to talk now. She wanted to make love, and afterward she would find the courage to completely kill the relationship with the truth. "Let's go to bed, and we can talk in the morning."

"Not on your life, darlin'." Despite their differences in physical appearance, the brothers looked very much like each other as they sat on the couch staring at her. They both sported identical frowns of disapproval.

"Why? I thought you wanted to make love." They didn't want her?

"Get over it, baby. You know we want you. We've been fighting like two dogs over you, but all that stops here and now. This is the way it works. No more lies. And don't give me crap about how you didn't lie. You withheld some important truths. Now, who is this asshole?" James wasn't going to be moved.

Tears welled again. She pulled her sweater around her as though she could block them out.

"It won't work," Noah said, his voice a bit of honey in the gloom. "We're not going anywhere. Tell us everything, and then we'll take you to bed and make love to you until you believe us. This is your home now, here with me and Jamie. Nothing you say is going to change that."

"I didn't think you were naïve, Noah."

"And I didn't think you had so little faith," he shot back.

"But that's the sad thing. I did have faith." She said it with a humorless laugh, thinking back to the idiot girl she'd been. "I had a lot of faith, and it got me in so much trouble."

"When did you meet him?" James asked.

Hope began to pace, her feet shuffling along the hardwood floors. She felt caged. She should have done this back in the station house. "I ran away when I was almost seventeen. My mother and I had a terrible fight, and she told me to get out."

"I doubt she meant that," Noah said.

Hope shrugged. "Her boyfriend hit on me. He'd scared me, but

245

she didn't want to hear it. She threw a fit and ordered me to leave. I walked away that night with nothing but my backpack and a hundred and fifty dollars I had saved up from babysitting."

"Did you go to your dad's place?" Noah asked.

"My dad didn't stick around after my mom told him she was pregnant." She had a name, but not even a photo. She'd never tried to look him up. He wouldn't welcome her, and she didn't want to know if he'd ever settled down, if he had a couple of kids and was happy, if it was only her he hadn't wanted. "Mom didn't talk to her sisters, so I didn't know them. I got on a bus and went to Atlanta. I was a dumb kid."

She talked in a monotone about those first days. She'd found a motel and lied about her age. She'd tried to find work but didn't have the proper papers. She'd been alone and terrified and too stubborn to ask for help.

And then she'd met Elaine.

"Was she your age?" Noah asked.

"A little older." She could still see Elaine with her henna-dyed hair and hippie clothes. Her laugh had been like a little wind blowing through Hope's misery. When Elaine had walked in a room, everyone looked at her. "I met her right after I got kicked out of the motel. I had gone back to the bus station. I have no idea what I was thinking. I didn't have the money for a ticket, but I was scared of everything. It seemed like a safer place to be than just walking the streets."

"You were a child, baby. Of course you were scared." James watched her, his eyes filled with compassion now that she'd started talking.

"Anyway, Elaine was meeting someone. Or she said she was. I know now that Christian recruited people at bus stops. I guess it makes sense. Desperate people take the bus. Not everyone, of course, but enough for him to get what he needed."

"She recruited you?" Noah asked.

"Christian ran a small company called Nature's Coalition. He had an office in Atlanta that functioned as a charity, but he had bought a large tract of land outside Atlanta. There he had a farm that supposedly experimented with greener farming practices."

246

"Con artist," James said, shaking his head.

"Worse. He had about fifty people living on the farm. His family." She winced because they were going to make the leap.

James laughed, the guffaw spitting out of his mouth. "You were in a cult?"

Noah smacked his brother. "This is serious."

James held his hands out in an apologetic gesture. "I know. I know. I'm trying to envision Sister Hope. I mean, wow. I thought Mel was the only one who had been in a cult."

Hope's eyes widened.

Noah shrugged. "It was a long time ago. It was the Church of the Immaculate Abduction. Mel left when he found out they actually worshipped aliens. He thought they were a crack alien-fighting team. I've often wondered what the sixties were like for Mel."

James slapped a hand on his knee. "We're wrong. Teeny was a Hare Krishna for a while."

Noah shook his head as though remembering a time. "Oh, and do you remember when Callie tried selling Amway? It was the same thing. And, hell, Nell is a cult in and of herself."

"Don't forget what Max used to call the Naturist Community," James said with a laugh.

Both James and Noah spoke at the same time. "The Cult of the Overly Hairy Potbellied Penis."

Hope took a deep breath, trying to find her patience. "I'm glad the two of you are having a nice trip down memory lane. It's not the same."

James stared at her, his laughter fleeing. "The point wasn't that it was the same, but that we all try some crazy-ass stuff when we're young. So this guy was all 'save the earth, line my pockets,' I take it?"

At least they understood that much. "Yes, but he was very believable."

"He would have to be." Noah settled back down. Butch put his head in his master's lap as though he was watching the show, too.

Christian had been spectacular. And Hope had been dazzled. "Elaine offered me a place to stay. I went with her because I didn't have any place to go. I worked on the farm for two weeks for room and board and a small salary. I liked it. I liked the fresh air and the work. I liked the people. I had lived in the city all my life. I had no siblings. I had spent my whole life coming home to an empty, colorless apartment, and suddenly I had space and people who were interested in me. And then I met Christian. He was beautiful, and listening to him talk was a revelation. He talked about the work the group was doing and how it was helping all these people."

"You were idealistic, and he was a combination of attractive man and authority figure. It's easy to see why you would fall. You were alone and looking for a father figure." Noah summed it all up in a neat bundle.

Hope continued. "He gave this speech, and afterward, he invited me to have dinner at the main house. He kissed me that night. I hadn't been kissed before. I had been very studious. All A's. I wasn't exactly a beauty queen, and I was easy to ignore."

"Never," Noah said.

But he hadn't known her then. "So I was completely innocent. I was shocked when he tried to put his hand on my breast. I was scared. And then I was terrified that I had pulled away because I was certain he would throw me out."

James's tone went hard, his quiet words cutting through the room. "He didn't throw you out. He liked the fact that you were innocent."

"Oh, yes." She turned away, unable to look at them. She stared out the window at the dying day. "He became a perfect gentleman. He walked me back to the cottage I shared with three other girls, and then he showed up for dinner the next night and every night after that. He barely kissed me again, but after a month, he asked me to marry him. He told me I was everything he'd wanted in a woman."

"He wanted a little girl, the bastard," Noah stated.

"He wanted someone pure," Hope corrected. "Don't all men want that? Someone without baggage? Someone whose mistakes don't follow them around?"

James shook his head. "Our momma told us mistakes were how a person knew they'd lived. And cleaning up after them proved what kind of a person they were."

Yes. She'd failed at both. "I married him. Toward the end, I was unhappy because he didn't seem to want me for who I was. He didn't want me to change and grow. He wanted the innocent girl to be that way forever. But then I didn't see him for what he was either. I was his wife for almost two years and not once did I suspect that my husband was a con artist, a thief, and finally, a killer."

She stared into the burgeoning darkness as she told her tale, but her mind saw something different. Some place different.

* * * *

Outside of Atlanta, eight years before

Hope walked through the double doors quietly, not wanting to alert Christian to her presence. She needed a few minutes alone before she started performing for her husband. That was how she'd started to think about the time she spent with him. A performance.

The two times she'd argued with him, tried to stand up for what she'd wanted, he'd scared her. Once she'd been sure he was going to hit her, but he'd stopped himself and taken her into his arms, murmuring that everything was fine, that she was still his angel.

She didn't want to be Christian's angel anymore.

How was she going to tell him that she didn't want to be married anymore? Her stomach churned. She didn't love him, but she also had no idea where she would go, what she would do. She had a GED, but no college because Christian didn't think she needed it. He'd said he would educate her, but he seemed to like to keep her in the dark.

"I don't think that's a good idea, Elaine."

She heard Christian speaking, his low tone prowling down the hallway. The main house was a lush temple to nature. There was green along the walls and a small fountain in the foyer. The fountain bubbled, but she could still hear him. There was a thin line of light from where his office door stood barely cracked open.

"I think it's a brilliant idea, Christian. I'm sick of this shit. I'm going to tell her, and then we'll see where your perfect little princess's loyalty lies."

Elaine's voice was shrill, on the edge of something manic. Hope walked cautiously down the hallway, careful not to make a sound. She had slipped out of her shoes on entering the house so she could feel the coolness of the floor beneath her feet. Someone had left a window open. A slightly chilly breeze rode through the house, carrying the words to her.

"She will always side with me. Hope is my wife. She's not a slut like you. She's a true lady. She came to me as a virgin and will remain by my side no matter what. I haven't allowed her feminine weaknesses to have sway."

Hope felt sick. Once Christian had found her reading a romance novel. He'd tossed it in the fireplace and chastised her for reading anything so idiotic. He'd said her mind was too good to waste on such drivel and handed her a treatise on communal living.

What if it wasn't about how smart she could be? What if he didn't want her to know what she was missing?

"And what about your masculine weakness? Does the perfect princess know you fuck me every chance you get?"

Hope stood stock-still outside the door, Elaine's words cutting her in ways she couldn't have imagined. She could see them standing there through the opening in the door. They were close, intimate even. After all the lectures on marital fidelity, Christian was sleeping with her best friend?

"Well, I'm certainly not going to fuck my wife's ass, and I'm not going to ask her to blow me. She's not a whore. Let's stop the bullshit, dear. Neither one of us believes in any of the crap we push, but Hope is different. Hope is innocent."

Her hands shook. Innocent. It was a word he used a lot. He treated her like a child half the time, like an idiot child who couldn't be trusted with anything like responsibility. She'd tried to become more involved in the organization, but the most he let her do was talk to potential investors.

And what did he mean he didn't believe?

"I need Hope." Christian's voice softened, cajoling. Through the crack she could see him put a hand out, touching Elaine's hair. "You have to see that. I love her. She's perfect, but you know as well as I do that men are imperfect. I have needs that I could never ask her to meet. It wouldn't be fair to her."

"But it's fine to ask me because I'm a whore." Bitterness dripped from Elaine's mouth. Her eyes narrowed even as Christian caressed her hair. "I like Hope. I actually feel guilty about bringing her here. I should have left her in that bus station."

Christian's hands tightened on her hair. "For the vermin of the world to devour?"

Elaine hissed as Christian's hands tightened. "Well, better vermin than a snake. She's going to find out about you. She's going to find out about the theft and the scams. What are you going to tell her when we shut everything down in a year or two? We always have to. We'll get close to getting caught, and we'll pull up stakes. What are you going to tell Hope when we have to flee the authorities?"

Christian's lips curved in a humorless smile. "She's a good girl. She'll do what I tell her to do."

Because she always had. Like she'd always obeyed her mother, right up to the moment she'd told her to get out.

Christian wasn't some white knight.

"What is she going to do when the feds come in? And eventually they are going to come in, Christian. This is a good setup, the best you've ever run, but can't you see you're skirting disaster? You're getting too much publicity and you're buying way too much into your own cover. Hope isn't good for you. She's a sweet girl, but you're obsessed with her. It's going to cost us all."

Christian's eyes grew cold, though Elaine wasn't looking into them. She was staring at his chest, her hand possessively on his arm.

"Leave Hope out of this," Christian said, his voice a silky threat. "She's mine, and it's going to stay that way. I'll take care of the authorities. You know how this works. We'll close up this operation if it gets too hot. It's already netted several million. I can't get out of here yet. I made a deal with certain people to get them information."

"I know what Jerry does. I'm not stupid. He's fleecing people out of credit card numbers, and you're selling them to the fucking mob. Hope will love that."

Hope didn't love anything about this conversation. Rage churned in her gut. Used. She'd been so used. Her anger was directed at anyone and everyone, including herself. How long had Christian and Elaine been partners? She wasn't sure who she was more angry at, Christian for being a duplicitous snake, or Elaine for making her think she was Hope's friend. Or herself for being the idiot who believed it all.

"And what about all these followers, Christian?" Elaine asked. "Some of them know too much."

Christian stepped back and shrugged as he opened a drawer of his desk. "I have a list of people to get rid of when we leave town. We've been careful. Most of the idiots on the farm don't have anyone looking for them. When they disappear, no one will care."

"Yes, I believe that's why we selected Hope."

"And if I have to dispose of my wife, I will." Christian's cold words broke through Hope's anger. He would kill her. God, he was talking about killing all of her friends. He couldn't really do that. He wouldn't do that. No way. Christian might be a criminal, but he wasn't a killer. She had to know him well enough to know he wasn't a killer. She had to.

He walked back to Elaine with a deep sigh.

Hope stood there unable to move. She needed to get away, but she couldn't force her feet to work. She felt frozen, as though she had to see this scene play out or it wouldn't be real to her. Christian had one hand at his side, but the other came out to caress Elaine's cheek. A sweet gesture he'd performed for Hope a million times.

"I will handle everything, El. I always do. I always clean up my loose ends. You should know that by now."

He turned her in his arms, her back to his chest. Elaine's eyes closed, and a dreamy look came over her face.

"I love you, Christian. I've loved you so much longer than that stupid twit. Let's get rid of her and take the money and run." Elaine's hand disappeared around Christian's backside.

Christian's hands tightened, and his left arm came up. A flash of silver caught Hope's eye, and Christian pulled a knife across his mistress's throat. Her white neck split, gaping open before a waterfall of life began to gush from her.

There was a terrible gagging sound and then a thump as Elaine hit the floor.

A scream curdled inside Hope. She swallowed it down, backing up until she couldn't see anymore. Unfortunately, she could still hear.

"Yeah, it's Chris. Jerry, I don't give a fuck about that. I just killed Elaine. Because the bitch was going to tell my wife everything. I can't have that. Get someone here to clean up. Now. Bitch bled all over my rug."

Her hands shook as she backed up, desperate to not make a sound. He couldn't find her. If he found her, he would have to kill her, too. Tears made the world a watery mess as she hurried down the hall and back out into the night. She was supposed to be at a friend's house, but she'd walked back up the hill to get her sweater. She ignored the cool air and braced herself.

She hid behind a shed as Jerry and his men walked by. There were three of them. Men who had laughed with her, worked with her. Men who claimed to be her friends. They were going to clean up after Christian's crime. They would dispose of Elaine's body, and then come tomorrow they would smile and laugh with her again.

All lies.

When she was alone, she calmed, forcing a placid smile on her face. Hope walked back to her friend's house, wondering all the while if the devil she'd married was watching her, planning her own death.

Chapter Fifteen

Hope forced herself back to reality. She could almost feel the Atlanta night around her, but she was here in Bliss. She wasn't the same girl Christian had fooled. Not by half.

"Let me get this straight," James began. Hope finally turned to look at him, and sure enough, there was anger on his face. "You watched him kill someone, and then you went back to him?"

"What was I supposed to do?" She sniffled, trying hard not to cry. She'd expected his anger. Noah was sitting and listening, but he hadn't moved from the couch. He wasn't jumping up to hold her. They were in their corners, and she was in hers. "If I had left, he would have searched for me. I had planned to gather some money and go to the police, but something happened that night."

"Did you try to kill him?" Noah asked, his voice steady and even.

She swallowed before answering, the affirmation of her crime stuck in her throat. "Yes. I tried. I suppose it was more of a case of I didn't try to save him. It was chilly that night, and Christian couldn't stand the cold. He also had trouble sleeping. He'd taken a pill when he came to bed."

"You fucking slept with him again?" The question tore from James's mouth.

James's vitriol was going to be worse than Christian's. She forced back the tears that threatened, shoving the emotion down. "No. I claimed my period was coming. Christian wouldn't touch me when that happened. He went to sleep after turning on the space heater. I got up in the night and got dressed. I stole money from the safe after I found the code. My birthday. As I was leaving, I stumbled over the heater. It was so dark. I was terrified, but Christian didn't stir. Not even when the curtains caught fire."

She'd watched them light up. The frail, filmy curtains had caught fire quickly, orange-and-red flames blooming and bouncing around. It had been like a dance. She'd thought for a moment that she should stay and watch, that this wouldn't be a terrible way to go out. The world had been cruel.

But something stronger had taken over. The world had been cruel because she'd allowed it.

"I walked out. I didn't wake Christian. I walked away and didn't look back. I took the car and exchanged it for another one outside of Little Rock. And then I wandered for years until I came here."

"What did you do with the money?" Noah asked.

James had gotten up. He started to pace, his hands on his hips.

God, she didn't want to get into this, but she'd promised honesty. Trev's words came back to her. He'd been right, of course. Words had power, and holding the story deep inside herself had taken her to the brink this time. The only way to get herself back was to tell the truth, to let the poison out even though it would cost her their love. She'd never really had it in the first place. They hadn't known her.

"I drank most of it. I stayed in motels and I drank because it seemed like a good thing to do. I had never had so much as a glass of wine until the night after I left Christian. I was only twenty, but I managed to get into a bar and some man bought me a drink and then two, and then I wasn't seeing Elaine anymore. I wasn't seeing Christian. I woke up the next morning in a strange bed, and I ran to the next town."

"Fuck all, do you have any idea how dangerous that was?" James asked, his eyes narrowed.

She shrugged. James, it seemed, was beginning to get the picture. "I didn't care. I didn't care about anything. I thought the cops would find me. I thought Jerry might figure out how much money I'd taken and come after me. But mostly I wanted to erase that picture in my head. I wanted to erase me."

"You know Trev from AA, don't you?" Noah seemed calmer than James, but then distance could do that. Noah was doing the right thing. He was distancing from her, putting up a wall between them.

"I only met him the day my car broke down, but he's been kind to me. He's right about what he said. I needed to have this conversation with you both. Honesty is the only way to stay sane. And it's the only way to live. You needed to know this. I spent years trying to find a way to eradicate myself. I used alcohol and sex to do it. I drifted wherever the wind or guy I was sleeping with would take me. Nate found me one night. I'd passed out in my car. He brought me home, and he and Callie and Zane sobered me up and got me to a meeting. Nate knows about Christian. Zane and Callie know, too, though I avoided talking about all the sex stuff. I couldn't be innocent anymore. It was stupid, but I wanted to obliterate the idiot girl who married a monster and didn't even know it."

A silence fell over the room, and she swallowed down her misery. She'd told them. She'd done it, and there was a certain peace that came with it. The worst was over. She was prepared for their reactions. They would stumble over words and try not to look her in the eyes. They would be gentle because they were good men, but they would ease her out of their lives.

And she would make it easy on them because she loved them. If she could go back and change things, she would. She would have made all the right choices to bring her here to this place in the right way, but she couldn't. The past had caught her, and she was done.

She took a deep breath and tried her damnedest to look calm. "So, if you don't mind, I should probably get back to the station. If this is Christian, I need to talk to Nate about what to do next."

James walked straight up to her. He took her shoulders in both hands and shook her lightly. "You are never leaving this ranch again. Do you understand me? After that story, if you think I will allow you to step one foot off our land, you're insane."

"James." She couldn't let him do this. "I need to get on with my life, and you and Noah need to move on with yours."

"What are you talking about?" He didn't release her, but he turned back to his brother. "Noah, what the hell is wrong with her?"

Noah stood, a sad look in his eyes. "Guilt."

"About what?" James asked, obviously perplexed.

Had he not listened? "Everything, James. Did you hear a word I said? I was willfully ignorant. I can look back now and see all the signs. They were there, but I didn't want to see them. I wanted the world to be sugarcoated, and Elaine died because of it. Whatever she did, she didn't deserve to die. I left Christian to die. I didn't even think about getting him out. I took that money. It was blood money, and I still took it. I didn't go to the cops. I can't even tell you about the years before I came to Bliss because they were a blur of alcohol. I'm everything Christian didn't want me to be. I'm a slut and an alcoholic and, in the end, I'm a coward because I never stood up."

James turned back to her, his fingers tightening. There was a tic in his jaw, and then she saw it. A single tear balancing on his eyelashes. "I ever hear you talk that way again, and that spanking you got earlier will feel like paradise. I will tear you up. You listen to me and you listen good. There ain't nothing wrong with you, girl."

"I slept around." She had to make him understand.

"There ain't nothing wrong with you, girl." Softer this time, but just as insistent.

"I'm an alcoholic." She was breaking under his gaze. She'd held up when she'd been sure he would turn from her, but seven little words were finding the cracks in the walls she'd built. Seven words were splitting her open and exposing her.

"There ain't nothing wrong with you, girl." Noah came behind her, his body crowding her, his hand in her hair.

"Don't you say it." It wasn't true. It couldn't be true. After everything she'd done, everything that had happened, it couldn't possibly be true. She couldn't do it. She couldn't let it happen. She didn't deserve it. Forgiveness. She didn't deserve it.

James pulled her close. The anger had fled his tone in favor of a loving, peaceful sigh. "There ain't nothing wrong with you, Hope."

"There ain't nothing wrong with you, love." Noah whispered the words against her ear.

And she was broken. The flood that had been dammed for years, that she had bottled up and fought against with only self-loathing and alcohol as her weapons, escaped like a cork popping open after years of tension. Horror flooded her, and she saw it all again. Felt it again. But she could cry this time. She could scream when before she'd been silent. It came out of her in a long wail, and they held her, surrounding her with safety.

She cried for the child she'd been, for the woman she was, for the person she could never be. She screamed for the injustices she'd seen. She let it out, her voice ringing through the room. Tears poured out, and they said it over and over again.

"There ain't nothing wrong with you, girl."

They said it, taking turns. They whispered it and spoke it out loud, and slowly it began to seep in, their words forming a promise she had never been able to make.

She was strong. She would survive. She was worthy.

They followed her to the floor when her legs gave way, never leaving her for an instant. She cried until she had nothing left, and she was empty.

So how was it that she felt so very full?

She sagged against James, his strength a welcome anchor now that the storm had passed. Noah leaned against her. The room was quiet, only the sound of their mingled breaths disturbing the silence. She closed her eyes and savored the sweetness of the moment.

"You're still here."

"I'm not going anywhere, baby." James tenderly forced her head up. "I told you, we're getting married. Now the way I understand it, you're not legally attached to this dickwad, but I think Noah and I should make damn sure he understands that you're divorced."

"Permanently," Noah added, his hand sliding over her hip.

She shook her head, still shocked at the outcome. "I don't understand you."

"That's funny, darlin'," Noah said. "Because I understand you."

"Explain it to me, brother." James sounded so calm, his breath easing in and out of his chest. "I would ask Hope, but I think I would get pissed off at the answer."

"More than likely," Noah replied. "You can't understand, Jamie. You've never done anything that genuinely hurt someone, not even yourself."

James frowned. "Hell, I ain't perfect."

Noah laughed. "Not even close, but you've always done your duty. You even did it for a snot-nosed brother who doesn't share an ounce of blood and who left you behind."

"We're past that," James said firmly.

"See. You forgive easily. But it's harder to forgive yourself. Think about it, Jamie. What would have happened if I had stayed in town, if I had been Bliss's vet? What would have happened the minute she walked into Stella's? Did you know you wanted her?"

James's hands stroked her hair. "Hell, yeah. I knew."

"And you stayed away for a year because you had nothing to give her. You wouldn't have felt that way if I'd been there." Noah's voice dripped with regret.

A deep sigh came from James. "The ranch would have still needed work. The fire would have still happened. We still would have needed money."

"But you would have trusted that between the two of us, we could give her what she needed." Noah leaned against her. "A year gone. We would have gotten married by now. She would be pregnant. We would have a family. And we don't because I got it in my head that I could finally get something you didn't have only to find out that it didn't mean shit because you weren't there to share it with me."

Hope smiled. "You two are taking a lot for granted. Maybe I would have played hard to get."

A light joy threatened to take her over. They were still here. She'd told them the worst, let them see the depths of where she'd sunk, and they held her. They were talking about a family. They'd seen her worst and loved her anyway.

James's smile turned distinctly wolflike. "Hard to get? I doubt it. I remember the way your pretty face flushed the minute you saw me. You wanted me. Now it might have taken longer because you would have known you had to take Noah's ugly mug along with mine. I got all the looks."

"Asshole." Noah laughed.

James stood up and offered her a hand. "Come with us, baby. We want to show you just how little we care about your past beyond the fact that we love the woman you are now. You made one mistake. I forgive you for it, but we need to talk about it so you never make it again."

She nodded, willing to listen to anything he had to say.

Noah took over. "You should have made damn sure the fucker was dead. Next time, shoot him, darlin'. Don't leave things to chance."

"We'll even help you hide the body," James offered helpfully. "A body can get lost on this land."

"I don't deserve you." But she would take him and Noah and whatever family they were blessed with.

James looked deep in her eyes. "I have a past, baby. If I haven't fucked up quite as much as you and Noah, it's only because I didn't have time to. I've made a mess of a lot of things in my life. I should have gone after my brother, but I let my stubbornness cost us."

"He's also slept with half of Southern Colorado," Noah supplied.

James slapped at his brother and then looked back down at her. "He's right. I'm not pure, baby. I'm not some perfect man, but I promise I won't touch another woman after you. I don't give a fuck who was in your bed before us, but from now on, it's me and Noah. We're your men."

He took her hand and started toward the bedroom.

Hope followed, reaching behind for Noah's hand, leaving her past behind for good. Now there was only her future ahead.

* * * *

Noah's hands trembled as Hope led him through the quiet house where he'd grown up. He knew every floorboard and wall of this house. Every inch contained a memory. There wasn't a room in the house where he couldn't remember his parents or some blissful piece of his childhood. Even the bad times now held a certain bittersweetness, as though time and age had taken the poison, leaving only the beauty behind. Yes, there had been hard times in this home, but each one had been met with his parents' grace, his brother's steadfastness. Though Noah had been born somewhere else, he couldn't remember that place. The Circle G seemed like the only home he'd ever had, as though his life hadn't begun until he'd walked onto this land.

And it had ended when he'd left.

He'd been a dead man walking, a ghost trying to get back to life and failing until one petite woman turned her eyes to his.

He loved Hope.

James opened the door to the master suite, the one their fathers had renovated to share with their momma. An aching sweetness pierced him.

"Do you remember standing outside in this hall, giggling?" James asked. He stared at the room as though he could see their parents in there once more, loving and laughing and building a home for them.

Noah missed them with his whole heart, but they were still here in every board and wall, in every acre. "Well, they made an awful lot of noise, brother."

Hope laughed. "You two would listen to your parents making love?"

Noah nodded, the memory coming to him. "It was hard not to, darlin'. Sometimes we could even hear them down the hall. When we got older and it was gross because parents shouldn't do that sort of thing, we would blast music. Our dads were always going after Momma. They were crazy in love. Twenty years they had together on this earth."

James became solemn. "And forever. They have forever."

Forever. It was all he could ask for. More than he deserved.

James walked through the door and sat down on the huge bed

that dominated the room. So much of it had been left untouched, a shrine to the love that had surrounded Noah and his brother all their lives. Three dressers and Momma's hope chest. Three rocking chairs and Dad's bookshelf. Papa's cowboy hat still hung on a hook near the closet.

"This is our room now. We're going to fill it with love the way they did. You remember what Dad did after their wedding?" James turned his head slightly and looked at Hope. "We weren't there, of course, but he told us all about it. Dad and Papa gave us the speech about sex. And then they told us how they felt about our momma and what words they used on their wedding night because sex, they said, went far beyond bodies."

Noah nodded and reached down, shoving his arms under Hope's knees, hauling her high on his chest. He loved the weight of her in his arms. He carried her over the threshold and to the bed where his brother waited. "Jamie and I loved this story. Papa carried Momma over the threshold, and Dad was waiting for her. Papa sat her on Dad's lap and told her something nice."

He settled Hope onto James's lap, his brother's arms going around her waist.

James held her close. "He said this is our home now. This is our place, and we will never leave it again. Our bodies can walk around, but our hearts and souls are here. Always."

"Always," Hope repeated, tears in her eyes. "I love you, James. I love you, Noah. I love you both so much."

She loved them. The words threatened to unman him utterly. She loved him, and she loved James. The family Noah had longed for was within his grasp. The ghost that was Christian Grady still lingered, but it was easy to brush him away for now. They would have to deal with him. If he'd truly fled the area, he would find a way to hire a private investigator to track him down. He wanted that man out of Hope's life permanently, and he would find a way to do it. He looked at his brother and could see plainly that James was thinking the same thing.

They would deal with Christian Grady, but tonight was all about Hope.

"Kiss me, baby." James leaned in, and Hope's arms floated up to circle his neck. She pressed her mouth to his.

James waved toward the nightstand. *Of course.* They would need a few things. Noah opened the drawer and found a box of condoms and a tube of lubricant. Yep. His brother was always prepared.

James and Hope kissed as James's hands pulled at her shirt, exposing creamy skin. Noah placed the items on the table and couldn't help but reach out and touch her shoulders. Such delicate muscles and bones to have had all that weight pressing on them. Hope had been drowning for years, but she'd fought her way back. She'd clawed and sacrificed, and she deserved the best life he could give her. They could give her.

He pushed her soft hair to the side and knelt down. James had gotten the buttons undone, his tongue still tangling with hers. Noah pulled the shirt away and the bra that came after. He ran his hands all along the skin of her back, memorizing its feel and the dips and hills of her flesh and bones. He marveled at the fact that he had a lifetime to get to know this woman, to adore every inch of her, to leave no piece of her unloved.

He kissed his way down the length of her spine, reveling in the way she shivered at his touch. Her skin was heating up, and he would bet once he got that dowdy skirt off her that her pussy would be wet, creamy, and tangy with juice. She was ready for them. She was ready to truly become their woman. Though they had each had her, knew how sweet she was, until they had taken her together, the promise remained incomplete.

"Come on, baby," James said, finally coming up for air. His face was flushed and his voice hoarse with arousal. "You don't need this skirt. In fact, you never need clothes in this room. This room is our world, and you don't need to hide yourself here."

She laughed, the sound a balm to Noah's soul. The whole time she'd screamed and cried, he'd felt pieces of himself breaking with her. He'd held her so tight, as though she might float away on a sea of pain, but she'd come through it, and now she was laughing. She was okay because they were together.

"It gets cold here," she protested. "I think you should know better than anyone what a Colorado winter is like. I can't run around in the altogether."

James put a hand on her breast, and when Hope gasped, Noah could bet on exactly what his brother had done. A nipple tweak could bring a sweet sub back in line. If she misbehaved too much, he would clamp those sweet nipples and his baby would feel the burn. And it was time to back his brother up.

Noah hardened his voice, using his best Dom tone, the one guaranteed to have his sub's eyes widen. "You heard what he told you. No clothes in our bedroom. You're allowed to get dressed and undressed, but if you're spending any amount of time in here, your lovely skin is the only cover that's required. And we'll keep you warm, darlin'. You won't need anything but your men to keep you warm. And trust me, there will be nights when you aren't allowed to wear clothes anywhere in this house. When we're alone, you'll sit at the dinner table in one of our laps while we feed you and feast on the sight of your gorgeous body."

"What about the two of you?" Hope asked, her voice shaky as James set her on her feet.

Noah took the opportunity to slip his fingers under the waist of her skirt and drag it off her body. She slipped out of the skirt and immediately put her arms over her chest.

Not happening. It was time to start making things clear to his almost wife. He pulled her hands to her sides. "No covering up. And we'll get undressed soon enough. But god, Hope, I think Jamie should be dressed most of the time. I can handle it when we're making love to you, but I do not want to see that on a regular basis."

His brother shot him the bird, one side of his mouth tugging up in a sarcastic grin. "Fuck you. I sincerely hope the years have taught you proper grooming techniques. The last woman we shared begged you to shave down there."

"Really? You had to go there?" Was nothing at all sacred in this house? Sometimes he thought the other partners of this town had it easy. Though he hadn't known them long, Noah would bet Alexei couldn't tease Caleb about his youthful grooming habits.

Hope held her hands up, laughing. "Stop, both of you. I can plainly see that I'm not merely the wife, I'm the referee. I'm starting a support group with Rachel Harper. You two are as bad as Max and

Rye. Fine, I'm naked. Someone better start kissing me. And I mean now."

James came to stand beside Noah. He slid his brother a long look. "That sounds awfully bratty. She's going to be demanding."

Noah loved the way Hope's skin flushed. She was obviously still self-conscious, but that would be gone soon. No amount of sex would ever take her innocence away. It was a lovely part of her soul, and Noah would kill to protect it. "She's going to learn her place."

Hope gasped, an irritated sound. "And where is that?"

"Between us, baby," James said, taking over where Noah had left off.

"Always between us," Noah finished.

It was his turn. Noah let his fingers skim across her skin, starting at her shoulders and settling finally at her waist. He pulled her to his body, her skin against his denim and the cotton of his shirt, but nothing could mask the heat of her or the hardness of those nipples against his chest. James crowded her from behind. She was caught in between them, and they would never let her escape.

"I think I can handle that," Hope said, her voice breathless.

Her hands were on Noah's waist, and she slowly let them drop to cup his ass. Noah's cock responded with a twitch as she pulled him close. *Message received.* She would give as good as she got. She would be strong enough to handle them both. And that was a damn fine thing. Noah didn't want a woman he could walk on. He wanted a woman he could walk beside. But that didn't mean he wouldn't put up a bit of a fight.

"Darlin', you are itching for a spanking." He loved slapping that glorious ass and watching it get hot and pink. He'd thought he would die while he'd watched her with James. He'd stared at Trev's wall of perversion and wondered how fast he could work her up to a paddle or a flogger. He would spank her until her cunt was dripping with cream, and then he would fuck that pretty ass of hers.

"My bottom is still sore from the last spanking," she whispered, her brown eyes wide. The little hitch in her voice made Noah remember how she'd whimpered every time James's hand had struck. How would she take to the St. Andrew's Cross, his whip whispering across her back?

Noah bit back a growl of frustration. He had to take this slow. He couldn't let his fantasies take over. This was about Hope. He had to remember that. There would be time later to introduce her to such pleasures. "Then you should obey us both for the next little bit or your ass will be a whole lot more sore. Darlin', when we're in this room and we're making love, you're our sweet little sub."

James shook his head. "And we both know damn straight that you're going to give us hell outside this room, so we demand some submission, because I get the feeling it's going to be me and Noah who are your slaves outside of it."

Hope's head fell back, rubbing against James's. "Yes, James. That's what you like to hear, right? Yes, James. Yes, my Noah."

Yes. For so many years, he'd heard "no" and "don't" and told himself the same thing. But now he realized that Ally could have told him yes a thousand times and it wouldn't have meant a damn thing because she hadn't been Hope. Hope, with her soft eyes and strong heart, was the one for him.

He'd finally come home.

"Noah?" Hope looked up at him, her brown eyes sympathetic.

"I love you." It felt good to say the words. They felt right.

He'd said them before, but he'd been a silly child. He'd been searching for something, and he'd said the words in the hopes that he could find it. The words weren't a road map, but a destination. Hope had always been his destination, the end to his searching and the beginning of his life as a man. The boy who had fought and clawed in a fit of jealousy and self-absorption had to go. Noah had to be a man because he was going to be a husband. Hope's husband. His brother's partner.

He could never, never let them down.

"I love you so much. You're going to legally marry Jamie, but I'm going to be your husband, too. I'm going to love you until the day I die, and long after that."

Tears pooled in her eyes. "And I'll be wife to you both. Oh, I'll be the best wife, Noah. James, I'll try with everything I have. I'll give this marriage and this ranch everything I have."

"Baby," James said, his arms hugging her from behind. "Noah and I are going to take such good care of you. We won't ever let you down."

Never again. He wouldn't let either one of them down ever again.

Noah tilted her chin up and took her mouth, molding his lips to hers. So soft. He sank his hands into her hair and let his tongue surge inside. Hope's mouth opened beneath his, her tongue dancing. He kissed her over and over, reveling in the feeling. He loved the little sounds, her gasps and moans. His cock was practically begging to be released, but he wanted this to last. This was the first time. Oh, he'd had her before, but this was the first time they were complete.

And there were several things he wanted from his wife-to-be.

He delved into her mouth one last time before reluctantly letting her go. James's hands were on her breasts, cupping her, his fingers playing with her nipples. They were swollen red berries as James pinched and pulled at them. Noah had the sudden urge to taste them.

"Her tits are so beautiful," James said, his hands offering them up.

Noah took the bait, not for a second willing to let the chance get by. He dropped to his knees in front of her and leaned forward. Her nipple lengthened as though there were a magnet between her breasts and Noah's mouth. Noah licked at it, brushing the areola with his tongue. He flicked at the hard bud and was rewarded by Hope's moans as she struggled against James's hold.

"You be still, baby. Noah wants a treat. You're our treat, and you're going to let us have you." James's arms were a cage holding her still for Noah's delectation.

God, it was good to have a partner again. He gave in and gave Hope what she wanted. He pulled her nipple into his mouth and sucked. He tugged at the nipple, laving it with his affection before letting it go and starting the process all over again with her other breast. He could smell her, a soft, tangy scent that had his cock aching. He sucked on her nipple and let his hand find her pussy. Sure enough, she was slick and wet, her folds swollen and wanting. He ran his hand across her labia, skimming her clit.

"Noah, please, please." She was still in James's arms, but her voice was shaking.

"Nasty old Noah is giving you a hard time, baby." James

chuckled against her neck. "Let me make it worse."

His brother's hand slipped down her torso, joining his own. James's fingers caught her clit, and Noah knew just what to do. He pressed the petals of her pussy apart and slipped two fingers up inside.

"Oh, oh." Hope tried to move, but James held her torso, and Noah wrapped his free hand around her waist. There was nowhere to go, no relief from their torment until they decided to release her. She was trapped, and that was where they wanted her to be.

"Give it to her, brother. We're going to make her come all night long. Now's as good a time to start as any," James vowed.

Noah worked his fingers up, hooking high inside her, seeking that magical place that would make her go off like a rocket. The muscles of her pussy gripped him, fighting his fingers. He slid in and out, fucking her with his fingers as James milked her clit.

Hope's whole body shook as she came. A delicious rush of cream coated Noah's fingers.

"What do you say, Hope? What do you tell your men after they give you an orgasm?" James asked.

"Thank you." Her voice was sweet and a bit dreamy, her eyes soft and languid.

Noah reluctantly allowed his hand to slip from her pussy. He brought his fingers to his mouth and sucked them inside. She tasted so fucking good. He loved her scent and the tangy cream that coated her sex. He licked off every inch of her arousal, reveling in her taste.

"We need to get her ready." James's voice sounded guttural. "I'm going to work on her ass. You need to try her mouth. Oh, she's got the sweetest mouth."

That sounded just about perfect to Noah. His brother was practically reading his mind. "On your knees, darlin'. James is going to get your ass ready. We're going to take you together."

As it should be.

He took her hand and helped ease her onto the floor. Her body seemed soft, and now that she'd had an orgasm, she complied without a single complaint or worry. She got to her knees, her head coming up and those eyes staring at him. He felt twelve feet tall when she looked at him.

"Take my cock out, darlin'." He could barely breathe thinking about her mouth on his cock. She stared up at him, her lips turning up slightly in a sweet siren smile.

Her hands came up, and with only the slightest of trembles, she undid the fly of his jeans.

He was going to die. He forced himself to stand there, to not shove his jeans down and his cock in. Her mouth was a masterpiece. Soft, pillowy lips. That pink tongue that darted in and out. He couldn't wait to feel it on his cock.

James picked up the lube from the nightstand. "I should make you do this, but I got a blow job earlier."

"You're a damn good brother, man." He was the best. He always had been. And James had always known how to share.

"You remember that when her mouth is around your cock. Our woman is damn fine at sucking a cock."

"I have had practice." She looked up at him, a gleam in her eye. As though she'd realized what she'd said, she flushed and her eyes turned down.

He was not having that. "Give her two, Jamie."

Two loud smacks cracked through the air as his brother delivered the punishment.

Hope shrieked a little, letting Noah know James hadn't held back. "What was that for?"

"We're going to spank the guilt out of you, darlin'. I loved you joking about it. I did. It made me smile. Trust me, you'll hear me and Jamie joke about the dipshit things we used to do twenty times a day. I will not have you be ashamed of your past. I love you for it."

"But, Noah—" she began.

"No. No buts. I hate what you went through, but it brought you to us. It made you the amazing woman you are. I won't allow you to be ashamed."

"Not for a minute," James said, his hands caressing her cheeks. "We're proud of you."

She bit at her lip before her hands came back up, and she started on his zipper, slowly dragging it down, making him crazy. His cock pulsed, desperate to be released. He shivered a bit as she pulled down his boxers and his cock finally sprang free. He hissed because his cock was so hard, he could pound nails.

He watched as James gently began to work her ass. Her shoulders shook a bit even as she took his cock in hand.

"Tell me how it feels," Noah demanded. Her hand gripped his dick gently as she moved, her breasts bouncing as James worked behind her.

"It burns, but I don't want him to stop." Her hand fluttered across his cock. "He's stretching me, but not as much as this thing will. And he's perfectly groomed, James."

Noah was damn glad he'd thought about that in the shower this morning. He should have known something was going right. He'd been ridiculously optimistic when he'd showered this morning and carefully shaved himself. From now on, he would let that be Hope's job. She could get on her knees in the shower and make sure he was properly shaved. And he would do the same for her. "I did it for you, darlin'. Now you let Jamie do his job and you do yours. Lick me. Suck me."

She nodded and leaned forward, her tongue coming out and lapping delicately at his cockhead. Noah stifled a groan. So good. It felt so good. His cock throbbed. Hope lapped at him before sucking the head in, the tip of her tongue delving inside the tiny slit of his dick. It felt amazing, but he wanted more.

He sank his hands in her hair, pulling her forward. His balls drew up as his cock began to dip inside. He forced his way in inch by inch, all the while watching his brother work. James squeezed more lube between the cheeks of her ass, causing Hope's spine to shiver as he opened her wide.

"This ass is going to be heaven." James stared at her, and Noah could only guess at what he was doing.

"Is she tight?" Noah asked, knowing the answer.

"So fucking tight. You should have seen how pretty she looked with a plug earlier. This tiny little asshole tried to keep me out, but I wasn't having it. I worked her hard, brother, until that plug finally slid right in." James's fingers pressed into Hope's ass, his wrist twisting between her cheeks. He pressed deep, shoving Hope forward, and Noah's dick sank inside.

Heat and moisture surrounded him. Different than a pussy. He loved this, too. Hope's mouth was a pleasure palace, her tongue dancing around his cock in whispery flutters. He gritted his teeth, enjoying the feel of her groaning around him as James added another finger.

"You'll be lucky to last a minute and a half, but you better fucking find a way because we're going to come together." James's hand moved in and out, fucking her in rhythmic time.

Noah pulled on Hope's hair, his eyes widening at the thought of working his dick into the tight hole of her ass. "No, Jamie. It should be you."

James's hand fucked in and out even as Noah started to get serious about her mouth. Hope's full lips wrapped around his dick as he began to thrust.

James shook his head. "No. I got to play first. I got to take my time, and you're gentler than me. I want her to love this. I need her to crave it."

"I don't feel gentle now." He felt like a marauder.

"But you will be. You'll be what she needs—what we need. You'll take care of her, and I'll fuck that sweet pussy until I can't see straight."

And then they would change places.

Hope's tongue whirled, and her cheeks hollowed out. She sucked him deep. Heat threatened to overwhelm him. His balls drew up, a warning that he could go off.

"Give in, Noah. You'll have more control. I intend to. I'm going to have her suck me deep, and I'm going to fill her mouth before I fill her pussy."

"I don't want to hurt her." Noah kept his hands gentle on her hair, allowing her to decide how deep and far she wanted to suck. Despite what he'd seen James do to her in Trev's dungeon, he was still worried about introducing her to BDSM. He wanted to go slow, to make her love it as much as he did.

James stood up, seemingly happy with his prep work. He frowned at Noah, looking down at the place where Hope's mouth worked over his dick. "She's not some fragile flower. She's strong, and let me tell you, this ass is going to take a pounding. If you can't do the job, then I will. I'm not holding back. She's going to understand what it means to be my woman. Sometimes it means a spanking and getting tied up six ways from Sunday while she takes my cock any way I want her to. You're telling me you want to keep the relationship vanilla?"

His brother was right. Noah held her head in his hands and thrust in, using her mouth because she was his. She should know what that meant. He would take care of her in bed and out, but he needed this. He needed to feel her submit to him. He needed the trust that went with the exchange. He craved it, and he hadn't been whole without it. He'd filled the hole in his life by prowling the dungeons of New York, spanking subs and giving them what they needed, never taking for himself. It hadn't been right because they hadn't belonged to him. He'd held fast to an empty vow, keeping himself apart from everyone out of guilt and pain.

He released it all now. He hadn't stood before a judge or a pastor and vowed to love Hope forever, but he didn't have to. He'd made the vow in his heart. He'd spoken it aloud in three words. *I love you*. He'd been blessed to receive them back. She was his, and he belonged to her heart and soul.

There was no room for regret or guilt. There was only the future to look forward to, and that included the deep bond that came from dominating Hope.

Noah felt like he was finally off the leash. He thrust hard into her mouth, and Hope groaned, the sound a sizzling sensation on his skin. James walked by him on the way to the bathroom, but it didn't matter. Nothing mattered except the humid pull of Hope's mouth as she struggled to take him.

"More," Noah demanded. He forced his cock in another inch. His balls were tight and high, nearly hitting Hope's chin with every thrust of his hips.

She sucked harder, seeming to take up the challenge. Now that James had walked away, she brought her hands up and cupped his balls, rolling them in her small palm as she tongued him and sucked, bringing him to the back of her throat before pulling away.

"That's it. Oh, darlin', I am going to come. I want you to suck it all down." He would be a part of her all day, his taste on her tongue the way hers coated his senses.

She growled around his cock as if to say "bring it on."

She sucked in long passes and finally worked his cock to the very back of her throat. Just as Noah felt his spine tingling, Hope swallowed, engulfing his dick in warmth and pleasure, and his balls shot off.

Pure joy shot through his system as his every nerve lit with sensation. Hope sucked, her mouth working as Noah gave up everything he had, his hips pumping out every ounce. He let it sweep over him, his eyes rolling back, sweet release suffusing his body, his every muscle heavy with a languid peace.

Hope sat back, a smile on her face as she licked her lips, devouring everything he'd given her.

And he knew. She was more than enough woman for two men, and she would love everything he had to show her. Hope would be his wife, his friend, his lover, his bratty, gorgeous sub.

His grand passion.

And it was time to show her just what was in store. Noah shoved his jeans off and tossed his shirt aside.

"You look like the cat who got all the cream," he said with a smile on his face. "I'm telling you something, darlin'. There's more where that came from."

He picked her up and tossed her on the bed. There was way more where that came from, and he would never stop giving it to her.

* * * *

Hope watched as Noah crawled onto the bed. Though he'd just come, he stalked toward her, his muscles moving in a sleek, predatory fashion. He reminded her of a hungry tiger stalking his prey.

And she'd never wanted to get eaten more in her whole life. Being Noah's meal was a pleasure beyond anything she'd known.

"Spread your legs." Noah growled the command.

When his voice rumbled deep from his chest, everything feminine inside her tightened.

"Not a chance, brother," James said, coming out of the

bathroom, drying his hands. "It's my turn."

Noah's eyes narrowed. "Fine. Spread your legs and let Jamie taste that pussy of yours."

"Damn straight. I'm going to look at it first." James stood at the foot of the bed. He'd shed his clothes, and he looked like a Greek god staring down at her.

She was big, her stomach curved, and her breasts too large. She had stretch marks and imperfections, but she forgot about them all because James's eyes were eating her up. His cock stood at full attention. Thick and hard, its length reaching up almost to his navel. Her nipples tightened, and despite the orgasm they'd given her earlier, her pussy felt empty. She was practically twitching like a cat in heat, desperate for them.

She spread her legs, watching James down the length of her body. Noah lay down beside her, his head close to hers.

"I love the way you taste. You spread those legs and let Jamie feast on you. When he's had his fill, we're going to pack you full of cock. We're going to fill you up and make you come until you can't anymore." Noah's fingers flitted across her breasts.

James put a hand on either ankle and pressed her legs far apart, her pussy on full display. He climbed between her legs and stared down. He pulled apart the lips of her pussy, his thumb sliding inside. He skimmed around, avoiding her clit.

Noah kissed her, his tongue coming out to trace the curve of her lips. She felt drugged as James got on his belly and pressed his nose into her pussy, breathing deep and groaning with pleasure.

"I love the way you smell." James kissed her clit, a light tap that got her hot and bothered and begging for more. "Is all this cream for me?"

He pinched at her clit when she didn't answer immediately. The sharp little pain bloomed into something more, and she responded as quickly as she could. "Yes, James. It's for you and Noah."

"That's right," he said with a sigh. "It's all for me and Noah. No one else."

"No one else." She let them have their way. There would be no one else besides them, and there had been no one who had truly mattered before. Anyone who had come before had been a means to an end. Even Christian had merely been a safe harbor, a port in the storm that had been her childhood. She loved these men. These men owned her heart and soul, and no matter what happened, she would never be apart from them. Death could come and would someday, but these men and their love would abide inside her until she joined them again.

"Hope, are you all right?" Noah looked down at her, his face grave. His hand came up to whisk away the tears on her cheeks.

All right? She'd never been all right. Not once in her life. But now she was better. She had finally found her place. "I love you."

He nodded. "I love you, too. So fucking much."

He kissed her, their lips meeting with passion and promise.

"Hey, don't you leave me out." James climbed up her body and took her mouth. She loved his weight pinning her to the bed, her taste on his mouth. "I love you, Hope. I love you, wife."

James Glen was going to be her husband. James, the gorgeous, heroic cowboy of her dreams, and he came with an amazing brother who would share her love. They could share it easily because in that moment, Hope realized her love had no limit. It would simply grow, like a tree unfurling its branches and reaching for the sun. Her love was boundless. It would include their children, their friends and neighbors, the great and beautiful family she'd found in Bliss.

"You're going to ride me, baby," James said, turning on the bed, hauling her with him. His hands were on her hips, guiding her where he wanted her to be. At some point in time, he'd slipped a condom over his cock, and now he took himself in hand, pumping a couple of times before guiding himself to the lips of her pussy. "When you're ready and we have you right and properly married, I'm not going to wear this, Hope. I want to see you pregnant. I want our kids to run across this ranch like the little wild boys Noah and I were."

She wanted that, too. So badly. Boys like James and Noah. Girls who loved books and music and riding horses. Children were a promise, an outward sign of inward passion. She prayed as she lowered herself on James's thick cock that she would be as good a mother as theirs had been, that she would teach her children to love as James and Noah had learned and then taught her.

She sighed as James filled her pussy. She balanced herself, her hands on the hard muscles of his chest. He was so beautiful, and somehow he'd chosen her. Noah had chosen her. Somehow, someway, she was worthy. She'd made mistakes and screwed up and fought her way back, and they were her reward.

"You feel so good, baby," James groaned, pulling her close. His hands moved across her skin, and she felt Noah moving in behind her.

"Spread her cheeks for me, brother. Help me make her ours," Noah said.

She let her head find James's chest, reveling in the strong beat of his heart. She sighed and gave over to them as James spread the cheeks of her ass, and Noah dribbled lube onto her anus. He pressed a finger in, but she was ready for that. James had stretched her, his fingers making her burn and long for the time when a cock split her open and claimed her.

"It's going to be all right, darlin'." Noah's soft Western accent soothed her as his fingers stretched and opened her asshole.

"I know. It's going to be perfect. Take me. Take me, I'm yours." Forever and always, she would be theirs.

He groaned behind her, and she felt something far bigger than a finger at the rim of her ass. Noah pressed in, and she whimpered. It burned, but she flattened herself against James and pressed out, trying to welcome him inside. James's cock throbbed, lighting up her pussy, but she was empty without Noah. Incomplete. Slowly, inch by delectable inch, Noah worked his cock inside.

Stretched. She was split and laid bare, no part of her unexposed, and it was all right because these were her men.

Noah moaned as he finally slid in, and she could feel his balls against the cheeks of her ass. She was full. She was full of them.

"We ride, brother," James said, his hands tightening on her hips.

"Yes, oh fuck, yes, we ride," Noah echoed.

And they were off, pulling and pushing her between them, the pleasure and pain mixing until she couldn't discern one from the other. Every second was a new sensation. Blinding emotions swamped her. She felt them in her pussy, her ass, her fucking heart. They filled and claimed each inch of her, including the soul she would have sworn she'd lost so long ago. It had merely hidden, and now it roared to life, and it was theirs.

Hope rode the wave. She bucked and thrashed and fought for every moment with them. She ground herself against James and then pushed her ass back to accommodate Noah. Something dark and forbidden flared inside her ass, sparking with dangerous pleasure, and she welcomed it. She thrust herself back and forth, taking each of her men until the orgasm swelled, and she screamed as it overtook her.

She felt James swell inside her, and his gorgeous face contorted as he came. Soon, she thought, soon she would be filled with him. She wouldn't wait. She wanted their babies in her belly. Noah shouted behind her and spasmed as he gave up his seed, driving deep and releasing inside her.

Hope fell forward, Noah right behind her. Sweat made a sticky, lovely glue that bound them together. Later, she knew, they would shower and wash each other, loving hands cleaning her body, but in the moment, she wanted the bond that held them together.

The new mistress of the Circle G fell asleep between her men, her thoughts no longer on the past, but dreaming of the future.

Chapter Sixteen

Christian Grady looked at the woman cowering at his feet. Actually, she wasn't cowering as much as he would have expected. It was another annoying moment in an already annoying week in a ridiculously annoying town.

"Do you understand what I'm telling you?" He wasn't sure the bitch understood English at this moment.

Lucy Carson turned her arctic-blue eyes up toward him. "Fuck off."

Yes. She was proving to be something of a nuisance, but then this whole goddamn town was out-of-its-mind crazy. The fiasco at the sheriff's office had proven that to Christian beyond all doubt. Luckily little Lucy hadn't caught sight of him at the station or he might have been completely fucked.

"I'll tell you again. I'm going to call your friend, who happens to be my wife. I'm calling her from your phone, you dumb bitch. She's going to pick up, and I'll explain to her that I will kill you if she doesn't come to me. You will cry prettily and beg for your life."

"I will say it again. Fuck you."

Lucy, it turned out, had quite the mouth on her. Christian felt his anger swell. He hated vulgar females. Lucy had seemed a sweet, accommodating sort. When he'd taken her out to pump her for information about Hope, he'd actually thought that she was innocent. But no innocent cursed in the face of danger. No innocent spat at her abductor. Lucy was a whore. Only whores fought.

"We'll get to that, I'm sure." Whores always wanted a good fucking, and it was nothing less than they deserved. Christian fought his urge to slap the bitch. He held up her phone and took a picture, making sure the lighting was all right. Morning light filtered into the cabin he was holed up in, lighting every cut and bruise he'd already given Lucy. He examined the picture. A person would be able to tell who she was and that she wasn't exactly in a happy place. It would certainly do.

"Smile for the camera." One more should do it. He made sure to hold up a newspaper with the date on it. The Bliss Gazette was a waste of the paper it was written on, but it did the trick. Hope would know he had her friend, and that soft heart of hers wouldn't be able to handle it. She would come to him.

And she would know what he planned to do with her.

Little Lucy fought against her bonds. She looked down at her hands, twisting them, the friction marring her skin. She'd been easy to catch, harder to hold. She'd fought like a wildcat, but he had help. It had taken all three of them to hold one small woman down after she'd tried to close the door in his face. He'd hoped he would be able to ease her into the car, but apparently she'd figured out who he was. Still, he'd managed to get her out of her place without anyone seeing.

"Do you want me to stay, boss?"

Christian sighed as he looked up at his flunkie. This man had been with him a short time. He missed Jerry. Jerry wouldn't have asked. Jerry would have known what to do. Unfortunately, Jerry was also very close to his height and his weight, and when he'd woken and realized that his home was going up in flames and he had the chance to start again, he'd sacrificed Jerry for the greater good. For Christian's good. Jerry's body had been his second chance.

"No. Go out to the ranch, and be there when Hope gets my

call."

The man nodded. He was an idiot, but a useful one. Christian had found him and his friend outside of Duluth. They were small cons, but fairly decent at bringing in the ladies. Their Western charm had worked well, and when he'd needed them to find jobs, they'd gotten it done. They could get close to Hope. They could bring her home.

Where he would decide if she lived or died.

"Sure thing, boss."

"You said she spent the night with them." Christian wanted to call the words back the minute they came out of his mouth. It was a weakness, but he couldn't help it.

"That's what I heard."

He didn't mean to ask the next question, but he couldn't quite help himself. "No one saw her sleep with them?"

The man in the cowboy hat shook his head. "No one was in there with her. No one knows what happened."

But Christian had his suspicions. He waved the man out, his brain whirling with unsavory possibilities.

His employee strode out of the purloined cabin. It seemed empty enough. From what Christian understood, it was a summer place, and summer was over. The nearest neighbor was a mile away, and no one in town thought Michael Novack gave a crap about anything but his own grief. He wouldn't notice Christian's domestic drama play out.

He was alone with Lucy, and soon Hope would be here. Hope would stand before him, and he would look into her eyes. He would know the truth.

And he would be her judge and her jury, and possibly her executioner.

* * * *

Hope let the water wash over her, a light joy infusing her. Every muscle ached, but she'd slept better than she had in years. She'd cuddled down between James and Noah, their bodies heating her skin and offering a bulwark against the world outside. Their arms had wrapped around her, and she'd been encased in their unique warmth.

Now the water was warm, sluicing over her body, washing her as clean as her words the day before had washed her soul.

Trev had been right. The truth was the only way to cut through the pain, to find the path. And the truth had brought her home.

She shut off the water to the shower and heard James and Noah arguing in the bedroom about who had to make the bed and who should go and fetch the coffee. She smiled, her heart full. They were obnoxious and all hers.

She thought about breaking up their fight but decided to concentrate on making herself presentable. If she walked out now, she would be forced to drop her robe, and then she was screwed. Literally. They were insatiable.

Twenty minutes later, she glossed her lips and walked into the bedroom. Peace. Quiet.

It wouldn't last long.

She got dressed in jeans and a T-shirt. Someone had moved her clothes from the guest room. A sweetness pierced her heart when she realized all three dressers had clothes in them. The boys had moved in, and they had moved fast.

The door opened, and James poked his head in. "Hope? Baby, come to breakfast. We have to eat fast this morning. Noah's got a load of cattle to check out. We're taking them to market in a week or two. I want to make sure they're damn healthy before we sell them."

She took a deep breath because she'd spent way too much time with Nell. James wanted to make sure his cows were healthy and in good shape before he slaughtered them and turned them into burgers. She shrugged. She liked burgers. "I'll be there in a minute."

At least she got to get dressed this morning. She'd been a little worried that they would want her running around naked at the breakfast table, but apparently the herd's medical checkup trumped the need to see her boobs while devouring pancakes.

She stared at herself in the mirror, not quite recognizing the woman who looked back at her. She was a rancher's wife. Well, almost. And a vet's wife. She had better get used to working with animals because they would dominate her life.

"Goddamn it." James's voice rang through the house.

Hope sighed and opened the door to the bedroom. She hoped James and Noah weren't fighting again. She would have to get some advice from Rachel on how to handle them when they started acting like five-year-olds.

"We need to start barring the gates at night. That's a nice car, though." Noah stood at the front window, his brother at his side.

"It's a dumb car for the mountains." James peered out the window and then whistled. "Whoa. Is that really what I think it is?"

Noah's voice was hushed and reverent. "1969 Camaro."

"Holy crap. That's a beauty. Z28," James breathed. "You know the horsepower that has?"

Hope looked out the window, too. "It's a car."

Both of her men turned to her like she'd said something utterly sacrilegious.

"That is a classic muscle car," Noah explained. "It's eight cylinders of pure power."

Hope wasn't impressed. She bet it didn't even have a CD player. Even her piece of crap had a CD player.

The Camaro charged up the road, churning dust behind it. It stopped at the long, circular drive, and the door opened. Out of the passenger side, Cade Sinclair unfurled his long, lean body, his eyes covered with mirrored aviators. Jesse McCann got out of the driver's side and said something to his partner that made them both smile.

"That ruins everything," James said, frowning.

"Now it's a douchebag car," Noah agreed.

Hope sighed. "I'm sure they're here to give me an update on my car. Will you give them a break?"

Noah held up her small cell phone. "They could have called. Phones work here, too."

"Not always and she probably doesn't have any minutes left on that thing. We're going to have to put her on my plan," James agreed. "Well, hell, let's get this over with."

Hope grabbed her phone and shoved it in her jeans. He was wrong. She had a couple of minutes left. Two or three. It didn't matter. She would let him take care of her. The heavenly smell of coffee wafted in from the kitchen. God, she needed coffee. She took another look at the two gorgeous mechanics walking up to the porch. Cade and Jesse were hot as hell, but James and Noah had ruined her. She sighed as she heard the door open and the men begin to speak. She decided she didn't want in on that conversation. They would talk cars and parts, and if she was there, they might do that chest-thumping gorilla thing, and she really needed some caffeine.

She pushed through the doors to the kitchen and found it already occupied. Two cowboys stood in the middle of the room. Tall and muscular, both wore boots and jeans and Western shirts.

"Morning, ma'am," the taller one said politely. The shorter one was on his phone, proving Jamie's earlier point.

She smiled and nodded their way. It was odd. The man sounded Southern. She'd gotten used to flat, Western accents, but this man's slow speech made her think of home.

"Good morning." She would have to get used to ranch hands being all over the place.

Her cell phone rang. Hope pulled it out of her jeans and looked down. *Lucy. Damn it.* She hadn't talked to Lucy in days, hadn't explained why she'd missed their dinner plans nights before. She was sure that someone had filled Lucy in on what was going on, but it wasn't fair to her friend to not hear it from Hope's own mouth. She slid the bar to answer the phone and stepped away from the cowboys.

"Lucy, sweetie, I'm sorry I didn't call. Things have been crazy here."

"Have they, love?"

Hope froze in the middle of the kitchen, her heart threatening to stop.

That voice. The one that haunted her nightmares. Christian.

She started out the door, ready to call out to Noah and James, but a large hand stopped her.

"Don't you think you should talk to your husband, Mrs. Grady?" The tall cowboy looked down on her with black eyes. "If you call out to those men, I'm afraid Brad and I will be forced to start shooting. Talk to the boss."

Her hand trembled. Christian had men on the Circle G? She supposed it would be easy. James had been desperate for new hands and hadn't had luck finding them. The minute Christian knew where she would be, he would have sent his own men in just for this occasion. Christian always had a plan.

But she couldn't risk Noah and James. She could hear them talking to the mechanics. If she so much as called out their names, they would rush in and be facing two guns.

"Hello, Christian. Why do you have Lucy's phone?" Hope asked, nausea churning in her gut. He was alive. She'd recognized the viable possibility, but now the truth hit her squarely, and she was reeling from it. Christian was alive, and he was after her.

"I have Lucy's phone because I have Lucy, dear. Talk to your friend." There was a moment of quiet, and then Christian growled. "You talk to your fucking friend, bitch."

A feminine voice moaned and shrieked in pain. Hope's eyes teared up. "Lucy?"

"I'm sorry, Hope." Lucy's voice came over the line, the sound fragile and tortured.

He had Lucy, and Hope knew what Christian could do to a woman. "Let her go."

"I will as soon as I have what I want." His voice had gone silky and smooth the way it did when he knew he had the upper hand. "As soon as you allow Jay to bring you out here to me, I'll release Lucy."

She didn't believe him, but what choice did she have? Lucy was utterly innocent. Lucy was twenty-five years old, and she'd spent most of her life taking care of her siblings in a single-wide trailer. This was the first time Lucy had been able to be on her own, and she was so excited about it. Lucy had sacrificed, and this should be her time to have fun, not to pay for Hope's mistakes.

"Do you honestly believe I won't kill her?" Christian asked. "I suspect you watched me eliminate dear Elaine. She'd outlived her usefulness." His voice went low, cajoling. "She was trying to come between us, love. You know I couldn't allow that."

"I watched you murder her."

He sighed. "I rather thought that was what made you run. Darling, you shouldn't have had to see that. You know men are just beasts. But I'm gentle with you. Always, because you deserve it.

Unless you've been doing something you shouldn't. We're going to talk about those men, Hope. Do you understand me?"

She understood him far too well. He wouldn't like the fact that she wasn't his pure little angel anymore. She also wasn't going to walk to him like a lamb led to slaughter. She moved toward the sideboard. Someone, most likely Beth McNamara, had set a lovely spread. There was a fruit tray that included apples and oranges and a single, small paring knife. It wasn't much, but she would take it.

The kitchen door banged open, and Hope nearly dropped the phone.

James stood in the doorway, an impatient look on his face. "Baby, do you want to come talk to these douchebags? They have an outrageous quote on fixing your car. You're better off letting me and Noah find you a new one."

She took a deep breath, remembering that the two men with her were armed and ready to shoot. "That sounds fine."

"Who are you talking to?" James looked down at her phone.

"Lucy," she replied, trying to sound nonchalant. "Catching up on gossip."

He nodded and then turned to the hands. "Shouldn't you two be out in the east pasture with Trev?"

The one named Brad nodded, but both men were staring at James. She took the chance to reach out and palm the small knife, wishing she had better access to the larger ones. While Christian's men replied to James, she slid the knife into her pocket and put the phone back to her ear.

"Lucy, I'll see you in a bit. I have to go. I have a couple of things I need to get done this morning."

"Yes, you do." Christian's voice was all threat now. "And, love, if you bring one of those men with you, I won't hesitate to kill him."

No, he wouldn't. "I understand."

She hung up.

James walked to her, tilting her chin up. "You all right, baby?"

Damn it. The last thing she needed was a curious James. "I'm fine. I'm a little tired. Now will you go and get rid of those men so we can sit down and have breakfast? I'm starving."

The smile that crossed his face threatened to light up the world.

He winked down before brushing his lips across hers. "Will do." He turned back to his hands. "And you two need to get to work. I'm not paying you to gawk at my woman, no matter how pretty she is."

James walked out, and she wondered if she'd seen him for the last time. She longed to get another glimpse of Noah, too.

"Let's go, Mrs. Grady," Jay said, taking her by the elbow. "We need to get going before those men come back."

She felt the hard bite of the barrel of a gun against her side as they walked her down the steps of the back porch and hustled her toward their pickup. They had been ready for her. The truck was parked and prepared for an easy getaway.

Brad buckled her in while Jay took the wheel. Brad looked at his partner in crime. "You send me the signal when it's all clear, and I can get out of here. I'll run interference on this end."

The door slammed, and Jay took off. Hope looked back as the Circle G's main house got smaller and smaller. Tears ran down her face. She'd briefly had a future.

But it was time now to deal with her past once and for all.

Chapter Seventeen

James smiled at the two mechanics who had obviously come out to deliver the bad news in the expectation that they would be able to get a glimpse of Hope.

Hope was having none of it, and that did amazing things for his ego.

"Where's Hope?" Noah asked, his eyes trailing back toward the kitchen door.

"Yes," Jesse said, his eyes following Noah's line of sight. "Where's the luscious Hope?"

Odd, now that he'd settled his relationship with Hope, James didn't feel the urge to bash the man's face in. "She's hungry. She had a long night."

"Yeah, she did." Noah held up his hand and offered a high-five.

James slapped at his brother's hand in a sign of male solidarity.

"So juvenile." Cade crossed his arms over his chest and sighed. "So, the rumors are true. You've settled your differences. The last time we saw you two you seemed to be at odds."

"We're brothers," James said. "We always figure it out. I've got some bad news for the two of you. I want you to stop working on her car. Hope said she's going to let her men buy her a new car."

Noah pointed out the front window toward the shiny car in the driveway. "You know they restored that beauty. Hope would look awfully nice driving around in something like that."

Yeah, and Noah would drive that sucker every chance he got. "Dipshit, our wife is not driving around these mountains in a sports car. Hell, Hope can barely drive as it is. No, we'll find her something safe."

Cade looked at him for a moment. "We'll keep our eyes open. Stop brooding, Jesse. She's taken, and it looks like she's in a good place. We're going to have to keep looking."

"Hey, maybe you can give Hope's friend Lucy a call." James was damn proud of himself for coming up with that plan. Lucy was a pretty little thing, and as far as James could tell, she was alone. She was friends with one of the local EMTs, but there was nothing romantic about her relationship with Tyler Davis. She worked doubles at Trio, and word was she sent most of her money back home. Lucy sounded like a woman who could use a couple of men looking out for her. And Lucy was Hope's friend. He had to start looking out for Hope's friends.

He would send these two River Lee's way if she hadn't recently gotten married. Of course, her husband was a massive ass, so he anticipated a divorce in her future.

Jesse shook his head. "Lucy? That waitress at Trio? The pretty brunette?"

"Yeah, Hope was just talking to her." James could guess what they had been talking about. Him. Noah. Hope was probably telling her friend all about the events of the last couple of days, and he was damn sure she was probably going into way more detail than he would be comfortable with. Women liked to talk more than men.

"I haven't met Lucy," Noah said, obviously curious about Hope's friends.

"Uhm, they were talking about her this morning at Stella's. She didn't show up for her shift last night. The big Russian guy was worried about her. I heard he and Holly and the doc were in the sheriff's office trying to convince Cam to start a search for her,"

Cade explained. "We were going to come out here, talk to Hope, and then we were going to head back and see if we could help with the search."

James shook his head. "I don't think you'll need to do that. Hope was talking to her a couple of minutes ago."

Jesse gestured toward the house phone. "Well, someone needs to let the Russian know. Apparently he checked her place this morning when he couldn't get her on the phone, and he said it looked like she'd been in a struggle. The whole damn place was torn up."

A cold fear ran along James's spine.

Noah looked toward the kitchen door. "Does everyone know Lucy is Hope's friend?"

James's mind was making some horrible leaps. "Yes. She and Lucy spend a lot of time together. It wouldn't take much to figure out that they're close. Hell, Lucy can talk a mile a minute, and she's not exactly discreet. She's not guarded. She'll tell anyone anything."

"What's wrong?" Cade asked, seeming to sense the tension.

"Hope?" Noah called out as he strode into the room.

"Bring her here," James ordered his brother.

They wouldn't let her out of their sight. Christian Grady was still close, and it looked like he was trying to find a way to get Hope. Since Grady hadn't been able to walk off with her yesterday, it looked like he might try to find a way to bring her to him. He grabbed his phone and started dialing Cam.

He cursed the ringing phone. What was taking Noah so damn long? He was going to grab a shotgun and lock all three of them in the bedroom until this fucker was caught. He had a deep desire to be the one who found him, but he wasn't about to turn his back on Hope.

The line picked up, and James started talking immediately. "Cam? Cam, listen to me. I think this guy has Lucy, and he's going to try to use her to get to Hope."

A calm feminine voice spoke back. Laura. Laura Niles was taking Hope's place at the station house. She, Rafe, and Cam were all there and all had extensive backgrounds in law enforcement. "James? We were about to call you. We need you to get Hope down to the station. Until we figure out where Lucy is, Hope needs to be under lock and key. Rafe is out talking to Lucy's neighbors, but we don't have anything right now except a wrecked apartment. Cam thinks this is all about Hope."

Noah walked back in the room, his face a pale white.

"Where's Hope?" James asked before he realized things had gone very, very wrong.

Noah wasn't alone. One of his new hands followed behind Noah, and James caught sight of the metallic gleam of a gun at his brother's back.

James felt his heart flip, adrenaline beginning to pound through his system. He couldn't lose his brother. He'd just gotten his brother back. And Hope. Where the hell was Hope?

And where had Jesse and Cade gone? He looked around, hoping for some backup, but the mechanics seemed to have slipped away while he was talking to Laura. Cowards. Or were they something more? How long had this Christian person been watching them? How many people had he put in this town?

Just how fucked was he?

"Where's Hope?" He had to force the words out of his throat. All he really wanted to do was scream.

"Jamie, I'm sorry. I think she's gone." Noah's voice sounded tortured.

The cowboy Trev had hired just a day before kept a hand on Noah's shoulder. "She's on her way to see her husband. And I'm not about to let you two screw up that reunion. Your wife never met me, but I've worked with the boss for a long time. He's obsessed with that dumb bitch. We aren't going to move on and get back in business until he deals with her, and I would like to get back in business. So I'm afraid I can't let the two of you go after her."

James met his brother's eyes.

"Jamie, she's more important and you know it," his brother said.

"Shut up," the cowboy said, shoving the gun deeper against Noah's back. "We're going to wait here until I get the all clear. It won't take long, and then we can all go about our business."

The man with the gun was lying. There was no way he would

leave them alive. He was simply waiting until he was sure he didn't need them for anything else. James could wait and pray that he was wrong, but he knew he couldn't.

"She's out there, brother," Noah said, his eyes fairly pleading with James.

Damn it. Did Noah know what he was asking him to do? Fuck yeah, he knew. He was asking James to make good on the promise they'd made. They might not have said it out loud, but they had grown up knowing this was the way a family worked. Hope was theirs. And Noah was willing to sacrifice himself if it meant James had any shot at saving her.

"I forgive you." James let go of all of his anger in that moment. He loved his brother—the man who shared a life, if not blood, with him, his constant companion, the other odd half of his soul.

Noah nodded and closed his eyes as though he didn't want to see it coming, wanted his last moment to be something private. He would be thinking of Hope.

James braced himself because if he could save his brother, he would try, but there was no way he could stand there as Hope got farther and farther away.

James felt the yell build inside, and then his eyes widened.

"I would drop that if I were you." A calm voice cut through the tension. Jesse McCann came from the left, his feet moving far more silently than any man who weighed somewhere over two hundred pounds should be able to.

The cowboy who held Noah flushed, his breath panting in and out. "I'll shoot him. I will."

"And then we'll shoot you." Cade Sinclair moved in from the kitchen, his SIG Sauer aimed at the cowboy's head. "Look, we don't care about the vet. We've been tracking your boss for eight years, ever since the minute we figured out he hadn't died in that fire. Once we found Hope McLean, we knew it was only a matter of time. So don't think we'll kill you. We'll merely incapacitate you, and then the torture begins until you tell us exactly where he is."

"I'm looking forward to the torture," Jesse said, his lips curling in a faintly cruel smile. "It's been a long mission. So, what's it going to be? Are you going to let the vet go and we'll have a reasonable discussion, or do I prepare to cut your balls off slowly? Don't think I won't. I'm comfortable with my sexuality."

"Fuck." The man dropped the gun and shoved Noah away.

Noah stumbled, but got to his feet. He turned back to Jesse and Cade. "You two are assholes. Who the fuck are you?"

"Men who have been waiting a long time for revenge. Christian Grady hurt someone we cared about. And we're going to bring him to justice. Now, where can we torture this guy?" Cade asked.

"He's in a cabin. He had Jay take her to a cabin." The cowboy was talking quickly now.

"There are hundreds of cabins, asshole," James pointed out. "You're going to have to narrow it down."

The cowboy swallowed. "I don't know. I…it was close to the lodge. Yeah, it was close to the ski place. The boss found it a week ago. It's supposed to be a summer cabin."

Jesse looked at James. "Ring a bell?"

"There are summer cabins all across the valley and up the mountains." He wracked his brain. "It's late in the season. Most of them are empty. We could ask Mel. He often checks in on the cabins to make sure they're locked up for the winter." And to check for aliens, who apparently loved empty vacation homes.

"I know the road it was on. I don't remember the name, but I remember where to turn," the cowboy said, the words pouring from his mouth. "Don't kill me."

"We won't if you're not lying," Cade promised. "Let's head out. We need a quieter vehicle. You can hear the Camaro from a mile away."

"We'll take my truck," James offered. "I need to call Cam. The sheriff needs to know. If we can't find her, I want everyone else looking."

"Call him while we're on the road," Jesse said, holstering his weapon.

"I'll get the guns," Noah said, his voice still shaking. He looked at James and took a deep breath. "We're going to get her back."

"I don't know if we should trust them." James wasn't sure he trusted anyone but his brother at the moment.

Cade pulled a gun out of the back of his jeans. "Use this on me if you have to. Look, we've been tracking this man for a long time. He hurt the woman we consider to be our mother."

"And he has the woman I consider to be my wife." He wasn't going to let anyone's need for revenge cost Hope her life.

Jesse and Cade nodded at each other, and Jesse finally spoke, his hand on the back of their prisoner's neck. "We would be doing our mother a great disservice if we were willing to sacrifice someone like Hope. I promise we will help you get her back. I promise. We won't allow this asshole to kill another woman."

James nodded and looked at his brother. "We'll get her back." He took his brother's hand and finally did what he should have done the minute he'd seen him. He pulled his brother in and hugged him. This was his baby brother, and it would always be up to James to be strong. "We'll get her back."

* * * *

Hope wished she'd managed to keep hold of her cell phone, but they had taken it from her when they put her in the car. Jay kept his gun trained on her, and she wondered why they hadn't tied her up. She'd learned that her captors names were Jay and Brad. Brad had stayed behind, and she had to wonder what he was planning to do.

"Don't try anything." Jay turned up the unmarked road. There were many such roads all over the county. This one ran up the mountainside that held the Elk Creek Lodge. Bliss was surrounded by mountains, but this particular one was mostly used by tourists, and it hadn't started snowing yet. It would be isolated. It would be perfect for a man with his mind on murder.

"He doesn't want you to hurt me, does he?" Hope asked. "He wants me pristine and perfect."

It would play into his disturbed psyche. No one could hurt her except him.

"If you run, he'll kill your friend. And by now, Brad will have those two dumb cowboys under control. If I don't call him in ten minutes, he'll kill them, too. Do you want that?"

She was in a corner, and she didn't see a way out. "What does he want?"

Jay frowned as he drove the truck up the steep hill. "You, though I have no idea why. He could have any woman he wanted. I guess he's mad you left. Did you really try to kill him?"

"No. It was an accident, though I did leave him to die."

"He said as much. He seems to think you're some perfect princess who couldn't handle seeing his masculine side."

Hope shuddered. "It wasn't his masculine side that bothered me. It was his psychotic side. He killed a woman. He slit her throat."

Jay shrugged. "I don't give a fuck, sweetheart. I'm in this for the cash. I'm going to drop you off and then go help Brad out. I have no idea what Chris wants to do with you, but he wants some privacy to do it."

She could imagine. She clenched her fists against the image. She wouldn't let him touch her. It would be a brutal violation for him to touch her. Now that she knew what it felt like to truly be loved, she couldn't stand the thought of even seeing Christian again.

Would she ever see them again? She would give anything to see them, to touch them, to tell them she loved them.

"He's going to be surprised when he finds out you've been playing around. If I were you, I would lie about what you've been doing with those two men. Maybe he'll be satisfied if he thinks you were just staying with them. I would come up with some reason, any reason that doesn't involve screwing those two guys."

He wouldn't believe her. She might try, but she doubted Christian was going to let her live. It would be up to her to survive.

Jay pulled the truck up the gravel drive, and she saw him.

Christian stood in the doorway of the small, neatly kept cabin. He was dressed in khakis and a loose-fitting button-down. His hair was shorter than it had been when she was with him, his eyes older, but there was no question the man in front of her was the man from her nightmares.

"Get out," Jay said. He had the gun in his hand.

With trembling hands, she opened the door to the truck. The paring knife she'd slipped in her pocket poked her in the hips, but she ignored the minor pain. She smoothed her shirt down, praying he couldn't see the outline of the knife. She would get one shot.

"Where's Lucy?" She was pleased at the even tone of her voice.

Christian smiled. Once she'd thought it was a beautiful thing, but now it seemed ghoulish. "She's still alive. Would you like to keep her that way?"

"Yes." She would do everything she could to save Lucy, but now she was worried about her men. Had Brad lain in wait for them? James had a gun, but he didn't carry one in the house. He packed a shotgun when he rode out, but he would be utterly unarmed, and Noah hadn't even fired a gun in years. Had they walked into the kitchen to find her only to get shot?

"You look good, Hope." He smiled as he said it, as though they were old friends who hadn't seen each other in a while.

"You look alive. I thought you were dead," she stated flatly. God, she had to force her feet to move. She didn't want to get near him.

Christian looked over her shoulder. "You may go, Jay. Do your job."

Was his job to clean up after Brad or to help Brad get rid of Noah and James? She needed to deal with Christian and find a phone. She prayed the cabin had a working phone. She would call James, and if she couldn't get hold of him, she would call Cam. *God, please let them be alive.*

"Come along, love. We have a lot to talk about."

She would have to get close. Her heart felt like a hummingbird inside her chest as the adrenaline started to pump through her system. Christian weighed roughly one hundred and seventy pounds. He was incredibly fit. There was no question he was stronger than she was, but she had two things on her side.

She had her knife.

And he had never really known her. Not for one instant. He saw what he wanted to see. Softness. Sweet innocence. He saw someone who was weak, but she was strong enough.

Though her every instinct told her to run screaming from him, she had something far deeper urging her on. It wouldn't matter if she survived only to find out James and Noah were gone. She had to fight. For herself. For them. For the future they could have.

He held out a hand when she reached the stairs. It was a courtly gesture, the type Christian was good at. He'd seduced her with his pristine manners. He'd never failed to open a door or pull out her chair. Hope doubted Christian would ever scratch his belly the way James did after a meal or talk about spaying pets at the dinner table like Noah. Christian was the perfect gentleman and the perfect person to draw in stupid young girls.

There was nothing wrong with her. It was Christian's fault. All of it. He'd targeted her. He'd been older, smarter. She'd been barely seventeen. Stupid, but she'd meant no harm. He'd been the one who lied, who manipulated. Hope had believed she was doing good, had loved the people around her.

She'd been foolish, but well meaning. She wasn't the reason Elaine had died. But she would be the reason Lucy lived. And she would do whatever it took to save her men.

She put her hand in his and allowed him to help her up. She hoped her distaste didn't show in her face.

"You were hard to find." He kept her hand in his.

"I stayed under the radar for a long time." She hadn't been able to keep a job for years after that night. It had made it easy to live off the grid. By the time she'd made it to Bliss, she'd been secure that no one was looking for her. She'd given Nate Wright her real name, and she'd started a job.

"I was surprised you managed to do that."

"How did you survive the fire?" She asked the question not only because she was curious, but her mind was racing with scenarios. She had to put off the moment when he put his hands on her body. If he found the knife, it was over.

"My friends saved me. I woke up when the heat got to be too much, but it was difficult to breathe. I stumbled out, but the house was on fire. Thank you, by the way. The office went up in flames. I didn't have to worry about the blood stains from poor Elaine. Jerry and Reginald pulled me out, but Jerry was hit by a beam. It was fortuitous. He died, but there was enough of him to identify. I took over his identity and identified his body as mine. Reg backed me up. We got out with most of the cash, though we owed a lot to certain factions. I had to hide for years before I could come after you. Luckily, a couple of months back, my mob connection landed in jail. He can't come after me from jail. I immediately started looking for you."

Alexei's trials. God. Alexei had put away several major mobsters by testifying against them. She'd never dreamed his courage would bring her own monster out in the open.

"Show me Lucy." She needed to know her friend was still alive.

His eyes narrowed. "I don't know if I want to do that. The last time you saw that side of me, you ran. I would never have hurt you. I loved you. A man has to do what he has to do in order to protect the things he loves. Can't you see that?"

She didn't want to listen to his half-baked explanations. "I just want to see Lucy. I want to make sure you haven't killed her yet."

He gestured to the door. "Fine. See her. I find your lack of faith in me sad."

He was off-the-wall, butt-fuck crazy. "If you told me the sky was blue, I would still think you were lying."

She walked through the door and gasped at the sight in front of her.

Lucy lay on the floor, her hands tied in front of her. Hope looked down at those hands. Christian had tied the rope tight, but it looked as though Lucy had fought. There was blood on the rope. Her face was swollen, bruises making an insult of what was her usually sweet expression.

"She's alive. I gave her a tap, and she went right out. Women are fragile creatures." He stood frowning as though the entire scene was distasteful. "You're too compassionate. She's a whore. She tried to kiss me after one date."

She dropped to her knees and felt for a pulse. It was there, strong and beating. Lucy's eye cracked open, and she whispered.

"Run, Hope. He's going to kill us both."

"Is she awake?" Christian asked.

"No," Hope said quickly, standing up. "But she's alive. Barely. I was telling her I'm sorry for getting her in this, and I won't leave her here."

He sighed, a deep movement of his chest. "Like I said, you're too compassionate, my love. You truly were the better side of me."

She needed a distraction. Her time was running out. She needed to get him angry. If she could get him to hit her, perhaps in the chaos she could get her knife. It was too small to be threatening. She would have one shot. One shot at saving Lucy, herself, her men.

"Well, if you're referring to the side of you that doesn't steal, lie, and murder people, then yes, I'm your better half."

His face hardened. "You know I don't like sarcasm. I'm being indulgent. I'm offering you a chance to come back to our marriage. I'm willing to forgive you for running. I shouldn't have killed Elaine in our home. I should have kept it far away from you. I don't expect you to understand why I had to do it. You're far too innocent."

And that was what he valued. And that was where she could attack. "I'm not so innocent anymore."

His jaw went tight, the gleam in his eyes stubborn. "I don't believe that. I heard the rumor about you. I've dismissed it as mere gossip. Even your friend there admitted that you don't date. You're a good girl. You go to work and you go home. Can't you see why you haven't taken a lover? Because we're married, and it's not in your character to break the vows we made."

Oh, the bile was starting to build. "We aren't married. That marriage certificate means nothing. It wasn't legal because you knew damn well I wasn't of age. As for the innocent part, oh, I could tell you stories, but let's stick to the most recent indiscretion. The gossip is true. I'm sleeping with James and Noah. Well, not sleeping with them. I'm fucking them. As often as possible, and together when I can convince them."

"Hope, I will not listen to this," Christian barked.

This was why he'd always been gentle. He'd never even tried to bring her a moment's pleasure because he didn't want her tainted by it. He was terrified of real women. He was a pitiful man who couldn't handle a woman, so he went after girls and tried to keep them innocent and ignorant. He was the pathetic one. She put one hand on her hips and let her right hand slip under her shirt. If she had any luck, he would think she was hooking her thumb in her jeans in a show of brattiness. "Yes, you will. You'll listen to everything because you should know what your sweet, innocent little wife has been doing. I took it up the ass last night, Christian, and it was good."

"You're lying." His face had turned a mottled red. His fists clenched at his sides. "You're lying, Hope. You're trying to punish me."

She shook her head. The freedom of finally telling him the truth was almost overwhelming, but she concentrated on the knife's hilt. The plastic edge brushed at her fingertips. "I'm not trying to punish you. I thought you were dead. And I have gone through more men than I can count trying to wipe away the stain of being your wife. And I absolutely love my men. Men, as in more than one. It's a way of life here in Bliss. I'm not ashamed. I love James and I love Noah, and you can't touch them."

"I'll kill them."

"No." She was sure of it now. She felt it in her soul. James was resourceful, and Noah was smart as a whip. They wouldn't wait blindly for some call to have them killed. They would fight, and they would win.

"I will," he promised. "I'll kill any man who touches my property."

"Then I'll have to make you a list. Be prepared. It might be long. I found a whole new world, and I will never be your girl again."

His face turned ugly, and he started across the room. "Then you've made my decision easy. I won't have a whore in my life."

She started to back up. The knife was stuck in her jeans. Christian came close, and she had a moment's breath before his hand came out to slap her viciously. The sound cracked, and the pain bloomed.

"You like that? You're such a slut. You probably like a little pain. I'm going to kill you and your friend." He bore down on her, his hand pulling at her hair. She felt the ache in her scalp as he forced her head back. His crystal eyes looked down at her, but she now saw that they were empty of humanity. He was nothing but a sociopath out for his own strange needs. "But I like a slut as well as the next man. Maybe you can show me what you've learned."

His mouth started to come down on hers. Hope gagged. She tried to push him away with her left hand while her right desperately attempted to pull the knife free. Panic threatened to overtake her. His lips slammed against hers. Her scalp ached as he forced her into position.

And then a loud *thwack* filled the room. He screamed and let her go. Lucy stood behind him, the remnants of a chair in her hand. It had cracked across Christian's skull, but he wasn't out. He let Hope go, the sudden loss of balance causing her to fall back.

Christian roared and turned on Lucy. Petite, sweet Lucy still had her hands tied and one eye had swollen shut, but she screamed as she wielded what was left of the chair. She brought it down on his head right before he drove a fist in her gut.

The distraction gave Hope just enough time to pull the knife free. Lucy fell back with a groan, and Christian fell on her, his fist rearing back. He would kill Lucy and then turn on her. Without a second's hesitation, she got to her feet and prayed her aim was true. Christian's neck was exposed. She could see his jugular. It stood out against the muscles of his neck, throbbing with exertion. She gripped the knife and plunged it in, forcing it through flesh. She pulled it out as he flailed and struck again. He tried to swat her away, but the blood was flowing now. He stood and tried to come at her even as his neck gushed. She kicked him away. He fell back, and she stood over the man who had been her first lover, her husband, the man who had almost ruined her life.

"That was for Elaine."

He coughed, blood sputtering. "She was a whore."

No. She'd been a woman who fell for the wrong man. "No. She was innocent."

Innocence had nothing to do with the state of her virginity but with the state of her heart. A woman could screw a thousand men, and if she still was able to love, she could hold her innocence in her soul.

Christian's eyes glazed over, and he was gone.

Hope turned to Lucy, who was struggling to get up. Hope dropped the knife and held Lucy, balancing her. "Oh, sweetie. I am so sorry."

Lucy shook her head. "I'm good. He couldn't kill me. He couldn't break me. He thought he could, but he couldn't break me."

Her words came out on a sob, and Hope held her close.

Lucy sniffled and turned her battered face up. "I want in on that club, though. It was a tag team, but it counts."

"Club?" Hope asked.

"Rachel's club. 'I killed a son of a bitch.' She was talking about making T-shirts. I want my T-shirt."

Hope nodded. "I'll make sure, sweetie."

She hugged Lucy to her. They were alive. They were alive.

There was a ruckus outside. Hope could hear a vehicle pulling up. Her heart froze. Had Jay come back?

"Hope!"

"Goddamn it, Noah. Don't you fucking let him know we're here."

She laughed through her tears. Her men were here, and they were fighting again.

All was right with the world.

Chapter Eighteen

"I am never working Woo Woo Fest again," Cameron Briggs vowed. He put his head in his hands and breathed a deep sigh. "I swear to god, I am going to make sure no one impregnates Callie for the next year."

"I will have to admit," Rafe began, "the FBI might have been a quieter job."

Cam frowned Hope's way. "Goddamn it, Hope. You are not to do that again."

Hope grinned from her perch on Noah's lap. Since they'd stormed into the cabin hours before, Noah and James had passed her between each other as though neither one was willing to let her go a single minute without one of their hands on her. Noah's finger brushed against her cheek.

"I wish he could die again. I'd like a shot at him," Noah said, staring at the bruises.

"Too bad," she said, leaning over to kiss him. She couldn't stop. She kissed them whenever she could. "Lucy and I took care of it." Hope turned to look at Laura. "Has Doc said anything yet?"

Laura came out from behind her desk. "Caleb says all of her wounds are superficial. He's cleaned her up and given her his best dose of Valium." She sobered. "Ty and River are staying to watch over her. Cam will take her statement later. She needs to rest now. I think we have enough to call this self-defense."

Cam ran a hand through his sandy hair. "I do. And I called Atlanta PD. They're sending a rep tomorrow to see if they can close a couple of cases. And they'll want to talk to Brad back there. We're on the lookout for the other one."

The cowboy who had tried to kill her men was safely in a jail cell.

Jesse McCann stepped forward. "Thank you. It would mean a lot to both me and Cade if we could get it on the record that Christian Grady was a criminal."

Hope turned to him. The superhot mechanics had showed up with her men, guns in hand. "How did you know him?"

She felt Noah's hands tighten around her waist, and suddenly James's hand was on her knee, both of her men providing support as though they knew what she was thinking. If Christian had hurt Cade and Jesse, she might have inadvertently aided in some criminal acts against them.

Cade leaned against the wall, his whole body seemingly weary. "Sweetheart, nothing that man did was your fault. Jesse and I grew up in Florida."

"Tallahassee. But we're not related or anything," Jesse admitted. "Not by blood."

"Sometimes you don't need blood to be brothers," James said, his voice deep. He and Noah exchanged looks. Hope felt her heart swell.

Cade nodded, and his breath hitched slightly. "We met in foster care. I'd been in the system for a long time, but Jesse had just been placed."

"I got lucky," Jesse said. "So fucking lucky. I got placed with a woman named Nancy Gibbs. She was an older woman. She'd never been married. Never had kids of her own. I thought she was doing it for the money. You know it happens."

"Not Nan." Cade shook his head, his lips curving up in a

reminiscent smile. "She believed. She really believed she could make a difference. She took care of us. She made sure we finished high school and got into college."

Jesse frowned. "If we'd stayed with her, maybe it wouldn't have happened."

She could guess. "She was an older woman? I ask because Christian loved to talk to older people. He would take tours of retirement facilities."

Cade nodded. "Our sophomore year she had a series of minor strokes, and we put her in an assisted-living facility. Just until summer. We were going to come home and take over her rehab, but she wouldn't let us quit school. Christian Grady convinced her to turn over her entire estate. He drained her dry, and when there was no money left, the state shoved her into some piece-of-crap home. We weren't her blood so no one informed us. We had to find her."

Jesse continued, his voice low and tortured. "She was our mother in every sense of the word but biology, and we weren't there when she died of pneumonia. She was an amazing woman, and she died in utter poverty, alone and unloved."

"Not unloved," Hope said, tears filling her eyes. "You loved her."

Noah rested his head on her shoulder. "They know. Our parents always know."

She took a deep breath. "I envy all of you. My mom doesn't care."

Jesse stepped forward. "That's not true. Hope, we haven't told you everything. When we started looking for the man who bilked our foster mom, we found out you were his wife, or he called you that. We didn't believe that he was dead. We started looking for you. We went to your mother."

She felt her eyes widen. "You talked to my mom?"

"Your mom bankrolled a lot of our search. She gave us what she could because she had been looking for you for years." Jesse got to one knee. "Hope, your mom has regretted that one moment for ten years. She's been alone. You've been the only thing on her mind, finding you. She loves you. She just wasn't good at showing it."

A sob tore from her chest. "My mom?" She couldn't finish the sentence. She couldn't.

"She wants you, baby," James said, kissing her forehead. "She wants you. How could she not? Does she know where Hope is?"

"Yes. We've kept her updated for the last month, but she's been afraid to call. She thinks you won't want to talk to her. She would rather get updates from us than lose track of you again," Cade explained. "She cried when we told her we'd found you. She cried like a baby and thanked god. She made mistakes before, Hope, but she is family."

And family meant something. "I want to talk to her."

"We'll bring her to the ranch," Noah promised.

Her mother wanted her. Years of pain slipped away. Mistakes had been made and forgiven. Family was what she made it. Noah and James were her family. Bliss was her family. And her mother was her family. Her heart was a huge, never-ending vessel capable of expanding with each new person she met.

"Thank you." James stood up and held out a hand to Jesse and Cade. "My brother and I can't express how much we appreciate your help. She's everything to us."

They both shook his hand. Cade gripped James's and then reached for Noah's. "We both hope you feel that way because we don't want to leave here. We've only been in Bliss for a couple of weeks, but this feels like home."

"We love it here," Jesse said.

"And it seems like you'll fit right in." Cam stood up, looking the two new men over. "But you two better stick to working for Long-Haired Roger from now on. No more vigilantes."

"Those days are over," Cade promised. "Just life from here on out."

Just life. It was all open in front of her. Life. In all its glories and wonders. Life, with its brilliant uncertainties.

She wrapped an arm around Noah and reached out for James, drawing him close. Their arms closed around her. Her future was defined by four hands, four loving arms, and two wide-open hearts.

"Take me home," she whispered.

"Always," Noah said.

"Forever," James added.

They took her hands and led her home.

* * * *

Jesse, Cade, and a new arrival in Bliss will return in *Chasing Bliss*, now available.

Author's Note

I'm often asked by generous readers how they can help get the word out about a book they enjoyed. There are so many ways to help an author you like. Leave a review. If your e-reader allows you to lend a book to a friend, please share it. Go to Goodreads and connect with others. Recommend the books you love because stories are meant to be shared. Thank you so much for reading this book and for supporting all the authors you love!

Sign up for Lexi Blake's newsletter
and be entered to win a $25 gift certificate
to the bookseller of your choice.

Join us for news, fun, and exclusive content
including free short stories.

There's a new contest every month!

Go to www.LexiBlake.net to subscribe.

Chasing Bliss

Nights in Bliss, Colorado Book 7
By Lexi Blake writing as Sophie Oak

Gemma Wells came to Bliss, Colorado, after a scandal cost her everything. Utterly lost, the disgraced attorney built walls so high that she thinks no one can get through them. She's given up on love, friendship, and all matters of the heart.

Jesse McCann and Cade Sinclair have floated through life, enjoying the world around them, but never allowing themselves to become a part of it. One look at the pretty attorney and Jesse realizes he's finally found a reason to stay put. Cade isn't so sure. He's crazy about her, but he also knows he doesn't deserve her.

As they begin to find their way together, a dark secret from Gemma's past threatens to wreck their futures. Her ex-fiancé is back, bringing danger with him, and their time is running out. Jesse and Cade have to melt this Ice Queen's heart, or she might not leave Bliss alive.

About Lexi Blake

Lexi Blake is the author of contemporary and urban fantasy romance. She started publishing in 2011 and has gone on to sell over two million copies of her books. Her books have appeared twenty-six times on the *USA Today*, *New York Times*, and *Wall Street Journal* bestseller lists. She lives in North Texas with her husband, kids, and two rescue dogs.

Connect with Lexi online:

Facebook: LexiBlake
Twitter: https://twitter.com/authorlexiblake
Website: www.LexiBlake.net

Sign up for Lexi's free newsletter.

www.ingramcontent.com/pod-product-compliance
Lightning Source LLC
Chambersburg PA
CBHW032126040825
30617CB00014B/40